2/4/24

WITH

D0513701

The
Wedding Dress
Repair Shop

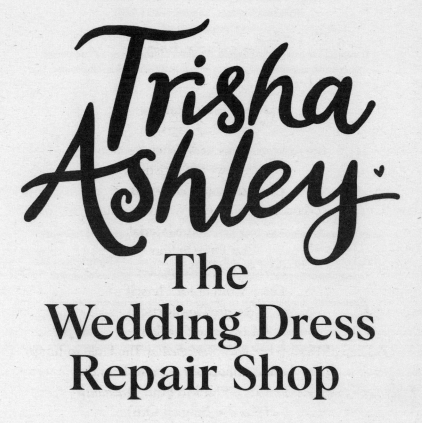

Trisha Ashley

The Wedding Dress Repair Shop

bantam

TRANSWORLD PUBLISHERS
Penguin Random House, One Embassy Gardens,
8 Viaduct Gardens, London SW11 7BW
www.penguin.co.uk

Transworld is part of the Penguin Random House group of companies
whose addresses can be found at global.penguinrandomhouse.com

Penguin
Random House
UK

First published in Great Britain in 2023 by Bantam
an imprint of Transworld Publishers

A CIP catalogue record for this book
is available from the British Library.

ISBN
9781787634749 (hb)
9781787634756 (tpb)

Typeset in 12/15pt Adobe Garamond Pro by Jouve (UK), Milton Keynes.
Printed and bound in Great Britain by Clays Ltd, Elcograf S.p.A.

The authorized representative in the EEA is Penguin Random House Ireland,
Morrison Chambers, 32 Nassau Street, Dublin D02 YH68.

Penguin Random House is committed to a sustainable
future for our business, our readers and our planet. This book
is made from Forest Stewardship Council® certified paper.

Dedicated to Helene Wiggin.
She was a wonderful friend and,
as Leah Fleming, an author who brought joy to many readers.
1942–2022

Character List

Garland Fairford, She works for the theatrical costumiers Beng & Briggs in London and specializes in historical costume.

Thom Reid, Garland's childhood friend. He later shot to fame as Ivo Gryffyn in a series of fantasy films.

Marco Parys, Garland's fiancé. A playwright and director, he is a former friend of Thom Reid's stepbrother, Leo Lampeter, and his wife, Miranda Malkin, who co-starred with him in the same popular fantasy film series. Miranda is cast in his latest play.

Rosa-May Garland, A famous Regency actress who mysteriously vanished after her marriage to Guy Fairford in 1816.

Wilfric Wolfram, Actor in Marco's play.

Mallory Mortlake and *Demelza Dartford*, Thom's friends from his time as an actor.

Characters living in or near Pelican Mews, Great Mumming

Honey Fairford, Bestselling revenge thriller novelist, Honey discovers that she and Garland are distantly related through Regency actress Rosa-May Garland.

Viv Greenaway, Honey's reclusive poet friend, who is staying with her after being recently widowed.

Pearl Morris, Proprietor of the second-hand bookshop, Fallen Idle.

Simon Speller, Hatmaker, who both lives and works in the mews.

Bruno Bascombe, A marionette maker, who is on a long sabbatical in New Zealand, leaving his young partner in charge of the business.

Baz, Art shop owner, and partner of Derek.

Derek, Honey's PA, and partner of Baz.

Ginny, Owner of New Age shop Spindrift.

Rev. Jo-Jo, The vicar of St Gabriel's Church in Jericho's End, near Great-Mumming.

Kay and Ella, Museum volunteers.

Rosa-May

Up-Heythram Hall, 22 May 1815

Recently my life has changed so dramatically – a very apt word in the circumstances – and in so short a time that I struggle to make sense of it.

My husband – and how strange it seems to be writing those words! – yesterday dashed off to the Continent to rejoin his regiment, leaving me here, with the promise that he would send for me as soon as possible . . .

This was not at all what I bargained for when, with unaccustomed impetuosity, I abandoned my stage career, at the very pinnacle of my success, for marriage to an army officer. I was in love both with Guy Fairford and the exciting prospect of a new life spent following the drum across the Continent. In fact, this very handsome calf-bound notebook, along with its fellow, were purchased expressly for the purpose of recording my impressions of my new life.

Instead, I find myself immured in this draughty and remote mansion, Up-Heythram Hall, high on the Lancashire moors, as the unwilling guest of my husband's older brother, Rafe, an

1

autocratic invalid of uncertain temper, and his sour and disapproving wife, Sophia. My suggestion that I return with my maid, Sara, to lodgings in London to await Guy's summons has been summarily dismissed by him, giving me the first intimation of the curtailing of the freedoms I previously enjoyed by the shackles of wedlock.

However quickly Guy sends for me – and I pray it will be soon – at the moment I feel that I have come almost full circle from where I began my life in Papa's draughty and secluded rectory, which is not so many miles away from here as the crow flies – although Papa, in his black cassock, reminded me rather more of some dark bird of prey than a crow.

Ten years ago, I most daringly made my escape in order to seek my fortune on the stage – with what success the theatre-going public well know – and really, I must have been quite inebriated with love to have thrown my bonnet over the windmill with such finality! Now the grim reality of my position has sobered me, though too late . . . and I have threatened to send Sara back to Town if she reiterates one more time that she warned me against my hasty and rash actions. A hollow threat, though, since she knows well she is truly my only friend in this chill mausoleum of a house.

But I can see there is nothing to be done now except wait impatiently for the moment when I can rejoin Guy and begin the new and exciting life he promised me. I will while away the time until that moment in writing a memoir of my life to date, though for my own amusement only . . .

1

Museum Piece

Garland
London, July 2018

Wednesday was my regular half-day off from Beng & Briggs, Theatrical Costumiers, a concession they grudgingly awarded to those of us expected to work on Saturday mornings, and often on into the rest of the weekend, if there was a rush job on.

As had become my habit ever since the Rosa-May Garland exhibition had opened earlier in the year at the V&A Museum, I was spending the afternoon with my nose practically pressed against the glass of one particular full-length display case.

There, arranged over two small, slender and faceless female mannequins, was not only that rarest of early nineteenth-century survivals, the actual costume Rosa-May wore for the reprise of her most acclaimed theatrical role, that of Titania in *A Midsummer Night's Dream*, but also the entrancingly pretty silk evening gown she had had modelled on it.

It was the latter that I was gazing at now, checking once again that the copy I was making at home was as alike as possible in every tiny detail.

I adored my job at Beng & Briggs, where I specialized in historical costume. It was my passion and I was a bit of a perfectionist where authentic detail was concerned.

The dress was in the high-waisted style of the time, with a skirt consisting of three overlapping tiers of gauzy white silk, the hems coming down in a series of points, each one embellished at the tip with a seed-pearl rosette. They lay like the semi-transparent petals of some fantastic flower over the pale lilac base layer.

Two rows of seed pearls edged the short, puffed sleeves too, and a kind of ruff effect had been cleverly created with a band of pleated lilac gauze, which stood up around the back of the neck and then edged the deep V at the front of the bodice.

The replica I was making employed concealed modern fastenings, so that the ruff could be easily put on and taken off in one piece, and I'd used fake pearls, rather than real ones. But I felt satisfied that, other than this, my copy was identical in every way.

I was even much the same size as Rosa-May had been – small and petite – but then, I *was* some kind of distant descendant, so perhaps I was a throwback. If so, though, it was only in my height and build, for if the hand-coloured prints of her and the rest of the cast in the fairy scenes, which were on display in one of the other cabinets, were anything to go by, she had had bright golden hair and blue eyes, whereas I am a green-eyed redhead.

I certainly didn't have any desire to go on the stage, either. I was definitely a backroom girl and was in line to take over my department when the present, very ancient incumbent, Madame Bertille, retired . . . if she ever did.

Beng & Briggs had been commissioned to re-create *all* the original fairy–costumes illustrated in the coloured prints, including that of Titania – the reproductions sturdy and made for effect from a distance, unlike the dress I was copying. They were for a new play that was to be staged in the autumn, and thereby hung a tale . . .

I moved along slightly to examine the Titania costume again, hearing as I did so the sound of footsteps as other visitors entered the so-far-deserted gallery.

Then, reflected in the polished plate glass, I saw the tall, thin figure of a woman loom out of the shadows, her pallid face, the dark pools of her eyes and a scarlet slash of lipstick making me immediately think of vampires . . . as you do, if you have an excess of imagination.

But then the slightly plummy voice of George, my friend in the V&A Theatre and Performance department, said, 'Garland?'

Swinging round, I saw that George, his small, portly figure attired, as always, in a natty three-piece suit, was steering the elegantly slim woman towards me, with one hand deferentially cupping her elbow. He reminded me inescapably of a small tug escorting a large and racy yacht into harbour.

Of course, I now recognized the woman. That black, sharply bobbed hair and the contrasting pallor of her long, angular face were familiar to me, not because she too was a descendant of the celebrated Rosa-May Garland, but from the jackets of her mega-bestselling novels and all the publicity surrounding them – and her.

Earlier in the year, when she'd loaned the Rosa-May Garland Collection to the museum, I'd realized I must be distantly related to her and, out of curiosity, I had bought the e-book of one of her novels, *Death Became Him*. But the ingenious revenge the jilted heroine took on her ex-fiancé was just too grisly for me. I was still having nightmares about it . . .

'Garland,' George repeated, as they came to a halt in front of me. 'This is Honey Fairford. Honey – Garland Fairford!'

He beamed impartially on us, as if he'd just performed a minor magic trick, while Honey examined me with as much interest in her dark eyes as I'd been devoting to the silk dress a few moments earlier.

'Hi,' I said, slightly nervously. I'd told George all about my connection through my father's family to Rosa-May Garland – hence my unusual first name, of course – but I'd only realized I must also be related to the bestselling novelist when she'd loaned the material in the exhibition.

But while I wouldn't have *dreamed* of contacting her on the strength of that, it appeared George was keen we became acquainted.

'Hello!' Honey said, her voice unexpectedly deep and husky. 'George has told me *all* about you and he thought you might be here this afternoon. Since it appears we're long-lost cousins, it seems more than time we met, doesn't it?'

'I think we must be only *very* distantly related,' I said. 'My parents died when I was ten, so I didn't really know much about the connection until the exhibition, except that I was named Garland after a Regency actress, of course, who later married into the Fairford family.'

'I expect we can figure out where we meet on the family tree,' she said. 'Look, if you're free, why don't we go and have tea at my hotel and then we can fill in some gaps?'

I looked at her uncertainly. She was perhaps in her late forties – it was hard to tell – and exuded a rather scary air of self-confidence, but when she smiled and her mouth twisted up at one corner, it made her seem suddenly more human and approachable.

I found myself smiling back and agreeing. 'That would be lovely.'

'I have someone coming to see me about a donation of

Elizabethan gloves, so I'll leave you ladies to it, then,' George said, slightly regretfully.

Then he shook hands with Honey and headed off, looking, with his silver hair and neat, pointed beard, like the British Consul to a small foreign nation: Our Man in Havana, perhaps.

*

Honey's hotel turned out to be Claridge's, not a venue familiar to me, since it wasn't one of my fiancé's haunts . . . though I wouldn't have been surprised to spot Marco's uber-posh and snobbish mother there, with her coven: all thin, bony women of a certain age, with taut, wrinkle-free faces and crêpey necks.

But there was no sign of her, even though it seemed that the rest of the world were eager to take their tea there that afternoon. I didn't see how they could squeeze us in, but at the sight of Honey, the staff immediately conjured up a table for two near a window. Such, I assumed, was the power of fame, presence, money and, it has to be said, a certain notoriety.

Still, I was quite sure that however scary my new-found relative appeared, the rumour that she ate her lovers when she'd tired of them was *grossly* exaggerated!

As if she'd read my mind, she looked at me over the top of her menu with that strangely attractive and raffish smile tilting one corner of her scarlet lips.

'This is my home from home. Do order whatever you fancy – this is my treat to celebrate finding a long-lost cousin.'

'I'm not sure I can claim to be a *cousin*,' I said, once I'd made my choice from the menu. 'But we must be connected *somewhere*.'

'My great-uncle Hugo was the one for genealogy,' Honey

said, lavishly requesting two glasses of champagne to accompany our tea, which would probably send me to sleep at that time of day, especially since I'd skipped lunch. 'I've recently inherited his house and there's a huge family tree hanging in the hall. I'm descended from Rosa-May's elder son and the last of that line. He was one of twin boys, but the younger brother vanished from the scene later. Hugo said family rumour had it that there had been a big quarrel and he'd run off to America, taking a piece of family jewellery with him to fund his new life, but Hugo never tried to trace him, so we don't know what happened to him. That could be where *you* come in, though, Garland.'

'If so, the younger son, or his descendants, must have returned to the UK at some point,' I said, interested. 'It would be fun to try and find out, though I wouldn't really know where to start looking, and anyway, I haven't got time.'

'Nor me, but I'll set someone on to it,' Honey said, decidedly.

A magnificent, tiered, porcelain cake stand had been set on the table and Honey now began wolfing down finger sandwiches, one after the other, as if she hadn't eaten for a month, although the plate seemed to refill itself every time I took my eyes off it. Perhaps the waiters were all members of the Magic Circle, temping between engagements. That would account for the way they'd squeezed our table into the crowded room, too.

'Do 'ave a butty, love,' Honey said, assuming a broad Lancashire accent and pushing the cake stand nearer to me. 'It'll make me feel less greedy, though I missed lunch after seeing my agent so I could catch George before his next appointment, and I'm *ravenous*. But I'm glad I did, as he's brought us together. So now, *do* tell me more about yourself,' she invited, before abandoning the sandwiches and biting into a miniature meringue, which exploded, enveloping her in a fine cloud of powdered sugar, which she waved away with one thin, elegant hand.

'What has George already told you?' I asked cautiously, when I'd finished a tiny smoked salmon sandwich.

I'd first met him at a weekend seminar on the conservation of historic costume and over the years we'd become friends. He was a great gossip – that air of ambassadorial reticence was *totally* misleading.

Honey wiped jammy hands on a napkin so snowy that it seemed like sacrilege to use it, and said, 'Well, for a start, he said that when he'd once commented on your unusual Christian name, you'd explained that you'd been named after your actress ancestor. So naturally, once I'd offered to loan the collection to the V&A, he knew we must be related and thought I'd be interested. He also told me you work in the historical department of Beng & Briggs, Theatrical Costumiers.'

I nodded, since I'd just put a delicious morsel in my mouth that seemed to be a yummy orange mousse concoction, coated in thick white chocolate, or 'enrobed', as menus sometimes put it, although I always feel then that whatever it is describing should have an ermine border and an embroidered fleur-de-lis about it somewhere.

Then I swallowed what was probably my entire normal calorie intake for the day and explained: 'I qualified in costume making and design, and did a work placement with Beng & Briggs. Then they offered me a permanent job and now I'm in line to take over the running of my department,' I said proudly. 'I've taken all kinds of courses in my free time, to broaden my skills, especially in historical costume construction, and I've also been involved in one or two projects to re-create gowns from old portraits.'

'Yes, George said you've already got quite a name for yourself, despite still being in your early thirties, and he often seeks your opinion on the authenticity of a piece.'

'I'm thirty-four,' I said, which didn't seem all that young to me, 'and it's very kind of George to say that, but he's the real expert. I do enjoy making accurate copies of historic clothing, although, of course, at Beng & Briggs we're only creating costumes that *look* historically authentic and effective on stage or on film.'

'It all sounds fascinating . . . and actually, that's given me an idea for a great way to kill someone,' Honey said thoughtfully. 'I mean, if you coated the inside of a suit of stage armour with something toxic, by the time they realized and got the actor out of it, it might be too late . . .'

While I stared at her in astonishment, she took out a pen and wrote *Armed with Poison* up the inside of her left forearm, in letters big enough for me to read upside down.

She put the pen away again and her dark eyes refocused on me. 'Where were we? Oh, yes, before we found you, George took me on a detour through the museum shop so I could see those miniature mannequins you have on sale there, dressed in copies of some of the costumes in the galleries. Lovely. I bought the one in the red-beaded Roaring Twenties flapper dress. George is going to have it sent to me.'

'I think you'd suit that style of dress yourself,' I suggested.

'True, but then, when you're tall and thin you look OK in pretty much anything,' she said slightly complacently. 'You obviously have a real talent for needlework.'

'Mum was a theatrical dresser before she had me, and she used to make period costumes for my dolls. Dad was a stage lighting technician, but his hobby was woodwork and he carved three little wooden mannequins to display some of

10

the dolls' dresses on. That's where I got the inspiration. I don't sell many of them – they're too expensive for the mass market – but fun to do and a good sideline.'

'I can see why they're expensive: all that hand sewing and fine detail on such a small scale,' Honey said. 'Those little black velvet-covered mannequin stands themselves are rather attractive.'

'I have them specially made, though the first ones were hand-carved from wood by a friend, Ivo Gryffyn, like those Dad made for me. They were lovely, but then Ivo . . . stopped,' I finished lamely, wondering, as I always did when I thought of him, where he was now and if he was happy doing whatever it was he had so suddenly abandoned his acting career and his friends for . . . including me, his oldest and, I'd thought, *closest* friend.

'Do you mean Ivo Gryffyn, the actor who played Gus Silvermann in those fantasy films?' Honey asked, looking at me with some surprise. 'He successfully transitioned from child actor to adult roles on the London stage, didn't he, before suddenly giving it all up a few years ago and vanishing?'

I nodded; my throat seemed to have closed up. It still hurt – to have found him again after so many years apart, only to lose him once more.

'You were friends?' she asked gently.

I swallowed hard and managed to find my voice again. 'We more or less grew up like brother and sister until we were nearly eleven. He and his mum and stepfather lived in the flat next to ours in Ealing and he spent a lot of time with us, especially after his mum died and it was just him and his stepfather. Mum worked from home, you see, so she was always there. Ivo and I were both arty and not academic. He loved messing about doing woodwork with my dad best, while I adored working with fabrics.'

11

I didn't add that when we'd met up again, years later, he'd still had that love of working with wood and had taken every course he could to learn new skills over the years, just as I had continued with costume courses.

I looked up to find her watching me, dark eyes unfathomable.

'Yes, you said earlier that you were orphaned at ten – was that when you lost touch with Ivo?'

I nodded again. 'I was on a half-term holiday abroad with my parents and there was an explosion in the block of flats where we were staying – a faulty boiler, I think. Mum and Dad were killed outright. I survived, badly injured, and by the time I left hospital, my parents' flat had been packed up and an aunt – my mother's older sister – whisked me away to Scotland, and that was that. I never went back to our flat, or got the chance to say goodbye to Ivo.'

Or Thom, as he had been to me then, though now it seemed to hurt less if I tried to think of him only by the stage name he'd hidden behind.

'That must have been a very traumatic time for you,' Honey said gently.

'I felt detached from life and everything seemed surreal for a long time. The aunt didn't really want me – my mum had been her adopted younger sister and they'd never got on. Once I started college, I moved out. There was some money from a life insurance policy and I managed. My aunt had invested that securely for me – she was always fair, even if she couldn't love me – and she'd also had most of the contents of my parents' flat put in a lock-up storage unit, so I could furnish a place of my own when I got the job at Beng & Briggs.'

'And I suppose, once you were working in theatrical costume, you ran into Ivo again?' she suggested.

'Yes, the theatre world is a very small one and one day we

just literally bumped into each other, although, of course, he was famous by then. But . . . it was like the years between hadn't happened and we just took up our friendship where we left off . . .'

Or we had, until I'd started seeing Marco, who I'd met through Ivo's stepbrother Leo. We'd argued about that. Ivo had never liked any of Leo's raffish London friends and couldn't accept that Marco had *totally* changed his way of life.

I came out of my reverie and thought I'd probably revealed more than I'd intended, for Honey looked at me closely and then said, 'I see!' as if she really did.

Then, to my surprise, she added, 'The fact that you knew Ivo Gryffyn makes yet another strange link between us. It's as if our lives have always been loosely woven together without our realizing it – very odd!'

'In what way does my having known Ivo link us?' I asked.

'Because *I* know Gus Silvermann, the author of those fantasy novels the films were based on. It's a small world!'

'But *no one* knows who he really is!' I blurted, shaken out of my thoughts of the past by this revelation. 'I mean, he wrote those books *as* the main character in them and his true identity is a big secret!'

'Not to me, because we were at Cambridge together. He was one of my crowd. However, I've sworn an oath of eternal secrecy!'

She gave another of her twisted but attractive grins and indicated the cake stand. 'Have another cake.'

'I shouldn't,' I said weakly, but I took a thin slice of Battenburg cake, which melted on my tongue like a sweet snowflake, and she put a tiny chocolate-covered choux bun in her mouth whole, chewed and swallowed it.

'George says you're engaged to the playwright Marco Parys?'

She glanced at the antique Art Deco emerald and diamond ring on my left hand, which made quite a contrast with my vintage Bakelite necklace and bracelet. 'I've seen a couple of his plays, but they weren't quite my cup of tea. I'm more of a *Woman in Black* kind of girl.'

To be honest, Marco's previous plays weren't quite *my* cup of tea, either, although they were undoubtedly clever, but I said loyally, 'He's a bit avant-garde, but I'm sure you'll love his new play, *A Midsummer Night's Madness*. It's opening in September at the Cockleshell Theatre and he's directing it, too. And, come to think of it, *that* is another strange coincidence, because the Cockleshell Theatre was where Rosa-May began her career and had her greatest success, wasn't it?'

'That's right. Ran off at seventeen from her post as a companion to an old lady in Bath to go on the stage and then found herself quickly catapulted into stardom as Titania.'

'Rosa-May must have had a lot of natural talent – *and* luck,' I suggested.

'The stars do appear to have aligned in her favour,' Honey agreed. 'And now in yours, too, it seems?'

'Yes, everything does appear to be coming together this year, and Marco and I are hoping to finally set a date for our wedding before Christmas. And you know,' I added, looking at her with a smile, 'that's all really due to you and Rosa-May Garland, because as far as my love life is concerned, the exhibition's been a real game-changer!'

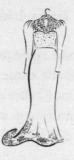

2

Animal Spirits

'How intriguing!' said Honey, as the waiter filled my champagne glass up again. 'Do tell me more.'

And after we'd toasted each other with a second, or maybe third, glass of champagne – for a bottle in an ice bucket had appeared beside the table – I did just that.

In fact, once everything took on that champagne shimmer, I could hear myself happily babbling away in a very out-of-character fashion for me, especially with a stranger. But then, somehow, by that time Honey didn't really *feel* like a stranger any more. Perhaps that was because she was the first blood relative I'd ever met, other than my parents.

'Of course, when George told me about the exhibition, I came to see it as soon as I could, though not on the opening day, because I was at work,' I explained.

'You work on a Saturday?'

'Yes, in the mornings, but I get Wednesday afternoons off in lieu. Sometimes, if there's a big rush job on, we keep going *all* Saturday, but you don't mind working long hours when you're doing something you love, do you?'

'No, that's very true,' she agreed, with that tilted grin. 'Stephen King says writing is the most fun you can have on your own, and I agree with him. I never tire of mutilating beautiful young men . . . though only in print, of course.' She grinned again. 'But go on: why did the Rosa-May exhibition change everything for you?'

'Well, for a start, the collection's unique, isn't it? I mean, just the survival of the actual early nineteenth-century costume Rosa-May wore as Titania is amazing, since they so often repurposed costumes for other plays – and, of course, frequently still do.'

'It was made especially for her, when she reprised the Titania role in late 1814, along with new costumes for Oberon and the other fairy characters, though we've only got the hand-coloured prints showing those,' Honey said. 'I found all the details in that journal that's in the display – part memoir, part diary.'

'I've seen it, and the blown-up excerpts on the boards around the room.'

'She began writing it in 1815, after she'd married Captain Guy Fairford and he'd left her with his brother and his wife in a remote house on the Lancashire moors while he rushed back to rejoin his regiment – just in time for the Battle of Waterloo! Rosa-May had expected to go with him to the Continent, so she wasn't very pleased.'

'I can imagine! Rural Lancashire must have been very boring after her life in London.'

'She said she only started the memoir to while away the time. Then it turns into more of a diary when she hears her husband has been injured. The entries stop on the last page, on the day he arrives home, so I don't know if she wrote any more and that book didn't survive.'

'It did say something in the exhibition leaflet about

Rosa-May mysteriously vanishing from the family records in 1816,' I said.

'That's right. According to Uncle Hugo, where she went is a family mystery,' Honey agreed. 'The costume itself only survived because the owner/manager of the Cockleshell Theatre gave it to Rosa-May as a wedding gift, along with those prints of the other characters, when she left the stage to get married. I found the journal actually tucked inside the dress, in one of the chests I discovered in the attic of Uncle Hugo's house when I was moving in.'

'It is amazing it should survive – and even more so that the dress she had had made to the same design did, too,' I said.

'She wore that evening dress to Vauxhall Gardens on the fateful evening she met Guy Fairford for the first time,' Honey told me. '*That's* in the journal, too. He was a handsome army officer, on leave to recover from an injury, and she fell for him instantly and gave up her career for him.'

The tone of her voice clearly intimated that she didn't think much of *that* choice.

'I'd love to read the whole journal,' I said wistfully.

'We seem to have strayed from your story to Rosa-May's,' Honey said with a smile.

'They are connected, though, because once I'd seen the exhibition, I enthused about it so much to Marco that he wanted to see it too. Then, when we got back to my flat, he said it had totally inspired him and he was going to write a contemporary play, based on the theme of *A Midsummer Night's Dream*. Only *his* would be *A Midsummer Night's Madness*, with a sort of ghost version of the Regency fairy scenes running through it. The actors will be dressed in replicas of the original costumes from the prints – Beng & Briggs are making them. All those scenes will be in black and white, which Marco says you can create using stage makeup and lighting.'

Marco liked to bounce his ideas off me, so by now I knew this all by heart. In fact, I'd had more than a little influence into getting him to create something slightly more mainstream than his usual work . . .

'That sounds original,' Honey said.

'The fairy characters will be half-seen by the contemporary cast, but then, gradually, the past overlaps with the present . . . or something like that,' I finished. I wasn't entirely sure I'd quite grasped the whole concept, despite my involvement in it.

I didn't think Honey looked as if she'd grasped it all either, for her straight black brows were drawn together in a frown over her dark eyes.

'Marco's already started auditions for the cast of the play.'

'So *that's* why you keep coming back to the exhibition and were studying those dresses so intently!'

'Partly, but not entirely,' I confessed. 'Because the moment I saw Rosa-May's Titania-inspired evening dress, I fell in love with it and I've been making myself a copy at home. Rosa-May must have been the same height and size as me, except that her waist was a little smaller – stays, I suppose.'

'Stay me with flagons,' Honey said vaguely, taking a gulp from her glass. 'The things women have put themselves through in the past to please men!'

'Well, I wasn't going to wear stays, even in the pursuit of historical accuracy,' I said firmly. 'So I just made the waist a little bigger. When it was almost finished, I put it on to show Marco and it certainly pleased *him*, even without the wasp waist, because that's when he suggested we should think about setting a date for our wedding! He'd had no idea I was even making a copy of the dress, because he'd hardly been to the flat for ages. First, he was writing his play and then in talks with the Cockleshell Theatre . . . I live miles out in Ealing Broadway, you see, while he has an apartment in the basement of his mother's house in Mayfair.'

'Swanky address,' she commented. 'So, absence had made the heart grow fonder, and seeing you in that beautiful gown knocked him all of a heap?'

'Something like that,' I admitted, though I didn't add that, until that moment, I'd started to be afraid we were drifting apart because we'd seen so little of each other. 'I said something about the dress making a really unusual wedding gown, but it wasn't a hint – just a passing thought – and that was when he said: "Why not?" and that we'd set a date once the play opened.'

Of course, he'd then somewhat marred the romance of the moment by suggesting our wedding might provide a good bit of publicity for the play, what with my connection to Rosa-May Garland, who had inspired it . . .

'So, had you been engaged for a while?' Honey asked.

'Not all that long, although we've been seeing each other for a few years,' I said. 'Our different working hours make things difficult, especially now Marco has gone into directing, as well. Unlike me, he seems able to manage on practically no sleep. He's the brilliantly clever, edgy type, totally focused on his work.'

'He sounds a pain,' she said frankly, and I couldn't deny I'd often thought the same thing . . . especially when his phone calls woke me up in the early hours so he could discuss the work in progress.

But on the other hand, he was also devastatingly attractive and almost impossible to resist when he turned on the charm.

I'd been amazed that he'd proposed to me in the first place. Actually, it turned out he'd never really intended to when he'd bought me the lovely Art Deco ring I'd fallen in love with when I saw it in the window of an antique shop. He said later he'd been surprised when both I and the shop owner had assumed we were buying it as an engagement ring, but that he'd gone with it because he'd suddenly realized he *did* want to marry me.

Honey's deep, husky voice recalled me back to the present. 'Did you say he still lived with his *mother*?'

'In a way. He's got a flat in the basement of her house and although it's not *entirely* separate, it does have its own front door on to the area and steps up to the pavement.'

I sighed. 'His mother loathed me at first sight. She's very rich, frightfully posh and stuck up, and obviously thinks I'm not good enough for Marco. She knows I stay over at his flat some weekends, but she's hoping the engagement comes to nothing.'

She'd made all that abundantly clear on the rare occasions when our paths crossed . . .

Marco called her 'Mummy', which always seemed odd to me, coming from a grown man. I mean, he's nearly thirty-eight!

Honey said, 'I expect you'll have your own place once you're married, and not have to see much of her.'

'Yes,' I said a little doubtfully, for the thorny question of where we were to live was yet to be resolved. Marco would have been quite happy to stay comfortably where he was, but apart from the fact that Mummy would be permanently hovering over our heads, as it were, there simply wasn't enough room in the flat for all my things and space for me to work.

Picking up my glass, I found it full to the brim again, and drained it. The shimmer around me now took on a rosy tinge and I suddenly felt sure all those little problems could be resolved . . .

Honey seemed to read my mind, for she said, perhaps slightly sardonically, 'So, once you've overcome a couple of minor hurdles, the future looks rosy all round? You're in line for promotion in a job you love, your fiancé is about to have a huge hit with his new play and then you'll get married and live happily ever after?'

'Yes,' I said firmly – but I still surreptitiously touched the wooden table under the cloth, for luck.

'Then I'm glad for you, of course, but from my point of view it's a bit of a shame, because otherwise I'd have offered you a job on the spot,' she said, to my great surprise.

'A *job*?' I echoed.

'Yes. I think you're just the kind of person I'll need to help me set up and run a project I have in mind, but it would mean relocating to west Lancashire. Pity, because it would have kept it in the family, too, now I've discovered I've *got* one.'

'Kept what in the family?' I asked curiously. And it was then that it suddenly occurred to me that we'd only talked about *me* and I hadn't asked her a single thing about herself!

'I'll tell you all about it anyway – you'll be interested,' she said, emptying the last of the champagne into our glasses before the waiter had the chance, and then upending the bottle in the bucket.

'About eight months ago I inherited my great-uncle Hugo's house in Great Mumming, which is a small market town in west Lancashire.'

'I've heard of it. Mum came from Ormskirk, which isn't far away. But do go on,' I added hastily, before I started monopolizing the conversation again.

'Hugo was ninety-six and an old rip – an ex-naval man – but we always got on well together and, anyway, I'm the last of the Fairfords in our branch of the family. Pelican House started life as a Tudor inn called The Pelican, hence the name. The original signboard is even still hanging in the hall. It's been a private home for centuries, though, and much remodelled and extended over the years. The Fairford family relocated there when they sold Up-Heythram Hall, their great, draughty barn of a house up on the moors, to a Victorian mill owner with social aspirations.'

This *was* all very interesting, but I didn't see where it was taking us, or where *I* might have come into the scheme of things – but I was about to find out.

'As I mentioned,' Honey continued, 'when I was moving in, I had some of my things taken straight up to the attics, to sort later – and it looked as if the Fairford family had simply transferred the contents of the manor attics to those at Pelican House. They're crammed with the junk of centuries, although so far I've barely looked beyond the first room. But *that's* where I spotted the two old trunks with the initials R-M.G. on them and immediately thought of our famous ancestor. So I had a look and – *voila!* – treasure trove!'

'That must have been *so* exciting,' I said. 'I suppose when you realized the importance of what was in them, that's when you offered to loan the collection to the museum.'

'That's right. I thought it would be a nice idea to have it all on public display while I decided what to do with it in the long term. The house needed a lot of renovation and updating, so that's taken quite some time.'

'George was delighted when you offered him the chance to put the exhibition on,' I said. 'I think he hopes you might make the loan permanent.'

'No, I'm afraid I'll want everything back eventually because I've got plans for it, as part of that project I mentioned.'

She grinned at me. 'I don't know if you're aware of it, but as

22

well as my novels, I've also written a few non-fiction books?' She reeled off some titles: '*Almost a Bride, Great Wedding Disasters, Wed, then Dead*?'

I nodded. Once I'd realized we must be related, I had, of course, checked her out on Amazon, as well as googling her.

'They're very popular and, over the years, readers have sent me several wedding gowns from their own bridal disasters, and even one or two antique ones that have been passed down in families, along with their stories. And, of course, I have my own dress, too, because I'm also a member of the Jilted Brides Club.'

That I also knew from my internet research, though I hadn't gone into it much.

'I'm sorry to hear that,' I said, but Honey quickly shrugged away my sympathy.

'I haven't known quite what to do with all the donated dresses,' she said, 'so they're packed away—'

She broke off, seeing my expression and said quickly: 'No, don't worry – they're carefully wrapped in acid-free tissue paper and stored in moth- and damp-proof boxes!'

'I *was* about to ask that,' I admitted. 'What *are* you going to do with them all?'

'That's the bit that will interest you, because now I've settled into Pelican House, I've decided to open a little wedding dress museum and put them on permanent display!'

I stared at her; this was the last thing I'd have expected.

'A . . . bridal museum?' I queried finally.

'Yes, although, of course, it won't be the hearts, flowers and happy-ever-after kind, but one dedicated to bridal disappointments and disasters.'

'That sounds . . . a fairly unique concept, Honey.'

'That's what *I* thought! The museum will incorporate the

Rosa-May Garland Collection, too, because although she wasn't jilted, according to that journal it might have been better if she had been. It's clear that by the time her husband left her in Lancashire, she'd started having doubts about her decision to marry him.'

'Really? It's frustrating we don't know what happened to her later, isn't it?' I said. 'Wikipedia says only that she retired from the stage on her marriage, in 1815.'

'I've scanned her journal, so I'll email you a copy when I get home,' Honey promised. 'Her handwriting is really terrible, though. I might get my PA, Derek, to type up the whole thing, at some point.'

'Great! And, you know, I think the museum's a really interesting idea, Honey,' I said, now I'd had time to get over my initial surprise. 'But you'd need to find suitable premises, of course. And then, if it's to open to the public, there are all kinds of rules and regulations to comply with.'

'Ah, but there's something about Pelican House you don't know, that makes it all possible,' she announced triumphantly. 'It has a later wing behind the main house, backing on to a mews, and, up to my uncle's death, it *was* a museum and open to the public on weekday afternoons.'

'Really? What amazing good luck!' I exclaimed. 'What kind of museum was it?'

'They *called* it a natural history museum, but really, it was just a repository for all the dead, moth-eaten, stuffed creatures collected or killed by my ancestors, along with cases of birds' eggs, insects pinned to boards . . . all sorts of grisly long-dead stuff. I wanted to make a bonfire of the whole lot, but it turned out that there's all sorts of red tape about disposing of that kind of collection, especially the remains of any endangered species. I've had to get an expert in, and clearing it is still an ongoing thing, though we're getting there. No one,' she added, 'seemed to want a full-sized stuffed water buffalo, with or without its glass case painted with a scene of its natural habitat.'

'No, I don't suppose there's a lot of demand for that kind of thing,' I agreed. 'Still, the fact that the building's been a museum of any kind will make things so much easier for you. It sounds perfect.'

'There's even a cottage, attached to the far end of the museum, where the former curator lived. He was also a taxidermist, so he had a workroom there, too.' She paused, then said musingly, 'I might have to have someone go through the museum and cottage with bell, book and candle, to cleanse the air of any lingering animal spirits.'

I looked at her uncertainly, wondering if she was joking, because that novel of hers I'd read didn't make me think she would be particularly sensitive to that sort of atmosphere, but she seemed to be serious.

'I like animals so much more than most people,' she mused, which went some way to explaining it.

'So, I've already got an expert disposing of the collection and someone else checking what health and safety rules, public liability insurance and anything else we'll need to sort out before opening. I believe in delegating all the tedious stuff to other people.'

'If the building was open to the public, does it need much doing to it?' I asked.

'Quite a bit, because it was just as run-down as the rest of the house, but it does have lovely parquet floors throughout, which I want to preserve. Some of the glass display cases might have been reusable, but I'm going to get rid of them and start afresh. I've found a place in North Wales called Priceless Interiors who will take them, and they're on the track of the kind of thing I want instead. That's where you would have been so useful, because I'll need expert advice on the storing and display of the wedding dresses and then a permanent curator/conservator to look after them.'

'It would be a dream job for a lot of people,' I said, rather wistfully.

'Once the museum is open and publicized – which will also give my novels a boost – I suspect I'll be sent even more wedding disaster dresses.'

'I'm sure you will,' I agreed, and sighed regretfully. 'If it weren't for Marco and my current promotional prospects, I don't think I could have resisted it.'

'It *is* a shame. You could have lived in the attached cottage with the workroom and been able to carry on with your own work when the museum was shut. I'll probably open it just weekday afternoons, like the old one,' she said. 'But I mustn't tantalize you with what might have been.'

'I'm sure you'll find someone else,' I said, 'but meanwhile, if there's any help or advice I can give you, I'm more than happy to do that. I'm very sure George will, too.'

'Great – and we must keep in touch now anyway,' she said.

We exchanged contact details, before I thanked her for a wonderful tea and staggered out to the taxi she'd summoned from the firm she used, which whisked me off in unaccustomed luxury to my not-very-des res in Ealing Broadway.

Rosa-May

22 May 1815

I was born in 1789, in my father's parsonage in the small rural and remote Lancashire village of Nettlefold, which lay at an inconvenient distance from the nearest town of any size.

The parish covered a wide area, even though the sheep vastly outnumbered the people dwelling there, but Papa had obtained the living through the good offices of the Taggarts, who lived at the big house, the Grange, and were related to my mother. Mama had, against all advice, married a handsome but impecunious cleric and lived to regret it . . .

But more of that later, although I cannot but help reflect that I am now dwelling only a short distance from the place I grew so very eager to leave.

Papa, with his hawk nose and flapping black cassock, may have looked like a bird of prey, but I have no fear that he will swoop down on me now, for my family have long since cast me off and expunged my name from the family Bible.

Not that I had been a welcome addition to the family in the first place, for I was a belated sixth daughter (though two had died in infancy), and seventh child, who had, so Mama informed me, set the seal on her ill health. Certainly, after my birth she took to the sofa and left the running of the household to my eldest sister, Betsy, even then an embittered old maid.

Of my other sisters, being also so much older than I, one had married the curate, who had later secured a living of his own in another part of the country, and the other, Martha, had secured a teaching post in the school for the children of poor clerics, where she had been educated.

What money we had went to educate and support my only brother, Edwin, though with some assistance with school fees and the like from Squire Taggart at the Grange. The family there provided our only excursions into society, since my parents and Betsy would be summoned to dine, when no other guests of any consequence were to be had.

So, with my sisters already out in the world and my brother embarking on his education, my unexpected and belated arrival was considered by Papa to be some kind of Holy punishment, though he bore this cross with Christian fortitude, christening me Mary Rose (Rose being my mother's maiden name) Swan, though I was always called May.

My mother, in the broken tones of an invalid, reminded me daily that my birth had completely ruined a constitution already frail after years of childbearing. Her manner would have rivalled that of the great Sarah Siddons herself in one of her most famous tragic roles . . . and perhaps I inherited my love of acting from her, along with my small stature, slight frame and fair colouring.

How horrified she would be at the thought!

In any case, it was an inauspicious start for one whose future destiny was to burst forth upon the London stage as that celebrated actress and darling of the theatre-going public, Rosa-May Garland!

3

Missed Connections

To my surprise, when I let myself into the flat I found Marco there, pacing up and down my living room-cum-workroom in a caged-panther kind of way. His dark curls were dishevelled, as if he'd been running his hands through them as he does when he's overwrought or angry, and the brown eyes he turned intently on me held a strangely accusatory expression.

I reflected, as I often did, that it was a pity someone had once told him he looked like Lord Byron in that famous portrait, because he'd rather cultivated the resemblance ever since – and I can't say Byron would be my idea of a role model, because he sounded a nasty and self-centred piece of work . . .

'Hi,' I said cautiously. 'I thought you were holding more auditions for the new play all day today?'

'I was, but they finished ages ago. Do you know how late it is?' he demanded. 'I've been trying your phone for hours and you've been ignoring me.'

'Oh!' I said guiltily, and fished my phone out of the depths of my bag. 'Sorry. I switched it to silent when I went into the museum and I've had such an interesting afternoon that I forgot all about it.'

'Evidently,' he snapped, throwing himself into one of the old armchairs that I'd covered in a fifties furnishing fabric with a pattern of clipped poodles and Eiffel Towers. 'Mummy spotted you in Claridge's having tea with someone, though she couldn't see who he was, because he had his back to her. Tall and dark-haired, anyway.'

'You know, I *thought* Claridge's was one of her haunts, although I didn't see her,' I said, dropping my bag on to a small table – or at least I meant to, but entirely missed it. Champagne didn't seem to have done much for my coordination.

'She only glimpsed you from the doorway, because they were full. She and her friends had to go to Fortnum and Mason instead.'

'Tragic!' I said sarcastically, but he ignored this, as he does most things he doesn't want to hear, especially about Mummy.

'Naturally, she rang me to say she'd seen you—'

'Because she was avid to know who I was having tea with?' I suggested.

'You look as if you've been drinking more than just tea,' he said, eyes narrowing suspiciously.

'I have – champagne! *Oodles* of champagne,' I said. 'Isn't "oodles" a lovely word? I don't think I've ever used it before.'

'Are you *drunk*?'

'No, just a bit fuzzy round the edges. And you can tell Mummy it *wasn't* a man I was having tea with – though it certainly wouldn't have been any of her business if it was – but Honey Fairford.'

'*Honey Fairford?*' he echoed. 'But . . . when you told me you'd realized you must be related to her and I suggested you contact her, you refused point-blank!'

'Of course I did! I mean, she's a very famous novelist and probably gets people claiming to be long-lost relatives all the time.'

'So, how come you ended up having tea with her, then?'

'I went to the V&A after work and George – you know, my friend from the costume department – introduced us. He'd told her all about me. She's staying at Claridge's, so she invited me back with her for tea. She's very tall and her hair is quite short, so I suppose from behind, across a crowded room, your mother *might* have mistaken her for a man.'

Especially since Mummy had the kind of mind that would jump immediately to that conclusion.

Marco visibly untensed and looked interested. 'Well, even if you didn't write to her, I'm glad you've met at last. I mean, she's such a mega-bestselling author that she must be *loaded*, and the family connection could potentially be useful with the publicity for my new play.'

I stared at him in astonishment. 'Marco, we can only be very distantly connected, and it was kind of her to invite me to tea so we could get to know each other better, but I mean, she's not about to take out adoption papers or anything! And nor,' I added firmly, 'do I think she's likely to want to help you promote your play.'

Ignoring this, he got up and began pacing the room again. Behind him, in the open doorway to the kitchen, the skinny blue-grey wraith of a cat materialized and, eyes malevolently fixed on the hated intruder's back, pulled a hideous face, just like that Munch painting *The Scream*. Then he vanished again, with only the faint rattle of the cat flap on to the fire escape indicating he'd actually been there and I hadn't imagined him.

Marco, lost in his own thoughts, had heard nothing. 'She might agree, if it promoted her novels, too,' he suggested. 'I told you the fact that I am engaged to a descendant of the Regency actress who inspired my new play would make a great publicity angle, and the story of your discovery that you're a long-lost relative of Honey Fairford would be the icing on the cake.'

'I really don't think she'd like being used as a promotional tool and *I* certainly wouldn't want my private life used in that way, Marco,' I said crossly. 'I'd prefer my connections with Rosa-May Garland and Honey Fairford kept out of it – and our wedding, too, because I want it to be small, quiet and strictly private.'

'You're *so* unworldly and naïve,' he told me impatiently. 'You want my play to be a huge success, don't you?'

'Of course I do! And I'm sure it will be – entirely on its own merits.'

He stopped pacing for a moment and looked at me searchingly. 'Do you *really* think so?'

These occasional glimpses of his underlying lack of confidence in his work were one of the things that endeared him to me – he *needed* me – and I hastened to reassure him.

'Yes! It's a brilliant play and it'll have so much more popular appeal than your previous ones.'

'Oh – *popular*,' he said, as though it was a dirty word, which it was among some of his more highbrow friends, but I knew he was pleased.

'Perhaps I could just *mention* in the publicity that I was inspired by the exhibition, after being taken to see it by my fiancée, a descendant of the famous actress,' he conceded. 'Although if Honey Fairford did agree to let us use her connection with you, too . . .'

'You can ask her, if you want to – I'm certainly not!' I told him.

'It would give the play a boost, even if it only came out later, when we got married,' he mused.

'If the play is still running by the time we actually set the date,' I said slightly acidly, but I don't think he'd heard a word I said.

'Perhaps she'd even like to come to the wedding?' he continued.

We appeared to have gone round in a circle and he still seemed unable to understand where I was coming from.

'Who says romance is dead?' I commented sardonically. 'And I don't somehow think Honey is a big fan of weddings.'

'Did you get her contact details?' he asked, single-mindedly.

'Yes, but I'm not sharing them with you. If you want to contact her, you can do it through her agent.'

'I suppose I ought to discuss it all with the Cockleshell Theatre management first, anyway,' he said. 'They're delighted I've got a Big Name to play Titania and we're casting for Oberon tomorrow.'

'Oh, yes – how *did* the auditions go today? Who have you got for Titania?'

'Miranda Malkin!' he announced triumphantly.

'Mirrie Malkin?' I repeated. 'But I thought she was firmly fixed in the States, making films?'

'She was, but the last two didn't do that well at the box office and then she got divorced from that film director she dumped Leo Lampeter for, so she's moved back to London and wants to return to her stage-acting roots.'

'I didn't realize she had any! I know she and Leo went straight from stage school into starring roles in the Silvermann Chronicles films, before they were even teenagers, along with Ivo. In fact, I first met them at Ivo's house in Hampstead – and you, too, Marco, though you didn't remember me when we met again later.'

'I don't think we were every really introduced – you were

just Ivo's old friend, hanging out with him,' Marco said, before adding resentfully: 'Ivo *never* liked me.'

'He didn't like any of Leo's London friends. He thought they were all afloat on cocaine and alcohol and a bad influence on him,' I said, although it was true that Ivo had always seemed to have a particular animosity towards Marco, even if he would never tell me exactly why.

'That's all in the past. You know I'm a changed man now, darling, sober and industrious,' Marco said with one of his more winning smiles.

'Yes, I do know,' I said, though six years ago it had taken him some time to convince me of that and persuade me to go out with him.

'We all sow our wild oats in our youth, and it wasn't *my* fault that when Leo went to the States, he took to the drink-and-drugs lifestyle there like a duck to water.'

'No, of course not, Marco,' I agreed, and I remembered how distraught he had been about his old friend's death following an overdose. We had comforted each other, for I was both shocked about Leo and devastated that afterwards Ivo had vanished from my life without a word.

I'd started going out with Marco only a few weeks before Leo's death. Ivo had warned me against him, so that we argued. But I was sure that he'd come round eventually, when he realized Marco really had changed and settled down.

With hindsight, that might have been optimistic, given that Ivo thought Marco and his friends had introduced Leo to drugs in the first place. Ivo was always bound to put some of the blame for Leo's death on to Marco. *And* on to Mirrie, for betraying the close ties the three of them had built up on the Silvermann film sets, when she had dumped Leo.

Marco must have been thinking about the past too, for he

said now: 'What happened to Leo was all very tragic, especially for Ivo – I mean, his coming home and finding Leo dead – but that was six years ago and people move on with their lives. Mirrie certainly has, and she really wants to make a success of a stage career now. She's going to be *perfect* in the Titania role, which is the main thing.'

And to him, I suppose it *was*.

'Oddly enough,' he continued, 'I was thinking earlier that it is a pity Ivo left the stage, because he'd have made a great Oberon. It was amazing, the way he could slip under the skin of any character.'

That was true, at least – it was being *himself* he'd had the problem with.

'Even if he was still acting, I don't think he'd want to work with you or Mirrie,' I told him.

'No, perhaps not. He cut Mirrie dead at Leo's funeral, just before he vanished,' he agreed. An unfortunate choice of words in the circumstances . . . 'Still, I have someone else in mind for Oberon, and we're lucky to have Mirrie as Titania. She'll pull in the punters.'

'I expect she will,' I said. I'd probably have a chance to see how good she was at the dress rehearsal, if I could get time off work then, but that was some way ahead yet.

Then it suddenly occurred to me that it would be Miranda Malkin I'd be making the copy of Rosa-May's Titania costume for. She was, I remembered, small and petite – and also golden-haired and blue-eyed, like the Regency actress herself.

I'd been looking forward to copying that costume, but this rather took the gilt off the gingerbread. But still, it was my work, my profession, and I'd make it as perfect as possible.

'Are you staying for dinner, now you're here?' I asked Marco hopefully. 'I could make something, or we could—'

'I can't,' he interrupted, picking up his jacket and shrugging into it. 'I've got a dinner engagement and I'm going to be running late by the time I get back as it is. Business – networking, you know?' he said quickly, seeing my disappointed face.

I nodded, but I wondered who he was networking with and had a probably unfair suspicion it might be Mirrie Malkin.

*

Once Marco had gone, the energy seemed to drain out of the room – and out of *me*, too, for the heady bubbles inside me had all popped.

After a couple of strong mugs of coffee, though, I revived enough to make an omelette and salad, before removing the dustsheet from a dressmaker's dummy in the corner, revealing my beautiful, soon-to-be wedding gown. Of course, Marco had seen it, but since that was before it was completely finished, I hoped that didn't mean bad luck!

I sat in one of the shabby little armchairs that had come from my parents' flat and ran a critical, professional eye over the dress. However immodest it might sound, I saw it was perfection and looked identical to Rosa-May's evening dress in every respect, even though there had been a little adaptation with the fastenings and materials.

I wasn't going to wear a veil, just a simple band of white silk flowers – and 'simple', 'small' and 'private' were going to be the key words when it came to my wedding, whatever Marco wanted.

I might not be able to stop him mentioning our engagement and my relationship to Rosa-May in his pre-opening publicity, but I was damned if he was going to turn our special day into a publicity stunt.

I had no family to support me on the day – I didn't really think Honey would go to the wedding – and few real friends, now Ivo had vanished from my life. I somehow seemed to have lost the knack of making close friends after my parents' death.

I did have people I was on friendly terms with, mostly from work, and one or two from my college days, but they were all busy getting on with their own lives.

Still, there was always George, who would lend distinction to my side of the wedding guest list. I might even ask him to give me away!

I expected Marco would want to fill the church up with his friends and any celebrities and journalists he could persuade to attend . . . and then, of course, there would be Mummy and her coven, too. She'd probably wear black!

With a familiar wrenching pain of loss, I thought how much it would have meant to me to have Ivo at the wedding. But then, he had so disliked Marco that, even though time had proved him wrong about his changed character, and even if we had made up our quarrel, he might not have wanted to be there.

It was pointless to speculate, for Ivo was gone.

I'd thought our friendship was unbreakable, so precious to both of us that we'd never lose each other again . . .

I had been so wrong.

4

Three-Act Tragedy

Perhaps it was the lingering, undermining effect of the champagne, but I couldn't stop my mind from wandering back to that wonderful, magical moment when, after more than a decade apart, Thom and I had found each other again . . .

After we'd bumped into each other and started talking, I'd suddenly really looked at him and seen that the reserved, quiet boy I'd known had morphed into the adult man before me.

When he'd told me that some of his happiest memories had been doing woodwork with my dad, and that he still loved working with wood, I'd said on impulse, knowing how much it would mean to him, that I'd give him Dad's woodworking tools. I'd known Dad would have loved Thom to have them, just as Mum would have been so happy to know that I was using her old sewing machine and dressmaking equipment.

Then he'd taken my hand and said he'd show me his workshop.

And as I'd followed him down to the basement, I'd realized that in showing me his private sanctuary, he was acknowledging that our old close friendship had resumed, even if the years between had left a few invisible scars and a secret or two.

We were still so young then, in our early twenties . . .

*

The sound of an email pinging into my phone pulled me back from the past and, when I checked, I saw it was from Honey.

> Great to meet you, Cousin Garland – and don't even think of calling me Aunt, because it's too ageing!
>
> We must keep in touch now and I'll be picking your brains about the museum project once I get home.
>
> Honey xx

I replied:

> Lovely to meet you, too – Cousin Honey! And I'll really enjoy helping you with the project, so ask me anything you like.
>
> Garland xx

I sent that off, then I thought for a moment and pinged off another one.

> PS. I told Marco I'd met you – actually, his mother had spotted us in Claridge's – and I'm afraid he might contact you via your agent re involving you in publicity for his new play, the angle being the whole coincidence of him being engaged to a descendant of Rosa-May, who inspired his

new play, after seeing an exhibition about her, loaned by his fiancée's long-lost cousin, the famous novelist Honey Fairford . . . or something like that! I told him I wasn't keen on having my personal affairs dragged into the PR and that he should certainly contact you before mentioning your name, so I thought I had better warn you.

She replied almost instantly, and I grinned, hearing her deep, husky, sardonic voice in my head as I read.

Forewarned is forearmed! But I'm a total media tart when it comes to publicizing my books, so will see what is in it for me!

If ever I'd met a woman who could take care of herself, it was Honey Fairford!

Rosa-May

I was lucky enough to have a kind young nursemaid, Sara, a girl of some education, whose family had fallen on hard times. Her older sister, as I later learned, had eloped with a strolling player, who had been performing with his company in the village where they then lived. But this, of course, had to be kept from my parents, and only to me did Sara confide the interesting information about the exciting world beyond the bounds of Nettlefold that she received in her sister's occasional letters.

The squire's family at the Grange included a daughter, Kitty, almost my own age, so it was arranged that I should share her lessons with her governess and be her playmate.

Sara, meanwhile, had become quite indispensable to Mama's wellbeing, bathing her head with lavender water when she had a headache and reading aloud books of tedious sermons and the like. My sister Betsy was at first inclined to be jealous, but was at heart glad to be relieved of some of these duties.

Sara dreamed of escape from her humdrum existence as much as I did when I grew older, for earning a living in some menial capacity was the only alternative to marriage open to either of us, and marriage was unlikely in the extreme, given our situations.

Besides, Sara was very tall and bold-featured, which, together with a very decided air and her superior education, set her apart from the local villagers.

Meanwhile, my lack of interest in scholarship — other than an ability to memorize and recite long pieces of poetry and prose — had caused my parents to think that, once I was old enough, I would be fit for nothing more than the post of companion to some elderly or invalid person.

I got on well enough with Kitty Taggart, who was a little lazy and stupid, but very good-natured. Kitty and I kept mostly to the nursery wing, but when the family were having one of their lively house parties, which often occurred when her two older brothers were at home, and decided to get up a play, we were sometimes bidden to take on minor roles.

I enjoyed this very much and my facility for learning a part quickly meant I was given longer roles than Kitty, from whose head the words, once learned, seem to pass out again with the utmost rapidity.

*

I was not, of course, on an equal footing with the daughter of the house, but at her beck and call as well as that of the rest of the family: useful for small tasks and errands.

Life continued in this not unpleasant, but humdrum fashion, until the year I turned sixteen . . .

5

The Stage Is Set

Time seemed to flash by me during the next few busy weeks, as a dry, dusty July turned into an unseasonabl cool and damp August.

Marco and I spent even less quality time together than before and I began to worry again that we were drifting apart . . .

But then, he was so absorbed in the production of his new play, which was to open at the start of September, while I was working overtime for Beng & Briggs: not only did we have the fairy scene costumes to reproduce for Marco's play, but also those for a TV costume drama.

I did manage one or two overnight stays with him, but they weren't a resounding success since he was now writing a new play and so kept vanishing up to his study, which was in Mummy's part of the house.

Then, when he did reappear, he only wanted to exhaustively discuss his new ideas with me, demanding my support and encouragement as usual, which was a bit draining . . . as was his habit of ringing me in the early hours for the same reason when we were apart.

Mummy ignored my presence in her basement, though I'm certain she knew whenever I was there and I was sure she was still hoping the engagement would fizzle out eventually.

It was not a very satisfactory situation, but I comforted myself with the thought that once *A Midsummer Night's Madness* actually opened, our workloads would have eased a little for both of us.

My wedding gown was completed, the mannequin carefully covered by a cotton dustsheet, and I'd now begun on a miniature version of an Elizabethan dress for the V&A Museum shop . . . and if you've ever tried to make an authentic-looking lace ruff scaled down to mouse size, you'll know how tricky that was. Still, I like a challenge.

Sometimes my neighbour's cat, Golightly, would appear, silent as a ghost (unless he was hungry, in which case he would scream like a banshee), to keep me company for an hour or two.

I *call* him my neighbour's cat, but actually Miss McNabb found him in possession of her flat when she moved in. The previous occupants must have shared him with whoever lived in my flat before me, for there was a cat flap in my kitchen door that gave on to the fire escape leading up to Miss McNabb's, and Golightly was obviously used to moving between the apartments as he liked.

He was a detached, unaffectionate kind of cat, so I might still have felt a bit lonely if I hadn't been in constant contact with Honey ever since the day we met. She'd quickly become a cross between a best friend and (though she had forbidden me to call her by the title) an acerbic and amusing aunt – a far cry from Aunt Rhona, who had brought me up!

It felt strangely comforting to have someone who was actually related to me, who cared about what was happening in my life. And she did seem as interested in me as I was in her. She said she always enjoyed exploring new worlds, and mine, the behind-the-scenes work of theatre costume making, was entirely novel to her.

True to her word, she'd had someone trace my family connection to her, working back from my father. I'd given her what information I'd found in the papers that had been stored in the lockup, particularly Dad's birth certificate. They'd tracked the line back to the younger of Rosa-May's twin sons, the one who'd run away to America, so Honey's guess about that had been right.

'Uncle Hugo said the reason for the family row was because he wanted to marry the blacksmith's daughter,' said Honey, on the phone. 'So they eloped and then eventually their son returned to England, though never making contact with the rest of the Fairford family. That was probably because his father had stolen a piece of family jewellery to fund his new life!'

'If his older brother came in for everything else, he probably felt entitled to it,' I suggested.

'I expect he pawned it before they even got a ship to America,' she said. 'Anyway, your father was the last of that line – it's amazing how so many big Victorian families do dwindle away to nothing. Mine did, too: I'm the last descendant of Rosa-May's eldest son.'

Then she added – and I could imagine the wry, tilted grin – 'But don't get the idea you're the long-lost heir to a fortune, because the estate was never entailed, but always willed directly.'

'I'm just grateful you aren't suing me for the lost family bauble,' I told her, and she laughed.

'This means we really are very distant cousins, which is nice.'

'Yes, it's lovely to have real family, however remotely connected,' I agreed.

True to her word, she'd emailed me the scanned-in copy of

Rosa-May's journal, but I hadn't got very far with it yet because the writing was crabbed and hard to read, even blown up on my laptop screen.

I enjoyed all our exchanges by phone, email and text. However strange it might sound, I had felt almost from the moment we met as if we'd always known each other.

Honey seemed to feel the same way too, for one day she said: 'It's odd, but once we started chatting in Claridge's, it felt as if I'd always known you, Garland! I suppose blood is thicker than water – we're family!'

'I know, me too. Believe it or not, I don't usually pour out my life story to someone I've only just met.'

'We're getting to know each other even better every day, if only by way of the phone and emails,' she said.

I thought, rather guiltily, that I'd also learned a little more than she knew about *her* past, because I'd felt curious enough to chase up that reference I'd found about the time when she was jilted.

She appeared to have almost got herself arrested for assaulting the best man, but then the story seemed to fizzle out when it became evident that he'd simply been injured in a drunken argument with the groom, which was why they'd both missed the wedding.

It was quite intriguing, though, and I'd have liked to have asked her about it, if I'd dared!

*

I'd become totally involved with the development of the museum project right from the start, because Honey and I exhaustively and enthusiastically discussed every aspect of it and she also sent me videos and pics of everything that was going on, including the last horrible examples of the taxidermist's art, ready to be packed off to a new home.

The photos of the museum showed it to be a long, two-storey stone wing, backing on to the main house, which was black and white Tudor. They were connected by a short passage on the ground floor and there was access to it from the curator's cottage at the other end of the building, too.

Repairs were now well in hand, the walls being painted and new blinds made for all the windows. George had advised Honey about those, because you have to be so careful to block out harmful light when displaying costume.

There was a large reception area and the front door of the museum gave on to the cobbled mews behind the house.

'I'm going to have a shop in the foyer,' Honey told me.

'What are you going to sell?'

'The usual stuff: postcards, a guidebook, souvenirs with our logo on – though I haven't thought one up yet – but also we'll stock *all* my books, both the novels and non-fiction. We could sell some of your little mannequins, dressed in replicas of the gowns on display, if you fancied the idea. But we can discuss that later, when you have time to visit.'

'I can't wait!' I said.

*

George had been roped in by Honey to give his expert advice on the setting-up of the museum, and we had fun discussing it all if he was free for a coffee and catch-up when I called in at the V&A.

Because we were so busy at work, George was the first to visit Honey, which made me quite jealous, even though they did their best to keep me in the loop.

The next time I visited George in his cluttered little office, he showed me the pictures he'd taken on his iPhone.

'This is the museum foyer – quite a spacious area, with the stairs rising up from it. Honey says she's going to install a lift, too. On this side is the room that will house the Rosa-May Garland Collection, and on the other, a staff room, with a door on to a workroom and then into the attached curator's cottage.'

The cottage, built in the same stone as the museum wing, looked quite cute, tucked into its corner of the cobbled mews.

He moved the images forward. 'Then the upstairs consists of three large rooms opening out of each other, so you can see from one end of the upper floor to the other.'

'What are all the bright yellow lines on the floor?' I asked, squinting at the screen.

'Tape. The antique reclamation place that took all the old showcases have found some suitable costume ones and we were measuring and marking where they would fit.'

'Honey doesn't let the grass grow under her feet,' I said, impressed. 'She says she's going to write the guidebook herself, too.'

'She has already begun a catalogue of the dresses sent to her and scanned in any information that came with them – or rather, she got her PA to do it.'

'She does seem very good at delegating, but she's really enjoying the whole project.'

'She's certainly been throwing money at it, although I warned her she would never recoup it from the entrance money, especially if the museum only opened in the afternoons!'

'I don't think she's exactly short of money and this is more of a hobby for her,' I said thoughtfully. 'But, being Honey, she will do it all as professionally as possible!'

Then we had a long and interesting discussion about where to order the right kind of museum-quality mannequins, the temperature and humidity control, and the importance of doing as little work on historic garments as possible – conserving what was there, not repairing.

George knew so much more than I did about all that kind of thing.

When we had finally exhausted these engrossing topics, George asked me out of the blue if Marco and I had named the day for our wedding yet, because he hoped for an invite – which I assured him he would get. Then I asked him if he would give me away and he seemed quite overcome.

'Of course, dear Garland. It would be an honour!'

'Thank you so much, George. But don't get out your best suit yet, because we're still no nearer naming the day.'

He eyed me acutely over the top of his half-moon glasses. 'I do hope everything is all right between you?'

'Oh, yes,' I assured him – and perhaps myself – then managed a smile. 'I'm just so totally run off my feet at work at the moment, and Marco's directing his new play as well as writing the next one, so there simply hasn't been a lot of time for us to get together recently.'

I sipped my coffee and then sighed and confessed: 'There's something we need to sort before we set the date, anyway: the thorny problem of where we are to live after we're married. His mother's suddenly come up with the suggestion that she turn the whole of the upper floor of her house into a flat for us. Part of it is currently occupied by the live-in married help, but they could move into Marco's basement instead.'

'That seems a generous offer, but I thought you told me she disliked you?'

'She does! In fact, she loathes me and I'm sure is still hoping our engagement will fall through. And converting the house would take quite a long time . . .'

'Ah, the Machiavellian touch,' he said.

'I've told Marco there's no way I'm living under his mother's roof. I want us to start our married life in a home of our own, even if it isn't an all-expenses-paid apartment in swanky Mayfair!'

'House prices *are* rocketing,' he observed.

'They are, but I can sell my own little flat and I'm sure Marco and I could manage a mortgage on somewhere a bit more central than Ealing,' I said. 'But he's so used to living rent-free, with everything done for him, that he can't see my point of view at all.'

'That's tricky,' George said sympathetically.

'I'm digging in my heels, and I'm sure he'll come round to my way of thinking eventually,' I said quickly, because I'd suddenly remembered what an old gossip George was. He looked so entirely discreet that he lulled you into telling him much more than you'd intended.

I'd probably already said too much and I was sure he'd soon be relaying it all to Honey!

Mind you, I suspect she'd already picked up on my worries during our chats on the phone, because I found her just as easy to talk to as George!

*

One lunchtime, I managed to slip into the theatre to watch part of a rehearsal for Marco's play, sitting alone in the dark auditorium. I knew Marco would be too busy to talk to me, even if he remembered I was going to be there, so when it was time to get back to Beng & Briggs, I just left as quietly as I'd arrived.

It seemed to be going well.

I knew Mirrie Malkin was two years my senior, but she looked much the same as when I'd last seen her several years before, and even then she hadn't looked her age.

Marco had told her he was engaged to Garland Fairford, Ivo's old friend, and she'd said she remembered me, though I doubted that. We'd only met in passing in Ivo's house when she and Leo were visiting, and although I'd been introduced and Leo had been friendly, she had given me the briefest of artificial smiles before turning away.

I have to admit that she was excellent in the scene they were rehearsing and, even without the Titania costume, managed to look as insubstantial as the Fairy Queen herself.

I recognized her Oberon, who had a dark and puckish face, as a well-known character actor, although I'd forgotten his name.

Marco stopped them mid-scene because he and Mirrie seemed to be jostling for position, and I heard Mirrie say, in a sweet, high, carrying voice: 'Marco, darling, wouldn't it be *much* better if I moved centre stage at this point, instead of Wilfric and—'

I thought, probably ungenerously, as I got up quietly to leave and go back to Beng & Briggs, that Mirrie Malkin would always expect to be centre stage, wherever she was.

6

Party Animals

One Friday evening, not long before the first dress rehearsal, Marco's mother threw a drinks party for the cast and the theatre management.

There was no time for me to get home before it, so I had to change at work, then dash over.

Even then, I was a little late and the rooms were already crowded and noisy, which I found quite daunting. Marco spotted me coming in and took me over to meet Mirrie Malkin.

She was standing with the slight, handsome actor playing Oberon. I might have maligned her character earlier, because she graciously said that she'd recognized me at once! 'That bright red hair – so unmistakable,' she said, with a trill of musical laughter. 'That hasn't changed.'

'No, and *you* don't seem to have changed much over the last few years, either,' I said politely, though actually, once you were up close, you could see a network of fine lines forming under the perfect makeup. We were of a similar height and build, but she was golden-haired and blue-eyed, just as Leo Lampeter had been, earning them the newspaper headline 'The Golden Couple' when they married.

Mirrie was wearing a slinky one-shouldered jumpsuit that clung to her, leaving little to the imagination, so I was glad I'd put on a dress that I knew did flattering things to my colouring and figure, even if in a more subtle way.

It was a deep topaz-yellow noil silk, with a bit of a waisted and full-skirted fifties vibe to it, and, for once, I was wearing heels. I'd teamed my outfit with amber earrings and a long necklace from my Bakelite collection – linked flat squares with holes cut out of the centres, in amber and dull green.

Marco introduced me to Oberon, too, whose acting name was Wilfric Wolfram. He seemed very taken with my dress – or rather, with me in it – because there was an unmistakable glint in his eyes when he said: 'That colour is *wonderful* with your pale skin and copper hair, not to mention the sensational green eyes! Where have you been hiding all this beauty, Marco?'

Marco turned and looked at me as if he was seeing me with different eyes. I suppose he'd been taking me for granted for so long that it took another man's interest to make him sit up a bit. And now I came to think of it, it had been ages since he'd paid me any kind of compliment.

Then Marco gave me a warm smile and said, 'Wilfric's right, darling, and you do look extra gorgeous tonight.'

I felt myself blushing, but Mirrie appeared to resent the men's transfer of attention to me. I saw her brows twitch together in a frown before she gave that trill of empty laughter again and said lightly, 'I suppose costumiers know how to make the most of themselves. Interesting jewellery choice, though, Garland,' she added. 'Not every woman would choose to wear *plastic*.'

'It's Bakelite – I collect it,' I explained.

'Oh, really? But that *is* a kind of plastic, isn't it?'

'An early form,' I agreed. 'I like the smooth texture and colours, though those were much brighter when they were made. Some collectors have them polished back to the original shades, but I quite like mine mellow.'

Mirrie rattled the diamond bracelets that encircled her thin arm like beads on an abacus wire. 'I prefer something with a bit more sparkle,' she said, which you didn't have to be Sherlock Holmes to guess.

Then she conceded, rather grudgingly, 'Your dress is lovely, though.'

'Thank you. I made it myself.'

'Marco told me you work for Beng & Briggs and your department are making the fairy costumes for the play, including mine, of course. But someone else took my measurements and did the first fitting.'

'My boss, Madame Bertille,' I said. 'We've finished most of them, but we're waiting for some more of the seed pearl trimming for your Titania dress. I was working on it today and, really, it only needs a few finishing touches now. A different department is making your gilded floral crowns and all the fairy wings.'

'Fascinating,' said Wilfric, smiling at me, though whether he meant me or my work, I wasn't entirely sure.

He moved a little closer. '*Do* tell me—' he began, but just then Marco, who had gone to find a drink, returned and handed me a gin and tonic, though by now he ought to remember that I loathe gin in any form.

Mirrie immediately reclaimed his attention, smiling enchantingly up at him, one small hand on his arm.

'Garland tells me my Titania costume is almost completed and I can't wait to try it on. I do hope it looks just like the original, which is so pretty.'

'Have you been to see the Rosa-May Garland exhibition?' I asked her.

'Oh, yes, Marco took me himself,' she said, which wasn't something he'd mentioned to *me*. 'The costume is wonderful, but that evening dress she had made to the same design is *fabulous*!' she enthused.

'It certainly is,' I agreed, and then Marco told her I'd made an exact copy of it for myself.

'Well, I haven't actually seen it since it was *almost* finished,' he said, 'but knowing what a perfectionist Garland is, I'm sure it will be identical.'

'And you aren't going to see it again, Marco, until our wedding day, because it's supposed to be unlucky for the groom to see the bride's dress.'

'It's going to be your wedding dress?' Mirrie said, sounding surprised. 'How original! But I'd just *love* to see it!'

'Then we'll have to send you a wedding invitation, when we've set the date,' I said, and she gave that trill of empty laughter once again, even though that didn't seem to me remotely amusing . . .

I remembered Ivo once telling me that Mirrie had changed so much from the girl he'd grown up with on the Silvermann film sets, especially once she and Leo had moved to America. He'd said she'd taken on the mannerisms of stardom almost instantly, and embraced the shallowness and glitz of Hollywood.

Mirrie's mind must have moved back to the past too, for she said to me, huge blue eyes searching: 'So, have you seen much of Ivo since he gave up acting and left London? I mean, being such old friends, he must have kept in touch with *you*?'

'Ivo Gryffyn?' exclaimed Wilfric, looking surprised. 'You knew him, Garland? I had a minor part in one of the Silvermann films.'

'He and Garland were childhood friends,' Marco told him. 'But she hasn't heard a thing since he left London, have you, darling?'

'No, and I don't know anyone who has, or who knows where he is now.'

'Oh, I thought *you* might have known, but then, perhaps you wouldn't tell me even if you did?' Mirrie said.

Then, without waiting for a reply, she took hold of Marco's arm again. 'Marco, darling, there's just a *little* point about that final scene I wanted to discuss with you and Wilfric, if we can find a quiet spot.'

She glanced at me, with a sweet smile. 'I just *know* you'll excuse us for a few minutes, Garland!'

And Marco, blinking at the dazzling smile directed at him, obeyed the tug on his arm and went off with her without a backward glance, though Oberon, flitting obediently off in their wake, did turn and give me an almighty wink. I wasn't quite sure what that signified . . .

They vanished through the open double doors into the next room and, turning, I saw that Marco's mother had watched my abandonment and now gave me a smug, satisfied smile that made cracks across her *maquillage*, so that her face looked as if it urgently needed retreading.

For a moment I simply stood there, with the increasingly loud and raucous sound of the party going on around me, a slightly menacing, feeding-time-at-the-zoo noise, feeling as unwanted as the gin and tonic in my hand.

I was not really part of the theatrical crowd and certainly didn't have anything in common with Mummy's friends.

And was I imagining it, or did Mirrie have designs on my fiancé? But then, she was probably flirtatious with all men, especially one who had both written and was directing the play she was in. I don't suppose it hurt that he was handsome and attractive, too, and of course, when she and Leo were married and living in London after finishing the Silvermann films, he had been part of their crowd, so she knew him well.

You can feel more alone in a crowd than in any wilderness, I thought, looking at the doorway into the back room where they'd vanished.

Then a hand touched my arm and I turned to see the famous and very elderly actor couple who Ivo had ranked among his few real friends.

They were the ones who had taken him under their wing on that very first film shoot and become almost like family to him. In fact, they were the only people I knew who might still be in touch with Ivo . . .

'Garland, my dear – how lovely to see you,' said Sir Mallory Mortlake and his wife, the equally celebrated actress Demelza Dartford, smiled at me and admired my dress.

Ivo had once, long ago, introduced us and ever since then, on the rare occasions when our paths had crossed, they had always remembered me and asked how my work was going, as they did now.

We chatted for a few minutes and it was balm to the soul, but when they moved on and Marco still hadn't reappeared, I went to look for him.

He was standing in the back room with Mirrie still hanging on his arm, at the centre of a group of the cast and a few of his less desirable old friends who I hadn't realized till then were even at the party.

As I watched, Mirrie looked up at him with those

enormous, sparkling, celestial-blue eyes and gave him a particularly intimate smile . . . and I turned on my heel and made my way out, depositing my untouched glass on a side table as I went.

I felt as much a fish out of water as I had at ten, transported from my cosy Ealing life to a remote and insular Scottish village – but now I was all grown up and I didn't have to put up with it. What's more, I was very, very bored, though of course that was partly my own fault, because I find it hard to talk to people I don't know well, but it would have been hard to break into a group of actors all happily talking shop.

In the hall I unearthed my coat and the bag with my work clothes in it, doubting that Marco would notice I'd gone for hours. I hadn't intended to stay over that night, tomorrow being, for me, another working day and an early start.

As I was replacing my heels with a pair of comfortable flats, Wilfric came out into the hall and I thought he might have had a little too much to drink, because his dark eyes were glittering as he tacked towards me, as if caught in a crosswind.

'Spotted you, darling – you aren't off already, are you? I was hoping to talk to you about those wonderful costumes you've been re-creating, especially mine!'

'Yes, I'm afraid I'll have to go. I'm working in the morning and it's always an early start,' I said. 'I'm so glad you like your costume, though.'

'I do, and you're talented as well as beautiful,' he said. 'Marco is a lucky man!'

The door behind him opened and a high and carrying voice called his name imperatively.

'I'd better get back before the she-devil comes and drags me off,' he said ruefully, and darted back into the room.

My pride had been a little assuaged by his evident admiration, drunken or not, but it was still with a huge feeling of release that I stepped out into the street and headed away.

When I let myself into my cosy and shabby little flat later, it was with a sigh of relief to be home again.

7

Changeling

I changed into jeans and T-shirt, then made myself scrambled eggs on toast, which I ate sitting in front of the telly, though since my mind was elsewhere I couldn't have told you what was on it, until the news came on, when I surfaced to find myself holding an empty tub of cookie-dough ice cream.

Golightly oozed in at that point and stared meaningfully at the tub like a famished orphan, all huge yellow eyes.

'It's ice cream, not mouse cream,' I told him. 'And if you haven't eaten your dinner today, it's your own fault for being so picky.'

He pulled one of his gargoyle faces, but came and jumped on his favourite chair, where he crouched like some very odd heraldic beast. A blue-grey cat *couchant*.

I was feeling a bit better, though I couldn't suppress a suspicion that Marco, with his theatrical star in the ascendant, was getting too good an opinion of himself lately and perhaps valued my support and reassurance much less than he once had.

As to my own profession, I'd always suspected that he thought costumier was nothing more than another name for a dressmaker, and that Mummy did too, which made me a totally unsuitable candidate as a wife.

I pushed down the small voice in my head that whispered that, in that case, perhaps *he* wasn't the right kind of husband for *me*.

Tonight had been something of a reality check, and the thought of a lifetime of socializing with his friends – especially the old ones he'd still kept up with – made my heart sink. I'd never make a good social hostess like Mummy, that was for sure.

Recently I'd seen less and less of the side of Marco that had endeared him to me and made me fall in love with him: the vulnerable, unconfident side under the bravado and sophistication, the Marco who had wanted my constant reassurance and support.

And I mean, although I know not everyone likes red hair, I am aware that I can look quite striking when I make the effort and Marco used to be proud to be seen with me.

But tonight, it had taken Wilfric's interest to make him sit up and take notice, and even then I was almost immediately sidelined and forgotten.

I turned off the TV and switched on the radio, tuned to the BBC World Service instead, which is like a kind of lucky dip: you never know what you're going to find on there.

While I listened and Golightly purred in a bronchial wheeze, as if he had a leaky gasket, I started quilting a miniature silk underskirt for one of my mannequin costumes. It was to go under a panniered seventeenth-century overdress, which would be open and looped back at the front to show it off – all very fiddly on that scale!

I was so engrossed in my work that I lost track of time, until my mobile suddenly buzzed like an angry bee and almost made me swallow a mouthful of tiny, glass-headed pins.

The phone was still at the bottom of my tapestry shoulder bag, but when I fished it out, Marco was on the other end of it, sounding exasperated.

'Garland? What took you so long to answer – are you at home?' he demanded. 'And why on earth did you sneak off early from the party like that, without a word to me?'

'Oh, you've finally noticed I'm not there?' I said sarcastically, looking at the clock. 'It took you a while.'

'The party's over now, but when I couldn't see you earlier, I just assumed you were in one of the other rooms talking to people. You're so small I'm never surprised if I can't spot you.'

'I'm not *that* small *and* I had heels on,' I said crossly. 'Since I knew practically no one there and most of them, like you, were in a huddle talking theatre shop, I got bored when you didn't come back and couldn't see any point in staying longer.'

'*Bored?*' he repeated, sounding incredulous. 'How could you be bored? And in any case, why not tell me you were leaving? I only knew you'd headed home because Wilfric told me you'd said so when he'd spoken to you in the hall earlier.'

'I *would* have told you if you hadn't still been in a huddle with Mirrie and some of the rest of the cast, and *she'd* already made it plain she wanted to discuss something *important* with you and I was surplus to requirements, hadn't she?'

'You could at least have told Mummy you were going, since she was your hostess, but she says you didn't even thank her for the party.'

'Your mother hates me, Marco, and she didn't invite me – *you* did. I'm surprised Wilfric didn't tell you straight away that he'd seen me leaving, but he probably forgot. He's very nice,' I added, feeling cross enough to stir the pot a little, 'and rather handsome.'

This was true enough, for I did think he looked fun, in a possibly malicious kind of way, though he really wasn't my type . . . and I was starting to wonder if Marco wasn't either!

Love makes you believe you can paper over the cracks in a relationship, but the chasms are still there, ever widening, just under the surface.

'I suppose Wilfric asked you for your phone number?' Marco demanded huffily.

'Of course he didn't. Don't be an idiot! He's acting in your play and you're directing it, so he's hardly likely to make a pass at your fiancée, is he? And I wouldn't have given him my number even if he *had* asked – what do you take me for?'

'No, of course you wouldn't, darling, sorry,' Marco said hastily. He went on, in a slightly more conciliatory tone, 'Look, sweetheart, I'll have to go now because I'm following the crowd on for dinner. So unless you want to jump into a taxi and join us—'

'Yeah, right – even if I wanted to do that, it would cost me half my week's wages,' I said, probably unfairly because he usually offered to send a taxi from the firm Mummy patronized to collect me. 'And you've forgotten that I have to go to work tomorrow and I quite like to sleep occasionally.'

'Oh . . . yes, I had forgotten, because it's ridiculous that you have to work at weekends.'

'We're busy – I'll probably have to carry on after lunch, too – though I'll still come over to your place when I've finished and stay. I think we really need a quiet evening in, because there are lots of things we ought to discuss—'

'Ah, tomorrow night . . .' he broke in. 'Well, that's another thing I was going to tell you, if you hadn't dashed off earlier:

I'm driving down to Suffolk after lunch tomorrow, to stay with Roy Digby at his country place. We have some business to discuss.'

'*More* business? Really?' I said coldly, because Roy is the manager of the Cockleshell Theatre and what could they possibly have to discuss that was so urgent it couldn't wait till Monday? The price of tickets and what colour the programmes should be?

Marco's voice dropped a couple of octaves into the mellow, more intimate tone that usually melted my heart, and sometimes my knees. 'Don't be cross, darling . . . and it's wasted when I can't see you, because you look beautiful when you're angry.'

'That is such a total cliché, I don't know how you can trot it out!' I snapped.

'Sweetheart, you know I love you, but our future really does hang on the success of my new play. I'm doing these things for *both* of us. And as for Mirrie, I have to keep my leading lady sweet, don't I?'

'I don't think she needs sweetening; she already reminds me of one of those Venus flytrap plants,' I said. 'All honey to lure you in, before snapping you up.'

He laughed and said lightly: 'It's just her way! Look,' he added, 'I've had a thought: why don't I pick you up from Beng & Briggs at twelve tomorrow for lunch? I can go down to Roy's any time that afternoon.'

'I can't! I'm sure we'll be working all day, so they'll probably get in sandwiches.'

'You're entitled to a lunch break, so they'll just have to do without you for an hour, so I'll see you at twelve,' he said. 'Must dash now – love you!'

And with that, he was gone, leaving me feeling as unsure and unsettled as I'd been when I first got back from the party.

*

Lunch next day didn't help matters much. For a start, I was in the middle of something really intricate, and my department head, Madame Bertille, clearly thought badly of my dashing out for an hour when everyone else was working on.

Not good, especially since I was hoping to become head of department when she retired – if she ever did, because she was so ancient that I expected her to wither to dust one day, like that She character from a Rider Haggard novel that was made into a film.

Then, to make matters worse, Marco was fifteen minutes late, so we had a fast and scrappy – in every sense of the word – lunch in a Pret a Manger, before I rushed back again.

Marco had looked more than a bit rough, especially when he took off the dark glasses he was wearing for a moment and revealed bloodshot eyes with dark lavender shadows underneath.

'Heavy night?' I suggested sarcastically, over my sandwich and coffee, and he winced and asked me to speak more quietly.

'I've got a bit of a headache, darling.'

'You mean a hangover?'

'Well, a bit,' he confessed. 'We went on to Wilfric's flat after dinner and he was making absinthe cocktails.'

'I thought as much. Insisting on wearing your dark glasses indoors is a bit of a giveaway.'

'If *you'd* been there, Garland, I don't suppose I'd have drunk so much.'

'I'm not your keeper, Marco, or your mummy. You're fully adult and in charge of your own actions. Besides, you know very well I can't do late nights before a working day, and my work is very important to me – just as important as yours is to you,' I said pointedly.

'I'm starting to think your work is more important to you than *I* am,' he said, like a sulky adolescent.

'That's rich, when you're so obsessed with your own work I'm only surprised you occasionally remember I exist! Look how long it took you last night to notice I wasn't at the party!'

'Darling!' he said reprovingly, in a hurt voice, taking my hand across the table. 'I know you think it's an old cliché, but you really are beautiful when you're angry and flashing those green eyes at me!'

That didn't soften my mood in the least, but luckily for him I had a mouthful of sandwich.

Before I could speak, he gave my hand a squeeze and said, in a wheedling tone, 'Come on, Garland! I admit I neglected you at the party and I was lucky Wilfric didn't try and snatch you away from under my nose! But I'm really sorry.'

I looked back at him, all melting smile and ruffled dark Byronic hair, but somehow the charm wasn't having the usual effect, probably because the dark glasses kind of made me feel he'd blanked me out. If eyes are the windows to the soul, he'd drawn down the blinds.

'Of *course* I think your job is important – and you are brilliant at it! I can't wait to see the finished Titania costume.'

'You'd have had it already, except we had to wait for more of the pearl trimming and the lilac gauze for the neck ruff,' I said, slightly mollified to the point where I might have begun to thaw slightly.

But then he blew it by saying, 'Mirrie kept on and on about

66

that replica of the evening dress you've made – she's dying to see it.'

'You'd better invite her to our wedding, then, if we ever finally set a date for it, because I'm not showing it to anyone before then,' I said firmly. 'And speaking of our wedding, there are a few important things we still need to settle first, Marco. I'd hoped we could have a quiet evening in together tonight and make some decisions.'

'Darling, we'll have lots of time to talk things through and decide on a date,' he promised, giving my hand another squeeze and then letting it go. 'It's hard to think of anything else with opening night so close. The success of this play is important to both of us, isn't it? If it *is* a success,' he added, in one of the sudden descents into self-doubt that usually endeared him to me.

'It will be,' I assured him automatically, because my mind was elsewhere. I'd checked my watch and was already gathering up my bag, ready to go.

'I'll have to leave you now, Marco, or I'll overrun my hour and Madame Bertille will kill me. Have a nice weekend in the country,' I added insincerely, and then dashed off.

I didn't wait for a kiss, which would have been bristly, since he didn't appear to have got round to shaving that morning . . . and the vogue for designer stubble has long since passed.

Our meeting had made me feel even more jangled and out of sympathy with him than before, so it was a relief to get back to my workroom, with the strangely comforting smell of a costumier's: a mix of fabric, warm machine oil, and wooden cutting tables and benches. It brought back memories of Mum's sewing room and my happy childhood . . . and Thom, though I pushed that thought firmly away.

*

I didn't sleep well that night, because the moment I laid down, all the disquieting thoughts and doubts about my future with Marco came rushing up to the surface.

Marco had looked so ghastly earlier that it even occurred to me that he might have slipped back into his old ways and, while I was sure some of his old friends still snorted fairy dust as if it was no more harmful than alcohol, he had sworn to me before I agreed to go out with him that all that was long behind him.

Ivo hadn't believed that, of course – it was mainly what we argued about when I told him I was seeing Marco – but then his views of him were for ever coloured by Marco's having been one of that group of Leo's friends that he blamed for first leading him astray.

I may never have been part of that scene, but I wasn't a fool and knew what went on – and probably still does – when so often a nose job seems to mean turning a mono-snout into two nostrils again.

Then I felt a bit ashamed of myself because Marco, apart from over-indulging in drink occasionally, has never given me any reason to doubt his assurances that he had changed his ways.

Finally I drifted off into an uneasy sleep, but I woke early on Sunday morning and, after breakfast, tried to distract myself with work.

I'd just started cutting out the satin overdress for my miniature mannequin when Honey rang me, sounding a lot fresher, brighter and cheerier than I felt.

'Garland, are you at home? Just say if you're at Marco's and it's not convenient, and I can catch you later.'

'No, I am at home, it's fine,' I assured her, putting down my smallest pair of dressmaking shears with a dull clunk on the worktable.

I glanced at the clock and said, surprised, 'It's only eight o'clock, Honey! I didn't have you down as a morning person.'

'I'm usually not, but I finished the final draft of *Bloody Young Men* in the early hours and emailed it off to my editor, and then I was too wired to sleep. I'm still buzzing, but I expect I'll slump later, though it doesn't matter because I'm taking the rest of the day off. I'll start a new one tomorrow – that *Armed with Poison* idea, which I had when I was talking to you over tea in Claridge's. Do you remember? The poison dust is coating the inside of the suit of stage armour.'

'Yes, I do remember! It's a really ingenious idea.'

'It's a bit *subtle* for me, really, but I expect I can get a bit more gore into it as I go on. Maybe there could be an iron maiden that turns out to be lethal, not a stage prop, too?' she said thoughtfully. 'Anyway, I didn't ring to talk about my books but because I want to know all about this drinks party you were going to on Friday after work. It might be useful, since the new book will be set around actors and the theatre. So – tell me all!'

I told Honey about the disastrous party, and how Marco had gone for dinner without me.

'You know, Marco does seem to take you too much for granted,' she commented. 'It's just as well you're too independent to let him trample all over you!'

'Definitely! Prickly, reserved and self-sufficient, that's me . . . and, I'm afraid, a bit quick-tempered.'

'I think most of those traits are assets,' she said.

I sighed. 'I'm starting to think Marco's become so self-obsessed, I'm not really important to him any more.'

'Perhaps he's simply increasingly involved in directing his play and so everything else, including you, is taking a back seat? If so, once the play opens, I expect he'll be entirely different.'

'I suppose so,' I said, with a sigh. 'But only if it's a success!'

'We'll hope it's a *huge* success and then he can finally turn his mind on to your wedding – and see sense about where you set up your first home together, too.'

Then Honey changed the subject to one that engrossed us both, the wedding dress museum. I asked her if she'd advertised yet for the job of curator/conservator, or if she'd like me to ask around for anyone interested.

'No, I haven't advertised yet, but there's no rush,' she said. 'With you and George to advise me, I can leave it a little while longer. I haven't decided yet when to open, either, but the renovations are coming along so quickly that might be as soon as late autumn.'

'Wouldn't that be too much of a rush, getting everything finished and the displays set up by then?'

'A rush, but not impossible. It would be good to open then, because I've just had another donated dress and it was for a winter wedding. It has a great story behind it that would be interesting for publicity.'

'I can see the attraction of opening early, Honey, but we're on the brink of September now and there's still some interior work to be finished, isn't there?'

'Oh, I'll just cross the workmen's hands with silver and they'll move up a few gears. I'm hoping, too, that once that damned play of Marco's opens, you'll finally have time to come down for a weekend, or even a few days, if you have any holiday due, to see how it's going for yourself.'

I admitted that I was *dying* to see the museum in the flesh, as it were, rather than just all the pics and videos she'd sent me, helpful though those were.

'And I'll show you the winter wedding dress, too, and tell you its story,' she said enticingly.

'The way things are shaping up at the moment, I won't be *having* a wedding, winter or otherwise,' I said gloomily.

'I can see the course of true love has hit a bit of a bumpy patch,' she said, and then we went back to discussing everything that still needed to be done before the museum could finally open, so it was quite some time before the call ended.

When I finally put the phone down, I suspected that during our conversation I'd given away a lot more of my feelings and my worries over Marco than I'd intended – and I expect George had gossiped, too – but then, Honey was very quick to read subplots and underlying worries and pick up on them.

I did love Honey's acerbic edge and sardonic comments and I could see that *I'd* let Marco blunt my own edge.

Time, perhaps, to hone it sharp again . . . ?

Rosa-May

In appearance I was an unremarkable child, other than my fair hair and blue eyes, being a small, skinny slip of a thing until I neared my sixteenth birthday. Although I did not grow any taller, as Kitty did, I took on a womanlier shape, and found myself invited, when it was decided by the younger members of one house party to put on scenes from A Midsummer Night's Dream, *to take the role of Titania, Queen of the Fairies!*

This was mainly at the urging of Kitty's brothers, which surprised me, since they had previously taken no more notice of me than of Kitty, teasing us both impartially.

This invitation was not universally popular with some of the young ladies of the party, and Kitty was also a little inclined to be jealous, but I revelled in it.

I found I could recall all the words perfectly and pronounce them clearly and, I thought, dramatically, although of course, I had never in my life seen a real theatrical performance! Papa was very much against such things, and had he not been under an obligation to the Taggarts for his living I am sure he would have forbidden me from taking part, even in such a private affair.

Sara had continued to share descriptions of the London theatre world, culled from her sister's letters. She was now widowed and let out lodgings to actors, especially those from the company at the Cockleshell Theatre. She was also sometimes employed there as a needlewoman and to help the ladies of the company to dress. She saw and described many performances, and these, together with my own modest success as Titania, fired in me a secret ambition to go on the stage myself!

Given my situation, this seemed a most impossible dream.

*

I said little about the play at home for fear Papa would find some way of preventing me taking part in it, and the mere thought of him ever discovering my desire to become a real actress and pursue a life treading the boards made me shudder!

However, he and my sister Betsy were present at the Grange when I took the stage – or rather, one end of the drawing room – as Titania, for he could not refuse the invitation, although Mama had felt herself unequal to it.

I so revelled in my part that, although I am sure they sat there emanating extreme disapproval, I was not aware of it until we were walking home together . . .

8

Dark Reflections

I spent most of Monday working on Mirrie's Titania costume, finishing off the fiddly task of creating the neck ruff and bodice edging from lilac gauze, before I began sewing on the last of the pearl embellishments.

I came home late and tired, and opened the door to my flat with all the relief of a rabbit diving into its burrow.

But as I stepped into my tiny hall I was sure I caught a trace of an alien scent on the air . . . something musky and strangely unsettling.

Then I opened the door to my living room and the first thing I saw was a cellophane-wrapped bouquet of long-stemmed roses on the coffee table, so I assume Miss McNabb, the putative owner of Golightly, had taken the delivery and left them there – we had keys to each other's flats.

That explained the lingering scent too, because my elderly but sprightly neighbour was prone to cruising the perfume aisles of the big stores, spraying herself lavishly with the testers and sometimes blagging free samples. She did usually tend to go for the more flowery end of the perfume ranges.

I dumped my big tapestry shoulder bag on the table next to the roses with a heavy thud – carrying around a pair of dressmaking shears in a leather holster and an extensive emergency sewing kit was an ingrained habit – and then, looking up, noticed that the dustsheet covering my wedding dress on the dummy in the corner wasn't draped in the way I'd left it.

Miss McNabb must have been overcome with curiosity and had a peek! She was a retired university librarian, with an interest in history, so I'd shown her the dress in the early stages, but not since. I hadn't actually seen her for ages, although that's how it often is in flats: sometimes you seem to bump into your neighbours every day, and other times, you can go a couple of months without seeing them.

She did post cat-related messages under my door occasionally, and vice versa.

I sniffed the air and thought I could detect a trace of that odd scent in here, too, so I opened the windows and then picked up my bouquet of tall, straight and stiff roses, which looked entirely unnatural and had no scent at all. The wrapping bore the name of a florist near Marco's house where I'd been with him when he was ordering flowers for Mummy, and there was a card in his writing attached, so he must have actually gone into the shop to order them, rather than just rung up.

The card said: 'So sorry about the weekend, darling – make it up to you! All my love, Marco.'

'You mean, all the love not devoted to yourself!' I muttered sourly, but still, I felt slightly mollified.

He used to always buy me flowers but, thinking back, I now realized he hadn't done so for a long, long time so I'm sure Honey was right and he *had* been increasingly taking me for granted. Perhaps my walking out on his party, and Wilfric's evident admiration, had been a bit of a wake-up call.

I hoped so, because I could see now that the Marco of six years ago, who had persuaded me to go out with him, had been entirely different: happy to potter about junk shops with me on Sundays, go to small, untrendy restaurants, walk in the park . . . simple things.

Not that he'd ever entirely abandoned all his old friends, of course, but he didn't usually inflict them on me. He'd been so cut up when Leo died, too, that I'd known he'd really cared about him, whatever Ivo thought.

I found a tall vase for the roses and shoved them into it, where they looked as interesting as cheap plastic ones: I liked *real* flowers, natural and with their own scents, just as I liked what I hoped was the real Marco, under the surface of the present incarnation, and hoped he would reappear after the launch of what could well be the crucial play that would send his career to the top level.

I'd have to try and be patient and understanding, though patience in anything other than my work did not come easily to me. Still, I'd *try*.

I knew the first full dress rehearsal was called for Thursday, hence the rush with the last-minute finishing touches to the remaining costumes. There was to be a photo-call the day before it for advance publicity shots in the theatre foyer, where already two large display boards showed photos of the original Regency costumes from the prints, with a bit about the Rosa-May Garland exhibition and how it had inspired the play.

I knew that even if I managed to get my half-day off this week, Marco would probably be too busy to see me, but it did occur to me that, since the Titania dress and the two floral crowns would be finished by then, I could offer to deliver them to the theatre when I got off at lunchtime. They'd be sure to send me in a taxi, too.

That way, I *might* get to see Marco – even have lunch with him – because, after all, he still had to eat!

I texted him thanks for the flowers and he replied that he was glad I liked them and, though he was sure he'd been so busy he'd been neglecting me lately, once the dress rehearsal and opening night had been successfully negotiated, he'd make it all up to me. That was reassuring.

I didn't mention my plans for Wednesday, because I thought it would be a nice surprise if I just turned up with the dress and crowns. Then, if he really couldn't do lunch, I could go to the V&A and catch up with George instead.

*

By late Wednesday morning, the Titania costume hung ready to go in a zipped plastic cover, and the fabric and jewelled flower crowns for the Fairy King and Queen were carefully packed into a hatbox.

My offer to deliver everything to the Cockleshell Theatre, before taking my afternoon off, had been well received and I was dispatched with my precious cargo in a taxi.

I directed it to the stage door and went straight in, the zippered dress bag draped over my shoulder and the strap of the hatbox in one hand.

I said hello to the elderly doorkeeper, who I knew vaguely by sight, and who was, as usual, in his warm and fuggy little cubbyhole just inside the stage door.

'The last of the costumes for the new play,' I told him. 'I'll just go through, shall I?'

I thought there was bound to be someone about to relieve me of my burdens, even if Marco wasn't currently backstage.

The doorkeeper, who had barely looked up from his newspaper, simply nodded, so I wafted past with a rustle of plastic.

I'd been backstage at the Cockleshell a few times, so knew my way about *and* where the star dressing rooms were. Sure enough, one of them had Mirrie's name tacked to the door.

There was no one in sight, though I could hear distant voices in the direction of front of house, so I wondered if they were still doing publicity shots.

If so, they surely must finish soon, and if I took my time perhaps Marco would appear.

I tapped on the door, but opened it when there was no reply, to find the dressing room empty, though there were signs of occupancy: a smart silk jacket and skirt hung on a rail and a handbag had been tossed on to a small table.

The room smelled of a musky scent that seemed oddly familiar – perhaps Mirrie had been wearing it at the party when we met.

I put down the hatbox on a chair and then removed the costume from its cover – Beng & Briggs would expect to have it back – before hanging it on the rail, where it swung gently.

I left Mirrie's crown in the hatbox, but took out Oberon's, hoping I could find his dressing room too or, even better, someone to take charge of it.

I cast one last, appraising look at the costume and thought I'd done a good job. It was sturdier than the evening dress version, of course, but still gave the impression of airiness necessary for the Titania role.

I'd left the door slightly ajar and now a faint current of air stirred the floating layers of pearl-embellished gauzy white silk that lay over the lilac under-dress, so that it seemed to take on a life of its own.

Footsteps sounded now, approaching along the passage and then voices coming from somewhere nearby.

I was sure I recognized Wilfric's, so I picked up his crown and went to find him.

The door to the next room along was open and I could see Wilfric standing with his back to me, talking to someone out of view. I was about to tap on the door when my hand was arrested by what he was saying.

'You certainly upstaged me in the publicity stakes by wearing that dress, Mirrie darling,' Wilfric drawled, 'but unless I'm very much mistaken, it's the copy of the original evening gown from the Rosa-May Garland exhibition that Marco's fiancée told us she'd made to wear for her wedding.'

'It is that one. I thought it would be *such* a good twist to the publicity, if I was pictured wearing it in front of that photo of the original. After all, I couldn't wear the actual costume, because it hasn't been delivered yet.'

'But we weren't supposed to be in costume, anyway,' Wilfric pointed out as my hand fell numbly to my side and I stood frozen in the doorway. 'And I'd like to know how you persuaded Garland to lend you her wedding dress, because it didn't sound to me as if she wanted anyone else to see it before the big day!'

'I didn't even try persuading her, because Marco said there was no way she'd lend it. I got him to take me over to her flat to see it on Monday, while she was at work, and it was just so *perfect* . . . So, we hatched a plan and Marco went to the flat with my dresser this morning to fetch it for the photo shoot, and now he's sent Annie straight back with it in a taxi with his door key, and she'll put it back exactly the way it was. Garland will never know. But it had to be returned before lunchtime, because apparently this is her half-day and she might go straight home.'

Wilfric seemed too stunned to speak for a moment – which made two of us, because my lips were as numb as the rest of me – but then he said incredulously, 'You took Garland's wedding dress without permission? And Marco helped you? I think that's *really* underhand, darling. And think how she's going to feel when she finds out, because she's bound to see the publicity photos eventually, isn't she?'

Mirrie must have moved because I could see her now, dressed in a cotton wrapper, reflected in the big mirror over the shelf at the back of the room.

She shrugged impatiently. 'I suppose she might see it eventually, but it won't matter by then, because she won't need a wedding dress. Marco is just keeping her sweet until the costumes are finished – he says she has quite a temper and we don't want any mishaps. But then, once the play opens, he's going to tell her about *us*.'

My legs had begun to tremble now and I was suddenly so cold my blood felt as if it had turned to ice in my veins. I couldn't have moved if I'd wanted to.

'I thought you and Marco were having a bit of a fling,' Wilfric said. 'Though I couldn't understand why, when he has such a gorgeous fiancée.'

'You and your redheads,' she said. 'And it's more than a fling – it's serious. He and Garland were never suited.'

'They seemed to have been together a long time and were planning their wedding, so the relationship must have had something going for it.'

'I expect he just drifted into it. I mean, she's only a glorified dressmaker – there's nothing special about her. I expect she grabbed him when he was at a low emotional ebb after Leo died. He and Leo were old friends. We all used to hang out together in London before we moved to the States.'

'Sleeping with the director seems to be your speciality, darling, doesn't it?' Wilfric said maliciously. 'But poor Garland!'

'You can console her, Wilfric! I'll get her phone number from Marco for you, shall I? Just don't make your move until Marco's ended the engagement.'

'You're such a complete bitch,' he said dispassionately.

'Thanks a bunch,' she replied coldly. 'All is fair in love and war.'

'And where is Marco the love rat?'

'He wanted a word in the front office with Roy, once he'd put Annie and the dress into a taxi. Then we're going out to lunch . . . a long lunch. He might pop back later to see how the understudy rehearsal is going.'

'I'll see you for the dress rehearsal tomorrow, then, Mirrie.'

'Yes. I wonder if Beng & Briggs have sent my costume over yet?'

'Beng & Briggs always deliver,' Wilfric said, turning away from her – and that was when he caught sight of me in the mirror. His expression went totally blank for a moment, then he gasped: '*Garland!*'

He whirled round, but the spell holding me had broken and, without conscious thought, I turned and dashed back into Mirrie's dressing room, turning the key in the lock behind me.

9

Left Hanging

The cold, shivery shocked feeling was quickly replaced by a hot tide of fury. I have a quick temper but I'd never before flown into such a berserk rage that I had no idea what I was doing.

But the next thing I knew, I was standing panting, with my dressmaking shears in my hand, and the beautiful Titania costume had been slashed to ribbons.

Long tendrils of gauzy white and lilac silk hung from the bodice, swaying slightly like some monstrous jellyfish.

While I stared horrified at it, I became aware that the door was rattling and voices were demanding to be let in – one of them Marco's.

Then I heard him shush the others before saying, persuasively: '*Please* open the door, Garland! I know you must be upset that we borrowed the dress without asking you, but it's back in your flat again and hasn't come to any harm.'

'I think she's upset about a little more than you borrowing the dress,' Wilfric's voice said drily. 'She also heard Mirrie tell me you two were in a relationship and you were just waiting till the play opened before ending your engagement.'

'Oh my God!' exclaimed Marco. 'Mirrie, you didn't, did you? I mean, I never said—I didn't mean—'

'Has Mirrie jumped the gun in more ways than one?' came Wilfric's voice.

'Oh, shut up!' snapped Mirrie, and then Marco must have put his shoulder to the door, because it burst open and crashed off the wall.

*

'Then they all just stood there goggling at me,' I said on the phone to Honey later, with a shudder of recollection. 'And *then* they spotted the costume hanging in tatters and their faces looked like a still from a horror movie.'

The moment I'd reached the sanctuary of my flat, Honey had been the only person I could pour it all out to. I didn't know what I'd have done if she hadn't answered her phone.

'Very graphic – I can picture that,' she said. 'Go on, what happened next?'

'It all got a bit confused after that – I think I was in a state of shock – but they couldn't have been more horrified about what I'd done than I was. I know I have a quick temper, but I've never totally lost it like that before, to the point where I can't even remember doing something!'

'A true berserk rage,' she said. 'Interesting! And you did have good reason to be furious, of course. None of them seem to have any inkling of how much love and hope you poured into making that wedding dress, not even Marco. It was a double betrayal.'

'I know, but even so, to destroy the costume I'd spent weeks working on was totally unprofessional! Beng & Briggs are going to *kill* me.'

'Tell me what happened after that,' she coaxed.

'It's all sort of blurred, like an old film, but I do remember Mirrie screaming: "Oh my God, is that my Titania costume?" And then Wilfric said: "It *was*, darling," after which Mirrie became hysterical and threw herself on to Marco's chest.'

'Well, that would help the situation along,' said Honey drily. 'I think I'm warming to this Wilfric, though.'

'It was Wilfric who took the shears out of my hand. I hadn't realized I was still holding them. Then he said, "Garland, darling, I can't say Mirrie didn't deserve that, but you've torn it now – quite literally, what with the dress rehearsal tomorrow and opening night a week on Monday."'

I swallowed hard. 'Marco was still holding Mirrie, but he looked at me as if he hated me and said he'd never have believed I could do something so vindictive and that he could have me charged with wilful damage! Then he ordered me to get out of his sight and said he never wanted to see me again.'

'I'm sure that bit about charging you with wilful damage must have been an empty threat,' Honey said judiciously. 'I mean, he wouldn't want the whole unsavoury story of why you'd done it to come out, would he? That wouldn't exactly be good publicity.'

'I don't know . . . but he also said he'd be ringing my employers immediately to tell them what had happened. I can see now that I should have taken the costume straight back to Beng & Briggs and told them myself. Only . . . by then I wasn't hanging together very well.'

'Of course you weren't. I'm only surprised you managed to get yourself home.'

'Oh, that was Wilfric! He was so kind, and sort of steered me out of there and put me in a taxi, and he gave the driver some money, which was just as well, really, because I didn't have enough on me for the fare all the way out. I'll have to find a way of paying him back.'

'I'm definitely liking the sound of Wilfric more and more,' Honey said.

'He gave me his card and said to ring him if I got in a lot of trouble over this, although, of course, we both knew he wouldn't be able to help because I've done the unforgivable and Beng & Briggs will fire me.'

'Is there time to repair the costume, or replace the parts you slashed?' she asked. 'Obviously, not for the dress rehearsal, but for opening night?'

'The bodice and sleeves are all right, but the whole skirt is in shreds and will have to be replaced. Something could be put together in the time, but not an exact copy of the original, or with the same quality of fabric and embellishments, which had to be ordered in specially. They'd have to work day and night, even so.'

They – not me. After this, I'd have no future in the job I loved.

My landline rang, which it did so infrequently it made me jump.

'The other phone's ringing – could you hang on a minute?'

'OK.'

I think I knew what the call would be about, even before I picked up the receiver and the clipped voice of Mrs Beng's secretary said that she and Mr Briggs would like to see me at eight a.m. next day.

'And she told me to bring something to put any personal belongings in, so I could take them home with me. Which means I'll be fired and out of there before the rest of the staff arrives, with no job, no fiancé and no future,' I told Honey.

'Well, I don't think Marco is much of a loss, to be frank.'

'You're right,' I said bitterly. And so, it appeared, had Ivo been: right about him all along.

I looked across the room at the sheeted shape of my wedding dress on the dressmaker's dummy.

'I feel I'd like to destroy my wedding dress now, too,' I confessed. 'It's . . . despoiled. That's the only word for it.'

'No, don't!' Honey said urgently. 'I'll put it in the museum and it will be a link between the other wedding dresses and the Rosa-May exhibition! Just pack it away in a box out of sight, for the moment.'

'All right,' I agreed heavily. 'I'll do that in a minute.'

We talked a little longer and then she told me to try not to worry about the future too much, but to ring her in the morning as soon as I got back home again.

And after packing away my hopes and dreams in a nest of acid-free tissue paper, I found the bottle of emergency whisky, downed a couple of stiff shots and then fell into an uneasy sleep until the alarm woke me in the early hours of next morning.

*

In the briefest of interviews, I was fired, given five minutes to collect my belongings and then escorted out of the building.

'So, my career just went down the pan,' I said to Honey, after ringing her when I returned. 'And once what I did to the costume gets out – and my bosses made it clear they were going to warn the other big theatrical costumiers – no one is going to want to employ me, are they?'

'*They* might not, but *I* certainly do!' Honey stated. 'I can't say I exactly *hoped* for this, but it had begun to sound as if Marco had gone off the boil as far as getting married was concerned, and also, a few things you'd said made me wonder if you were getting cold feet, too. It's why I've held back from advertising the museum job. So, how about it? A fresh start here, in Great Mumming, a little cottage all of your own, with a lovely workroom waiting for you?'

'But would you still want me, knowing what kind of thing I'm capable of doing when I lose my temper?'

'Of course! What you did was a totally understandable one-off. I felt much the same when I was jilted and can't even remember the drive to the cottage where my fiancé was staying, so it's just lucky for him he wasn't there when I arrived . . . though, of course, all the blood on the doorstep and up the hall brought me to my senses.'

'Blood on the doorstep?' I echoed.

'It's a long story. And, of course, when he turned up much later to apologize, I *did* assault him, but he didn't press charges. The Fairford women are clearly dangerous when provoked.'

I felt just a little better after that. And, after all, if it hadn't been for my promotional prospects and Marco, I'd have been tempted when Honey first told me about the job, when we were at Claridge's.

'What *is* that strange sort of wheezy rumbling noise in the background?' Honey suddenly demanded.

'Oh, that's Golightly, my upstairs neighbour's cat. He often visits, but when I got home I found him here with all his food, bed and litter tray. Miss McNabb was urgently called away because her sister in Edinburgh has had a stroke. I don't know when she'll be back.'

I looked at Golightly, who was asleep on his favourite armchair.

'I think you did mention the cat and I expect he'll be a bit of company for you till she gets back,' Honey said, then went back to the original topic.

'So, what about it? Do you want the job? I think you'd enjoy the work. Once the museum is open, it will just be part-time, so you'll be able to do your own work, too.'

'If I have any work,' I said.

'You will – those lovely little costume mannequins you make for the V&A, for a start.'

'George will hear what happened on the grapevine eventually, even if I don't tell him myself.'

'Yes, but I'm certain he wouldn't tell the shop to stop stocking them. He's your friend.'

I thought about it and decided she was right. George might be a big gossip, but even though he would be shocked by what I'd done, he would understand.

'You can sell them in the museum shop here, too: not just copies of the wedding dresses, but perhaps replicas of Rosa-May's costume and evening dress.'

'Maybe,' I agreed, although I wasn't sure I'd ever want to look at Rosa-May's costume and dress again.

I thought about leaving my tiny flat, a safe haven in the area where I had lived as a child, so that it had felt like coming home, but there was nothing else to keep me in London now.

I could run away, just as Ivo had done, for there was nothing and no one to hold me here. I'd miss George, but perhaps he'd come and visit.

'If you really mean it, I would love the job,' I said. 'It would not only be a fresh start in a new place, but also exciting to be closely involved with the new museum from the beginning.'

'Salary to be negotiated, cottage rent-free – you can pay the utilities,' Honey said briskly. 'Is your flat rented or your own?'

'Mine – or rather, it belongs to the mortgage lender.'

'You could let it, then?'

'I think I'll burn my bridges totally and sell it, no going back. And all my furniture will fit easily into a small cottage.'

'There we are, then. You'll have a busy few days, putting the flat on the market and packing up, and then you can move in whenever you want to – the sooner the better! It will be great to have a fellow enthusiast on the spot. We're going to have so much fun with the museum, just you wait and see!'

Rosa-May

Papa said he hoped such shallow admiration as I had received for my play-acting would not go to my head.

'Especially the attentions of the young gentlemen, who are so far above you in station and can mean nothing by it,' said Betsy with a jealous titter.

'No, indeed,' said Papa gravely, and added that he had not realized before that I had now grown up and it was high time I was sent out into the world to earn my living, instead of indulging in frivolity.

He was quite wrong to think that the admiration of the young gentlemen – however surprising to me – might have gone to my head, for I had neither encouraged it nor taken much heed of it, as I assured him.

And this was true, for even then, having overheard some of Mama's descriptions of childbirth, I had been filled with a huge dread of it and a resolution that I would rather die than marry and expose myself to this fate.

My small and slight stature, so like Mama's, would surely mean I would undergo the same agonies.

I assured Papa that I was very eager to make my own way in the world . . . which I was, although not at all in the way he meant me to!

*

After the play, our usefulness to the house party at an end, Kitty and I returned to the schoolroom under the careful eye of the governess.

Kitty would have a London Season the following year and be presented at court and I hoped Papa would not seek a post for me before then, for the prospect of being a companion, at the beck and call of an elderly employer, was not a prospect to gladden my heart!

Our education now concerned the accomplishments expected of a young lady, including singing. I found I had quite a pleasant, if light, voice and thought this might be an asset if ever I achieved my desire to go on the stage.

However, life was to take a sudden and unfortunate turn, only a few days after my acting debut . . .

*

It was late one afternoon and I was making my way home through the grounds when, on entering the rose garden, I perceived Piers, the younger son of the house, standing alone by the lily pond, moodily tossing pebbles into the water.

I made to withdraw, but before I could do so he looked up and, seeing me, swiftly approached, saying: 'May! I had been wishing I could see you – and here you are, like the embodiment of my dreams!'

And then, to my great astonishment and dismay, he declared he had an undying passion for me and, seizing me in a rough grip, attempted to kiss me!

Surprise made me immobile, for, until that moment, he had been nothing more than one of Kitty's teasing brothers. But then my senses returned and I struggled mightily and fetched him a great box on one ear!

'Little spitfire!' he said, panting and attempting to embrace me again. He was so much stronger and larger than I that I do not know what might have happened had not the squire's voice suddenly rung out, saying with astonished wrath: 'Piers!'

10

Listing

I had a largely sleepless night, not helped by Golightly's decision to join me in the early hours, when he attempted to kick me over to the edge of the bed, so he could stretch out luxuriously and snore. Before I met Golightly, I hadn't even realized cats *did* snore.

Scenes of what had happened at the theatre flashed across my mind every time I closed my eyes, like bits of a half-remembered nightmare, and at four I abandoned sleep as a lost cause and got up.

I sincerely wished it *had* been a nightmare, but it wasn't and there was no going back. But Honey had come to the rescue by generously offering me a way out and I resolved to make a fresh start in Great Mumming.

There was something strangely reassuring about the name of the little market town, probably because Mum came from somewhere round there and had talked about it. I wondered if there was also a Little Mumming, or even a Not-so-Great Mumming, too.

I put on my oldest and most comforting fleece robe – one I'd never let Marco see me wearing – and made some coffee, before beginning to compile a to-do list. My motto is, when in doubt, write a list.

Things to do immediately:

1. Return engagement ring to Marco.

Of course, if I'd been thinking straight on Wednesday, I'd have thrown it in his face . . . but then, if I'd been thinking straight, I would have simply walked out of there with my dignity and professionalism intact.

2. Repay taxi money to Wilfric, with thanks.

He'd been so unexpectedly kind that, really, I should email him thanks, too. I remembered he'd given me his card, which must be in the bottom of my bag, somewhere.

3. Ask Honey for the postal address of the mews cottage.

I'd need that so I could sort out the utilities and send it to all the other people who would need to know my change of address.

4. Go to estate agent and put flat on market.

I'd go to the one I bought it from, that would be easiest . . . and use the same solicitor, too, because I'd liked her and she was very efficient.

5. Clean flat for viewers and start to pack.

6. Find removal firm.

I would only need a small removal van, because I didn't have that much furniture and most of what there was had been my parents'. Our old flat hadn't been a lot bigger than this one.

It was all coming with me, anyway, along with my sewing machines, dressmaker's dummies, bolts of cloth and racks of thread . . . the tools of my trade.

7. How will I get to Great Mumming?

I didn't drive, so I supposed I'd better find out where the nearest train station was . . .

8. Confess to George about what happened and that I'm taking Honey's job offer.

I hated the thought, because I knew he'd be disappointed in me, but it would be better if I told him myself.

9. Give the V&A shop my new address.

I'd need the sales of the little costume mannequins to augment my part-time income.

And, memory jogged, I added:

10. Finish off current costume mannequin and deliver to V&A.

I made more coffee, then started a fresh sheet with slightly less urgent tasks. It all felt quite empowering: I was now the captain of a ship about to set sail to new horizons, not clinging to the mast of a sinking hulk.

1. Ask Honey if she could possibly measure the windows in the cottage, to see if my curtains will fit.

She'd sent me a short video of the interior of the cottage ages ago, after it had been renovated, replastered and painted, and the walls were all now plain cream with the woodwork picked out in white, so it would be a blank canvas when I moved in.

2. Tell Miss McNabb on her return – or when she rings – about my imminent move, so she can make arrangements for Golightly.

Unless whoever bought my flat was a cat lover, she'd have Golightly all to herself. I can't say I would miss him, because Golightly had never shown any signs of affection towards me, but he'd miss being able to range between the two flats whenever he fancied a change of scene . . . or of menu, if he thought I was cooking something more interesting than his cat food. I was also used to looking after him when Miss McNabb was away, or out late . . . but then, there *are* catteries.

I'd come to a halt, pen suspended. I was sure there were lots more things I needed to do, or to know . . . but perhaps I'd got enough to be going on with.

I showered and changed into jeans and a green T-shirt. Apart from having lavender shadows under my eyes from lack of sleep, by the time I'd darkened my lashes and brows and added a bit of rose lippy, I'd lost the zombie elf vibe and looked *almost* human.

Golightly had demanded breakfast the moment I'd got out of the shower, but then had gone back to bed – *my* bed – so I didn't think he'd miss me if I went out for a while. He'd be able to get through the cat flap on to the fire escape, if he wanted to, though not into Miss McNabb's flat, because her cat flap would be locked. Experience had taught her that when she was away, Golightly would sit in the empty flat and scream horribly for hours, which wasn't popular with the neighbours.

I found a small, padded envelope and put my engagement ring inside, wrapped in a bit of tissue paper. It was beautiful, but somehow it had never seemed really *me*, like the Bakelite jewellery was. I was obviously a plastic kind of girl and falling in love with both the ring and Marco had just been a temporary aberration.

I didn't bother with a note, just addressed it to Marco, but I did write a brief thank you to Wilfric to put in an envelope with some money to repay him for the taxi.

It was now almost six, and promised to be a fine day. London was never entirely quiet, even this far out, but in the early morning hours it was as close as it ever got.

I filled Golightly's water bowl, put some dry food in his dish and scattered around a few of the cat treats he loved, for him to find when he eventually decided to get up.

Then I shrugged into a cotton jacket, put the two envelopes in my big tapestry bag and went out.

*

No one in the theatre world was likely to be stirring at that time of day, so I dropped Wilfric's envelope in at the theatre first of all, before heading for Mayfair, where I tiptoed down the steps to Marco's basement door. I slid the small padded envelope through the letterbox without letting it make a betraying rattle, though since the blinds were down and there was no sign of life, Marco must still be in bed . . . with or without Mirrie.

Mission accomplished, I strode off up the street with a feeling of having escaped peril, and caught the tube back to more familiar territory.

I treated myself to a comforting full-fat breakfast and two huge cappuccinos while waiting for the estate agent's to open.

Over the second coffee, I emailed Honey about the cottage's postal address and the window measurements.

It took a bit of rooting around in the bottom of my bag before I found Wilfric's card and emailed him, too, to say there was an envelope waiting for him at the theatre, with the taxi fare in it and thanking him again for his kindness. I finished with the hope he'd have huge success in the play.

I paused for a moment, thinking he was already bound to know I'd been fired by Beng & Briggs, and then added that I'd already accepted a new job and would be moving out of London almost immediately.

Then, girding my loins, I went to put my beloved little flat on the market. It felt as if I was abandoning it and, with it, the link to the past and my happy childhood that it had represented.

*

Wilfric emailed me back later, saying I really shouldn't have bothered repaying him for the taxi. It was his pleasure and he entirely understood my actions, because I'd been tried beyond reason, which was sweet of him and rather soothing. Then he went on, more waspishly:

There were such ructions after you'd left and I'm sure Mirrie has now told anyone who will listen about what happened, because she's too stupid and self-obsessed to see how badly it reflects on her. Marco did realize it, once he'd calmed down, but it was too late then and anyway, he'd already rung Beng & Briggs, so I expect it will all come out anyway.

Marco was angry with Mirrie for letting the cat – or cats – out of the bag to me, too, so that you overheard.

Now the penny has finally dropped that Marco'd never intended dumping you for her at all, so currently the producer/star actress situation is just a trifle fraught.

The next bit made me smile, despite myself, because I'd been guiltily wondering how Beng & Briggs were getting on with a temporary replacement for the Titania costume, at such short notice. Charles, the assistant who would be hoping to step into my shoes, really wasn't up to the job, especially any hand sewing, but that was no longer my concern.

Mirrie had to wear a Sugar Plum Fairy costume from stock for the dress rehearsal and I can tell you now, she was the sourest plum I ever saw!

Do keep in touch and let me know if I can ever do anything at all to help.

Will xx

'Will' sounded a lot friendlier and less precious than Wilfric, but I wasn't sure *how* friendly I wanted to be. He might have been unexpectedly kind and thoughtful, but he most definitely wasn't my type. But then, if I didn't answer his email, that would be the end of it because our worlds would not, in future, overlap . . .

*

I embarked on a whirlwind of activity that at least had the effect of making me so exhausted I collapsed into bed each night – only to wake up hanging off the edge, with Golightly in sole occupation of the middle of it.

I'd quickly reached the bottom of those first lists, but written at least two more since.

The flat was now tidy and as clean as a sea-scoured shell. The estate agent photographed the flat and put it on the market the same day I'd been in to see them, and the Signboard Fairy had sneaked up while I wasn't looking and planted a 'For Sale' sign in the few feet of gravel that passed for a front garden.

Honey had sent me the address of the cottage, which was 1 Pelican Mews, and a new photo of the exterior, showing the small stone cottage tucked into the corner of the mews next to the museum, an open-trellised arch over the door. There seemed to be a narrow passageway dividing the house from the next building.

Honey, ringing me up on Saturday afternoon to see how things were going, said oatmeal Berber carpet was being laid as we spoke, the last thing to be done. 'Though there are vinyl floors in the kitchen, bathroom and utility room, and the floorboards in the hall were so good, I just had them sanded and sealed.'

'It all sounds wonderful,' I said. 'I really think you ought to charge me rent for it.'

'Oh, it's a perk of the job, which won't be hugely well paid,' she said airily. 'I'll expect you to work all hours for a pittance, especially leading up to the opening day!'

'I will – but for love of the work, rather than money,' I assured her. 'I'm so looking forward to unpacking all those dresses and finding out their histories.'

'You'll be as fascinated as I was,' Honey agreed, but *she* was clearly working down a list of her own, for she now said: 'There's a new boiler and radiators in the cottage. You've lost the second bedroom and gained a utility room because I removed the horrible bathroom from next to the kitchen and had a new one put in upstairs. The cottage *is* very small,' she added rather doubtfully.

'It's still going to be a lot bigger than my current flat,' I assured her.

'Well, that's good, and of course, you also have the adjoining big workroom, which runs under part of the museum.

100

Hugo had that done, to give the last curator a workroom for his ghastly stitching and stuffing activities, but that's all a thing of the past,' she added hastily. 'I had Ginny, who has the New Age shop across the square, go through it and do some kind of cleansing ritual.'

'Sounds fascinating!'

'It seemed to involve a bowl of burning herbs and a gong, and she yelped a few times, but that might have been the bowl burning her fingers,' Honey said vaguely. 'It smelled quite funky when she'd finished, but in a good way.'

I thanked her for the measurements she'd emailed me, not only of the windows, but the rooms, too, so I could decide in advance where things would fit.

'Oh, Viv did all that. It gave her something to do.'

'Viv?' I didn't think I'd heard her mention a Viv.

'Viv Greenaway, one of my oldest friends. She's just lost her husband and is staying with me.'

'The name sounds vaguely familiar,' I mused.

'She's a poet. Her late husband, Brad Whittenstall, was too, and a much better-known one, probably because he was more outgoing, while poor Viv has always been shy and reclusive. It's so rare for two creative souls to make a go of a marriage, but they were very happy, so I won't be adding *her* wedding dress to the exhibits.'

I could imagine Honey's grin when she said this.

'Do thank her for me,' I said. 'I really appreciate it.'

Then Honey asked me tactfully if I was OK for money to pay the mortgage and bills until the flat sold, and also the removal expenses, which was so kind of her, though I still had enough savings to cover everything.

'How are you getting here yourself? I never asked you if you had a car.'

'I haven't. I've never learned to drive. I'll get a train to the nearest station, wherever that is.'

'Oh, nonsense! I'll arrange a car and driver when I know the date!' she said, and wouldn't take no for an answer.

So that was that sorted. I would travel up like a lady on the day I wanted to move and be there when my belongings arrived.

Despite my inner turmoil over everything that had happened and the suddenness with which my life had so radically changed direction, it was all starting to get very exciting!

*

I'd told Honey that I hadn't heard anything from Marco directly, but described what Wilfric had said in his email, and that I'd also posted my engagement ring through Marco's door.

But then I was woken in the early hours two nights running by my phone buzzing on the bedside table.

Each time, it stopped before I could get to it, and each time it was Marco's number.

I suspected he was writing late in his study and, as he'd done so often in the past, rung me to angst about his new play, bounce ideas off me, or just wanted me to tell him how brilliant he was.

It had only been a reflex action and he'd cut the connection as soon as he'd realized what he was doing.

It was all jangling to the nerves, so after the second time I severed even this tenuous connection between us by turning my phone off at night.

He'd have to finish this play without me and, unless he'd been listening to my advice about following up *A Midsummer Night's Madness* with another supernatural thriller, and instead gone back to the stuff his arty friends told him he should be writing, this one might just be his swansong.

Despite the lack of sleep and all the other things I had to do, I'd worked hard on the little costume mannequin over the weekend and finished it, ready to deliver to the V&A. I arranged to see George while I was there: confession time.

And then there would be nothing to stay for, so I'd decided to move on the day the play opened: Monday, 3 September. A time for new beginnings . . .

11

Cat Flap

I delivered the costume mannequin to the museum shop as soon as it opened on the Monday morning, then had a quick last look at the Rosa-May Garland exhibition, which was to close at the end of September, when everything would be returned to Honey.

Then I had coffee with George in his tiny little office – behind the scenes at the museum, as it were.

His first words, once the coffee was poured and a plate of those scrummy biscuits with a thick coating of dark Belgian chocolate offered, were: 'I've been hearing some very odd rumours about you, Garland – quite unbelievable.'

The cat had apparently already jumped out of the bag.

'I think you may have to believe them, although I meant to tell you myself,' I said, putting down my cup and then resolutely describing what had happened. *All* of it. I didn't hold back on the details.

He heard me out, sipping his coffee and occasionally shaking his head, or murmuring 'Dear, dear!' in a mildly shocked tone.

'Do drink your coffee before it goes cold,' he said when I

finally came to a stop. 'And have a biscuit – chocolate always seems very calming, somehow, and you do seem to have been having quite a time of it.'

'That's the understatement of the year!' I said wryly, taking one. 'And I still can't believe I behaved so unprofessionally. I mean, destroying the costume after all that painstaking work! But I must have been in a blind rage, because I don't even remember doing it!'

'Of course I can't condone your actions, but clearly you acted under extreme provocation and I expect, after what you overheard, in a state of shock.'

'Yes, when I overheard Mirrie telling Wilfric how she and Marco had plotted to borrow my wedding dress for the photo shoot and that he was intending to finish with me once the play opened – well, I went sort of numb and icy cold. When I'd dashed into Mirrie's dressing room and locked the door behind me, the next thing I knew, I had the dressmaking shears in my hand and the costume was in tatters.'

'That must have been a terrible moment for you, dear Garland, but as I said, you acted under extreme provocation and weren't really responsible for your actions.'

'I could hardly believe what I'd done!'

He shook his head again. 'Well, it *is* done. But what will you do now?'

'The saying that every cloud has a silver lining is true,' I told him. 'Honey Fairford has offered me the post of curator/conservator at the wedding dress museum, so I'm moving there almost immediately.'

I told him all about Honey's kindness and how I could live in the cottage attached to the museum. 'And there isn't anything now to keep me in London, so I've put my flat on the market and I'm packing up.'

'I think you're quite right to make this move, Garland, and a fresh start. In fact, I quite envy you! Great Mumming is a nice, quiet, little town. I'll be up to visit from time to time – dear Honey has given me an open invitation to stay whenever I want to.'

'I know she's really valued all your advice and input into the museum plans,' I said. 'I'll look forward to seeing you there.'

Then, over more coffee, we fell into a discussion of all the various aspects of costume display, which was very soothing.

I described the latest mannequin I'd brought for the shop and mentioned that Honey had suggested I should sell them in her museum shop, too.

'Copies of some of the wedding dresses on display – though I'm not sure how popular those would be! But also of Rosa-May's costume and gown . . . when I can look at them again without feeling sick.'

'You know the V&A will take as many of the costume mannequins as you can make,' George assured me.

'That's great, because I'll have time to do my own work, too, and I'm not sure how much call there will be for a costume maker up there.'

'I'll be sorry to lose the Rosa-May Garland Collection at the end of the month,' he said sadly, as I finally got up to leave. 'And I'm sorry to be saying goodbye to you, too, Garland. I'll miss you.'

'I'll miss you too, George. But at least we'll still see each other whenever you visit Great Mumming.'

And as I left the museum, I thought that George was the only real friend I had in London – and the only person, other than people like solicitors and estate agents, to know my new address.

*

The removal firm I'd chosen – the same one that had moved my parents' furniture from the storage unit to the flat – had dropped off a few packing boxes and I'd raided the nearest supermarket for more.

My flat was really only a one-bedroom, because you couldn't have got anything larger than a baby's cot in the other, it being the size of a large broom cupboard. I'd used it as an extra work-station and storage for my fabrics, so I dismantled and packed up all of that room first, so I could use what was left of the floor space to pile boxes on as I filled them in the rest of the flat. The heavy stuff first: my collection of Victorian novels and children's books, the tiny wooden case full of Beatrix Potter books and all my costume reference books.

Then there was the set of orange Le Creuset pans that had been one of Mum and Dad's wedding presents, and which weighed a ton.

My life slowly vanished into boxes . . . and I soon discovered that Golightly found empty ones irresistible, so that I was always finding a pair of yellow eyes and a grimacing furry face looking up at me as I was about to put something in.

I'd replaced my favourite curtains with some old ones, so I could wash them, then remove the old curtain tape and replace it with new, having turned them sideways. It was really lucky they would fit the cottage windows that way! I'd made them myself, from lengths of vintage furnishing fabric bought from eBay; I was always on the lookout for anything interesting.

Most of my Bakelite jewellery collection was displayed in one of those glass-topped curio tables, a very battered one I'd picked up from a junk shop and relined with blue velvet, but the brooches were all pinned to a matching heart-shaped velvet pad I'd hung on the wall – hearts, anchors, Scottie dogs . . .

and a couple of clear Lucite ones, with flower shapes pressed into the back and painted, giving a sort of 3-D effect.

I bubble-wrapped the padded heart without taking any of the brooches off, but emptied the table and packed the pieces separately. My few valuables, like my laptop, would go in the car with me.

While I'd tried to confine most of the boxes to the spare room, so the flat looked more homely for viewing, the packing had begun to overflow into the living room by Wednesday, when there had been eight viewings in total and three offers, though none of them tempting! I wasn't taking less than it was worth and I wasn't reliant on the sale to be able to move, so I was in a good position.

I'd been so busy that it was only after I'd thankfully closed the door on the last of the viewers that it occurred to me that Miss McNabb had now been absent for several days without a word and I was just thinking I'd better give her a ring to tell her I was leaving on Monday for a new job and she'd have to arrange something for Golightly if she wouldn't be back before then, when *she* rang *me*.

I didn't recognize her voice immediately, because her accent had become infinitely more Scottish than before, so that she was in full flood with a report on her sister's health before I twigged who it was.

It appeared her sister was making a good recovery from the stroke, but wouldn't really be able to live alone any more.

'So since she has this big house and there's nothing to keep me in London now, we've decided I should move up here permanently. Of course, I only rent my flat and I've already given the landlord notice, so I'll just have to pop down briefly at some point to pack up and arrange the removal. There's plenty of room here for all my things.'

'I can see the sense in that,' I agreed, when I could finally get a word in. 'And oddly enough, I've put my flat on the market and I'm moving out of London almost immediately, too.'

'But – your work! Your engagement!' she exclaimed in surprise.

'I've broken my engagement and taken a new job in west Lancashire. I'll be moving there on Monday.'

'This is such a surprise,' she said. 'And all very sudden.'

'I know, that's why I was about to ring you, because of Golightly: will you be down before I leave, so you can take him back with you?'

There was a slight pause. 'I was ringing because I hoped you could take him on,' she said. 'He can't come here because my sister has Patterdale terriers and they're little devils for chasing cats. Anyway, to be honest, I'm not that fond of him! As you know, he just came unexpectedly with the flat.'

'Oh,' I said blankly. 'Well, that's a non-starter now I'm moving too, so what *are* you going to do with him?'

Golightly had oozed back in and was sitting bolt upright on the other armchair, giving me a narrow-eyed look as if he was aware we were discussing his future.

'I really don't know . . . unless perhaps you could take him to a cat rescue place before you go?' she suggested.

I looked at Golightly again and he pulled one of his hideous faces at me, which was not the kind of thing that would endear him to potential new owners. Besides, he was an old boy and had already had to start again with Miss McNabb when his previous owner left him behind.

'Or . . . perhaps you could take him with you,' she suggested hopefully.

'Take him with me? I don't think he'd like that, especially

since I'll be living in a small cottage in a town centre with no garden.'

'But he can't get down into the garden now, and he isn't really an outside cat,' she pointed out, which was true because the fire escape was the sort that had to be let down manually from my level to the ground.

'But he likes sitting on the fire escape and watching what's going on,' I said. 'And he wouldn't even have that. And you know what he's like – he hates change of any kind and would probably scream his head off for days, if not weeks.'

'Oh, well, it will have to be a cat rescue centre then,' she said. 'If you could possibly take him I'd be very grateful, and I'd pay for a taxi, of course.'

It all sounded a bit cold-blooded and, at that inconvenient moment, I suddenly realized I'd managed to become attached to the weird creature who haunted my flat. I wasn't sure I could bear to stuff him into his travel basket and dump him in a cat rescue centre, probably never to be adopted.

Before I knew what I was saying, I'd agreed to take him with me to Lancashire.

I must have lost my senses, though the cheerful young man who came to view the flat the very next morning hadn't, because he said he'd give me the full asking price, so long as Golightly, who had been deterred from his usual escape by heavy rain, was not included.

Rosa-May

Piers released me immediately and, though I was relieved to be free, I felt the utmost mortification at being found in such a situation. Without staying to hear what the squire might say, I fled for home.

The squire rode down after dinner and was closeted with Papa in the study for some time.

I was extremely apprehensive, but when the expected summons came, I was not called upon to defend myself, for Piers had taken the whole blame on himself – as well he might! He had told his father that he had fallen headlong in love with me on the evening I played the role of Titania and, on coming upon me alone in the rose garden had, with no encouragement from me, decided to declare his undying passion on the spot.

It was fortunate that Mr Taggart had arrived in time to see me box his son's ears and my attempts to repulse him, for it lent truth to the tale.

'His intentions may have been honourable, but Piers, as a younger son with his education to complete and his way to make in the world, is in no position to marry, even were the match a suitable one,' said the squire.

'I certainly do not aspire to such an unequal match and, I assure you, I have never shown Piers the least encouragement. The thought never even entered my head,' I said, my voice trembling despite my best efforts, for Papa still looked like the Wrath of God. 'I hope nothing I inadvertently said gave him to believe I would welcome his attentions, sir.'

'No, I don't expect you did,' the squire said, looking at me kindly. 'The trouble is, you have suddenly turned so deuced pretty, you have turned the silly young cub's head!'

When he had gone, Papa gave me a long and severe lecture on all the faults he perceived in my character and demeanour, but otherwise did not punish me.

But the upshot was that my schoolroom days were at an end: I was no longer to share in Kitty's lessons, but instead stay home until a suitable situation could be found for me.

My godmother, Lady Bugle – a distant relation of Mama's – was appealed to for advice and she being at that time without a companion, I was to be packed off to Bath forthwith, to fill this post.

I had only once met Lady Bugle, despite her being my godmother, and on this occasion she had struck me as autocratic and coldly formal in her manner, although my heart had been somewhat softened towards her by the gift of a topaz cross on a gold chain, which was still my only ornament.

This recollection made me hope that she had a warmer heart than appearances suggested.

*

Piers having been sent to visit friends for the rest of the Long Vacation, I was permitted to go to the Grange to say goodbye to Kitty, after which I had a brief interview with Squire Taggart, who, to *my complete astonishment, bestowed upon me a purse containing ten guineas as a parting gift! This seemed to me such riches beyond compare that I could barely stammer out my thanks.*

He seemed pleased, though, and pinched my cheek, saying I was a taking little puss, before adding, on hearing Mrs Taggart's voice outside the door, that we need not tell his good lady of the money: it would be a little secret between us.

12

In the Basket

I emailed Honey to explain about the cat and she raised no objections at all, though I strongly suspected she'd paid the taxi firm extra to transport the cat basket along with me and my various downmarket bags and boxes.

Honey's email had said she would unfortunately be away on the day I moved in, doing an author event and taking Viv with her, but she'd put a note with the info about anything I'd need to know urgently in the cottage kitchen and she'd leave the keys at a workshop two doors along.

On the final morning, the removal men packed all the contents of my flat into their van in about an hour . . . and very forlorn it looked when empty, too. The removal men were going to drop off a couple of large items for someone else a bit further north first, then would be with me just after lunch, which suited me very well.

I wouldn't say the taxi driver was enchanted to have a yowling cat in the back of his smart car – and it has to be admitted that there were some horrendous rending noises as Golightly attacked the wickerwork basket – but luckily he soon gave up and went to sleep.

London had put on its sunniest September face, as if to show me what I would be missing, but as we drove further and further north, the sky clouded and by the time we reached the outskirts of Great Mumming you could hardly see out for great sheets of rain, and the fast beat of the windscreen wipers had sent me into a hypnotic trance.

I peered out when the driver told me we were nearly there and had a brief impression of a market square surrounded by buildings, before we turned through a narrow archway and bumped over the cobbled yard of the mews.

I told him the cottage was at the top left side, and he skirted some kind of little central garden and came to a stop in the corner. When he turned the engine off, the rain drummed on the roof like giant fingers and Golightly woke up and said something grumpy in Cat.

'I've just got to fetch the keys – I won't be a minute,' I said, pulling on an inadequate cotton jacket.

'Don't rush. With a bit of luck, this rain might go off . . . or an ark float by,' he said sardonically.

'I think the sky might be a bit lighter now,' I said optimistically as I stepped out on to wet, shiny cobbles, and indeed, the deluge seemed to slacken at that moment and turn into a fine rain that swept across the courtyard in wet, grey curtains, revealing glimmers of some of the stone buildings surrounding it.

I didn't hang about looking, though, but hurriedly followed Honey's directions, passing the end of my cottage and the narrow passageway, then knocking at the second door along, where there were lights on behind the wide windows. The knocker was shaped like a jester's head, complete with traditional belled tricorn cap, and I let it drop with a heavy thump.

The door swung open immediately, as if the person behind

it had been listening out for me – or perhaps had heard the slam of the car door.

I pushed wet hair out of my eyes. 'Hi, I'm Garland Fairford and I've come to collect the—'

I broke off, looking up into the face of the man who had opened the door: a very familiar, straight-nosed, handsome face, the dark amber eyes suddenly seeming to flash with a spark of golden light.

'*You* – here?' we both said simultaneously, and then, for a long moment we just stared at one another as the smile of welcome died on his lips.

Thom . . . My heart had given a great leap of joy at the sight of him, but now I was filled with a conflicting desire to both hug him and pummel him hard.

I recovered from the shock first; the fight-or-flight instinct must have kicked in. I snatched the keys from his hand, turned on the spot and ran back to the car, slipping and sliding on the cobbles.

Behind me, I thought I heard him call my name.

*

Ten minutes later, I was standing in the hall of the cottage, my belongings scattered around me and the car was gone. The driver had cheered up; I think I must have overtipped him because I hadn't really known what I was doing.

I locked the front door, then closed my eyes and leaned my forehead against the smooth wood, taking a few deep breaths and wondering if I'd just conjured Thom up out of thin air.

But no, he'd seemed real enough, casual and relaxed in jeans and a loose blue chambray shirt with the sleeves rolled up. His dark honey-coloured hair was longer than I'd ever seen it, tucked behind his ears . . .

And how quickly the old, familiar name had sprung to my lips, my first line of defence already crumbled away to nothing.

He really *was* here, in Great Mumming; had probably been here all the time, for he'd looked at home and relaxed before he recognized me.

A thought struck me: Honey knew about my connection with Thom, so she had concealed the fact that he was here from me. And, remembering the stunned look on Thom's face, I concluded he'd had no idea it was me who'd be collecting those keys, either.

It was some slight consolation to realize that at least he couldn't think I'd found out where he was living and followed him up here because, as far as he knew – assuming he was still hearing things on the theatrical grapevine from Mallory and Demelza, who I'd always suspected of keeping in touch with him – I was about to marry Marco and was in line for promotion at work.

Now I felt *really* confused, my mind in chaos. Was the workshop where Honey had left the keys his? Did he actually live nearby?

I urgently needed to speak to Honey, and I was already groping in my shoulder bag for my phone when I remembered she was off doing her book event and I'd have to leave it till later.

A sudden and horrendously loud scream of rage reminded me that actually I *wasn't* alone and I was dripping on to the doormat, while poor Golightly was still confined to his basket and beginning to sound like a kettle coming to the boil, or possibly about to explode.

Duty called, and also I remembered that the removal van would be here before too long. I'd simply have to try and put what just happened out of my mind for the present and get on with things.

I hung my jacket on the doorknob to carry on dripping and then turned to take stock of my new home. The heating must be on because the wooden-floored hall was warm. A narrow staircase climbed steeply up from it, but there was only one door off it, to my left, which I pushed open to reveal a long sitting room with a window on to the mews.

I carried Golightly's basket in there and, setting it down on the wool Berber carpet, cautiously opened the door and stepped back.

He did not, however, shoot out in a fury, but instead stared at me for a long moment and then, putting a paw gingerly out, patted the carpet as if suspecting it was quicksand in disguise, before slowly emerging with a 'What fresh hell is this?' expression on his furry face.

'This is our new home,' I told him, then followed as he stalked towards the open door to the kitchen, at the other end of the room.

It was all dazzlingly white in there, both the tiled walls and the units. I could see at once there would be just enough room for my little pine table and two chairs, and there was a corner for my fridge-freezer.

'All mod cons, see,' I told the unimpressed Golightly, 'and through here' – I threw open another door – 'is the utility room that used to be a bathroom. Washing machine, new boiler . . . and space for a litter tray.'

And on that thought, I fetched it and the bag of cat litter and set it up. I didn't want anything to mar that beautiful oatmeal living-room carpet.

Golightly sat and watched me as I did this and then filled his water bowl.

'Right,' I said to him. 'Are you staying here, or do you want to come and explore?'

As if he'd understood me, he got up and led the way back into the living room, which was bare apart from a small fake woodburning stove on a stone hearth. There was a door on that side of the room too, which must lead to the workroom, but I'd save that for last.

Golightly vanished upstairs, and when I followed, there was no sign of him on the landing, or in the shower room, which was another symphony in white, with the sort of curved glass shower cubicle that would probably beam you up to a *Star Trek* spaceship if you pressed the wrong button.

The cat was in the bedroom, lying in the middle of the pale carpet like a small puddle of dull, grey-blue cut velvet. He got up when I opened a door to reveal a built-in cupboard with a hanging rail and shelf, but he didn't find anything of interest in there and backed out in disgust.

'If there were ever any mice, they're long gone,' I told him, then went to look at a small, original cast-iron fireplace with a scallop-shell-shaped top, now painted white and very pretty. The front window looked out on to the mews, like the room below, but you still couldn't see much of it clearly through the veils of fine rain, just a glimmer of lights on the other side of the courtyard where the tall, black-and-white shape of Pelican House loomed.

I stood there for a moment, feeling the welcoming warmth of the cottage envelop me – and no trace of the previous occupant lingered there.

Back downstairs again, I opened the door to the workroom. With the gloomy day and the rain beating against the windows, the room seemed dark, but I found a wall switch and big strip lights illuminated a much larger space than I'd expected, with another smaller room at the back, with a Belfast sink and draining board.

The flooring was practical vinyl and the walls painted a soft, pale dove grey. It was empty, apart from some fixed shelving on the far wall, which had another door that presumably led into the museum. I'd wait for Honey to show me over that, although I had a bone to pick with her first: a mammoth-sized one with Thom's name on it.

If it hadn't been for that, I'd have thought I was in heaven, with so much room for all my sewing machines, dressmaker's dummies and other equipment. I'd even be able to have something I'd only ever dreamed of before: a cutting table of my own.

I itched to start a list. It might prove a bit expensive, so I hoped the flat sale would go through quickly, so my small remaining nest egg wasn't reduced to fragments of shell.

I checked my watch: maybe there was time for coffee and a sandwich before the van arrived.

This time, I noticed the heap of mail on one of the kitchen worktops, with a note from Honey, welcoming me to my new home and giving me a few bits of vital information. When I located the mini fridge behind a dummy cupboard door, it contained butter, milk, cheese and bread. It was all so kind; she'd shown me nothing *but* kindness, apart from the small fact that she'd concealed Thom's presence in Great Mumming from me.

On the bottom of the notes she'd scribbled that she'd be back later and not to bother cooking tonight, just come over to Pelican House for dinner at seven. I would have things out with her about Thom, then, I decided.

Meanwhile, I tried to put him out of my mind and, after a cup of coffee and a sandwich, I read the meter and sent that to my new electricity supplier.

Then I was ready for the arrival of my furniture . . . after I'd had a long search for Golightly, only to find him in the utility room, curled up asleep in the bottom of the cardboard carton I'd brought his cat litter, food and bowls in.

*

The living room seemed lighter by then, and when I went to look out of the front window for any sign of the removal van, I saw that the rain had eased off to a very fine haze. I could see the buildings enclosing the rectangular cobbled yard now, all built of warm stone like my own cottage, with doors and window frames picked out in black and white, which sort of tied it in with the rambling Tudor rear façade of Pelican House, with its gables and overhanging, diamond-paned windows. It seemed to have its own little railed garden behind, but there was also the oval of shrubs in the centre of the yard, too, which would be nice to look out on in spring.

The long museum building loomed to my right, making up one whole side of the mews, and had shallow steps leading up to double wooden doors.

My attention was caught by the van squeezing slowly through the arch that led on to the market square and I dashed back to the utility room, tossed a few cat treats into Golightly's bowl, then shut the door on him and went to let the removal men in.

*

Like the driver of the taxi, the removal men didn't seem to want to hang about after they'd brought in my stuff and deposited everything in the right rooms. They even declined my offer of tea and biscuits, although that might have been because of the eldritch shrieks coming from the utility room.

They had been kind, however, even putting my little white bed together for me and not complaining about having to manoeuvre my very heavy industrial-sized sewing machine into the workroom. It had its own load-bearing table on castors, but those aren't a lot of use on cobbles. Or up and down steps.

I gave them a generous tip, too – at this rate I'd have to find a cashpoint soon – then waved them off.

A watery sun was now struggling to push aside the dove-grey clouds, and far from presenting a slightly dismal appearance, the mews now looked positively charming. I could just read the words 'Hetty's Hats' on a signboard over one of the windows of the buildings on the left-hand side, which looked like a mixture of workshops and cottages. I suppose originally these were all stables and housing for the grooms and coachmen.

From my porch, I couldn't see much more of the buildings along the same side as the cottage, other than the end of the first one, on the opposite side of the passage – and I certainly wasn't about to step out and risk being spotted by Thom!

But even as I glanced that way, he came out of a door further along with a white bull terrier on a lead. I was rooted to the spot and, as if feeling my eyes on him, he turned from locking the door and stared at me . . . or perhaps it was just the sound of Golightly's screams, audible even through a locked door and two rooms, that had caught his attention.

Whatever spell had frozen me to the spot suddenly broke and I went back in, slamming the door behind me.

Then it was just me, an angry and confused cat, and a lot of thoughts that I kept pushing down under the surface, although they soon bobbed back up again.

13

Poetic Licence

Golightly was sitting just inside the utility-room door and ceased screaming the moment I opened it, then pulled a gargoyle face at me, before calmly returning to his dish to polish off the last cat treats.

'I thought I'd left my involvement with self-obsessed, volatile males behind me in London,' I told him sourly, but he took no notice, even when I hauled in the boxes containing the rest of his paraphernalia and began unpacking his gourmet dinners, more bags of treats, scratch mats and his furry igloo bed.

Then I set up the cat litter bin and lined it, before cleaning up his tray . . . and I definitely felt that the way he used it, the moment it was all clean again, was a gesture of contempt.

'Thank you *so* much,' I said. 'Glad you're so grateful I didn't dump you in a cat rescue place.'

He made a sound that was probably the Cat equivalent of 'Huh!' before stalking purposefully off into the living room and settling himself on one of the two small, shabby armchairs. It was lucky he always favoured the one covered in a vintage design of donkeys wearing straw hats, instead of my favourite, with the Eiffel Towers and poodles, because I suspected he'd have won any argument.

This might be a small cottage, but it was still twice the size of my flat, and what furniture I had was now dotted about the room: a small desk in front of the window; the glass-topped curio table; a TV unit; a small wooden chest that did service as a coffee table; a little tub chair I'd had as a child; and a lot of bookshelves.

The back wall was stacked with boxes and bundles waiting to be unpacked, after which there would be even more space and I could invest in the luxury of a sofa.

It was still only early afternoon, so I started unpacking, which is a much speedier process than packing it all up in the first place.

In only a few hours, the curtains were hung in the living room and bedroom, my bed made up and my clothes all neatly put away.

I laid my small pink and blue Chinese rug next to the bed, found the reading lamp for the bamboo bedside table, and then everything was ready for me to just fall into bed in a stupor of exhaustion at the end of the day. There were a lot of things to do before then, however . . .

Downstairs, Golightly snored noisily and obliviously on, even when I started clattering pots and rattling cutlery into the kitchen drawers.

There was another small oriental rug to go in front of the hearth, this one in shades of faded coral and duck-egg blue. I switched on the fake log burner to try the effect, and it flickered cheerfully, giving the impression of comfort and warmth. The place was starting to look and feel like home.

The curtains in here were patterned in roses against a trellis. I do love roses, but real old-fashioned ones with crumpled, scented petals – most definitely not the artificial-looking ones in that bouquet Marco had sent me . . . or perhaps just left in my flat when he showed Mirrie my wedding dress. I should have smelled a rat – a love rat – and not just assumed it had been Miss McNabb who'd put them there.

Feeling tired and grubby, I flattened out the boxes I'd emptied.

The bookshelves were still empty, the display cabinet and glass-topped curio table ready to be filled, but I could take my time over those.

I decided the fridge-freezer had had enough time to settle and cautiously switched it on. It came to life with a hum and then started trying to communicate with me in what sounded like Dolphin, but then, it's always done that from time to time, so I wasn't particularly worried.

When I checked my watch I was amazed at how late it was, although I had stopped earlier just to give Golightly his dinner.

Now I just had time for a quick shower and a change of clothes into black leggings and a long, drapey, moss-green tunic. Then I was ready to go out for dinner, although, truth to tell, I was so tired that all I really wanted to do was put on my old robe and slippers in front of the stove.

But still, I had an urgent need to talk to Honey, and the sooner the better!

I left the downstairs lights on, including the hall, picked up my jacket and went out into the cool of the early dusk. Everything smelled damp and fresh.

*

Skirting the central garden on the museum side, well away from the workshop where, even now, Thom might be lurking,

I did glance back but there was no sign of anyone about, and although some windows glimmered on the opposite side of the cobbled yard, there were none in the two buildings on the same side as my cottage. I could see now that the one nearest my cottage had a large board fixed to the front, that read: 'Pelican Puppet Theatre'.

Puppets – I remembered that Thom had become interested in carving marionettes, so perhaps that was the connection that had led him here? I couldn't make out the sign over the workshop next to it, other than a name 'Bruno Bascombe'.

Somewhere, a clock began to chime the hour and I hurried on, going through the arched passageway to the market square, before turning right to the front door of Pelican House.

The lamps on either side of an ancient-looking studded wooden door were already lit and as I approached it was thrown open, revealing several people in the hallway.

This was definitely Pelican House, but I wondered for a moment if I'd mistaken the time, or even the day.

I stood watching for a moment as two elderly women emerged and walked briskly off together across the square, then a youngish man with a cockatoo-like crest of fair hair assisted three rather more infirm visitors down the steps and into a taxi that had drawn up outside, calling a cheerful goodbye before he went back in again.

I hurried to reach the door before he closed it and heard Honey's familiar voice saying: 'Thank you, Derek.'

'Not at all. I'll just clear away the sherry glasses and then I'll be off home,' he said, and vanished up the dark hall as Honey spotted me hovering on the threshold.

'There you are, Garland! Did you get trampled by the march of the Zimmer frames? Come on in!'

'I thought I must be too early. Have I come at the wrong time?'

'No, not at all,' she said, closing the door behind me. 'That was just the remnants of Great-uncle Hugo's Genealogy Society. They always met here on Mondays, and even though Hugo has passed away, some of them didn't seem capable of grasping the idea that they'd have to find another venue, so in the end it was easier to let them keep coming. Derek pops over to see to them – they do love their sherry and sandwiches.'

'Derek?' I echoed, slightly at sea.

'The man you just saw – he's sort of my PA, secretary, house-keeper, cleaner, general factotum – totally invaluable! He has no set hours, just fits things in to suit himself.'

Slightly dazed by this flow of information, I let her take my jacket and hang it on a hallstand almost as dark and shiny as the wooden panelling on the wall, then followed her into a sitting room with more dark panelling, though the walls above it were white and a real fire burned in the stone fireplace. There were several plum velvet easy chairs and a vast and squishy-looking sofa, and the general effect was rich and cosy.

Honey, tall, slim and elegant in black trousers and top, gave me her tilted smile. 'It's lovely to see you again at last, Garland. I'm glad you're on time, so we can have a little catch-up before the others arrive. Viv's cooking.'

'Which others?' I blurted. 'It's not a dinner party, is it?'

'Well, not *really*. I just thought it was time I got everyone who lives in the mews together, so I can tell them about my plans for the museum. I've been too busy since I moved in to really get to know everyone, except in passing – mostly at the pub. But I thought it would be good for you to meet them all straight off, too, and break the ice.'

Before I could reply, she flipped up the top of a huge globe to reveal bottles and glasses and said, 'Speaking of ice, would you like a drink? Viv only drinks sherry, but I mix a mean Martini.'

I'd been about to broach the question of why she hadn't told me about Thom but I think she mistook my expression, because she said, 'I know the globe drinks cabinet is really naff, but it was Uncle Hugo's and it's sort of amusing.'

I found my voice at last. 'Honey, would one of these mews residents you've invited to meet me be Thom Reid, alias Ivo Gryffyn, by any chance?'

'He's just known as Thom Reid in Great Mumming, but yes, he works for Bruno Bascombe, the marionette maker, and lives in Pelican Mews.'

'Then why, since you know the connection between us, didn't you tell me he was here?' I demanded. 'I mean, you know he walked out on me six years ago, so you must have realized what a shock it would be for me to come unexpectedly face to face with him!'

I found I was holding a glass full of Martini, complete with an olive on a stick, and I took a great, steadying gulp.

'Cheers, and welcome to your new home,' Honey said, raising her glass in salute. 'And the reason I didn't tell you about Thom being here, once I realized you knew each other, was because he so obviously didn't want it known who he was, or where he lived now – and then later, I thought it might put you off coming here, if you knew.'

'It would,' I said bluntly, then thought about what she'd just said. 'But – surely everyone here knows who he is – or *was*?'

'Of course, but we're all pretending we haven't recognized him. Anyway, his glory days as Gus in the Silvermann films were a long time ago now, so I don't suppose he was still getting mobbed before he left London.'

'No, and somehow he always managed to look so ordinary even though he—' I broke off. 'I suppose he *has* been here for the last six years?'

'Uncle Hugo told me he'd been coming up to work with Bruno for some time before that and bought one of the mews cottages. Then, when he moved here permanently, he became Bruno's full-time apprentice. He's been here ever since.'

I felt my quick temper rising. 'So all those years when I was wondering where he was and if he was happy, he's been happily working and living here!'

'I don't think anyone can escape the past that easily, Garland, no matter how much they may try,' Honey said sombrely. 'You always carry the ghosts with you.'

I supposed she was right. I'd never quite managed to escape my past – first the death of my parents when I was a child, which illogically had felt like an abandonment, and then, later, Thom literally had abandoned me, though he at least had had a choice.

'I still think you should have warned me, Honey. What if he thinks I found out where he was living and only took the job here because of it? I mean, it all seems one hell of a coincidence. Doesn't it?'

'Oh, he doesn't think that. And life is full of the weirdest coincidences,' she assured me. She sipped her own drink and her dark, thoughtful eyes met mine over the rim of the glass.

'How do you know he doesn't think it?'

'He rang me earlier, shortly after I'd got back and said he'd had a shock when he saw you, because you'd known each other from childhood, though you'd since lost touch.'

'Yeah, right!' I said sarcastically.

'And he said you were obviously surprised to see him there, too—'

'Understatement of the year!' I put in.

'But he really did think it was a coincidence, because he doesn't realize that *I* know all about your shared history.'

That was true. During all our long exchanges by email and

phone, I was sure I'd revealed almost every detail of my relationship with Thom, not to mention the whole Leo/Marco connection that had caused our last quarrel before he left London for good.

'So, why did he ring you?'

'To find out what you're doing here, of course! I mean, he realizes you are my new museum curator, but he said the last he'd heard of you, you were firmly fixed in London, doing well in your profession and engaged to be married.'

'What did you tell him?'

'Well, first of all that we'd discovered we were distant cousins after we'd met at an exhibition about a mutual ancestor, a Regency actress.' Then, she continued blandly, 'I said that when I'd heard that due to a change in your circumstances you were looking for a new job out of London, I immediately offered you the post of curator.'

'"A change in my circumstances" is one way of putting it,' I said drily, and she gave that attractive, twisted grin.

'Of course, then he wanted to know *what* change of circumstances and I said he'd better ask you himself if he really wanted to know and I looked forward to seeing him with the other Pelican Mews residents for dinner at seven thirty.'

The realization finally dawned. 'So he *is* coming here?' I looked at my watch. 'Any minute now!'

'Well, he didn't say he *wasn't*, and he accepted the invitation earlier, along with the others. But I rang off then, anyway.'

'Who are these others—' I began, then broke off as a woman came into the dining room, visible through the folded-back double doors.

She was about Honey's age, small and slight, wrapped in a large flowered pinafore. She was setting down a stack of plates but looked up when our voices ceased.

She had a sweet, heart-shaped face with a broad brow, above which sprang two wings of wavy brown hair. She reminded me strongly of a portrait of Charlotte Brontë.

'Viv, come and have a sherry,' invited Honey. 'This is my cousin, Garland – I've told you all about her.'

Viv came in with seeming reluctance, darted a shy smile in my direction, then accepted a glass of sherry. She didn't stay and drink it with us, though, but without a word headed back through the dining room and out of a far door.

'Elective mute,' said Honey when she'd gone.

'What?'

'Elective mute, though they called it selective mutism when we were students together. She's been one from a child and it means that as well as being very shy, she literally *can't* talk to most people, only to ones she knows well, like me. We were at school together before university.'

'I've never heard of it,' I confessed.

'Not many people have. It's more common in children and then, with the right treatment, they usually manage OK as adults, but Viv's has continued all her life.'

'Won't she be a bit daunted by a dinner party of people she doesn't know, then?'

'She was used to presiding over dinner parties when her husband, Brad, was alive, so although she is unlikely to say anything, as long as no one expects her to talk, she'll be fine.'

'Her condition must make everything very difficult,' I said.

'It was all right when she was married, because her husband was outgoing. Big, brash, good-hearted and happy to talk for both of them.' She smiled. 'I think Brad adored her cooking, too – she's very domesticated.'

'I remember you telling me you had a poet friend staying

with you and I had vaguely heard of her, though I don't read a lot of poetry.'

'Nor me. Anyway, since she wasn't coping on her own after Brad died, I invited her here for a long stay.'

'That was kind.'

'Not really, because she'll do all the cooking! I'm not much of a cook. And if I'm away, she can help Derek look after my dog.'

'Which dog?'

'Rory, my Irish wolfhound – he's in the kitchen, hoping for titbits. Have another Martini,' she added hospitably.

'I'd better not, because I haven't had much to eat today,' I said.

Just then, the front door knocker echoed resonantly through the house like the crack of doom, making me jump.

'They don't make doors like that any more,' Honey said. 'That must be the others.'

14

Associations

Honey returned with three newcomers – or rather, two, plus one oldcomer, in the shape of Thom. Actually, he didn't look all that familiar, now I came to take a good look at him, with his long hair framing a face that was still handsome but older and more melancholy.

I looked away quickly when he glanced at me and Honey introduced me to a tall, pale, willowy, young woman with feathery, platinum-blond hair, light grey eyes and a rather cool and reserved manner.

'Garland, this is Pearl Morris.'

'Hi!' I said, thinking that never had a name suited someone more.

But she smiled in a friendly way and said, 'Welcome to Pelican Mews, Garland!'

'Pearl owns the second-hand bookshop on the far side of the entrance to the mews – Fallen Idle,' Honey said.

'Fallen Idol?' I queried, wondering if I'd heard right, and Pearl spelled it out for me.

'My late husband thought it up; it tickled his sense of humour. The shop fronts on to the square,' she added, 'but my cottage is behind it, in the mews, right next to Simon's hat workshop and flat.'

She gestured to the tall, sandy-haired man standing next to her who, I had noticed, had been watching her with an air of dog-like devotion in his faded denim-blue eyes.

He started when he heard his name and gave me a boyish grin. 'Simon Speller – I'm the Hetty of Hetty's Hats – and very pleased to meet you,' he said, and I found myself returning the smile, because there was something very appealing about Simon.

'I noticed the signboard,' I began, but before I could ask him how he came to be Hetty, Honey had lugged forward the elephant in the room in her usual impetuous way.

'Of course, I don't need to introduce you to Thom, since it appears you already know each other,' she said blandly, and I gave her a look that she met with feigned innocence.

'I did know Thom, but that was a long time ago.'

'You've met before?' Simon sounded surprised. 'You mean, when he was Ivo—' He stopped dead and looked guilty. 'Sorry, Thom, I forgot I wasn't supposed to mention that.'

'It doesn't matter. Garland knows, and I'm sure everyone locally does, too, so it's no big deal,' Thom told him.

'I used to work for a large firm of theatrical costumiers in London, so our paths were bound to cross,' I explained, shrugging, and left them to draw their own conclusions, although I caught Thom's dark amber eyes fixed on me with an unfathomable expression in their depths and looked away quickly. 'Of course, I had no idea he was living here, and he didn't know until I arrived that I was the new museum curator.'

'It's odd the way things come about,' said Honey. 'Garland is an expert in the recreation of historical costume, so I'm so lucky she was available to take up the post in my new museum. But I'll tell you how that came about, and what I'm planning for the museum, over dinner. I think we'd better go through to the dining room, because I see that Viv – my friend who is staying with me and kindly offered to cook our dinner – has just put the soup on the table.'

Viv must have crept in and set down the steaming tureen at one end of the table silently before vanishing again.

Honey lowered her voice conspiratorially: 'Garland already knows, but I must just explain about Viv! She's extremely reserved, especially with strangers, and is unlikely to speak to any of you. She has a condition called elective mutism.'

By their blank expressions, none of *them* had ever heard of it before either, but they got the idea anyway.

Honey led the way into the dining room and directed us where to sit. She was at the head of the table, with Simon and Thom next to her, on either side – 'hostess's perks', she called that. I was next to Simon, with Pearl opposite and the end chair on her side was left vacant for Viv, who now returned, divested of her pinafore and carrying a basket of small, warm bread rolls.

She set it down in the middle of the table before taking her seat, perching right on the edge, like a bird who might take flight at any moment.

'Thom, there's a bottle of champagne in that ice bucket behind you, if you wouldn't mind doing the honours?' said Honey. 'Apart from being my favourite tipple, this is by way of being a bit of a celebration.'

She ladled out and passed the soup, while Thom opened the champagne with a loud popping noise and filled our glasses.

'Smells delicious, Viv – Stilton and broccoli?' Honey guessed, and Viv gave a slight nod, without looking at her.

Thom leaned over to place a full champagne flute in front of me and I was suddenly very conscious of him in a physical way I'd never felt before. It was unsettling, but I suppose it was because our past connection had broken so completely and we were now meeting again on the other side of an abyss, like strangers.

Despite the inner turmoil, I suddenly realized I was ravenous and the soup smelled delicious. We all paid it the homage of silence while we savoured it.

'That was the most delicious soup I've ever tasted,' Simon said when we'd finished, and when we all agreed, I saw Viv flush slightly with pleasure.

'Viv is a wonderful cook, which is more than I am,' Honey said. 'My idea of a dinner party is to order in a big takeaway and lots of beer.'

'That's pretty much my idea of one, too,' said Simon. 'Real home cooking like this is a great treat.'

Simon was so patently open, friendly and unscary that I wasn't surprised to see Viv give him a timid smile, but then, the next minute, throw a terrified glance along the table at Thom's slightly brooding profile. He had tied back his hair with what looked like a leather shoelace to keep it, as he'd explained, out of his soup.

Simon sprang up to help carry out the empty dishes, knocking his chair over in his eagerness and apologizing to it as he set it back on to its legs. He came back with Viv, bearing a roast chicken and all the trimmings.

Honey said she didn't trust any man with a knife in his hand and deftly carved that up herself.

The gravy was rich and very thick, the way I remembered Mum making it, not the thin, dark fluid my aunt had called gravy. I was sure neither the stuffing nor the bread sauce had come out of a packet, either, and the roast potatoes were crisply fluffy. I can't really describe them any other way.

I began to feel a little more sober as I ate – that Martini on an almost empty stomach had probably not been a good idea – although I only took a couple of cautious sips of the champagne, in case I suddenly started babbling, like I had at Claridge's. Or perhaps more likely, since I was now feeling quite disorientated and spaced out with tiredness and everything that had happened during this long day, falling asleep in my chair!

'I think we could call this the first meeting of the Pelican Mews Residents' Association,' Honey suggested, with her twisted grin. 'We're all here except Bruno, who's on a long trip to New Zealand, Garland, staying with his daughter and her family.'

'My boss,' Thom told me.

I didn't look at him when I said, 'Yes, Honey told me all about him.'

'And he's not your boss any more, Thom,' Honey corrected him. 'You might have started off as his apprentice, but you're an equal partner in the business now.'

'I'll never know as much about marionettes as Bruno does. He's had a lifetime in the business,' Thom said.

'Bruno told me you were better at carving faces than he ever was, even before the rheumatism. You put real character in them,' said Simon.

'Yes, and he wouldn't have gone off for months, leaving you in charge, if he didn't think you were up to it,' agreed Pearl.

'Bruno was one of Uncle Hugo's cronies, so I know him quite well,' Honey explained to me. 'He lives above his workshop, next to the puppet theatre: that's owned by the Marinos, a big extended local family, but they don't live in the mews and

they're out on the road from spring to autumn, doing traditional Punch and Judy and marionette shows all over the
place, especially at the seaside.'

'They just use the theatre for storage most of the year, but
they put on shows at weekends over the winter,' said Thom.
'Some for children and some, like the one they're putting on in
October, more for an adult audience. This time it's going to be
a Victorian melodrama called *Maria Marten and the Murder in
the Red Barn*. I've been working on the marionettes for the
main characters.'

'I love a good Victorian melodrama,' said Honey. 'I'll look
forward to that . . . although I don't suppose they would like
me to rewrite the script, so that Maria murders her lover instead
of the other way round, would they?'

'I suspect they'd probably prefer to stick to the original,'
Thom said with a grin.

Simon suddenly looked at me with a strangely hopeful
expression dawning on his face. 'My grandmother used to
make the marionette costumes for Bruno and I've been doing
it since, but it's not really my thing. But if you are a costume
maker, Garland, perhaps—'

'Simon, let the poor girl settle in, before trying to load any
more work on to her,' Pearl said, and he looked abashed.

'Sorry!'

'Thom has the cottage in the corner between Bruno's workshop and Simon – and apart from the museum and your
cottage, Garland, that's it, as far as residents go,' said Honey.

'Yours is solely a workshop, isn't it, Simon?' I asked. 'You
don't sell hats directly to the public?'

'No, it's just wholesale at the moment. My grandmother
Hetty was the original Mad Hatter of the family and then it
skipped a generation and landed on me. Gran's retired to

Brighton now and I've taken over. I have wondered about trying to sell direct through my website at some point.'

'I've been trying to persuade Bruno to do that for ages,' put
in Thom. 'He didn't even have a website until I got Pearl to set
up a basic one for the business.'

'You designed and set up the website?' Honey asked Pearl,
with interest.

'And mine,' Simon put in. 'She's ace at that kind of thing.'

'It's a sideline, but I enjoy it,' Pearl said. 'You don't make a
huge living from second-hand books.'

'That's interesting, and could be really useful to me,' Honey
said.

'But surely you have a website already?' Pearl asked.

'Oh, yes, an author one – my publisher set it up and runs it.
But I really want an all-singing, all-dancing one for the
museum, when it opens, perhaps with virtual tours and an
online shop. If you think you'd like to take it on, we could get
together and discuss it.'

'Love to,' agreed Pearl.

'I made my own little website, though it's more like an
online CV,' I said. 'But I was thinking of starting to sell online
too, once I've settled and the museum has opened.'

'Garland makes the most wonderful miniature costume
mannequins!' enthused Honey. 'I bought one from the V&A
shop and I'm hoping she'll sell them in our museum shop,
too. She'll have plenty of time for her own work, once the
costumes in the museum have been catalogued and set up on
display.'

'Well, if you need any advice about online selling through
your website, Garland, just pop round and pick my brains,'
Pearl offered. 'Free coffee thrown in. I keep a coffee machine
and a comfy sofa in the back room to lure people in.'

'I missed the bookshop on the way here – I didn't look that way. But Fallen Idle is an irresistible name!'

I remembered she'd said that the name was her late husband's choice and thought how young she was to be a widow and that it probably accounted for the reserve and slightly remote air.

'Pearl runs a book group on Tuesday evenings,' Simon said. 'It's at the bookshop this time and you could come if you wanted, Garland.'

'It's just a small group,' said Pearl. 'Me, Simon, Thom, Baz from the art shop, the Rev. Jo-Jo, who's from the church I attend, and Baz's partner, Derek.'

'You've seen Derek already, Garland, letting out the members of the Genealogy Society, when you were arriving.'

'And I forgot to include Ginny from Spindrift, the New Age shop on the other side of the square,' finished Pearl. 'We don't always read the same book and then discuss it, like other groups. Sometimes we just each talk about what we're reading at the moment.'

'Sounds like fun,' I said, 'although, apart from Shakespeare, I mostly reread old Victorian favourites and children's classics. I spent my teenage years growing up in a house where those were the only books, apart from the Bible, and I sort of got addicted.'

'I have a big section of Victorian novels in the shop – you must come and browse,' Pearl suggested hopefully.

'I will,' I promised.

'Perhaps we should have regular Pelican Mews Residents' Association meetings now, too,' suggested Honey. 'I'd been meaning to invite you all round for ages, but I've been so busy, what with my book deadlines, organizing the house renovations and then all the museum plans. But we could make it a regular Sunday night thing, over a takeaway?'

'Sounds good to me,' said Simon, and the others agreed. They seemed already to be good friends, but prepared to welcome in the newcomer, and I could see it might prove quite impossible to cold-shoulder Thom as I'd like to.

'Let's clear the table ready for the dessert and then I'll tell you all about my plans for the museum!' Honey said.

And, over a delicious treacle tart, served with thick cream, she did.

I already knew it all, so sipped from my champagne flute, which seemed to have magically filled itself up, just like the ones in Claridge's.

When she'd finished, Thom said, 'Well, I thought a wedding dress museum sounded an unlikely thing for you to set up, Honey. I mean, I have read a couple of your novels and they aren't exactly a celebration of the joys of marriage.'

'Marriage is anything but,' agreed Honey cheerfully. 'But after I'd written a few non-fiction titles on the subject of bridal misfortunes, readers started to send me wedding dresses with stories attached, and suddenly it seemed the logical thing to do. And then there was the natural history museum, all ready to transform.'

'I prefer a museum full of wedding dresses of any kind to one crammed with dead animals and birds,' said Pearl. 'I only went in once, out of curiosity, and I soon came back out again.'

'I know – gross,' agreed Honey.

'So, how did you meet Garland?' Simon asked. 'I mean, given you have the same surname I'm sort of assuming you're related – or is that just a coincidence?'

'No, we're distant cousins, although we didn't know it until this July, when we met at the V&A Museum,' Honey said, then explained how she'd found the trunks belonging to our famous actress ancestor in her attic when she'd moved in and loaned the contents to the V&A.

'And my contact at the museum told me about Garland and I knew she must be related to me somewhere on the family tree, so I got him to introduce us and we became friends,' she finished, smiling at me. 'She and George – my contact – have been assisting me with the museum plans, but I'm so lucky that Garland has agreed to move here and take the curator job on.'

'It's a wonderful opportunity and I can't wait to see the dresses and find out their stories,' I said.

'There's going to be a Rosa-May Garland Room on the ground floor, next to the shop and reception desk,' Honey told them. 'The loaned material comes back at the end of this month. Rosa-May didn't have a bridal mishap, although from a journal I found with her costume and clothes in one of the trunks, the marriage itself was a misfortune she came to regret.'

'Did you find out how you and Garland are related, Honey?' asked Pearl, interested.

'Rosa-May had twin boys and I'm descended from the elder and Garland from the younger one. He ran off to America in his late teens, with the local blacksmith's daughter and vanished.'

'Now, that is romantic,' Pearl said. 'What happened to Rosa-May?'

'The journal she wrote during the first months of her marriage ends with her husband, who was wounded at the Battle of Waterloo, returning home. Uncle Hugo said she just seemed to vanish without a trace after the birth of the twins the following January, so what happened to her is a mystery.'

'It'll make a good story for the exhibition, though,' said Thom.

The long and draining day was really catching up with me now, and things were beginning to get a bit swimmy.

'Are you settling in OK?' asked Simon, and added, kindly, 'Just say any time if you need help with anything.'

'Thank you,' I said. 'But I came from a minute flat, so really, there isn't much to unpack and sort out.'

'If you need any extra bits and pieces of furniture, we might find something in the attics,' said Honey. 'I never got further than that first room, where I found Rosa-May's trunks. The other rooms look crammed. I think when the family moved here from their big house on the moors, they simply transferred the contents of the old attics into the new! I hate the idea of having all that clutter above my head, though, so I'll have to sort it out at some point soon.'

'We might find some more of Rosa-May's things,' I suggested, waking up slightly.

'We might find almost *anything* up there,' agreed Honey.

'The Pelican Mews Residents' Association could probably give you a hand clearing and sorting it, before these Sunday supper meetings,' Simon suggested, a boyish gleam in his eyes. 'A sort of treasure hunt!'

'I doubt they would have put anything valuable in the attic,' Pearl objected. 'You're such a boy sometimes, Simon!' she added, and he went a bit pink and looked hurt.

'I'd love some help, even if we don't find much more than trunks of old clothes – although that would be Garland's idea of treasure!'

'Yes, that would be wonderful!' I agreed.

By now, my eyelids seemed to be trying to press heavily downwards and there was a noise in my ears like the crashing of waves, so when Honey suggested we move into the sitting room for coffee, I said: 'Would you think me terribly rude if I just went home, without waiting for coffee? Only it's been such a very long and tiring day that I suddenly feel totally past it and will probably slump into a stupor shortly.'

'Of course not. I should have thought of that,' said Honey.

'There's the cat, too. He seems to have settled, but I don't want to leave him for too long in a strange place.'

'What kind is he?' asked Pearl.

'Grey, skinny . . . weird,' I said, and felt Thom's eyes on me; he'd known Golightly. 'He's only mine by default.'

'Sounds . . . interesting,' Pearl said. 'Pop in tomorrow, if you have time and if you've recovered enough,' she added.

'Thanks – I'll see how it goes,' I said.

Viv had quietly melted away into the kitchen, so I asked Honey to give her my thanks for a lovely dinner and headed for the hall.

'I'll walk back with you,' Thom said.

'No, don't. I'd much rather just go alone,' I replied quickly and probably rudely. 'There's no need to break the party up on my account. Goodnight, everyone!'

Honey saw me out. 'Just text if you need anything, but otherwise, how about if I come over tomorrow after lunch and show you the museum? Or would you rather leave it till you've settled in? I don't expect you to officially start work till Monday, by the way.'

'I'm dying to see it, so tomorrow would be great,' I told her.

'Then I'll come through the building and tap on the door to your workroom at one, shall I?'

'OK,' I agreed and, wishing her goodnight, went down the steps and turned through the arch to the mews, feeling a slight sense of escape, although I wasn't sure from what.

This time I spotted the swinging sign for the bookshop, even if it was too dark to read. There was just one lamp in the middle of the mews garden and the gleam of the lights I'd left on in the cottage beckoned me home.

I decided to buy a decent pocket torch tomorrow to light up the dark places . . . and there were still a few dark places in my life that needed illuminating.

But not tonight.

Rosa-May

Bath appeared to me bewilderingly huge and bustling, though I saw little enough of it for the first few days, for my godmother was confined to her bed with a head cold, assiduously tended by her aged, sour and very jealous maid, Hannah.

My sole excursion in those first days was to go, escorted by Hannah, to visit a reading room and circulating library in Milsom Street, in order to change Lady Bugle's books. It seemed also to be a fashionable meeting place where many fine ladies and gentlemen were gathered. I felt like a drab little sparrow, in my hand-me-down brown pelisse and an outmoded gown of Kitty's, which I had somewhat inexpertly adapted to fit my much smaller frame. Add to this an unadorned straw bonnet with brown ribbons and a pair of stout, well-worn country boots, and you will well understand why no one took the least bit of notice of me.

I, of course, took in everything! The modish clothes of the ladies and the window of a milliner's shop on the way home, where I would have lingered, had Hannah but let me.

However, things improved a little once Lady Bugle had recovered enough to leave her room, and, having tutted over my meagre and inadequate wardrobe, summoned a dressmaker to furnish me with clothing more suited to my new position.

I had no say in choosing the fabrics or pattern of these garments, of course, but even though everything was to be in depressingly dull shades, and cut with utmost modesty, it was at least all new!

A cloak, simple bonnets, walking boots, slippers, gloves and stockings were brought to the house for approval – my benefactor's, not mine.

There was nothing among my new possessions to excite the soul of a young girl – for I was then still but sixteen years old – and on examining my reflection in the spotted mirror in my chamber, I thought it was certain that no one would take me for anything other than what I was: a poor relation, at the beck and call of her employer, although there had not, in truth, been a great deal for me to do.

I read sermons and worthy and deeply tedious novels to her by the hour, while she dozed on the sofa, and I answered her correspondence at her direction.

Such duties were not onerous, just very, very dull, and I longed for a letter from Sara, bearing more exciting news than any I would have to impart in return.

15

First Nights

I'd shut the living-room door to the hall when I went out, leaving Golightly with the run of the kitchen and utility room, and since I intended doing that every night, he'd have to get used to it. I wasn't prepared to share my bed with him permanently . . . or any other male creature, come to that.

Right now, the single life and throwing myself into my fascinating new job seemed far more attractive prospects.

I found Golightly sitting just inside the living-room door, looking abandoned and pathetic, as if he'd been there for hours, although beyond him I could see a cat-sized dent in the seat cushion of his favourite armchair, and when I skirted round him to touch it, it was still warm.

'You complete fraud!' I told him, and he shuffled round to fix his yellow eyes on me, which still held a 'You left me all alone in a strange place and I didn't know if you'd ever come back' expression.

'I'm not falling for it,' I said, and he pulled one of his horrendous faces at me.

'If the wind changes, you'll be stuck with that expression,' I warned him, before going into the kitchen, where I could see through the open utility room door that he'd made use of his litter tray again and also polished off every last remaining morsel of his dry food. It's a mystery why he always looks half-starved.

I'd achieved a lot of unpacking already, but there was still so much more left to sort out, not to mention setting up my new workroom, which, to me, would count as fun.

The night air had briefly woken me up and I made a comforting mug of hot chocolate . . . and then almost fell asleep over it, thinking of the evening and of how, whenever I'd glanced in his direction, Thom's dark and sombre amber eyes seemed to be fixed on me with an unreadable expression in their depths.

He wasn't any longer the old Thom I'd come to take for granted in my life. I seemed to be seeing him now in a totally different light.

From what he'd said to Honey earlier, he evidently didn't know I'd been dumped by Marco and fired by Beng & Briggs, but if he was still in contact with Sir Mallory Mortlake and his wife, he'd find out eventually. It was a mortifying thought.

I remembered I'd turned my phone to silent before I went out and I fished it out of the depths of my bag, which I'd dumped on the kitchen table. I'd been so preoccupied with the move and then the emotional turmoil of coming face to face with Thom that it was only when I found an email from Wilfric – or Will, as I must now call him – that I remembered Marco's play had opened tonight.

Will sounded exuberant.

Darling! Play opened and four curtain calls – I just know it will get great reviews and run and run! Did my best to

150

upstage you-know-who and she's so dumb, I don't think even now she's realized that mine is the absolutely pivotal role! I'm the deus ex machina of the play – the Iago, as it were – and though I have fewer lines, they are much more important than hers.

Will xx

I didn't take the 'darling' seriously, of course, and I noted that, just like all Marco's communications, Will's was entirely about himself – written, I suspected, on a rush of post-performance adrenalin and euphoria.

Still, I was glad for his sake that it had gone so well, although, somehow, it felt like a world I had left behind a long, long time ago.

By now, unlike Will, I wasn't running on adrenalin or anything else, but instead had reached the stage of sheer exhaustion where my bones felt as if they had been filled with lead. There was a sound in my ears like the sea crashing against a cliff and the floor undulated when I got up.

It was all I could do to wish Golightly, who was curled back up on his favourite chair, goodnight, close the living-room door on him and climb the steep dog-leg wooden stairs to my familiar little white bed, in the unfamiliar cream-painted room, where I fell instantly into a deep and dreamless sleep.

*

I woke once in the night, with a horrible jolting, panicked feeling that I had no idea where I was, and lay there tensely, heart thumping, till everything came back to me.

All was silent, as it had never been in London, until an owl hooted somewhere not far away.

It was strangely comforting and, relaxing, I fell back into a dreamless sleep.

*

When I woke again it was very early morning and not yet light, but this time at least I remembered where I was.

I heard the sound of the central heating coming on – someone must have pre-set it, because I hadn't got round to it yet – and the room was still a little chilly as I dressed in practical jeans and sweatshirt and headed downstairs.

Golightly must have heard me moving about, for he was now slowly working up his vocal range from low cries to a full-throated scream.

I hoped he wasn't going to do that whenever I went out, too – or whenever he got bored – because here he wouldn't have access to any outside space at all, not even a fire escape to view the world from.

Apart from that, he'd never been an outside cat, nor even tried to escape by way of the front door. Would he *want* to venture into the courtyard, if I let him out? And if so, would he stay safely within the mews? The middle of a town wasn't really the ideal place for an old cat to learn how to be street-wise. And anyway, Honey might not be keen on my installing a cat flap in the pristine paintwork of the front door.

Golightly had changed to a different tune the moment I'd appeared, one with an imperative note that suggested I serve him breakfast immediately, which I did for the sake of peace.

While I was eating my toast and Marmite, I rifled through the junk mail to see if I'd missed anything yesterday and found a second sheet of notepaper in Honey's handwriting, on which she seemed to have randomly jotted down any bit of possibly useful information that came into her head. I learned in quick succession that Thursday was market day, the Sun in Splendour, on the other side of the square, did bar lunches and evening meals, there were three takeaways in town and an excellent fish-and-chip shop a few minutes' walk away.

Like Honey, I wasn't a great cook, so that was all interesting.

The nearest cashpoint was at the supermarket on the outskirts, because the bank, like the library, had closed up shop. There was still a post office, however, located in Rani's Minimart around the corner, in which, said Honey's angular black writing, you could get pretty much anything you wanted, unless you had exotic tastes and deep pockets, in which case the deli next to the Sun in Splendour would be delighted to welcome a new customer.

Rani's Minimart sounded more my cup of tea.

It was still a bit early for the shops to open, so I did some more unpacking. Also, I started a list of things I needed to buy, like picture hooks, though I felt nervous about hammering hooks into those freshly plastered walls.

I was in the utility room, flattening cartons that had held cleaning materials, when Golightly followed me in and jumped into the box he'd favoured the day before, where he sat glaring at me, as if daring me to flatten that one, too.

I couldn't personally see the attraction, or what that box had going for it that the others didn't, but anything that amused him had to be a good idea, and it must have done because when I showed no sign of trying to evict him, he curled up in it, emitting his wheezy purr.

Cats are weird and mine was weirder than most.

Sitting at the kitchen table over a coffee, I sent a brief

congratulatory email to Will, before beginning to add more things to my shopping list: eggs, butter, bread, cheese – including a piece of Parmesan – salad, fruit . . . and comfort food for the freezer, like fish fingers and tubs of ice cream.

I glanced at my kitchen clock, currently propped against a stack of Mum's old cookery books on the work surface, and thought the shops should all be open by now. I could hear Golightly still snoring from his box, so I grabbed the list and a couple of shopping bags and sneaked off, collecting my shoulder bag on the way.

I felt naked without that bag, though the thump of the smallest of my pairs of dressmaker's shears against my hip was no longer comforting. And why was I still carrying around the tools of my trade? Did I think there might one day be a sewing emergency, and someone would shout, 'Quick, send for a dressmaker!' or, from a stage, 'Is there a costumier in the house?'

No, I'd really have to break myself of the habit.

When I'd looked out of my window earlier, the sky had seemed undecided about whether it wanted to be blue or grey, but now the blue, a pale harebell shade, was winning, and a weak sun was gilding the rooftops and bouncing off the diamond-paned windows at the back of Pelican House. The old black-and-white building looked as if it had grown there slowly, a crooked, higgledy-piggledy structure that was rather charming and fairy tale.

I cast a somewhat furtive glance around, but there was no one to be seen, so I set off briskly past the closed wooden double doors to the museum, admiring the flowerbeds in the small central garden, between the shrubs. It was all very neat and tidy, behind white railings, as was the little square of garden behind Pelican House. I couldn't really see Honey as a gardener, so I expect she has someone in to do it for her.

It made the mews seem more familiar, knowing who was behind all the doors, even if one of them was Thom Reid. But after my first glance I didn't look again and went briskly through the narrow entranceway to emerge into the market square.

Like most of its kind, it was actually far from square and used, on non-market days, as a car park. A war memorial stood in the middle and there was a convenient convenience at one end. Several shops, the pub and what looked like a small town hall were grouped cosily around it.

I decided to do a circuit of the square first, just looking in the windows, before going to the nearby minimart on my way back.

I found the art shop and then the one called Spindrift, with a very New Age window display. The deli Honey had mentioned was on the far side of the square, next to the impressive square façade of the Sun in Splendour. This town centre seemed to be thriving, at least.

The few people about wished me good morning, so I felt I'd slipped back into some time warp, although it was very pleasant. In London, it's always better not even to make eye contact with anyone you don't know, let alone talk to them!

Once past the town hall, my circuit was completed and I headed down the narrow street that ran along the side of Pelican House and the museum, where I found Rani's Minimart, which had a narrow front but stretched back a long way and, as Honey had said, had pretty much everything anyone could need.

They had cute little miniature shopping trolleys too, and soon I had accumulated a lot more than I intended.

My bags filled, and with the cheerful goodbyes of the plump lady behind the till, I staggered back out into the street.

It was only when I'd hauled them all the way back past the front of Pelican House that it occurred to me there might be a quicker route back by way of the alley behind my cottage: the gate in the passage between that and the puppet theatre must open into it. I'd have to explore later. I also wondered if you could get funky wheeled shopping bags.

I gave my arms a rest by putting the bags down outside Fallen Idle, so I could gaze into the window. There were a few enticing books displayed there on Perspex stands, including a hardback of one of Honey's revenge thrillers, all shiny embossed bloodstains, a Victorian fairy book I hadn't got, and a large and interesting-looking tome on Venetian masks.

While I gazed, raptly, Pearl's pale face suddenly appeared as she reached over and placed a tiny Tolkien book, *Tree and Leaf*, on a smaller stand. Then she looked up and spotted me.

Her remote face was warmed by a smile of recognition, or maybe by the prospect of a potential customer, for she mouthed through the glass at me, 'Come in!'

16

Hidden Pearl

I mouthed back 'Later', holding up the shopping bags, but she was already heading to the door, which opened with the tinkle of a bell.

'Hi! Do come in and have coffee with me,' she invited. 'I've just put some on in the back room.'

'That's kind of you, but I can't right now, because I've been shopping and this big bag is full of frozen stuff,' I explained.

'Oh, that's no problem!' Pearl held the door wider. 'My cottage backs on to the shop, so I can just take the bag of frozen things through and drop it into my chest freezer till you go.'

'Well . . . all right,' I said, following her through the crammed bookshelves and into a back room which, though lined with bays of books, was also part office, part sitting room. A computer sat on a large desk in one corner and a sofa and comfortable chairs were arranged around a low table in the middle.

'Have a seat,' she said, taking my bag of frozen stuff and vanishing with it through a door at the back of the room, returning a moment later and going across to a coffee machine.

'I've got all kinds of coffee pods – what do you like?' she asked. 'Americano? *Café au lait*? Espresso?'

'*Café au lait* would be lovely,' I said, and leaned back on the sofa, looking round me. 'This is cosy . . . and I can see it's where you keep the Victorian novels! That's tempting, but I'll have to come back when I've got more time to browse.'

'I remembered you said you loved them, so I'm luring you in,' she said, smiling. 'I keep them all in here, as well as anything of value, although I'm not really an antiquarian bookseller, just second-hand. My husband was the real bibliophile, but he died four years ago, not that long after we'd opened the shop.'

'I'm so sorry,' I said, taking the mug she handed me. 'You're very young to be a widow.'

'Thirty – but cancer doesn't take any account of age.' She sat down opposite me on one of the armchairs, with her own mug, and pushed an open tin of shortbread biscuits in my direction.

'The bookshop was really Neil's dream and I feel I'm sort of keeping his memory alive by carrying on with it. We had such fun setting it up, even though it's never been exactly a money-spinner.'

'No, but the best work is the sort you'd do whether you were paid for it or not,' I said. 'You must have lots of happy memories to look back on.'

'I do. I don't usually tell people about Neil when I've only just met them,' she said, with one of the smiles that so transformed her usual cool, reserved face. 'But somehow I feel I've known you for ages. Perhaps it's because you already knew Thom, and he and Simon have been such good friends and a support to me through everything.'

'It's . . . several years since I last saw Thom,' I said carefully. 'He left London suddenly and I had no idea he was living here until I came face to face with him yesterday. Honey had left the cottage keys at his workshop.'

'Odd how these things happen, but it must have been quite a surprise,' she said vaguely. From her expression I thought she'd noticed the coolness between me and Thom the previous evening, but was tactfully not asking any questions.

Instead, she said, 'So, how did Honey manage to persuade a top-notch theatrical costumier to up sticks from London and move here to look after her wedding dress collection?'

I laughed. 'Honey was exaggerating my importance! I did work for years in the historical costume department of one of the leading theatrical costumiers, and I was even in line for promotion. I was also engaged to be married but . . . something happened to change all that. When the engagement was broken and Honey offered me the job, I decided on a fresh start here.'

'Yes, it was fascinating to hear how you met at the V&A and discovered you were related!'

'I've been involved in the plans for the museum ever since we met and so has my friend George, who works at the V&A and really *is* an expert on historical costume. He came up here on a visit a little while ago, to advise Honey on the plans.'

'Yes, he came in with Honey and she introduced him. I had a book on fans in the window and he couldn't resist it. Small and very dapper, with a silvery goatee beard and gold-rimmed half-moon glasses.'

'That's George,' I agreed.

'I'm sorry to hear about your broken engagement,' Pearl said.

'My fiancé turned out not to be the man I thought he was. Story of my life, really,' I added, slightly bitterly.

'You just haven't met the right one yet,' she consoled me. 'Neil and I were very happy and I'm sure we always would have been, if he hadn't been taken away from me . . . but now I have good friends instead, including Thom and Simon, and that's enough.'

From the devoted looks Simon had been casting in her direction last night, I thought it probably wasn't really enough for him, but I was sure Pearl hadn't realized that.

'The book group will be meeting here this evening, from seven onwards, if you can make it. You'd get to meet the rest of my friends, and they're all really nice people.'

'I don't know . . .' I began doubtfully. Did I want to be pulled into a circle of friends that included Thom?

'Oh, do come! We're not at all highbrow and we have fun discussing books because we all have such different tastes. If you're very busy, you could perhaps simply pop in for half an hour to say hello, or just leave it till next week, if you'd rather.'

'I'll . . . see how things go,' I temporized. It was becoming plain that living in such a small community, and with Thom, Pearl and Simon practically on my doorstep, it was going to be almost impossible not to get drawn into their company. There were Honey's Sunday attic-clearing and supper get-togethers, for a start, which, since she was my boss, I couldn't very well get out of, even if I wanted to . . . and actually, I secretly hoped we might find more of Rosa-May's belongings up there in the attic.

I may have reread my childhood collection of Famous Five books too many times . . .

I voiced something that had been puzzling me. 'You know, Pearl, I'm still surprised the news that Ivo Gryffyn was living here didn't get out. I know the films were years ago now, but it all got raked up just before he left London for good, when his stepbrother and co-star in the films died.'

'I remember reading about that – such a tragedy,' she said. 'Thom was already living here when Neil and I arrived, and he'd been visiting for a few years before that, so the locals had already gone through the stage of thinking he looked like Ivo Gryffyn, to realizing he actually *was*, but since he obviously didn't want to be recognized, no one mentioned it. By then, too, he'd just sort of seamlessly blended in. He's even got a touch of the local accent!'

'He's always been able to merge into any background, like a chameleon,' I agreed. 'I suppose that's what made him such a good actor.'

'The locals just take people as they come, really,' Pearl said. 'If he wanted to live quietly under a different name and make marionettes, that was his business.'

I could see that attitude would have attracted Thom to the place, almost as much as the marionette making.

'He never wanted fame or an acting career,' I said.

'You knew him quite well, then?'

'I'm not sure I ever really knew him at all,' I said, then got up. 'Thank you for the coffee, but I must get back now, because Honey's coming after lunch to show me round the museum and I've got a few things to do before then.'

'I'll get your bag out of the freezer.'

When she returned, Pearl said, 'Do pop in for coffee or a browse any time. I promise not to do the hard sell and talk you into buying anything!'

'I probably will anyway,' I said. 'And thank you for the coffee.'

The bell gave its musical chime as she let me out. '*Try* to make the book group tonight – you'd be so welcome.'

'I'll see,' I said noncommittally, and then headed off through the narrow entrance to the mews with my heavy bags, feeling that I might have made a friend.

As I emerged into the now sunny courtyard and paused to

get a better grip on the chillier of the two shopping bags, I heard the sound of quick footsteps behind me and then a hand closed on my arm.

Somehow I knew who it was even before Thom's voice said, urgently: 'Garland, wait a minute! I want to talk to you.'

I turned to him. 'I'm afraid the feeling isn't exactly mutual, Thom,' I began, but already he'd wrested one of the heavy shopping bags from my hand.

'I'll help you with these – give me the other one. They're way too heavy for you.'

'I don't need help, thank you,' I snapped, stepping back before he could grab the other bag.

He looked quizzically at me, the breeze sweeping in through the entrance passage tossing that unfamiliarly long hair about, as if at the direction of some unseen film director.

'I'm not sure the Johnny Depp look really suits you,' I said, the words out before I'd realized I'd even voiced my thoughts.

A genuine grin lit his face. 'I haven't gone for the whole Captain Jack Sparrow thing, though – wait till you see Baz, from the art shop!'

The white bull terrier I'd seen with him yesterday now sat on his feet, which I suppose was more comfortable than the cobbles. It had a comical aspect, with one ear up and one down, bright dark eyes and a grinning mouth with a lolling pink tongue, but it wasn't the sort of dog I'd have associated with Thom.

'This is Jester,' he said, seeing where I was looking. 'He's Bruno's dog really. I'm just looking after him. Jester, this is Garland,' he introduced us formally. 'She is small, but fierce!'

That had once been a joke between us . . .

'Shake a paw,' Thom was adding, and Jester obligingly lifted one front foot up. You can't snub a dog, so I shook it, feeling silly.

Then I said, 'Please give me back my bag, Thom. We have nothing to talk about and I want to get home.'

'Come on, Garland! We can't just carry on pretending we barely know each other.'

'Thom, I'm not sure I *ever* really knew you at all,' I said coldly. 'And right now, I have to get back to the cottage and put my frozen stuff away, then have some lunch, before Honey shows me round the museum at one.'

'It's barely half past eleven now, but if you like we can talk while you're putting the shopping away.'

'No! And anyway, you can't bring that dog into my cottage because I've got a cat.'

'I know, you said so last night, but Jester loves cats.'

'The feeling isn't likely to be reciprocated, because Golightly isn't your average cat.'

'Golightly? You mean that weird creature that used to haunt your flat sometimes? I thought he belonged to your neighbour.'

'He did, but Miss McNabb had to go and live with her sister and couldn't take him.'

'She probably moved just to get away from him,' he said. 'But he must be getting on a bit now.'

'He is, and too old to start again in a new place, but there wasn't really any alternative to bringing him with me. Honey doesn't mind my having a cat in the cottage.'

'I assume she hasn't met said cat yet.' He grinned again, and I felt the corners of my mouth *almost* twitch upwards before I got a grip on myself.

'OK, then, I'll put Jester in the workshop and join you in a minute,' Thom said, and then, seeing I was about to veto this idea, added impatiently: 'We're going to have to have things out sooner or later, so you might as well get it over with now.

After all, if we're both living and working in Pelican Mews, we aren't exactly going to be able to avoid each other, are we?'

He didn't wait for an answer, but strode off towards the workshop and, since he was still carrying half my shopping, I supposed I'd have to let him in.

And perhaps, I thought, it *would* be better to clear the air and get it over with.

By the time I'd put down my bag, found my key and opened the door to the hall, he was back again and followed me in.

The cottage had been quiet as I approached, but at the sound of the key an unearthly falsetto wail sounded from the living room.

'What the hell is that?' demanded Thom, dropping the shopping bag, which luckily didn't have anything breakable in it.

'Golightly, of course!'

'I don't remember him making any noise other than snoring,' he said, slightly nervously.

'He's been very vocal since we got here, probably because he isn't used to being left in a strange place.'

This time, Golightly had remained sitting on his favourite chair, but fixed his accusing yellow eyes on me as I entered the room. Then, spotting the visitor, his eyes narrowed before he pulled one of the most hideous faces in his repertoire – the Silent Scream – before jumping down and stalking towards Thom, who recoiled slightly.

But then, to my astonishment, Golightly simply twined himself around Thom's legs a couple of times, before leading him in the direction of the kitchen.

'I think he remembers you and he always did quite like you . . . or as much as he liked *anyone*.'

'I'd say it was more toleration than liking,' Thom said, dumping the big bag on to the table, before starting to unpack it. I washed my hands and then began putting the perishable stuff away.

'Can you give Golightly a cat treat? That's what he's after. There's an open bag on the worktop in the utility room. Just one, though, because I've been overdoing them to try and cheer him up.'

He did so and then sat down at the kitchen table, looking around him.

'It's odd to see all the familiar things from your parents' flat here, but nice, too.'

'It makes it feel more like home, just like it did my own flat,' I admitted, putting the kettle on.

'It has that effect on me too because your parents made me part of your family, especially after Mum died.'

He fell silent until I plonked a mug of coffee down in front of him – I hadn't asked what he wanted, just went with what I felt like. Then he looked up at me and said, quietly and very sincerely: 'I'm sorry, Garland. Really, really sorry.'

'For anything in particular, or just generally?' I asked.

'You know what I mean. For leaving London without a word and not keeping in contact with you, though I did have some idea how you were doing, because the Mortlakes passed on any news of you. They mentioned they'd seen you at a party quite recently.'

'That's more than I knew about what was happening to you, Thom,' I snapped. 'I got back from Scotland, having settled my aunt's estate as quickly as I could, after seeing the news about Leo, and I was worried to death because you weren't answering my calls or emails. Then the emails started bouncing and your phone number wasn't recognized!'

He tried to say something, but the pent-up feelings of the last six years swept me unstoppably on.

'As soon as I got back I went straight round to your house and it was empty, with a "For Sale" sign outside, and no one could tell me where you were.'

'Garland—' he tried again, but I ignored him. It felt good to finally let it all pour out.

'For the last six years, I haven't known if you were alive or dead, happy or sad . . .' My voice broke. 'I thought we were as close as any brother and sister – and you just cut me out of your life and walked away.'

He reached out a hand and covered mine on the table. 'I *know* – and there hasn't been a single day since when I haven't thought of you, and wondered if I'd done the right thing.'

'But *why* did you do it?' I demanded.

'Because I could see when we quarrelled that you were in love with Marco, and nothing I could have said would have altered that. Your future would lie with Marco in London, pursuing the career you loved and . . . at the time it seemed the best thing was to make a clean break. After Leo died, I wasn't really thinking too straight. I just desperately wanted to escape and leave it all behind me.'

'Including me!'

He ran his free hand through his hair. 'I didn't want Marco in my life after what happened.'

'I don't know why you've always had such a downer on Marco, because he wasn't any worse than the rest of Leo's London friends and he convinced me he'd totally changed before I started going out with him. I thought you'd see that eventually and we'd make our quarrel up.'

'I didn't believe the leopard had changed his spots that much, and I really didn't want to see you with him.' He sighed. 'I just hoped for your sake he really loved you and you'd be happy . . . but it doesn't seem to have turned out that way, or you wouldn't be here.'

'No, it all went resoundingly pear-shaped, and he showed himself to be a total love rat,' I said bitterly. 'So now you can say, "I told you so."'

I had left my hand under his warm one and he squeezed it now.

'I'm not going to, because I'm really, really sorry, Garland,' he repeated. 'I suppose that's why you broke the engagement off?'

I took a long swig from my hot, strong coffee, which put a bit of heart into me.

'There's a bit more to it than that, and I suppose I'd better tell you because you'll only hear about it from the Mortlakes.'

'They're mostly based on Grand Cayman now, but their friends keep them in touch with the theatre gossip,' he agreed. 'They don't pass most of that on to me, because they know I've left that world behind, but they always tell me when they've seen you, so I knew the party they saw you at was for the cast of Marco's new play, which was going to open at the Cockle-shell Theatre.'

'Yes, that's all part of the story. And Honey loaning the Rosa-May Garland material to the V&A is tangled up with it, too.'

I began to describe how the V&A exhibition had inspired Marco to write a new, and more commercial, play, and how I'd fallen in love with Rosa-May's lovely evening gown, which had been based on her Titania costume, and I'd made a replica, which was to be my wedding dress.

I paused uncertainly after that. 'I'm sorry, this probably isn't making a lot of sense.'

'No, it's fine! Don't forget Honey told us all about the con-nection you'd discovered between you, so I know the back-ground.'

'OK then. Well, Marco's play is a supernatural thriller called *A Midsummer Night's Madness* and it opened yesterday, with Mirrie Malkin in the role of Titania.'

'Demelza mentioned she'd been at the party, so I assumed she was in it.'

'Marco told Mirrie at the party about my copy of the Regency dress, which she'd seen at the exhibition, and she was really keen on seeing it. I told her no one was doing that until my wedding day, and I didn't think any more about it . . .'

'But she did?'

'Yes. I discovered she'd persuaded Marco to "borrow" my wedding dress for her to wear at a photo shoot.'

I told him how I'd been delivering the Titania costume to the theatre and overheard her talking to Wilfric Wolfram about what she and Marco had done.

'Marco had just put Mirrie's dresser into a taxi with the dress, so she could return it to the flat before I got home and realize it wasn't there. She seemed to think it was amusing, but to me it felt like Marco had betrayed my trust.'

'He had,' Thom said grimly.

'Then, as if that wasn't enough, she revealed that she and Marco had been having an affair and he was only waiting for the play to open before telling me our engagement was over.'

He pressed my hand warmly again and said sympathetically, 'The shock of hearing that, right after you learned they'd taken the dress, must have been devastating.'

'It was. I was literally frozen to the spot until they suddenly spotted me in the makeup mirror. Then I ran back to Mirrie's dressing room, where I'd just hung the Titania costume on the rail, and locked the door. I . . . sort of needed a breathing space. And then—'

I broke off, swallowing hard and then looked away from him. 'The next thing I knew, the Titania costume was slashed to ribbons and I was standing there with my dressmaking shears in my hand.'

I did glance at him then and saw him looking so understandingly at me that I managed to rattle off the rest of it in one quick burst: the final scene with Mirrie hysterical and Marco livid with rage.

'It was horrible. Will – Wilfric Wolfram – was just an onlooker, but he was *so* kind. He got me out of there and put me in a taxi home. But, of course, Beng & Briggs fired me first thing next morning and I knew no one else in the theatrical costumier business was likely to take me on, so it felt as if I'd fallen off a cliff.'

'Poor Garland,' Thom said, shifting his chair round the table so he could give me a hug.

I leaned my head against the comforting warmth of his chest, feeling his heart beating steadily under my cheek. All the anger, hurt and resentment I'd felt towards him seemed to be draining right out of me . . . or almost all.

He rested his chin on top of my head and there was just the hint of laughter in his voice when he said: 'You always *did* have a temper – up like a rocket and down with the stick – but this time you totally lost it for a few minutes and that's not surprising, given what happened.'

'A few minutes was all it took to end a career and an engagement, although I'd have broken off with Marco anyway once I'd found out about them borrowing my dress. There was another thing, too: from something Mirrie said, it sounded like she and Marco might already have had an affair at some time in the past, and were just picking up where they left off.'

Thom said, 'They did. I caught them together only a few months after she and Leo married. But she swore she'd been drunk and it was a one-off and I believed her. She and Leo had been close, ever since stage school. I suppose I *wanted* to believe her, just like I did when she came back to Leo after the first time she'd dumped him for someone else and said she'd made a huge mistake.'

'I suppose finding her with Marco that time was part of the reason why you never liked him and didn't think I should go out with him?' I said.

'Yes, but it had been a long time before, and I wasn't sure at the time how far it had gone. I should have told you.'

'It probably wouldn't have made any difference even if you had,' I admitted. 'I fell for him hard and I really believed he'd totally changed his life around and wanted to settle down.'

'I'm still sorry things didn't work out for you,' Thom said. 'And I *should* have kept in contact. I know you wouldn't have told Marco where I was, if I'd asked you not to. I made a wrong decision and hurt you badly – and myself, too, in the process.'

'All those years when I was worrying about you, you were happily living here,' I said, flaring up again.

'I was never entirely happy without you, Garland,' he said simply. 'The day we had that last quarrel, I'd meant to finally tell you about the cottage here and the puppet workshop, because I wanted to leave London and move up here permanently, even though I knew I would see so much less of you.'

'You were going to tell me?' I lifted my head and looked at him, though his arms round me didn't slacken. 'That was always your secret retreat, so I never asked you where it was. I respected your need to get away sometimes.'

'Just as I never asked you where you bolted to when things got too much for you,' he pointed out.

'Oh, that was just an old caravan on a farm near Tring, with no mod cons. It used to drive Marco mad when I vanished there, because I'd keep my phone off till I was home again.'

'Our last secrets revealed!' he joked, and this time he really did smile and I could see all the fascinating little gold specks in his amber eyes . . .

'It's serendipity that we're back together again,' he said, then gave me another hug and let me go, before looking more seriously down at me.

'Am I forgiven?'

'I'm working on it.'

'Good, because when I saw you on the workshop doorstep yesterday – was it only yesterday? – it felt exactly like the time we bumped into each other at the theatre, after you'd moved to London. I felt so happy,' he said simply.

'My feelings were definitely more mixed,' I said, and come to that, they still were! This was Thom, but somehow the relationship had changed. I pushed that thought away to examine later.

'Do you want to share my Cornish pasty and chocolate eclairs?' I offered, bringing the situation back down to earth. 'If so, you make some more coffee while I heat up the pasty.'

'Done,' he said. Then added, uneasily, 'That cat's been very quiet in the utility room, hasn't he?'

'He's probably in his box. He took a fancy to one of the cartons I brought his food in.'

And when we tiptoed in and looked, he was fast asleep in the bottom of it. He looked almost cute, apart from the asthmatic wheezing noises.

After lunch, Thom said he'd better get back to work.

'I've got two more faces to carve for *The Murder in the Red Barn*: Maria and her stepmother.'

'Oh, yes, I remember you telling us about that last night. I'd love to see them when you've finished, *and* the play.'

For some reason, Thom looked slightly uncomfortable, but perhaps I'd imagined it, because he said: 'Yes, you must see the workshop – and your dad's old tools are all there – another link to you I could never break. I've learned that you can never entirely escape your past, and some things, deep down, you don't want to.'

He turned on the doorstep as I was letting him out. 'Are you coming to the book group later?'

'I might, just briefly. I had coffee earlier with Pearl and she asked me again. I'll see how tired I am by evening, and I still have lots of unpacking to do.'

'OK – there's all the time in the world to get to know everyone,' he agreed, then gave me a smile that seemed to turn my heart over, and strode off, long hair blown about by the wind – not so much Captain Jack Sparrow as the *Last of the Mohicans*.

Rosa-May

Lady Bugle assured me that, once she felt herself equal to it, I could accompany her to the Pump Room, where she daily promenaded and drank the water, as well as other diverse entertainments, such as concerts of Ancient Music and the Sunday service at the Abbey. This sounded like a prospect of glorious dissipation compared to my current immurement in her tall, gloomy house!

And indeed, right from my first visit to the Grand Pump Room, life did take a turn for the better, for this most elegant building, near the Abbey church and the Roman springs, was evidently also a meeting place for the fashionable.

Music played as the visitors strolled about, greeting friends, staring at newcomers and sipping the water – which I tried and found to be quite disgusting.

Lady Bugle introduced me to those of her acquaintance present, including her greatest friend, Mrs Gorringe, who, most fortunately, had her granddaughter Leticia staying with her. Letty was a merry, brown-haired girl, only a little older than I, and was staying with her grandmother in order to obtain a little town polish before she came out during the London Season in the following year.

Practically from the moment we set eyes on each other, we became bosom friends and this added immeasurably to my enjoyment of Bath.

We were allowed to walk out together, accompanied only by Letty's maid, who was a young and silly girl who did not question where we went or what we did, in the way that Hannah had done, though our excursions were innocent enough: to the library, to promenade in the park, or gaze into milliners' windows. Letty, who had sufficient pin money to buy herself any small trifles that took her fancy, often made small purchases, but I was determined not to weaken and spend the money the squire had given me, which I was sure I would need for my eventual escape, should I find a way of attaining my dream of going on the stage.

*

Letty and I soon confided our secret dreams to each other, though they were, of course, very different.

Letty, who was both pretty and had a modest fortune, expected to make a good marriage after her first London Season. Meanwhile, her grandmother took her to dances held at the Assembly Rooms, as well as to the theatre. On one occasion, to my great delight, I was allowed to go with her, in order to see a benefit performance of Macbeth *with the inestimable Mrs Siddons reprising one of her most acclaimed roles.*

Though she was no longer young and at the height of her powers, I was nonetheless quite overcome by her performance. In this I was not alone, for I saw grown men weeping and several ladies in the audience fell into hysterics and had to be removed.

17

Ebb and Flow

I washed up and then went through into my new workroom, leaving Golightly fast asleep in his box. Perhaps he felt safe in there. Who knew? But I hoped it meant he was a bit more chilled about his new surroundings.

There were three keys on my ring, one each for the front door and the workroom, and the third, as I discovered when I tried it, for the door through into the museum.

I resisted the urge to open it because, tempting as it was to take a quick peek, I thought I'd leave my first glimpse until Honey arrived to show me round.

Instead, I filled in the time by starting to rearrange my workspace, which was so big that all the sewing machines, equipment and materials, which had taken up most of the living room and all of the box room in my flat, rattled around in there.

There was plenty of space along the walls for long work-benches, as well as that longed-for cutting table in the middle, and perhaps a computer workstation in the window. The storage room behind would easily take my two hanging rails, with plenty of room to spare for an ironing board – and what luxury it would be to be able to leave that up all the time and not have to put it away!

The removal men had lined up my three dressmaker's dummies in one corner, as if they were queuing for a bus and, for some whimsical reason of their own, had placed a polystyrene head at the base of each. They looked oddly grisly, palely loitering there, and I thought they might give Honey ideas for an even more gruesome plot, so I moved the heads to one of the shelves at the museum end of the room.

I began yet another list, headed 'Workshop', and wrote: cutting table, workbenches, computer desk . . . filing cabinet?

I had one trestle table, which I put up, but it looked pathetically small and lost, even with the sewing machines lined up next to it.

That still left a big stack of boxes, bundles and bolts of cloth sitting in the middle of the room like a strange island.

The list of things to source online had grown quite a lot longer by the time Honey tapped at the adjoining door and I let her in.

She was dressed head to foot in black, which seemed to be her favourite colour – a cowl-neck tunic over skinny jeans. The only bit of colour was a covetable pair of carved jade earrings.

'Hi, Garland!' she said, and then cast a look around the room. 'I see you're getting sorted out already. Are you settling into the cottage OK, too?'

'Yes, and I love it! I've unpacked everything in there except the books and bric-a-brac, but I was saving this room as a treat, because setting it all up ready to start work will be such fun!'

'If you say so,' she said. 'Has this room got everything you need? I had extra electric sockets put in and there's already a sink in the back room.'

'It's perfect and so *big*! I'll be able to have a large cutting table, as well as two longer benches and a desk – and still have lots of room to spare.'

'Do send me the links to anything you need to buy for work and I'll get Derek to order them as museum business expenses.'

'I think I should pay for anything I need like that myself, really,' I objected. 'I mean, I'll be using it for my own work, too.'

'Oh, we can swing it as an expense, don't worry,' she said. 'You won't have much time for your own work till the museum opens, anyway – and it sounds as if you might be making the costumes for Thom's marionettes, too, doesn't it?'

She gave her twisted grin. 'Simon was obviously reluctant to take it on after his grandmother retired to Brighton, and he sounded desperate to hand it over to someone else!'

'No, I don't think it's his thing, really, but I don't mind if I do get landed with it. It'll be a doddle after the miniature costume mannequins. Thom said I should go and see the first of the marionettes he's carved for *The Murder in the Red Barn*,' I added, and she gave me a sharp sideways glance.

'So, you and Thom have already made it up, then? When you were freezing him out last night, I wasn't exactly sure how deep the permafrost went and how long it might take to thaw. It felt not so much as if there was an elephant in the room as a Siberian mammoth.'

'We had a talk earlier today and I'm *partially* thawed,' I admitted. 'I still can't completely understand why he didn't trust me enough six years ago to tell me where he was going, because he must have known I wouldn't have shared the information with anyone else, if he didn't want me to. It was cruel.'

'It was just after his stepbrother's death, so he probably wasn't thinking rationally at the time,' Honey suggested.

'I suppose not. And we had just quarrelled over my going

out with Marco, who he always seemed to blame more for
Leo's drug addiction than any of his other London friends. It
turns out he had another reason to dislike and mistrust Marco
too: he suspected Marco and Mirrie had had an affair soon
after she married Leo.'

'Why didn't he tell you at the time?'

'He said he wasn't certain. Mirrie had told him they weren't
and he'd wanted to believe her. I told him, from what I'd overheard Mirrie saying to Wilfric at the theatre, he was right all
along.'

'So, one more thing you have to forgive Thom for!' she said
with another grin. Then asked, 'Has Marco tried to contact
you since the fracas at the theatre? I mean, other than those
late-night calls you mentioned.'

'I left my phone off at night after that, but they stopped
after a bit – he was probably too busy in the run-up to opening
night to work on his next play – but he did send me one text
message on the day before I moved here.'

'What did it say?'

I shrugged. 'No idea. I just saw who it was from and deleted
it without a second thought. I was really exhausted at the time
and, anyway, I expect he just wanted to rant at me again.'

'He might have come to his senses and wanted to apologize?'

'I doubt it, but he must want to say something because
when I turned my phone back on this morning I'd missed
another call from him, and this time he'd left a message too.'

'Which you also deleted?'

'Got it in one. I just don't feel interested any more and I
wish he'd leave me alone. I'd even forgotten his play opened
the day I moved here until Will emailed me after the opening
night to tell me how it went.'

'You know, I'd forgotten all about that, too!' she said.

'It seems to have been a success, and Will made a big hit in his role as Oberon, so I'm glad for his sake.'

'Yes, he was very kind to you at the theatre that time. Did he say anything else interesting?'

I told her what he'd said about Mirrie not realizing that his part in the play was the most important one, even if she did have the star billing.

'That's priceless!' she said, laughing. 'And it's good that you seem to be totally over Marco.'

'Yes, he's yesterday's bad news. I'm just sorry I wasted so much time bolstering up his ego and coaxing him to write something people might actually want to watch.'

'It wasn't entirely wasted, as far as Will goes.'

'There is that. But Marco can sink or swim with the next play without me.'

A faint, unearthly cry rent the air from the direction of the cottage and Honey started.

'Is that horrendous noise by any chance your cat?' she enquired. 'If not, I think we need to get the cottage exorcized again.'

I sighed. 'It is. Golightly must have woken up and realized he was on his own again. He never used to be this vocal, so I think it must be being in a totally strange place.'

'I expect he'll get used to it. Are you going to let him out into the courtyard?'

'You know, I was wondering about that. He's always been an indoor cat, but he might get bored shut in the cottage all the time.'

'If he's an old cat, he might be happy to have the run of the courtyard and not venture any further,' she suggested. 'You could try it and see. Have a cat flap put in the front door.'

'Wouldn't you mind?'

'No, not at all. Only Pelican House is a Grade II listed building, so we can do what we like to the cottage.'

'Perhaps I'll get one to try then, though I suppose he ought to be microchipped first in case he does stray.'

'There's a pet shop that might have cat flaps. If you turn left after you pass Spindrift, it's just down that road. I'll text you the vet's number, too. Happy Pets is only a few minutes' walk away.'

'Great, thank you,' I said.

'Well, I don't know why we're standing here talking when there is so much to see!' Honey said. 'Come on, I'll give you the guided tour of the museum, although really, you've been over every inch virtually and in on all the plans, anyway.'

'That's not quite the same as actually being here,' I said, following her through the adjoining door. 'I'm dying to see it!'

'We've got it to ourselves this afternoon, apart from the plumbers,' she said. 'Lock the door to your workroom behind you – you'll have to get into the habit of that when the museum is open, because you don't want inquisitive members of the public wandering into your cottage.'

'That's true, although I suppose out of opening hours I can leave all the doors unlocked if I'm coming and going.'

'This is the staff room, office and stockroom, all rolled into one,' said Honey, as we entered a room that was already equipped with a table and chairs, desk, a small sink with a kettle on the worktop next to it, but also – much more interesting to me – a wall of metal shelves on which reposed brown archive boxes big enough to take carefully folded items of costume. Not only that, but there was also a whole rack of what I was sure were wedding dresses in opaque plastic covers . . .

Before I could say anything, Honey continued, 'Those are all the donated wedding dresses in the boxes and hanging bags.

We can move them into your storeroom when you're ready for them. The empty shelves on the other wall are for stock to put in the museum shop, and things like leaflets, brochures and extra copies of my books. I should think the shop, and the online sales, will be what generate the main part of the museum's income.'

'I see you've numbered all the wedding dresses,' I said, hardly taking in a word of this.

'Yes, and as each one arrived, I added them to a catalogue on my computer, together with scanned-in copies of any photos or information that came with them. The originals are in the boxes. I'll email you the catalogue and then you can keep adding details as you work on the dresses.'

'That's really organized.'

'It was just easier to keep track of what I'd got. When George was up, he checked I'd packed and stored all the dresses properly, especially the older ones.'

'How many wedding gowns are there so far?'

'Eleven donated ones, plus mine – and yours will make thirteen.'

I was gravitating towards the first of the boxes when she took me firmly by the arm and steered me towards the door.

'No you don't! You'll have plenty of time to look at those later.'

I gave the boxes one lingering look of longing, then allowed myself to be ushered into the museum foyer, a large space with a dark polished parquet floor.

There was a window with the blind up and the big double doors at the front were open, letting in the light through a pair of glass inner ones.

I was trying to make out the design and lettering on them when Honey said: 'Baz from the art shop designed the logo on

181

the glass doors, to go with the name I thought up. It's a house with windows and a door, shaped like a wedding cake with the bride and groom on top, but cracked and divided down the middle. The lettering says: "The Wedding House: A Little Museum of Bridal Misfortune". I'm having a signboard painted to go outside, too.'

'That's all rather clever,' I said. 'The name and logo will look good on merchandise in the shop.'

'That's what I thought, and I'm having a Happy Never After line, too. There's loads of room for stock in here, as well as a big reception desk. I've got Priceless Interiors, the architectural reclamation place in North Wales, looking out for a decent desk and some display shelves and cupboards for in here, as well as the bigger cases for the costumes.

'We'll have some shelves behind the desk for higher value items, like your little costume mannequins, if you want to sell them here later.'

'I don't know if anyone would want to buy them, if the dresses are from bridal misfortunes, Honey.'

'I think you'll find you're quite wrong. In fact, it wouldn't surprise me if you were asked to make copies of some of the dresses for brides to wear to their own weddings!'

I couldn't imagine that, but she sounded quite confident.

'We'll need things like a till and credit card reader on the desk, and a phone.'

'I haven't really thought of that side of the job much,' I said uneasily. 'I mean, I've never used a till or sold anything directly to the public.'

'Oh, you don't have to worry about that! I've already got two volunteers lined up to man the desk and office: they're a pair of retired sisters. One is a former librarian and the other actually ran a small folk museum in Devon, so they are perfect!'

I felt a huge relief, especially when she added that Derek was going to add caretaking and cleaning the museum to his repertoire. 'And he will remove the takings at the end of each day and put them in our safe in the house, do the banking, and that kind of thing.'

'You already seem to have it all organized,' I said admiringly. 'Did you say the two ladies were volunteering?'

'Yes, although I'm sure they will have perks. We're negotiating those.'

'I feel guilty now that I'm going to be paid for doing a lot less!'

'But you are the expert and will be really busy behind the scenes – and *in* the scenes, if there are any booked guided tours. I imagine we will get a lot more donated dresses once we're open, so it won't be a static display but an ever-expanding and changing one.'

'Sounds great. Do you know what the opening times will be yet?'

'Almost the same as Uncle Hugo's museum: two till four on Monday, Tuesday, Wednesday and Friday afternoons, and ten till one on Saturdays. Closed Thursdays – that's market day – and Sundays. Your days off are Thursday, Saturday afternoon and Sunday.'

'That's half a day more than I got at Beng & Briggs,' I said.

While we talked, I'd been conscious of hammering and other noises from behind a door beyond the wide wooden staircase that rose from the foyer.

'Is that the plumbers you mentioned?'

'Yes, they're installing the toilet cubicle. We're just having a single purpose one, with disabled and baby changing facilities. There's a perfectly good public toilet just outside in the market square, so that seemed enough.'

'Is that a lift I see next to it?'

'Yes, neat, isn't it? Big enough to take a wheelchair and one other person and also handy for transporting heavy things up and down, too,' Honey added.

'You seem to have all the bases covered!'

'Not quite. There's always something I haven't thought of!'

She pulled a small notebook and pen out of her jeans pocket and scribbled something in it. I don't suppose there was enough room up her arm for all the book ideas *and* museum ones, although there seemed to be some crossover because she said now: 'You know, when I've finished writing *Armed with Poison*, I might just call the next one *Happy Never After*, to tie in . . .' Then she added, more briskly: 'Come on, we'll go upstairs next. Let's try out the lift and pop up like twin pantomime demons.'

18

The Bloody Bride

I felt more as if I was popping up encased in an ice cube, but the lift worked smoothly and almost silently and we stepped out on to the dark polished parquet floor of the upper storey, where the rooms all opened out of each other, giving a long vista to the other end of the building.

The walls were painted the same very light dove grey as my workroom, and there was a sense of light and space.

'There are blackout blinds on every window. George was insistent on those, and that they must be kept closed permanently once the displays are up.'

'Absolutely,' I agreed. 'Light would damage some of the exhibits.'

Looking round, I saw that the work was still not entirely finished, for bundles of electrical wires emerged in odd places, like strange sea corals.

Honey led the way through the rooms, familiar to me from the many videos and photos she'd sent, with tape marking the eventual positions of display cabinets.

'There's going to be one big central glass case in the final room, lit so it will be visible from the lift and stairs, and sort of beckon you towards it.'

Now I was actually there, it was much easier to imagine the space furnished, the pale shapes of the wedding gowns glimmering in their lit cases.

We wandered around, discussing the displays and all the behind-the-scenes details that have to be considered, particularly for costume displays. It was all more George's territory than mine, but I was learning.

'There's no access to Pelican House from this level?'

'No, it's only connected by a short passage from what will be the Rosa-May Garland Collection room, off the foyer. You'll see that in a minute. We've had to turn the door to it into a fire door and install another from the passage directly into the garden.'

As we walked back to the stairs I said, 'The dresses we have now will be well spread out in all this space, but I'm sure you're right and we'll get more donated to us later.'

'If we open early, it will probably still be a work in progress anyway, with dresses added as they're ready to put on view,' said Honey. 'Eventually, I thought this first room could house temporary exhibitions of dresses just on loan, or with a special theme.'

'Great idea!'

'And since people always love true crime stories, we'll dedicate the furthest room to that angle.'

'Have we got enough crime-related dresses for that?' I asked, startled.

'Two or three,' she said vaguely, and I thought I'd better skim through the catalogue as soon as Derek sent it over, to see which she meant.

'It's all a lot further advanced than I expected – practically down to finishing touches,' I said. 'I'll need to order the display mannequins as soon as I've measured the dresses, so we'll have to decide what type to have.'

'I'll leave that to you, Garland, and I'm sure George will advise you.'

'Some costume museums favour the clear plastic kind, but I like the solid black ones because the costumes stand out so much better, like those in the Rosa-May Garland exhibition at the V&A.'

'That's good, because I forgot to tell you that I'm purchasing those from the V&A as well as the information boards they had specially made. George arranged that, and it seemed sensible. I mean, they can't reuse the boards, and probably not the mannequins either, because Rosa-May had an unusually small and slight figure.'

'Tell me about it,' I said, because my size had made buying clothes off the rack difficult all my adult life.

'We should keep a few stock sizes of mannequins in, too,' I suggested. 'And I suppose we'll need all kinds of small stands for displaying accessories.'

'Just email me lists of what you need as you work through all the material, and I'll get Derek to put in the orders.'

We were back downstairs now and crossed to the door opposite the staff room.

'You have to imagine the brass plaque saying "The Rosa-May Garland Collection" because I've only just ordered it,' said Honey, opening the door to reveal a square room a little smaller than any of the others, but still spacious enough to take three tall glass display cabinets, their positions outlined in red tape on the floor.

'I thought the biggest cabinet, to the right, would be perfect for the Titania costume and the evening dress,' Honey said.

'Then the narrower one next to it could display your wedding dress, so the visitors can compare it with the original.' She turned. 'And over there, we can display the two silk dominoes we found in the trunks.'

The dominoes were loose robes that were often worn over evening dresses for masked balls, or other entertainments, although I didn't suppose Rosa-May had had any more use for those than for the lovely Titania costume, once she was transported from London to the depths of the Lancashire moors.

'Perhaps eventually I could make evening dresses to go under the dominoes and they could be left open at the front to display them,' I suggested. 'There are lots of Regency fashion plates to inspire me and it would be fun.'

'Good idea,' said Honey. 'It's a pity we don't have the dress and pelisse Rosa-May wore for her wedding, but she describes them in her journal, so perhaps you could try to re-create those later, too?'

'I must make an effort to read more of the journal, but I've been so busy and her handwriting is awful!'

'You sort of get your eye in for it, after a while, so it's easier.'

She gestured to a space outlined in yellow tape on the far wall. 'I'll have a glass-topped table with the journal open inside it over there, and a few odds and ends from the trunks . . . and then, that big rectangle of yellow tape in the middle of the room is another glass case, just tall enough to take both trunks, perhaps displayed open with a few Regency-style props showing.'

'That's an odd size for a showcase – I wonder what was in it originally?' I said.

'Oh, most of the cabinets are coming from an ecclesiastical museum and I think that one had those tall hats in it, that look sort of like origami – mitres? Or am I thinking of something else?'

'No idea. I'm not big on ecclesiastical vestments, but I know what you mean.'

'When everything comes back from the V&A, all we'll really need is an information board about *your* dress, Garland, describing how we discovered the family connection – the visitors will love that – and how you came to make a replica of Rosa-May's dress. But you can say as much or as little as you want about why you never wore it as your wedding dress.'

'I think I'll simply say it was never worn because the engagement was broken off,' I said, 'but I'm glad all my work on it wasn't entirely wasted!'

'I'm going to put my own wedding dress in that true crime room upstairs at the back,' Honey said with a grin. 'Not, as it turned out, that any crime had been committed, but it all looked a bit dodgy at the time with the dress covered in bloodstains. I'm thinking of calling that area the "Bloody Brides" room,' she added.

I stared at her, uncertain if she was joking or not, but she was now fishing a bunch of keys out of one pocket and handing them to me.

'These are your set of keys to the museum, so you can come and go as you like. I've got one, and Derek will have a set too, and Ella and Kay, the two volunteers. We'll keep spares in the staff room.'

'Unless there's a burglar alarm, I'll probably often work late and wander around,' I said.

'I didn't think it would be worth having an alarm, because there's nothing much burglars would want in here, and we'll only keep a small amount of money in the office at night, for the float.'

'That's fine, then, so long as we don't frighten each other to death, wandering around late at night!'

'Once all the dresses are on display I might well take to late-night prowling. And Viv seems quite interested by the whole idea, so maybe she'll be wafting about at night, too, looking for poetic inspiration.'

'Perhaps we should all be belled, like cats, to warn each other we're there!'

'I think I'd feel too much like a morris man,' Honey said seriously.

I heaved a happy sigh. 'I can see what the finished museum will look like now, in my mind's eye, and it's going to be such fun working on the dresses! I can't wait to start opening those boxes and bags in the stockroom to see what's there.'

I must have sounded wistful, because Honey smiled and said that although we really ought to go back to the house to sort out my terms of employment, we could just do a quick detour first, so she could show me one particular dress.

'It's that winter wedding dress I mentioned to you recently, the one that made me think we should open the museum much earlier than I'd originally planned.'

In the staff room, she selected a bag from the rail and unzipped it, pulling out a long, strapless gown with an ominous splatter of what could only be bloodstains across the pristine whiteness of the skirt.

'There's a *faux* swansdown cape thing and a crystal and satin flower headdress in the archive box with the matching number,' Honey was saying, as I stared, mesmerized, at the dress. 'The bride's mother sent loads of information with it, and that's all in the box, too.'

'That *is* blood, isn't it?' I queried, finding my voice.

'Yes, that's blood all right,' Honey agreed. 'The dress has

been stored for almost a year, so it's turned dark. Do you remember that story in the papers last November, about the bride who vanished on the eve of her wedding, and all they found was her bloody wedding dress?'

'I do, vaguely,' I said. 'Didn't they arrest the fiancé . . . or perhaps I've got that wrong?'

'They questioned him, then let him go, because apart from the few stains on the dress, which were the bride's blood group, there was no sign that anything had happened to her. She'd just come back to her mother's house after a hen night at a local restaurant and vanished, taking nothing with her.'

'That's mysterious!'

'You'll find the whole story written down by her mother in the archive box, including information not in the newspaper reports. Her daughter was – or, I hope, *is* – Amy Weston and she was twenty-nine and teaching history in a sixth-form college. She lived with her fiancé, but was spending the night before her wedding at her mother's house. The bridesmaid dropped her off there before eleven that night – and that was the last anyone saw of her.'

She paused. 'The groom was having his stag night with a few colleagues, and since he was the jealous, possessive type, he'd rung his fiancée several times during the evening to check up on her and wanted to know what time she was going back to her mother's house.'

'A bit obsessive and creepy,' I observed.

'That's what I think. Apparently, since they got engaged, he'd managed to cut her off from her old friends and they did everything together, which always sounds smothering to me,' said Honey. 'Her hen night didn't sound like a riot of fun, either, just dinner with a handful of colleagues from the college, though the bridesmaid, who worked there too, was a friend. The mother,' she added, 'still thinks the fiancé abducted her, but there was no evidence to prove it.'

I thought it over. 'Did the bridesmaid actually see her go in the house?'

'Good point. Yes, she did, and she says she also noticed a car parked at the end of the street that looked very much like the fiancé's. It would have been like him to check she was where she'd said she was. They found a card from him in Amy's room that said "After tomorrow, we'll never be apart again", but he said he gave it to her before she left their flat.'

'Even more creepy!' I said. 'But if she felt the same way, she didn't have to marry him, did she?'

'She might have been scared of him, I suppose,' Honey said. 'She sent him a message just after she got in, to say she was home and turning off her phone because she was going straight to bed. Which everyone assumed she had. Her mother had been out, and when she got back she thought Amy was in bed. It wasn't until she opened the door next morning that she found her missing and the stained dress. She'd gone in the clothes she was wearing that evening and hadn't even taken her phone or handbag.'

'It sounds like the start of one of your novels,' I suggested.

'I suppose it does a bit. Anyway, there was no sign that the house was a crime scene, or that the fiancé had ever been in there. He tried to reach her by phone a couple of times after she'd told him she was switching it off and the records place him at their flat, several miles away. So, for lack of evidence, the police just had to assume she'd left of her own accord and the investigation fizzled out. But nothing has been heard of her since and her mother naturally wants to know the truth of what happened. She still thinks the fiancé somehow abducted and killed her daughter.'

'And she sent you the dress, to put on display?'

'Yes, she'd seen a small piece I did for a women's magazine about how I'd been inspired by all the dresses from disastrous weddings that had been sent to me to open my own museum displaying them. She wants the dress and the story to have maximum publicity in the hope new evidence will be found. And, of course, the publicity will be great for the museum, too,' she finished practically.

Then, in her deep, husky voice, she sang something about it being a good day for a white wedding before asking me if I knew that song.

'No.'

'Listen to it on YouTube sometime. It's a good one. I like a bit of rock, or punk – very cathartic when I've been committing murders by proxy late into the night.'

'It sounds as if it would make good background music in the museum, played low,' I said. 'But I expect there would be copyright issues.'

'I'm sure there would be,' Honey said regretfully.

'Now I can understand why you want to open the museum as early as possible, so you can get maximum publicity about this dress and its story, so that's probably the one I ought to look at first,' I suggested.

'Yes, because it will be the central attraction in the Bloody Brides room, displayed in that spot lit central case.'

'Are you *really* going to call it the Bloody Brides room?'

'I certainly am,' Honey said. Then her dark eyes got that strangely abstracted expression I was becoming familiar with and she pushed her left sleeve up, displaying an arm covered in ballpoint pen, some of it faded like old tattoos, and added 'The Bloody Bride – or maybe Bridegroom?' to the rest.

'That would make such a good book title, though I have a

feeling I've already noted it down.' She scanned up and down her arm, then said: 'Yes, there it is, just a bit faint.'

I reverted back to the mysterious disappearance. 'I hope Amy left of her own accord and the fresh publicity solves the mystery . . . though the bloodstains do look a bit ominous.'

'I've got an entirely open mind about it,' Honey said. 'I know from my own experience that even a vanished bridegroom and a blood-soaked scenario don't necessarily mean foul play.'

She didn't enlarge on this, so I asked cautiously if she meant to reveal the story of her own jilting when her wedding gown was put on display.

'I think I might, because enough water has passed under the bridge since for it not to matter now if the whole thing comes out,' she mused. 'But not in a vindictive kind of way, because being jilted inspired me to start writing the revenge thrillers under my own name and then my career really took off.'

Her gamine grin reappeared. 'It was the best thing my fiancé ever did. I suspect you'll grow to feel much the same about the break-up with Marco.'

'I already do! My broken heart seamlessly mended the moment I grasped that not only had he let Mirrie take my wedding dress without permission, but he'd also been unfaithful with her. The double betrayal was unforgivable.'

It felt as if betrayal had been the story of my life so far. I'd even been unreasonably angry with my parents for getting themselves killed, leaving me to live with a stranger, but then, children aren't reasonable about these things.

And then there was Thom. Although on the surface we'd made things up, it was still hard to forget the years of loss and hurt he'd put me through.

'I'm entirely focused on my new job now and looking forward

to living a quiet life here in Great Mumming with Golightly, if he'll settle down. He wasn't ever really my cat, he just visited, and he's never shown any sign of being attached to me.'

'I look forward to meeting him; he sounds interesting.'

'That's one word for it – and he might soon be haunting the mews, scaring the visitors away!'

'Bruno's dog, Jester, has free access to the courtyard and, when it's fine, they leave the workshop door open and put a mat out for him to lie on. Perhaps Golightly will make friends.'

'Thom said Jester likes cats, but I suspect the feeling isn't going to be mutual,' I said dubiously. 'I'm not sure Golightly's even met a dog before.'

'Oh, I expect they'll get on fine,' Honey said with unfounded optimism, and then, zipping the Bloody Bride's dress back into its cover, suggested we adjourn to Pelican House for coffee and to sort out my employment details.

We went back through the Rosa-May Garland Room and Honey opened the fire door on to the short passage that led to the house. There was no window, just the second fire door on to her garden, which she'd had to put in to satisfy safety rules.

We came out in a scullery and I followed her into a large kitchen with low dark beams and a big central table.

It smelled scrumptious, probably because Viv, wrapped in a large black pinny printed with brightly coloured sugar skulls, was taking a tray of muffins out of the oven.

'What great timing!' Honey said, sniffing the air appreciatively.

A huge grey wolfhound, who I remembered was called Rory, seemed to agree with her, for he was sitting bolt upright in his large bed in the corner, following Viv's every move with large, soulful eyes.

'These are blueberry and the ones already cooling on the

rack are chocolate chip,' said Viv, in a pretty, light voice, before catching sight of me behind Honey.

I thought she'd immediately clam up, so I was surprised when, after a moment's hesitation, she smiled and whispered, 'Hello, Garland!'

Then she averted her eyes rather shyly and carried on transferring muffins on to the wire cooling rack.

Honey looked faintly amazed, but without comment switched on the coffee machine and got out mugs.

'Has the dogwalker taken Rory out for a run?'

Viv nodded.

'Good, because I want another session on the book before dinner and Rory will be too tired to want more than an amble round the market square later.'

We drank our coffee and ate a muffin apiece in the kitchen with Viv, while telling her what we'd been doing and about the Bloody Bride.

'I hadn't got round to telling you about her yet, Viv,' Honey said. Before adding to me, 'Viv's interested in all the stories connected with the dresses.'

'Yes . . . so fascinating,' whispered Viv.

'I'm hoping they'll inspire you to write a whole new poetry collection, Viv, just as your cooking will inspire me to write my novels even faster, which will make my agent a very happy woman.'

'I just might,' she said in a thread of a voice, as if she was confiding a secret.

Honey bit into her second muffin. 'Great! I'd like you to get so inspired you move in here permanently – make a fresh start, like Garland.'

Viv went pink. 'You're always so kind . . . but you can't really mean it!'

'Of course I do,' said Honey, looking astonished. 'When did I ever say anything I didn't mean? I told you when I brought you back here that you could stay as long as you wanted and, goodness knows, this house is big enough for us both to have our own separate spaces to live and work in, whenever we want to get away from each other. You think about it.'

Honey got up. 'Come on, Garland, let's go to my office and sort out the important stuff, like your salary. The workwoman is worthy of her hire.'

*

A little while later, I headed back through the museum carrying a box of muffins that Viv had left in the kitchen for me with a note.

I was thinking about the first list of purchases that I was to email over to Honey later – the cutting table at the head of it – and stiffening my resolve not to unpack any of the dresses until it arrived. Besides, I had received the catalogue of gowns Honey had compiled, so I ought to read through that first.

In the foyer I skirted around a porcelain loo, which stood in the middle of the floor like a piece of bizarre sculpture. The inner glass doors were now open and pinned back, and two workmen were unloading a lot of pipes and what looked like a packaged washbasin from a white van, so presumably the new convenience was getting to the finishing stages.

I actually turned my head away from the tempting archive boxes in the staff room and locked the door of my workroom behind me, as if I'd just passed a very difficult test.

There was no sound from the cottage now; it was almost ominously quiet. Nor was there any sign of Golightly . . . but then I noticed that the door to the hall was open a crack and eventually I discovered him luxuriously stretched out across my bed, fast asleep, making that leaky-bellows noise.

I tiptoed out. If I went now, I'd just have time to slip across to this pet shop Honey had told me about and see if they had a suitable cat flap . . . and buy more expensive treats to propitiate the Household God with.

I collected a shopping bag and then, after a moment's thought, put half the muffins Viv had left for me in a sandwich box of my own and took it with me.

Rosa-May

The whole experience of my visit to the theatre only increased my belief that I was destined to become an actress and made me even more determined, if that were possible, to achieve my goal, an ambition that Letty found both exciting and to be applauded.

We spent many happy hours walking about the gardens, discussing how this might best be accomplished. I also shared with her Sara's occasional letters from London, where, as well as helping in her sister's lodging house, she was sometimes employed at the Cockleshell Theatre, so had much of interest to impart.

The theatre had been newly refurbished and reopened and was, she said, set to rival both those of Drury Lane and Covent Garden.

My secret plans made it possible for me to tolerate the tedious hours I spent reading to Lady Bugle, or dispensing tea for her very unexciting circle of friends.

*

With the turning of the New Year and my seventeenth birthday, I resolved to put off my plans no longer.

I would run away to London and go to stay with Sara at her sister's house and they, with their connections to the Cockleshell Theatre, would endeavour to interest the actor-manager Aurelius Blake in my earnest desire to enter his company.

Sara warned me of the difficulties I would face in obtaining this end and also, should I be successful, the pitfalls and privations of the life, for actors, it seemed, would find themselves travelling the length and breadth of the country for weeks on end and all but the most renowned of the company earned little more than a pittance.

Then, too, there was the general poor opinion of the morals of actors and, most especially actresses, which might lead to attempts upon my virtue . . .

But she also told me that Mr Blake and his wife, together with his brother, were of a strict Methodist persuasion and their company was most respectable.

This would suit me very well, for having seen the effects of child-bearing on poor Mama, I retain the greatest terror of it and my resolve never to expose myself to the risk.

Letty finds my attitude on this matter very strange, for these things are women's lot and, to her, to be a spinster is a sad fate.

19

String-Driven Thing

When I tapped on the door of Bruno Bascombe's workshop half an hour later, Thom looked surprised but pleased to see me. His hair was tucked behind his ears, so he looked more himself, and was wearing a workmanlike heavy brown canvas apron with lots of pockets.

'Hi, Garland! Come in,' he invited, stepping back.

'I can't stop,' I said, resting a heavy carrier bag on the step, so I could fish the plastic box of muffins out of my shoulder bag.

I passed it to him. 'Viv was baking earlier, when I was over in Pelican House, and she kindly gave me some homemade muffins. They're huge and I can't possibly eat them all myself, so I thought you might like half of them.'

'I would. But surely you could come in for ten minutes, couldn't you?' he suggested and then, without waiting for my reply, picked up my shopping and led the way in.

'What on earth have you got in here? It weighs a ton!'

'Mostly tins of cat food. I've been to the pet shop across the square, though I only wanted to see if they had a cat flap – which they did – but when I saw they also had the expensive food Golightly prefers, I thought I'd better stock up on it. He never seems to put any weight on, but I don't want him to waste away.'

I found myself in a long workshop that held that familiar scent of wood, and perhaps linseed oil, together with other, less identifiable elements that I remembered from Dad's shed all those years ago, and then I spotted some of Dad's tools on the nearest workbench, next to the big, tiered, wooden toolbox with all the compartments that had been his, too.

I felt a lump come into my throat and had to blink back a rush of tears. Thom might have been able to leave me behind, but he'd treasured those enough to bring them with him.

Luckily Thom, having put down the bag, had his back to me as he switched on a kettle in a sort of little cubbyhole at the end of the room and unhooked mugs from a shelf above.

'You've got time for a drink? Tea, coffee?'

'A quick coffee, then,' I capitulated. 'I've already left poor Golightly on his own for most of today.'

I sat on a high, leather-topped, metal stool, and Jester, who had been sitting on a large furry cushion bed, tail thumping a tattoo, now got up and came to say hello.

I stroked his silky ears and said, 'I think dogs are probably a lot less trouble than cats, and this one always looks as if he's grinning!'

'He probably is,' Thom said. 'He's very good-natured and laid-back.'

He put a mug of instant on the bench next to me and sat on another stool, opening the plastic sandwich box.

'Chocolate chip *and* blueberry, my two favourites,' he said. 'Are you going to have one?'

'No, those are all yours. I've still got some at home.'

'Fair enough.' He took a great bite and made appreciative

noises, while I sipped my coffee and Jester switched the melting gaze of his dark eyes on to Thom instead.

'Did you say you'd been buying a cat flap, Garland? Have you decided to try letting Golightly out, then?'

'I'm going to give it a go because I think he'll be bored, with no outside space at all. I talked it over with Honey earlier, and she doesn't mind if I install a cat flap in the cottage door. I'm hoping he won't go beyond the mews, but I need to have him microchipped first, just in case. I'll give Honey's vet a ring as soon as I get in and make an appointment.'

'I can fit the cat flap for you, no problem,' Thom offered. 'I'll come over and do it in my lunch hour tomorrow, shall I?'

'That would be very kind, if you're sure you have time?'

'I'm my own master while Bruno's away, but I often work on into the evening when I'm making something interesting anyway, so I put the hours in.'

'OK. I'll probably spend all tomorrow at the cottage, finishing the unpacking and starting to set up my workroom,' I said. 'I must say,' I added, 'it's wonderful to have my own big workshop.'

'I know what you mean. It felt like I'd died and gone to heaven the first time I came here to work with Bruno,' agreed Thom. 'Room to spread out, leave my tools around and have everything I could possibly need to hand.'

'Bruno must think a lot of your work, if he's left you in charge for months.'

'He trained me, so he knows I can do the work, but I'll never know as much as he does. He comes from a long line of puppet makers, just as the Marinos, who have the puppet theatre next door, come from generations who travelled around the country with Punch and Judy shows.'

'I'm looking forward to seeing *The Murder in the Red Barn*.'

I looked around the workshop and, now my eyes had adjusted, could make out more of the details in the shadows away from the bright central strip lights. Marionettes in different sizes, clothed and unclothed, hung on pegs, or wooden racks. There were tools, wood, pots of paint and jars of brushes; machinery that might be lathes, heavy old metal vices fixed to the edges of the benches and open boxes of sandpaper . . . It was a clutter, but a workmanlike one, and I was sure Thom would be able to lay his hands instantly on anything he needed.

At the back of the bench we were sitting at was a long, shallow wooden box with the pieces of a marionette laid out in it, reminding me inescapably of photos of skeletons in archaeological digs. The carved head had its face turned to the wall, as if it had been naughty.

I gestured to it. 'Is that one of the new puppets you're making for the *Red Barn* production?'

He nodded, though for some reason looking slightly uncomfortable. Perhaps he didn't like anyone seeing a work in progress.

'That one's Maria's lover-turned-murderer, William Corder. He still needs jointing, painting and stringing. Stringing a marionette is an art in itself and took some learning!'

'I should imagine it's tricky,' I agreed. 'If you really want me to take over the costume making from Simon, I suppose I'll have to learn how to adapt them so they don't impede the movement of the puppets.'

'It would be a relief to Simon if you did take that off his hands, but there's no rush. And for this show, there will only be three characters to dress.'

'It'll be easy compared to making my mini costume mannequins,' I said, and then fell silent for a moment, thinking how odd it was to be sitting here with Thom, talking about things that interested us, just as we had all those years ago – except now there were differences, undercurrents . . . Too much had happened and we were not quite the same people any more.

Thom finished the rest of his muffin in one bite and then, when he could, said, following on from what we'd been saying, 'Simple costumes in bright colours work better for the performances. We paint the faces quite boldly, too. Honey suggested we collaborate to make puppets wearing copies of the wedding dresses in the museum, didn't she? Those could be more subtly painted.'

'I expect some of the dresses are lovely, but they must all have unfortunate stories behind them, so I don't know how popular they'd be in the museum shop.'

'There's always a market for the macabre or mysterious,' he said. 'Like the eternal fascination with the Red Barn murder!'

'I expect you're right,' I said. 'Do you make most of your marionettes for commissions?'

'Mostly, although we also renovate old ones and, when we have time, make stock sizes or characters to have handy. I'd like to expand our website to sell more through that, too. I persuaded Bruno to let Pearl set one up for us, but, so far, he's a bit reluctant to embrace internet selling.'

'Unlike Honey, who's dead keen! I'll be working full-time until the museum is up and running. Then it looks as if I'll have lots of my own work to fit in after that, what with carrying on with the V&A costume mannequins, some for our museum shop, and then the marionette costumes, too.'

'You won't miss your old life . . . or Marco?' Thom said hesitantly, looking at me from his unfathomable, dark amber eyes.

'I'll miss my old job, but as for Marco, you can't be serious, after what he did! I mean, even if he turned up wearing sackcloth and ashes and begging for forgiveness, there's no going back with relationships – and if you try, things are never quite the same again.'

'No,' agreed Thom. I knew he realized I'd meant *our* relationship too, twice so abruptly broken off, for he said, tentatively, 'But perhaps sometimes it's possible to build something new on the old foundations, if they were solid enough?'

'Perhaps . . .' I said, then got up. 'I must get back.'

He grabbed the handles of the heavy shopping bag before I could.

'I'll carry this back for you.'

'I can manage,' I protested, but not too much, because I thought my left arm was probably already several inches longer than the other one, just from carrying shopping since I'd got here.

Jester, pink tongue lolling out, accompanied us, though his steps slowed as we approached my door and a now-familiar unearthly screaming reached our ears.

'Golightly appears to have woken up,' I said drily. 'It's dinner time and he's feeling hungry and abandoned.'

'He has amazing lungs for something so old and skinny,' Thom said admiringly, but I noticed that Jester had stopped dead and was now slowly backing away.

'That must be what they mean by caterwauling,' Thom remarked gravely, putting my bag down in the hall once I'd opened the door. The noise from the living room, where the door was still ajar, stopped suddenly, as if turned off.

'Will I see you at the book group at Pearl's, seven tonight?'

'I don't really think I should leave Golightly again so soon,' I said doubtfully.

'If he settles, you could just briefly pop in to meet everyone,' Thom suggested. 'It's only an hour and then we usually go to the pub afterwards, but you could skip that bit.'

'I might. I'll have to see.'

'If not, I'll be over tomorrow lunchtime to fit that cat flap,' he said, then strode back to where Jester was anxiously waiting for him, reminding me of Nana, the dog in *Peter Pan*, another favourite old classic of mine.

*

Golightly, as I'd suspected, didn't display any sign that he'd been missing me, or feeling lonely; he just conducted me to his bowl in a no-nonsense way and demanded his dinner.

I opened a tin of his favourite food and he wolfed that down in record time, while I was still stashing the rest of the tins away. Then he retired to sleep it off on his favourite armchair. He said something in Cat to me in passing, which I'd like to think was a thank you for hauling his heavy cans of food home, but probably wasn't.

I rang the vet from my bedroom, where Golightly couldn't hear me, and made an appointment to take him for microchipping the following afternoon. Then I went back downstairs and made myself some cheese on toast, because it felt like a long time since lunch, before settling down to source the cutting table and the other things on my first list, with fast delivery. I sent that over to Honey, though it sounded like something she usually delegated to the all-purpose Derek!

I ordered a few smaller items myself – things that were more for my own work than the museum's: sets of little drawers for stowing odds and ends of sewing materials away, spool holders and flatpack storage boxes in pretty colours.

I made the mistake of checking what books there were on the history of wedding dresses too, which all seemed to be glossy, illustrated and expensive.

I had a brief reply from Honey, saying Derek had put in my order before he went home and would send over the delivery details when he had them.

I wasn't expecting delivery to be quite next day, but I'd chosen the suppliers for speed, rather than economy, so I hoped they'd get here soon.

It was half past six by then and the book group met at seven. I was in two minds about it, because I was tired and still had unpacking to do, but I also felt strangely wired and restless, so I thought perhaps I *would* just pop over and meet everyone. I needn't stay long. Perhaps next week, if Golightly had settled, I could go on to the pub as well. There were faint hopes of my developing some kind of social life, despite Golightly.

When I was ready to go out, I went back into the living room, where he opened his yellow eyes and looked at me accusingly.

'I'll only be an hour at the very most, and if you don't scream the place down, you can have yet more luscious cat treats when I get back,' I told him.

He seemed to consider this offer, then closed his eyes and put his head down on to his front paws again, so I hoped a bargain had been struck.

Simon, Thom and I all simultaneously stepped out of our respective front doors, as if we were taking part in a TV sitcom, then the other two waited for me to catch up with them, so we could go round to Pearl's together.

The bookshop displayed a 'Closed' sign, but Simon pushed the door open with a jangle from the bell and we followed him in.

There were already several other people in the back room, sitting round the table and Pearl was dispensing coffee from the machine.

She looked up and smiled. 'Garland! I'm glad you could make it.'

'I've only popped in briefly to say hello this time,' I said. 'I've got so much to do and the cat's getting really fed up with my constantly leaving him shut up alone.'

'Well, have a cup of coffee and meet everyone before you dash off again,' she said hospitably. 'Then we'll see you next week, when you and the cat have settled in properly, and perhaps afterwards you'd like to come to the Sun in Splendour with us.'

'It's a weekly rite,' agreed Simon. 'Tuesday is Lancashire hotpot night at the pub, followed by that northern delicacy, a slice of rich fruit cake accompanied by a chunk of Lancashire Crumbly.'

'Lancashire . . . Crumbly?'

'A kind of cheese – the best in the world,' said a small, portly man with a Lancashire accent. He had a black bandanna tied around his head, and a large gold hoop earring like a slightly run-to-seed pirate.

'I'm Baz, by the way,' he introduced himself. 'I have the art shop in the square.'

He indicated the slight young man with the crest of fairish hair sitting next to him on the sofa and added: 'This is my partner, Derek.'

'Oh, we know *all* about each other, even though we haven't met before,' Derek said.

'I saw you briefly yesterday, at Pelican House, when you were seeing some visitors out,' I said. 'Honey told me you are her PA.'

'PA, housekeeper, general dogsbody. Renaissance man, that's me,' Derek proclaimed. 'I'm on tap whenever needed.'

'Thank you for ordering all those things for my workroom so quickly,' I said.

'Think nothing of it – it's all part of the service!'

'This is Ginny, who has a lovely shop called Spindrift in the square,' Pearl said, introducing me to a woman with a dreamy expression and long, flowing, snow-white hair. She could have been any age from fifty to seventy. She was dressed in layers of the kind of clothes you see on the Gudrun Sjödén website, which I always admire but never know quite how to put together. In fact, with her angular body and thin, interesting face, she looked like one of their older models.

'And then there's just me you haven't met,' said a cheerful voice from beyond Baz on the sofa, and a woman with a broad, rosy face leaned forward to look round him and beamed.

'The Rev. Jo-Jo,' said Simon, but I'd already clocked the dog collar and remembered that Pearl had mentioned her.

The vicar had teamed the dog collar with a black T-shirt like the one Baz was wearing, but without the skull and crossbones, and a skirt in an improbable tartan of magenta, bright green and red.

'Jo-Jo isn't really a local,' explained Pearl. 'She lives a few miles away on the edge of a village called Jericho's End, but there isn't a local book group there.'

'There's one nearby in Thorstane, but they're very highbrow and I'm not,' Jo-Jo said. 'I can't always make it to this one and I'm afraid I'll have to dash off early tonight, too – a late meeting.'

Over coffee, it became apparent that they all knew who I was and why I was there, so either they'd arrived early and Pearl had filled them in, or the local grapevine was extremely effective. I suspected the latter.

We talked a bit about the museum, and Baz, Ginny and Pearl seemed hopeful it would bring more visitors to the town and into their shops.

'We have seen an increase in visitors to the area in the last few years, anyway,' Ginny said, sounding much more practical than she looked. 'There's a Christmas cracker factory nearby that's opened to the public and has all kinds of craftworkers, a gallery shop and a really good café. Then there's a woodland walk with some Roman ruins. Jericho's End, where Jo-Jo's parish is, is a bit of a mini tourist hotspot, with Fairy Falls and an old garden that's being restored and open to the public.'

'Yes, there's lots going on around here,' Baz agreed. 'Great Mumming is bucking the trend for empty town centres – it's thriving.'

'We're not much more than a large village, really,' Simon said. 'The town hall in the square is also the fire station, the police station and the tourist information bureau.'

'I had a little walk around the square, but I haven't really had time to find out where everything is yet,' I said.

'Time enough for that,' said Pearl. 'Now, why don't we have a quick round robin before you go, so you know what kind of books we all like.'

It transpired that Derek was a big Honey Fairford fan, which was just as well, really; Jo-Jo and Thom liked cosy crime; Simon loved big blockbuster thrillers; Pearl seemed to go for serious literary stuff, of the gloomier Booker-winner kind; Ginny, fantasy; and Baz, romcom.

When it got to me, I said apologetically, 'I'm not reading anything at the moment, it's been so hectic with the move and everything . . . but I'm afraid I'm addicted to Shakespeare, Victorian novels and old children's books.'

'That's a fairly rich diet,' said Jo-Jo.

'I spent my teenage years living in a remote village in Scotland, where those were the only books in the house, apart from the Bible. I sort of got addicted to the Victorian stuff, and I'm always looking for new ones. I'll come and browse your shelves when I have time, Pearl.'

'Do,' she said. 'And feel free to pop in for a coffee any time – no obligation to buy anything.'

She handed me a list of everyone's contact details and I gave her my mobile number.

'We take it in turns to host the group, so it's handy to have contact numbers if there's a sudden change of venue,' she explained.

I got up, my legs suddenly feeling tired. 'I'd better get back.'

'I'll have to go too,' said the vicar, and Pearl let us out into the darkening square.

'Lovely to meet you,' said Jo-Jo. 'Once you've settled, you must come and visit my church. It has a very special stained-glass window and a lot of history.'

'I'd love to, but I don't drive.'

'Oh, someone will bring you – Thom, or Simon, perhaps. Pearl doesn't drive, either, but Simon kindly drives her up for the service on Sundays.'

The town hall clock gave a tinny chime and she started. 'Gosh, is that the time? Must dash!'

And with that she sprinted across to a small lime-green Beetle, parked in the almost empty square.

*

I found Golightly exactly where I'd left him, though he woke enough to clock my return and demand treats with menaces.

I have yet to see the point of cats and I suspect he feels the same way about humans.

212

20

Message in a Bottle

I woke early after a good night's sleep, feeling much fresher and ready for anything: Tigger had got her bounce back.

I lay in bed for a little while, thinking over everything that had happened since my arrival – and there seemed to have been such a lot packed into just two days that I felt as if I'd lived there for months and had already known Simon and Pearl for ages . . . though perhaps the new Thom would take a bit more getting used to.

On the surface, we might have fallen back quickly and easily into our old relationship, but underneath things had changed. Although in slight and subtle ways that I couldn't yet quite understand.

During the years between childhood and our early twenties, when we had been apart, we had both been driven inwards by circumstances. Thom had always been quiet and reserved, and became even more so. And, of course, we both had our secrets from those years. We didn't confide everything to each other when we met again.

I had never told him what a bitter and angry teenage rebel

I'd been, which I'm sure must have made my poor aunt rue the day she'd taken me in. It was a sympathetic art teacher who had helped me escape the past and find a career I could channel all my energy and passion into.

As for Thom, growing up literally centre stage must have been hell, and I could understand why he'd formed such a strong bond with Leo and Mirrie, while all the time, like me, he must have been mourning my parents and the loss of our old, safe, happy life together.

We'd resumed our old, close relationship, and though we'd occasionally gone out with other people in the first couple of years, eventually our friendship seemed to be enough for both of us . . . until I so suddenly and unexpectedly fell for Marco.

By that time, Thom had been spending more and more time at his secret hideaway and I'd gone to the party where I met Marco only because Thom had been away for six weeks and I'd begun to feel very lonely.

Then, when Thom finally returned to London and I told him I was in love – and who with – I really expected he'd be happy for me, once I'd convinced him, as Marco had convinced me, that he was a changed man, ready to settle down.

Thom had seemed first stunned by my news and then, when I wouldn't listen to his warnings, angry.

Perhaps we would have made our quarrel up, had Leo not died from an overdose so soon afterwards, stirring up all Thom's old mistrust and animosity against Marco, and, of course, at the crucial time I was up in Scotland, occupied with organizing my aunt's funeral and sorting out her estate.

Of course, Thom suspected Marco had had that affair with Mirrie, and had he told me that at the time, it might have opened my eyes to Marco's true nature – or perhaps not, because I was so totally blinded by love.

Marco was devastated by Leo's death and I was desperately lost and unhappy when it became clear that Thom had cut me right out of his life, along with everyone else, so that we clung together . . . and that's when I saw his more vulnerable side, the lack of self-confidence that lay under his sophisticated exterior, and which endeared him to me.

Marco had needed me, even if Thom hadn't . . .

A clock chimed somewhere, jerking me back out of the past and I saw that pale gold rays of sunshine were sneaking in around the edge of the curtains.

I got up, showered and dressed, then went downstairs. There was no sign of Golightly anywhere, but he must have been asleep in his cardboard box, because when I looked in the utility room he popped up out of it so suddenly I nearly had a heart attack: cat-in-the-box.

I filled his bowl and then made myself a poached egg on toast, and afterwards, when I was drinking a second cup of coffee, Golightly came and wound himself around my ankles.

This was not something he'd ever done before, and nor did he usually make an odd rasping noise . . .

It took me a few moments to realize it was a variation on his usual wheezy purr.

Was this the first manifestation of a slight feeling of affection or merely cupboard love? I bent and stroked his odd, bluish-grey fur, which had the appearance and texture of an old Persian lamb coat.

'Are you feeling a bit more settled?' I asked him. 'This is your new for ever home and, from now on, it's just you and me, kid.'

His only response was to jump on to my knees and headbutt me under the chin, so that my teeth snapped together painfully. Then he jumped down and made off into the living room and his favourite chair, leaving me staring after him.

My relationships with the males of any species always seemed to be so complicated!

He watched me as I sat at my desk in the window, from where I could see the top of a small tree somewhere in the middle of the central garden, and opened my laptop. I thought I'd probably need a bigger desk, a decent printer and a filing cabinet in my workroom, something else to add to my interminable lists.

It was ages since I'd had a chance to read any more of Rosa-May's journal, which was easier to make out blown up on the laptop than on my phone, but that would have to wait for later, because I had a lot of business to sort out first.

There were emails from my solicitor and estate agent, and the sale of my flat seemed to be going through OK. I should come out of it with a decent profit, so one day I could buy a place of my own, if I wanted to. Prices up here were bound to be a lot cheaper than London.

I sent off some replies, caught up with a change to a standing order I'd missed and was just about to reply to a message from George, hoping I was settling in well, when Miss McNabb rang me.

I think her conscience was pricking her about having dumped her cat on me, as well it might, but I assured her that Golightly seemed to be settling down and that I was going to try letting him out, once I thought he was ready for it.

'But if he strays beyond the mews I may have to rethink that. I'm getting him microchipped this afternoon, in case he gets lost.'

'He's never *been* out, other than up and down that bit of fire escape, and he couldn't get off that,' she said doubtfully, but it clearly wasn't her problem any more because then she began to tell me how well her sister was doing and that looking after her and the dogs kept her busy.

After the call was finished, I was just about to turn the laptop off when I noticed there was an email in my junk box. When I looked, it was from Marco.

My hand hovered over the delete option while I stared at it. The subject was: 'Garland!!!', which wasn't informative, but finally I opened it, wondering if Honey had been right and he wanted to apologize to me. Not that anything he could say would make any difference, but perhaps I'd better find out.

It read:

Garland,

I've been trying to reach you without success – you don't even answer your phone.

'Well, *quelle surprise*, sweetie,' I muttered.

While I admit it was totally out of order of me to let Mirrie borrow your wedding dress, no harm was done to it and you'd never even have known had you not been in the theatre that day and overheard her conversation with Wilfric. This also seemed to give you the totally wrong idea about my relationship with Mirrie, which was strictly professional – and I certainly never told her I intended to end our engagement!

'Oh, pull the other one, it's got bells on it!' I said impatiently.

I may have flirted with Mirrie to keep her sweet, because she's so temperamental – a nightmare to work with – but that was all.

But even had you thought there was something more between us, your action in destroying the costume on the eve of the dress rehearsal was way out of order. I know your quick temper, but I still find it hard to believe you could have done such a thing.

'Well, that makes two of us, Marco!'

Leaving that aside, I had thought you'd want to know how the opening night of A Midsummer Night's Madness went, especially since it was your eye for the common touch that persuaded me to turn it into supernatural suspense.

The *common touch*? Thanks a bunch, I thought.

It was a huge success, but of course, that kind of thing isn't entirely me, and friends have said how much they preferred my previous plays, so I have returned somewhat to my roots with the one I am now writing. The opening night was such a success that I am sure my new audience will follow me, whatever direction I take.

He'd be quite mad if he took their advice and went back to the arty-farty stuff, because the audiences who had appreciated *A Midsummer Night's Madness* were going to expect more of the same in his next play.

I started to wonder if he'd been drunk when he wrote this email . . . and glancing back, saw it had been sent early on

218

Tuesday morning, probably in a mood of post-opening-night alcohol-fuelled euphoria.

> While I was justifiably furious at finding you had destroyed the costume, once I had heard from Wilfric what you'd overheard, and learned you had lost your job, I felt that was punishment enough and I am now prepared to forgive you.

That was very big of him – not!

> Fortunately, Beng & Briggs managed to create something passable for Mirrie to wear until a true replica of the original can be recreated.

I was quite sure they'd have come up with something in time for the opening night, but unless Madame Bertille herself took a hand in making the replica Titania costume, it wouldn't be anything near as good as the one I'd made.

Apart from his name, that was the end of Marco's email. There had been no enquiry about how I was going to manage without a job – it had been entirely about him.

I deleted the email, although I didn't go quite as far as blocking him. I assumed he had no idea I'd even left London yet, and it might be better to know if he finally discovered where I was. I also had a strong suspicion that soon he would come to miss my 'common touch' in his writing, even if he didn't miss anything else about me . . .

I felt unsettled after that, so I did a little research into *The Murder in the Red Barn*, which was based on a real crime, to check the date it had happened, so the marionette costumes would be historically accurate.

I'd have liked there to have been an alternative ending to the story, with Maria snatching the gun from William Corder's hand and shooting him instead, before escaping to a happy new life, but of course, there wasn't.

I suspect some of Honey's influence was rubbing off on me.

21

Where There's a Will

I thought I'd spend the rest of the morning finishing the unpacking in the cottage, starting with filling all the bookshelves with my beautifully bound old Victorian novels and the well-thumbed paperback children's books that I still comfort-read from time to time.

Until I could buy some picture hooks, I couldn't hang anything up, including the padded heart on which were pinned all my Bakelite brooches, but I could arrange the rest of my collection in the glass-topped curio table.

I didn't have much bric-a-brac, and most of what there was had belonged to Mum and Dad: a photo of their wedding day in a silver frame, vases, a box covered in shells, and an amusing teapot shaped like a snail, with a tiny version of itself on the lid.

I arranged these treasures carefully on the shelves and added the big album of family photos – mainly of me, from babyhood up to the age of ten, some including Thom.

Golightly watched me unpack, occasionally getting down from his chair to try an empty box for size, but none of them seemed to measure up to the one in the utility room.

I had acquired a few things besides Bakelite over the years, and put a big, saffron-yellow jug on the kitchen windowsill and an Art Deco coffee pot with a spout like a hooked nose on the living-room mantelpiece.

Honey had been right about everything finding its place, so that all that was left to do then was scatter around the cushions, made of oddments of vintage fabric, that had filled out the heavier boxes and – hey presto – it was home.

Now I had the room, I could do with a sofa and maybe another easy chair as well as a couple more kitchen ones, but I didn't think I'd find those in Honey's attic on Sunday. It would, however, be fun helping her sort out the accumulated junk of centuries. In fact, it might be like the start of a Blyton or E. Nesbit adventure. I suspected Thom, Simon and even Pearl would feel much the same way!

I flattened all the cardboard boxes, tied them in a big bundle with string and jammed them behind the wheelie bin in the passage next to the cottage, in the hope they would be taken away for recycling.

I spared Golightly's box, of course, and not only because he was now lying in it again and eyeing me beadily.

I don't know why unpacking makes you so grubby, but I needed a wash before lunch, and when I checked my phone afterwards I found a message from Derek with the delivery details for the cutting table and workbenches. The table was actually arriving tomorrow! Then the workbenches – I'd gone for the trestle kind – were coming on Friday.

That suited me, because it was the day when I expected some of the odds and ends for the workroom that I'd ordered myself to arrive.

Hopefully, by Monday, everything would be set up and ready for me to start work.

I would begin reading all the details of the dresses before that, of course, and I was also determined to read another page or two of Rosa-May's journal later on and pick up the story, which sounded intriguing.

I'd only just sent a reply to Derek when up popped a new email from Will. There seemed no escaping the past entirely, just as, I suppose, Thom never quite escaped his when he was receiving regular bulletins from Demelza and Mallory.

I have to admit that I do rather enjoy Will's slightly malicious and acerbic take on things. Events seemed to have moved on since Marco sent his email, because Will's was quite illuminating in several ways, including how Marco's next play was faring.

Darling!

Chez nous, relations between our leading lady and director are increasingly rocky. It started to go downhill the moment she had calmed down after the scene in the dressing room and grasped that Marco's attentions had not been serious ... Of course, he then immediately backtracked and told her she'd got it all wrong and he meant to tell you your engagement was at an end in good time, but by rushing things Mirrie had brought about a catastrophe that could have been avoided.

That went down like a lead balloon, I can tell you!

But, as they say, the show must go on and we all know in our hearts that the play is a huge success and will run and run, so Mirrie is not about to cut off her nose to spite her face by flouncing out ... especially since that would break her contract and she is so very money orientated.

At the theatre yesterday I overheard Marco telling Mirrie about the play he's currently writing, which seems to be about a woman turning into a swan, of all things. It sounds too dreary and arty for words, like the highbrow dross he used to write. Mirrie, of course, only wanted to know if there was a big part for her in it. From what he was saying, he'd just run the plot and theme of it past the management and they'd thought much the same as me . . .

Mirrie assured him it sounded brilliant, but though she's sharp as a knife when it comes to money, she isn't exactly going to win the Intellectual of the Year title, is she? Then Marco made the mistake of saying that you'd told him he should write another supernatural thriller and I popped my head out of the dressing-room door and said I couldn't help overhearing, but you were quite right. So then Mirrie had a tantrum and accused him of being sorry he'd broken off with you and I left them to it . . .

What larks!

Will xx

*

I'd found Thom's mobile number on the contact list Pearl had given me and I sent him a text suggesting he come for lunch before fitting the cat flap. I was just putting out salad, cold meats and cheese, a jar of pickles and some crusty rolls I'd bought the previous day, when he arrived, carrying a large toolbox.

'I wasn't sure what tools you had,' he explained, setting it down in the hall. 'And I thought even if you had an electric drill, it might not be charged up.'

'No drill and only the most basic of tools,' I said. 'We'll have lunch first, though. Come through, before Golightly beats us to it.'

As far as I could tell, Golightly was pleased to see Thom. At any rate, the faces he was pulling weren't as hideous as the ones he used to direct at Marco, who he hated.

'This looks good,' Thom said, following me into the kitchen and sitting down. The chair creaked.

'I think the joints are loosening,' I said. 'And these chairs definitely need repainting, but since Mum did them this sugared-almond-lilac shade, I can't bring myself to change it.'

'Shabby chic is very trendy,' he assured me, then fended Golightly off. 'I take it he isn't allowed any of this?'

'No, but I'll rattle a couple of cat treats in his bowl in the utility room; that should take his mind off it.'

It did, and we ate in mostly companionable silence, although I did tell him about my flat sale going through and Miss McNabb's bad conscience call. But I didn't mention the Marco email . . . or Will's, come to that, though I wasn't entirely sure why.

'I'd better get on with fitting that cat flap,' Thom said finally, after polishing off the last of the crusty rolls.

'You make a start, then. Just shut the door to the hall as you go, so Golightly doesn't escape, and I'll bring our coffee out there in a minute, when I've washed up.'

When I did, I found the cottage door open on to the court-yard, which was bathed in warm September sunshine, so different from the chilly, dark, rain-washed day when I'd arrived. Simon wandered across from his workshop to see what Thom was doing, mug of tea in hand.

'As cat flaps go, that's not a very big one,' he observed, as I put Thom's mug down on the step next to him.

'Neither is the cat and he's also very skinny, although he has enough character and lung power for a tiger,' Thom said.

As if to back up this statement, there was a demonic howl from behind the closed living-room door.

'What kind is he?' Simon said nervously, having slopped some of his tea down his jeans.

'I don't think he is any particular kind. My neighbour never mentioned it, but she might not have known because he just unexpectedly came with her flat.'

'I suppose he was marginally better than a poltergeist, but only just,' said Thom with a grin, and I gave him a look.

Simon offered advice, which Thom totally ignored, and very soon the new flap was installed and demonstrated. Being black, it didn't stand out too much against the glossy paintwork of the door.

'And you can lock it from the inside. I'd better do that now,' he said, 'so he doesn't get out before you want him to.'

'I thought Sunday might be a good day to try it for the first time and see what he does,' I said. 'It should be quiet then and he'll have got used to the idea that the cottage is his home . . . or I hope he will.'

'I'd better get back. I've got a van picking up a consignment of hats shortly,' Simon said. 'You must come and see the Mad Hatter's workshop some time, Garland.'

'Love to – thank you.'

'I'd better get back too,' said Thom, stowing his tools back in the box and then handing the empty mug to me. 'I was sent a very ancient Burmese puppet for restoration this morning and I want to make a start on it. They're lovely things – Mallory and Demelza would give their eyeteeth to add it to their collection!'

'I didn't even know there were Burmese puppets!'

'It's a very old tradition. Pop in and have a look when you've got a minute.'

'I will,' I agreed, and then stood there on the doorstep rather absent-mindedly watching him walking back to his workshop . . .

He didn't look back, but a moment after he'd let himself in, he reappeared carrying Jester's large, furry cushion and laid it outside in the sun.

Jester immediately flopped down on to it and Thom vanished again, back into his puppet world.

I wondered how Jester would react if he found Golightly sharing his courtyard. Or, perhaps more importantly, how Golightly would react to him!

There was still an hour before I needed to wrestle Golightly into his basket and I found myself wandering into my workroom, where my eye fell on the box containing my wedding dress.

I unlocked the door to the staff room, and added it to the shelf. I'd transfer it to an archive box and number it later. For the moment it just felt good that I'd moved the personal connection one step away from me simply by making it one more dress in the collection – number 12.

My mobile rang while I was still there. It was Honey, asking if I was at the cottage.

'Only if you are, could you pop along and open the staff room door, so the plumbers can get in and make tea? I usually leave it unlocked for them, but forgot to mention that to you.'

'OK – I'm actually in there now,' I agreed. 'Do they need milk?'

'No, there should be plenty of long-life stuff in the mini fridge under the sink.'

'I'm off to the vet to get Golightly microchipped shortly,' I told her, fumbling one-handed for the right key and inserting it in the lock.

'Have fun,' she said, and rang off.

Two workmen were hovering hopefully in the foyer, but when I invited them to come in and make themselves some tea, they insisted on showing me the new toilet cubicle first. They were very proud of it and I think just wanted an admirer, so I duly admired the gleaming white fittings and tiles, the two handbasins at different heights, to make one accessible for wheelchair users, and the flap-down baby changing unit.

'It is a thing of beauty and a joy for ever,' I assured them, and the younger of the two men gave me an attractive, gap-toothed grin.

I had to dash off back to the cottage then and get Golightly into his basket, which was not a fun experience for either of us. I pushed him in headfirst in the end, but it was a big basket and he could turn round quite easily, to hiss at me through the grille at the front.

He wasn't thrilled to meet the vet, either, but the pleasant young woman, who had introduced herself as Treena, handled him with the skill of long practice. He didn't really seem to notice when the microchip was inserted and then she gave him a quick check over, while I told her his history, as far as I knew it.

'He must be getting on for twenty, I think,' I finished.

'I suspect he's so skinny because he's an old cat, but you must try and get a bit of weight on him,' she advised. 'His teeth are in quite good condition, considering.' She gave him a couple of shots and filled in his brand-new vaccination card, while her assistant hung on to him with practised efficiency.

'He doesn't look like any other cat I've ever seen,' I told her. 'His fur sort of goes in whorls, like Persian lamb, and he's a weird colour.'

'Oh, I think he's mostly Devon Rex, but with a good dash of something else.' She shrugged.

Golightly gave her his best Silent Scream face.

'He pulls those faces all the time – you don't think he's in pain, do you?'

'No, I think he's just weird,' she said casually, then gave me some leaflets, including one about pet insurance, along with a hefty bill.

I tottered home with the cat basket, listing to one side. At this rate my arms would be so stretched my knuckles would drag along the ground.

In my absence, all the local takeaways had pushed menus through my door and I wondered if they somehow knew a potential customer had moved in.

I let Golightly out in the hall, then stowed his basket under the stairs, hoping I wouldn't need it again for a long time. He led the way through to the utility room, where he seemed to be indicating that treats were called for.

I'd bought some healthier high-protein ones in the surprisingly well-stocked shop part of the vet's reception and I tried him with those. He ate them, but didn't seem wildly enthusiastic.

The receptionist had also persuaded me to buy a cat toy – a feathery one on a string dangling from a stick. I thought Golightly would treat it with contempt, but the moment I trailed the bright feathers in front of him, he tried to grab them and then chased it all over the place, until after ten minutes he suddenly lost interest, or perhaps was simply tired, for he headed to his chair for a snooze.

I went to my desk and made a new folder marked 'CAT', in which I put the first of what I was sure would be many bills.

Then I decided to reply to Will's email. I wasn't going to tell him where I was. I supposed eventually Marco would discover I'd left the flat and might then think of my connection with Honey, but I hoped before then he'd have lost interest – and Will would have, too.

Rosa-May

Sara duly approached Mr Blake for me, and secured his promise that he would receive me and hear me in some part of my choice, which both excited and alarmed me!

But I was quite determined on my course, and Letty, although loath to have me leave Bath before she herself did, agreed to help me – and also loan me a little of her generous pin money to augment the ten guineas that the squire had given me, for I needed to obtain a seat in the Mail coach to London and then would need a conveyance to the house of Sara's sister. There would be other expenses, too, for I would not be able to leave the house carrying more than a small cloak bag.

Letty's maid was sworn to secrecy and dispatched to buy me a ticket for the Mail . . . It was often quite full inside but she managed to secure me the last place for the following day and I took this as a good portent.

I hoped Letty's maid would keep a still tongue so Letty did not get into any trouble for helping me. I have told her, if they should ask, that she had no knowledge of my plans.

With fear and trembling in case my plans might somehow be discovered, I packed a few necessities. It seemed to me best not to leave a note for Lady Bugle, but to write once I reached London, when there would be little chance of any pursuit.

Not that I thought she would stir herself much in this direction, once she found that I had run off, and when she and Papa had received my letter of explanation as to my intent to become an actress, I was convinced both would wash their hands of me.

*

The household went to bed early, but I did not. I put a bolster in the middle of my bed and drew the covers over it, so it seemed as if I was still asleep. Then, wearing the plain bonnet, dark gown, pelisse and cloak in which I had arrived at Lady Bugle's, I crept through the house, unlocked the front door and stepped nervously into the street. It was not an hour at which any respectable woman would have been abroad, especially alone, but to my great relief, the streets were quiet, until I reached the bustle of the coaching yard and claimed my seat inside the Mail, packed in between a fat countrywoman and a desiccated spinster with a disapproving air.

But I did not care, for, with shouts and the sound of a horn, the coach rattled over the cobbles and we were off!

22

Highly Strung

Before dinner I had a long and interesting three-way email conversation with Honey and George, when she told him of her determination to open the museum much earlier than she'd originally intended.

'The building itself was in good repair, and the redecorating, rewiring, new plumbing and having the parquet floors sanded and sealed has taken less time than I thought it would.'

'You do seem to have worked wonders in a short space of time,' George replied. 'Although there are still the display cabinets to be delivered and fitted and all the bridal dresses to be carefully examined, catalogued and properly displayed. You must give Garland sufficient time for that.'

'I'll begin evaluating them the moment my workroom is set up,' I wrote back. 'I've got a big cutting table and new workbenches arriving in the next two days, so everything should be ready for Monday. I can't wait!'

Honey remarked that when the Rosa-May material was returned to her at the end of the month, it would be ready to go straight out on display and George immediately demanded reassurances that it would be displayed in the perfect condition in which it left his care.

'Of course it will!' I assured him.

Honey put George's mind at rest on the subjects of heating, humidity and light, then went on: 'Setting up the Rosa-May collection and the Bloody Brides room will be our first priorities.'

'What Bloody Brides?' demanded George, baffled, and then she had to explain about Amy Weston and the bloodstained dress.

'I can see the publicity value, and that you'd like to get the museum open before the anniversary of her disappearance,' he replied, 'but I wouldn't want to see the opening rushed to the detriment of some of the older and – to me, at least – more interesting costumes.'

'I'll have a realistic idea of when we will be ready to open within a few days,' Honey said. 'I'll chase up Priceless Interiors for delivery dates of the display units. By then, Garland will have had a chance to make a preliminary assessment of the collection, so we can order the mannequins. After all,' she added, 'we don't need to put all the dresses on display at the start. It can be a work in progress. Once I have all the information I need, I'll pick an opening day and make it happen!'

I was sure she would, too.

'You will be very busy, Garland, because each dress will need careful examination and cataloguing, as well as any necessary repairs carrying out,' said George. 'But you can call on me for any advice you might need.'

I thanked him and said there were so many things I hadn't thought of until I got here, like information boards, leaflets and guidebooks.

'But I'll write those, once you've added all the interesting details to the catalogue,' Honey said. 'Anyway, George, I'll let you know when I've settled on an opening date, so you can put it in your diary, because I want you to be there. I might have a pre-opening party in the museum foyer for special guests before the doors open to the public.'

'Of course, I wouldn't miss it for the world,' George assured her.

'It's settled then. You can stay at Pelican House again. I have a friend here on a long visit, who cooks like an angel, so the catering will be a bit less slapdash than on your previous visits.'

'Dear Honey, where the company is excellent, I never notice what I'm eating,' he said gallantly.

*

I had lasagne *à la* freezer for dinner, followed by the last of Viv's muffins, and by the time I'd cleared away I was suddenly swamped with tiredness.

I sat in my armchair with my feet up on an old leather pouffe and the laptop on my knees, and began to read the next pages of Rosa-May's journal.

The room was warm and quiet, except for the odd hubble-bubble noise Golightly was making as he slept, and soon the crabbed, small handwriting began to waver and blur before my tired eyes. After a while I put an old romcom on the telly instead and dozed happily in front of that, until, to my extreme surprise and discomfort, Golightly woke up and decided to arrange himself on my knees, all bony angles. He did make the odd noise I'd come to recognize as his purr once he'd settled himself to his satisfaction, so this might be a sign of affection . . . On the other hand, he might just see me as an alternative cat bed.

Whichever it was, I felt strangely reluctant to dislodge him, even after the film finished, but fortunately he eventually took himself off and I could get up, my legs numb, and go to bed.

When I was drawing my bedroom curtains, I noticed a light on in a room high up at the back of Pelican House, where a window jutted out over the garden. I felt certain it was Honey, writing away into the night.

*

There were no unwanted texts, emails or missed calls when I remembered to switch on my phone next morning, but in the early hours, presumably after she'd finished her writing session, Honey had emailed across an update of the catalogue she'd compiled of all the wedding dresses and any paperwork that had come with them, this time with their wedding disaster stories written out in full as if they were chapters in her next non-fiction book, which they possibly might be.

She wrote in the email:

I'll give Viv a copy, too! I think she really *is* starting to feel inspired and I do hope so. She's a very good poet, concise and drily witty. If her muse does takes wing, she may haunt the museum. I hope you won't mind.

I emailed back, assuring her I wouldn't. Viv could come and go as she pleased. In fact, if she hung around enough, she'd probably get roped in to help, once I began to set up the displays.

After breakfast, I thought I'd better pop out to Rani's Minimart again, this time using the short cut through the gate between my cottage and the puppet theatre. It saved a long trek and would be handy for popping out for milk, fresh bread, or anything else I ran out of.

While I was putting my shoes on in the hall, Golightly seemed to notice the cat flap for the first time and headbutted it in a tentative fashion. When it remained closed, he looked disgruntled and stalked off back into the living room.

'Wait till Sunday,' I called after him, because there was no way I was going to try letting him out before that.

It wasn't yet eight o'clock, but I could hear all the noise of a market being set up in the square – the clang of the metal poles that held up the stalls, engines revving and voices. I ought to have a look round that later.

I was back with a loaded bag in no time and was surprised when I entered the mews to see Honey, standing with Viv at the front of the museum, admiring two huge terracotta garden urns at either side of the steps. They certainly hadn't been there ten minutes ago.

Honey called me over, so I left my bag on the doorstep and went to see.

'Aren't they splendid? I got them from Terrapotter and they've just dropped them off.'

'Terracotta?' I queried.

'Terra*potter* is the name of the business. They make all kinds of garden pots, but specialize in huge ones, in both antique and modern designs. They're up the Thorstane road out of Great Mumming, opposite a good junk shop.'

'These pots are made to a very ancient design, but with modern embellishments,' Viv whispered, but now I was closer, they looked more as if they had been dredged up from the sea-bed, because they were encrusted with seaweed, barnacles and all manner of sea life . . .

I said so and Viv replied, 'Yes, that's what I think, too. They're lovely.'

'I'm not sure what to plant in them yet, but I'll talk to Josh, who keeps the gardens tidy, and see what he suggests,' said Honey, then gave an enormous yawn.

'Sorry – I worked late last night and haven't had enough sleep,' she said. 'Look, there's Thom coming out with Jester. He ought to see my lovely pots, too.'

She waved and beckoned, but Viv made a small squeak like an alarmed rabbit, and scuttled off round the mews garden and through the gate to go behind Pelican House.

Thom, joining us, stared after her with faint astonishment. 'I don't think Viv likes me very much!'

'It's not just you, she's like that with most strangers, especially men,' Honey said. 'I'm only surprised she talks to Garland, but I think that's because she's related to me and I'd talked about her a lot . . . but also possibly because she's so small and appears unalarming.'

'"Appears" being the operative word,' said Thom, grinning. 'She's small but fierce, and has a fiery temper when provoked far enough.'

'Oh, don't remind me!' I said with fervour. 'I'm never going to lose my temper again, in case I turn berserk, like last time.'

Honey gave that attractive tilted smile. 'I think that was a one-off event caused by extreme provocation, though we women do need to keep a bit of edge or we get walked over.'

'It would be a brave man who tried to walk over either of you,' said Thom.

He duly admired the spectacular terracotta pots, then said, 'I'm working on an amazing antique Burmese puppet – the one I told you about, Garland. Why don't you both come and have a look?'

Jester got off his cushion to welcome us into the workshop and then sat grinning amiably with his tongue hanging out while Thom showed us the wonderful old marionette, which was on the workbench.

'There are twenty-seven specific characters in Burmese puppet theatres and this one is Zawgyi, the Alchemist. I think the clothes are basically original but have been repaired and new embellishments added later.'

The figure was dressed mostly in slightly faded red garments: a flared coat and trousers under a sort of skirt, and a matching red cap and slippers. Everything was trimmed with gold.

'That sort of skirt affair he's wearing is called a *paso*,' said Thom. 'He's one of the nicer characters.'

'It all looks a bit of a tangled mess at the moment,' said Honey.

'It needs restringing and some repairs – conservation rather than restoration. It was found jumbled up in a box of junk in an attic.'

'Wouldn't it be lovely if we found some like this in your attic on Sunday, Honey?' I said.

'I strongly suspect all we'll find is broken furniture, useless junk and spiders,' she said, and then her eye was caught by a marionette hanging on a peg right behind the bench, its face turned to the wall.

'Is that the William Corder marionette I saw before?'

'Yes, I've strung it now,' Thom said. 'I'll get on with the next one when I've finished with the Alchemist here.'

I was about to ask him if he could turn it so we could see the face, when Honey, who was still staring at it, said, 'I think I feel another plot idea materializing: *Strung Up with Hate . . .*'

She snatched up a biro from the workbench, pushed up her left sleeve and added it to the tracings of thoughts already there.

Thom looked slightly startled by this, but I was now quite used to it, although I didn't even want to *think* about where she'd run with that idea.

'I'm coming up the home straight with the first draft of *Armed with Poison* – I'm a fast worker once the ideas take shape. It won't take me long to beat it into submission after that, and then I can get on with the next.'

I shuddered slightly. 'Weren't you going to write *The Bloody Bride* after that one – or *The Bloody Bridegroom*?'

'Probably, but I've always got two or three plots simmering on the back burner.'

'When I was going to bed last night I saw a light on in the upstairs room at the back of Pelican House,' I said. 'I thought that was probably you, working.'

'Yes, I find my mind is most creative in the small hours, and also I like the feeling of being high up, and sort of perched over the garden. My desk is in the overhanging window and I often wonder what's holding it up.'

'Perhaps you ought to find out?' I suggested, slightly alarmed, although I suppose it *had* stayed put since Tudor times.

She shrugged. 'Live dangerously. Unlike me, Viv is a day-time writer. She's going to work in the garden room off the kitchen. It has an outside door, so she can potter about out there as the fancy takes her.'

'Is she going to make her home with you now, then?' I asked.

'I hope so. We're going to try it for a few months and see. Her husband's niece would like to rent her cottage, so we'll have to pop down there and sort things out at some point soon. We can have any furniture and personal possessions she wants packed up and brought here. There's plenty of room for it. She wants her own desk and bookshelves in the garden room, too, and all her favourite reference books.'

'I quite like being surrounded by big, illustrated reference books when I'm working on a new project,' I said. 'And I must get a big desk for the workroom and a proper filing cabinet.'

'Uncle Hugo was a silver surfer and I had his office furniture moved into the first attic when I moved in. That's when I spotted Rosa-May's two trunks. You could have a look on Sunday, Garland, and see if it is any use.'

'Thank you, that would be great.'

'We might find a few bits and pieces of furniture you'd like for the cottage, too – you never know – although most of what I could see was massive, dark mahogany and Victorian.'

She rolled down her sleeve and tossed the pen back on the bench.

'Well, I must love you and leave you. I'm doing a live radio interview by phone for a book programme in half an hour and I want to get into the right frame of mind, *and* warn Derek not to vacuum outside my study door while I'm at it.'

'And I've just remembered I abandoned my shopping on the doorstep,' I said, following her out into the sunshine, which still had a lot of warmth in it.

'It's Italian night at the pub on Thursdays – Pearl, Simon and I always go, so why not join us?' Thom suggested to me. 'I've seen you there a few times too, Honey.'

'I might persuade Viv to come, though she cooks so well the incentive isn't really there any more,' she said. 'But *you* should go, Garland – meet more people.'

'I'll have to see. I'm going to start setting up the workroom today. The cutting table will arrive this afternoon.'

'Text me if you decide to come to the pub and I'll wait for you,' suggested Thom. 'I usually go over just before seven.'

'OK, but don't wait for me if I haven't texted by then,' I said, and went off to rescue the abandoned shopping, which fortunately this time did not contain anything frozen.

*

Later, I had a quick look around the market before the cutting table was due to arrive.

There was the usual interesting mix of stalls and I bought some fruit and cheese, then found someone selling fabric remnants – always irresistible. On my way back, I impulse-bought a stack of inexpensive wicker wastepaper baskets, which I thought I could stand bolts of cloth upright in, instead of just leaning them in a corner.

When I took them into the workroom and tried it, it worked well.

I opened the doors to the staff room and foyer, ready for the delivery, and found the front doors open, so workmen must have been around somewhere. Then I went back to unpacking boxes until the sound of a van in the courtyard told me the table had arrived.

The delivery man brought it into the foyer but was so grumpy I didn't even bother asking him if he might possibly help me get it into the back room. Luckily, just then two men in painters' overalls emerged from the Rosa-May Room and were a lot more obliging: they not only carried the table through, but set it up for me. They even took the packaging away, saying it could join the stuff in the back of their van. Then they went back to painting the window frame in Rosa-May's room, so I took them cups of tea and biscuits through, as a reward.

It would be nice to be a strapping Amazon, who could heave heavy tables about without a second's thought. However, being the size of a Christmas tree fairy can sometimes have its advantages . . .

*

By the time I'd finished for the day, the room looked a lot more workmanlike, with most things either on the shelves or neatly stacked away in lidded storage crates.

Before I went back into the cottage for the night I returned to the staff room. I'd had second thoughts about my wedding dress and decided it would be better hung on the rail.

I removed it from its tissue wrappings, shook it out, then put it on a padded hanger inside a new zipped plastic cover, before hanging it between Honey's dress and that of Amy Weston.

There were others hanging there, whose stories I didn't know, but they were probably far sadder than mine . . .

The bags moved and whispered together as I closed the door to the workroom and locked it. Perhaps they were telling each other secrets.

23

The Sun in Splendour

A little while later, Pearl rang, and when I answered she said, 'You sound breathless – you didn't rush to answer the phone, did you?'

'No, I was playing with Golightly,' I said, and explained about the feathery cat toy.

'Hours of harmless fun,' said Pearl, sounding amused. 'What I actually rang for was to find out if you wanted to go to the pub tonight, because if so, you could pop round to mine at about seven and we'll walk over together. It's Italian food on Thursdays, and it's excellent.'

I hesitated for a moment. 'Yes, Thom mentioned it earlier, but, well . . . I had lasagne for dinner last night.'

'Unless you made it from scratch, it won't have been like the food you'll get tonight. It's authentic Italian home cooking. The publican's mother-in-law is Italian and she takes over the kitchen on Thursdays. There's usually tiramisu on the dessert menu, too,' she added enticingly. '*And* you get those little wrapped almond biscuits with your coffee afterwards.'

'Amaretti? I think that's the clincher: I love those!'

'So do come tonight.'

'OK, I will. The cat does seem to be settling down and, luckily, with the cottage tucked away in this corner, I don't think anyone will hear him even if he does start up his Soul in Torment performance. He's an old fraud. I'm sure he only wants to make me feel guilty. Whenever I reappear, he never seems pleased to see me, just . . . sort of accusatory and miffed.'

'You can't let him run your life, or you'll definitely be living under the cat's paw,' she said with a laugh, then added that she'd see me about seven and rang off.

It was a mild evening, so I just swapped my old jeans for newer ones and the now-grimy T-shirt for a jade top. A bit of makeup and some green Bakelite bangles, and I was good to go.

Golightly followed me into the hall and watched with narrowed yellow eyes as I put on my sandals and a thin cotton jacket.

'You know the routine by now,' I told him sternly. 'You saw me put treats in your bowl and I won't be out long.'

He pulled a face, though not one of the worst, then turned and vanished back into the living room, leaving me feeling strangely guilty. He had the knack of doing that.

I swung my heavy tapestry bag over my shoulder, the costumier equivalent of a doctor's bag, ready for any emergency. I couldn't cure myself of the habit of carrying basic sewing materials around with me, but since the affair at the theatre I'd been less comfortable taking the dressmaker's shears.

The puppet workshop, Thom's cottage next to it and Hetty's Hats were all in darkness, so Thom and Simon must already have left.

Pearl was waiting for me just inside the bookshop door and stepped out when she saw me, locking it behind her.

She looked cool and elegant in floaty layers of fine linen in a shade of misty blue-grey. With her tall, slim figure, she'd have looked like a model in anything, and the colour suited her pale skin and platinum-blond hair, too.

'You look lovely,' I said. 'Perhaps I should have dressed up a bit, too?'

'You look fine. I don't usually bother much about what I wear, but I made the mistake of popping across to Spindrift in my lunch hour, to speak to Ginny,' she said with a rueful smile. 'She's very persuasive, in a quiet way – even more than I am to *my* customers! – so I found myself trying on this dress and loose jacket and then I was lost.'

'It really suits you.'

'She has some lovely and unusual clothes – you should have a look.'

'I wouldn't suit that layered style – I'd just look like a heap of washing with legs. I'm too small and I need clothes that go in at the waist.'

'There were some nice, clingy tunics in cotton jersey you might like, but I expect you make a lot of your clothes yourself anyway.'

'I do for smarter outfits, but at Beng & Briggs, where I used to work, we all wore black – trousers and tops, in my case. I don't know why, because every bit of thread or fluff showed up against it. I mostly live in jeans otherwise, though I expect I'll have to smarten up a bit when the museum opens, even if I'm not actually manning the reception desk.'

'Honey seems to almost live in black jeans, so I can't imagine her caring what you wear.'

'She's the Woman in Black,' I said. 'Black jeans do look smarter, so perhaps I might go for those, but with brighter tops.'

Mentioning the title of Susan Hill's wonderfully successful spooky play suddenly reminded me of Marco's email. I'd told him to go and see it, then think about how he could instil some of that supernatural, scary element into *A Midsummer Night's Madness* . . . but if he reverted back now to his old style, it was none of my concern.

While we were talking, we'd walked across the middle of the square, where just a few cars were parked and the only remaining traces of the busy market were a few stray cabbage leaves and the lingering smell of hot, deep-fried doughnuts. I could practically taste them – oily and gritty in the mouth, the doughy texture as you bit into it and then thin, runny, dark red jam in the middle.

Lights illuminated the large pub sign with its smiling round sun circled by rays of gold, like a halo of corkscrew curls.

'Is it a hotel or just a pub?' I asked. 'It looks quite big.'

'It was a hotel at one time, but now it's just a pub, though they do have a big function room too. The landlord, his own large family and his wife's extended family, occupy the upper floors and they all help in the business.'

'Sounds very cosmopolitan!'

'The landlord's local. He met his wife when she came over to visit the Marino family, who own the puppet theatre. They have Italian roots and she was a distant connection. One night they took her to the pub and, hey presto, love at first sight and happy ever after!'

'I like the idea of happy ever after, even if it didn't happen for me . . . or for the poor brides whose dresses will be in the museum! But still, being jilted seems to have done wonders for Honey's career, and the end of my engagement led to my being free to take this job.'

'I hope you'll be very happy here, Garland. My husband and I were, even if we didn't have long together.'

'Time enough to have made many treasured memories, I hope,' I said gently.

'Oh, yes! He loved books and walking on the moors. Those were his main passions in life. And he loved me, too, of course,' she added, with a slightly melancholy smile.

I thought if Simon *was* cherishing hopes in her direction, he'd find her late husband a hard act to follow.

She led the way up two wide, shallow steps under a covered portico to a dark, metal-studded door. As she opened it, a great wave of light, warmth and sound rolled over us, then seemed to recede, pulling us inside with it.

I found myself in a large, crowded, brightly lit bar, with other smaller areas opening out of it, giving glimpses of people sitting at tables, or playing pool and darts. I thought probably the interior had originally been divided into several small rooms, but now they had all been thrown into one.

Pearl, so much taller than me, had been peering about and now she said, 'There's Thom and Simon, over in the bay window, with Baz and Derek.'

She waved. 'I'll buy you a Welcome to Great Mumming drink, Garland. What would you like?'

'Just ginger beer, if they have it, please,' I said. 'I'm not usually much of a drinker, though since I met Honey I seem to have got through a lot of champagne!'

'I can't run to champagne, but they do have ginger beer, the real, peppery stuff. I'll have the same,' she said, and when we'd got our drinks we made our way over to join the others, who made room for us. I found myself sitting on the window seat next to Thom, with Pearl opposite, between Simon and Baz.

Simon said hello to me absently, because he was gazing at Pearl in evident admiration.

Then he said to her: 'You look lovely tonight, Pearl. That shade of blue-grey really suits you.'

'Well . . . thank you, Simon!' she said, going slightly pink, as if she'd forgotten how to respond to a compliment. But then, with a return to her usual cool and reserved manner, she added, 'Ginny somehow managed to persuade me to buy the dress and jacket earlier today. I've warned Garland that though Ginny *seems* vague, you're lucky to get out of Spindrift without buying *something*.'

'That's true,' Thom agreed. 'I never intended starting a collection of brightly painted wooden frogs holding leaf umbrellas, but now I seem to have one in every room of my cottage.'

'They're very jolly, though,' said Simon. 'I have an indoor water feature I never intended installing, as well as a large carved wooden head of Buddha and a set of small Mexican pottery bowls, decorated with cactus plants.'

'You have been warned,' Thom said to me gravely. He was so close on the window seat that his arm brushed mine when he turned to speak to me and I felt a current run between us, like a sudden small electric shock . . . which was odd. Thom clearly hadn't felt it, however, for he was now teasing Pearl.

'In your own way, you are almost as bad as Ginny at making sales, Pearl. Once you start to browse her bookshelves, Garland, you've had it.'

'Books really sell themselves,' Pearl said, unruffled. 'I might just show a customer whose tastes I know one or two books I think they'd be particularly interested in.'

'I'm dying to see what you've got, especially among the Victorian novels in the back room,' I said. 'And there was a big glossy book in the window about Venetian masks that looked interesting . . . but I expect it's expensive, so I'll put off looking at that one, in the hope someone else buys it first and removes the temptation.'

'I've still got it and it's *very* reasonably priced, really. In excellent condition, too,' said Pearl enticingly. 'Shall I put it to one side for you?'

'No, don't bother,' I said hastily. 'I'll take a look at it when I come in, if it's still there, but it's not really my field.'

'Here's Honey and Viv,' said Simon, half-turning, and I saw Honey's tall, slim figure cutting a path through the crowded room, with Viv following in her wake.

They managed to squeeze on to the end of the next table and Derek, who was seated on the other side of Baz, handed them a couple of menus. Then he dealt the rest out between us, like a giant deck of cards.

'We'd better decide what we want. Not that it's difficult,' he added to me. 'There's always a choice of two dishes, one with meat and the other fish or seafood.'

'The great vegetarian and vegan wave hasn't exactly hit the Sun in Splendour yet,' said Baz. 'The nearest they get to it is the vegetarian-friendly ploughman's lunch, which they serve all day.'

'The seafood ravioli sounds good to me,' I said, scanning the menu. 'I don't eat a lot of meat now, and mostly chicken when I do, but I like to know it had a happy life first.'

Thom grinned at me. 'We'll have to find a local source where we can be sure the hens have a fun time.'

Viv leaned over and whispered something inaudible to Honey, who said, 'Viv says the chicken we had last Monday was organic and free range.'

'I often wonder what an *inorganic* chicken would look like,' Derek mused.

'Inedible, I should think,' said Simon, grinning.

'Ginny probably knows who has the happiest hens,' Pearl suggested. 'She's supposed to be a vegan, but you often find her here, tucking into a ploughman's, or in the teashop on the square, having a full cream tea after her shop shuts.'

'*And* she drinks coffee with ordinary milk in it, so at best she's a deluded vegetarian,' pointed out Derek.

'I'll eat pretty much anything,' Honey said. 'Especially if Viv's cooked it. She's the best cook ever!'

Viv went pink to the roots of her soft brown hair, reminding me again of the portrait of Charlotte Brontë, with her intelligent, resolute but sweet expression, and she murmured something only Honey could hear.

We ordered our food, which, when it came, was excellent, as was the tiramisu and coffee that followed. We paid our dinner the compliment of eating mostly in appreciative silence, but over the coffee and amaretti biscuits, the talk was wide ranging and interesting.

I learned quite a bit about the history of the area and the local sights, some of which I'd already heard mentioned. I told them about the Rev. Jo-Jo's suggestion that I go and look at her church in Jericho's End one day.

'It's not really *in* Jericho's End, which is a tiny village up a narrow valley. The church is ancient and perched high up on a hill overlooking it,' said Simon.

'I go to St Gabriel's for the Sunday morning service every week,' Pearl said. 'It has a lovely atmosphere and Jo-Jo's sermons are often quite lively! Simon kindly drives me up there, though I'm sure church services aren't really his thing.'

'Oh, I don't mind,' he said amiably. 'It's very calming, somehow, and you never know – one day the goat might turn into a sheep.'

'I haven't noticed any sign of a halo forming yet,' said Pearl, but she smiled at him.

Rosa-May

The journey was long, cold and uncomfortable, and I think I would have perished from hunger had it not been for the kindness of the countrywoman seated next to me, who shared her provisions.

But what joy it was when finally I fell into dear Sara's arms! She looked even more forbidding than I recalled from my last sight of her, but I knew her kind heart and deep attachment to me.

I was allotted a small attic room next to Sara's, but had little time to recover from the journey, for I learned that my interview with Mr Blake was to be the very next morning!

*

With what trepidation and excitement I set out with Sara for the Cockleshell Theatre off Drury Lane, drab as any house sparrow in my stuffy gown and brown pelisse. I meant to give Mr Blake some of Titania's speeches from A Midsummer Night's Dream, *in which I had made such a hit the previous year at the Grange – but even at seventeen, I realized that, supposing I should be lucky enough to gain a small place in his company of players, I had much to learn and, according to Sara, the enmity and jealousy of the older and well-established actresses to contend with, who assume the major roles as of right.*

Mr Blake was a rosy-faced, portly man with silver curling hair and a most abstracted expression, so that at first he did not seem interested in me.

But he invited me to take off my bonnet and step on to the stage, then recite something for him and his brother, Joseph, who had now joined him.

Sara gave me an encouraging push forward, for I seemed rooted to the spot with fear – but once I stood on the stage and began my piece, it was as if I became Titania and forgot my audience entirely.

There was a silence after I finished in which I returned to the realization of where I was, after which Mr Blake asked me to sing.

I thought the sound seemed a little lost in that great space and Mr Joseph Blake seemed to agree, for he said I had a pretty voice, though perhaps not very carrying. However, much could be done to improve it.

Then Mr Blake said indeed, and that I had much to learn about the profession before any speaking part could be allotted to me . . .

Then the brothers conferred in tones too low for me to hear and I came down from the stage to stand with Sara, my knees trembling, feeling that my fate hung in the balance . . .

But then, to my delight, Mr Blake gave me to understand that I might become a very minor part of the company that his brother, Mr Joseph, would be taking on tour that summer!

I would be paid little, of course, for I had everything to learn, and he also stressed the good name and reputation of his theatre and actors.

Sara, too, would be accompanying us, to help dress the ladies and other such tasks.

*

On our way home, Sara said her presence would help protect me from the advances of young men of fashion, who would inevitably cast their lures at such a young and pretty actress. I told her I would be very glad of this, for I was still of the same mind and intended to remain single and virtuous.

24

Ice Cream and Angels

'From what the Rev. Jo-Jo told me about Jericho's End, it sounded fascinating, with Fairy Falls and an old garden,' I said.

'It's a tiny tourist hotspot and there's an endless debate about whether there are fairies or angels inhabiting the local falls,' said Thom. 'There's a nice walk up to the falls, a really good ice-cream parlour, and the old physic garden that's being restored and opened to the public.'

'There's the ruin of a small early monastic settlement, too,' said Baz, 'near a really good pub called the Devil's Cauldron.'

'With so much going on there, I can see why it's a tourist hotspot,' I said.

'It was hugely popular for day-trippers in the Victorian era, and the ice-cream parlour was one of the earliest in the country, outside London,' Baz said. 'It fell out of favour a bit, after that, then became an artists' colony between the wars. Now it's back on the up again.'

'I'll take you up there,' offered Thom. 'In fact, we could all have an excursion, if anyone else wants to come?'

'Derek and I go up there all the time anyway. I like to paint near the falls and we take a picnic in good weather,' said Baz.

'I suppose I could come if it was a Thursday afternoon, when the shop is closed,' said Pearl.

'Thursday afternoon is the traditional half-day closing for the shops here,' Simon explained to me. 'The market packs up around lunchtime and then the town goes dead.'

'The museum will be shut on Thursdays, too,' Honey reminded me, leaning over to join in the conversation.

'We could have a late lunch in the Devil's Cauldron, or an ice-cream tea at the café by the entrance to the waterfall walk . . . or both,' Simon suggested rather greedily.

'Simon, since we're bound to be back here for dinner that evening, I think a coffee and an ice cream at Ice Cream and Angels should be enough!' said Pearl.

'Ice Cream and Angels?' I echoed.

'That's the name of the café,' she explained. 'They make their own delicious ices and soft drinks. Then afterwards, we can burn up some calories walking to the Fairy Falls.'

'Sounds good to me,' said Thom. 'And afterwards, we can drive up to the old church.'

'That sounds lovely,' I said. 'But do you and Simon have half-day closing on Thursdays too?'

'In theory. You know what it's like when you work for your-self: if we're busy, we just carry on,' said Simon. 'But we are our own bosses.'

'Bruno's still mine,' pointed out Thom.

'Not really, because you're partners now,' amended Pearl. 'And anyway, he won't mind what hours you put in, as long as the work gets done. He left you a free hand.'

'By next Thursday I'll be hard at work on the dress collection and probably won't want to stop, day off or no day off!' I said.

'We'll *make* you,' promised Thom. 'A bit of fresh air will do you good.'

'I'm only going to be paying you a part-time wage anyway, after the first couple of weeks when we're setting up the museum,' put in Honey. 'After that, I'll expect you to be there during opening times, but otherwise, you can arrange the hours to suit yourself.'

'Fair enough,' I said. 'Since working on the dresses will be my idea of fun, I'm bound to lose track of the time I spend on them anyway.'

Something I'd thought of that afternoon came back to me. 'Honey, I was thinking earlier that if the door from the cottage into my workroom was replaced by the kind of stable door Thom's workshop has, I'd be able to leave the top half open when I was working and keep an eye on Golightly. I wondered if you'd mind.'

Honey thought it was a good idea. 'If he takes to going outdoors, you might not see so much of him, anyway.'

'That's true, but I won't know until I've tried letting him out on Sunday morning, when things are quiet. I just hope he doesn't leg it out of the mews.'

'If he does, I expect we'll all be spending the rest of the day cat hunting,' said Baz, and then he and Derek went off to play darts.

'You know,' said Honey, 'I think I might have seen a stable door at the junk shop up near Terrapotter. It was out in that covered bit of yard.'

'Oh? I might measure up the doorframe and go up and look,' I said. 'Maybe on Saturday.'

'I'll go with you and hold the tape measure,' offered Thom. 'I like a rummage round there, anyway.'

'Happy hunting!' said Honey. 'Viv and I had better make tracks now, because I want to do some work. Are you all still coming to Pelican House on Sunday afternoon, to help me start sorting the attics, if I bribe you with a takeaway supper?'

'We'd do it without the bribe, because we're dying to explore your attics,' Simon told her. 'About half three, or four?'

'Great,' said Honey. 'But I suspect it's going to be dusty, grimy work, so wear something you don't mind getting grubby!'

She gave that tilted grin. 'The first official meeting of the Pelican Mews Residents' Association and Attic Exploration Society.'

'The prospect of finding a treasure trove will be what keeps us going,' said Simon. 'Like those metal detector societies, always hoping for a hoard of gold.'

'Live in hope,' she said with amusement. '*My* main hope is that the man from the junk shop will buy all the stuff I don't want. He's already had the brass bedsteads from some old servants' rooms.'

'You'll have to be careful not to let anything valuable go by mistake,' Simon warned.

'I have a reasonable eye for antiques, and Viv's good at spotting anything valuable, too, so I don't think we'll be letting any heirlooms go for a song.'

'Does the junk shop man have a name?' I asked.

'Yes, but I've forgotten it. It's Galahad, or something like that,' she said vaguely.

'He can't possibly be called Galahad!' I protested, laughing.

'No, he's called Arthur and the shop's Arthur's Cave,' said Thom.

'Same kind of name,' said Honey. 'Come on then, Viv – I've got a murder to commit tonight.'

*

I spent the next morning happily continuing to set up my workspace.

The first thing I did was to transfer the wedding dress collection to my back room, and while it was easy enough to push the hanging rail through, since it was on castors, emptying and moving the shelves took a lot longer.

Luckily, the metal racking was in narrow, tall sections, so fairly easy to drag through, especially after I put a bit of old material underneath, to help it slide over the vinyl.

I arranged the boxes on it and, finding a marker pen and labels with the spare archive boxes, I tagged the bag containing my dress with a large number 12.

I put together my own smaller hanging rail, but that still left plenty of room, even after I'd fetched the ironing board from the cottage and set that up permanently.

It was sheer luxury to have all this space! When you live and work in a very small flat, you're forever putting things away, or getting them out.

I contemplated the shelves of boxes and the bags on the rail from the doorway for a few minutes – that Aladdin's cave of exciting possibilities! Then I firmly took myself back to re-arranging things in the main room, although I may have fondled the cutting table once or twice, in passing.

At lunchtime, it struck me that though Golightly had yelled a bit when I shut the door to the living room on him, he'd been quite silent ever since. I found him upstairs, fast asleep on my bed again, totally and blissfully zonked out.

I made a tuna mayo sandwich and checked my phone while I ate. There was another email from Marco, which this time had not been consigned to the junk box, where it belonged.

I dithered a bit, wondering whether to delete it unread, but in the end I opened it, which was a mistake since it appeared that my lack of response to his previous attempts to contact me had seriously got up his nose.

There was no 'Dear Garland' about this email – in fact, it breathed out a miasma of aggrieved exasperation from every line. It started abruptly:

Garland, where on earth are you? Your lack of response to my email, when you must know how worried I am about you, is positively cruel!

Strange – I hadn't noticed any sign of interest in what had become of me at all!

I was so concerned that this morning I went all the way out to Ealing and found your flat not only empty, but with a For Sale sign outside – and a Sold sticker across it! Someone let me into the hall and I found a bouquet I'd sent to you, propped up dead against your door.

I went upstairs to see if your batty old neighbour, Miss McNabb, knew where you had got to, only to discover that she had vanished, too, and her flat is to let.

The estate agents refused to give me any information about your whereabouts, so I can only draw the conclusion that you have left London with Miss McNabb, though I can't imagine why, unless for some joint business venture, perhaps?

The man was mad – and I hadn't even left London at the same time as Miss McNabb! He'd have made a rotten private eye.

Beng & Briggs said they had no other forwarding address for you and would not have given you a reference for a new job, even if you'd asked for one. They also said that once the reason for your sacking got out, it was unlikely in the extreme that you'd find another position in London. Of course, I know how much your work meant to you and I'm sorry about that, but it was quite inevitable, given what you did.

'Tell me something I don't know, Sherlock,' I muttered.

Still, after all we've meant to each other, I can't comprehend how you could simply disappear without letting me know where you were!

'Join the club, buster,' I said, for that's exactly how I'd felt when Thom did it to me, though with more reason, for, after all, Marco had ended our engagement and told me he never wanted to see me again! Not to mention that he'd rung up Beng & Briggs in a white-hot fury, to tell them what I'd done without, I was certain, including any of the mitigating circumstances.

But Thom, whom I had loved more than any brother, had resolutely turned his back and walked off into a future that didn't include me – all because I'd fallen in love with the stupid, self-obsessed idiot who had emailed me this load of drivel!

I most certainly wasn't going to tell him where I was, and sincerely hoped he would never discover it, or that Thom also lived here, because he'd jump to the obvious conclusion that I'd known his whereabouts all along. He certainly wouldn't keep the news about where Thom was to himself, either.

I looked down at the email again and saw that he hadn't given up his quest quite so easily as I'd thought.

I managed to get hold of the phone number for that friend of yours at the V&A, George, but he said he had no idea where you were, either.

Thank you, George, I thought, and hoped that had exhausted all the lines of enquiry Marco could think of – or for the present, at any rate – although he was bound to think of contacting Honey, eventually. I'd have to warn her.

> Wherever you have gone, you have acted way too hastily. I said before that you'd entirely misunderstood the situation between myself and Mirrie. I am quite cross with her for giving you the wrong impression, as well as persuading me to let her borrow your dress, against my better judgement. However, it came to no harm – unlike the Titania costume.

That was a low blow about the costume, but clearly he was unable to grasp how I felt about my wedding dress.

He'd obviously switched to a charm offensive in the last line – offensive being the operative word, as far as I was concerned.

> Darling, I miss you and we so need to talk!

'Darling, we so *don't*,' I said aloud.

In fact, I'd no intention of opening any channel of communication with him ever again.

I called Marco a very rude word and looked up to find Golightly standing in the doorway. He seemed to be mouthing an emphatic, if silent, agreement.

*

I went over to the museum a few minutes before the delivery slot for the workbenches, to open and pin back the doors to the foyer. There had been no sign of any workmen about today and all was quiet.

Luckily, since the tables were trestles, I managed to drag them into the workroom myself, then put them together.

My Amazon delivery arrived just as I was about to lock the museum doors. I now had the wedding dress reference books and a tall, leather-topped stool, a bit like the one in Thom's workshop, which I'd rather liked.

Soon I had the arrangement of benches and sewing machines to my liking and sat on the tall stool, swivelling it round and round, as you do – small things amuse small minds – until Honey rang to summon me to go through to her office.

There was no sign of Viv when I passed the kitchen, though it was redolent with the smell of baking – something like cheese scones, I thought, sniffing appreciatively.

Honey wanted to show me the photos Priceless Interiors had just sent her of the first of the renovated display cabinets from the ecclesiastical museum.

'The first lot are arriving on the fourteenth and then the rest on the seventeenth, though they're still sourcing more to fill in any gaps,' she said.

They were all in dark glossy wood: full-length display cases and shallower units with shelves.

'They've got a big mahogany L-shaped desk for reception and some shelving and drawer units that will do for the shop.' She scrolled to another picture. 'This is a smaller desk and chair for the staff room.'

'I think they all look really good, and we'll have plenty of display space to expand into,' I said.

'I just want to make sure that huge desk *will* fit in the foyer between the staircase and the wall, with a gap to get round it,' Honey said, and came back with me to the museum.

I helped her measure up. The desk would fit quite nicely, so she rang Priceless Interiors on the spot and insisted she wanted it delivered on the fourteenth, with the first display units.

I could hear protesting noises from the other end, but she got her way, which wasn't surprising since she must be spending a fortune with them. She had sold them the glass cases that had housed the stuffed animals from the natural history collection, however, which might have offset some of her expenses.

'That's that,' she said in satisfaction, pushing the phone back into her jeans pocket. 'I tell you what, let's go up to the attic in the house and see what you think of Uncle Hugo's office furniture. If you like it, I'll get it brought down to your workroom and then it will be out of the way before our first Great Attic Hunt on Sunday.'

'OK,' I agreed, and followed her back through the corridor from the museum and up and up the tall, crooked old Tudor house until we finally arrived at a set of steeper and uncarpeted stairs that opened directly into the first attic.

'Here we are! The attics ramble up and down various levels, just like the rest of the rooms in the house, but the ones over the later kitchen wing used to be the servants' quarters, so there isn't much in those. Even less, now I've flogged most of the brass bedsteads and washstands to the junk shop man, Arthur. The door to the right leads into the older attics.'

'There's not a lot in this room,' I observed.

'No, because I had all my odds and ends and Hugo's office furniture moved into one of the servants' bedrooms. My cunning plan for our Sunday sessions is to shift anything I want to get rid of into there. But anyway, come and look at Hugo's stuff.'

In what must have been a very spartan bedroom she twitched off a dustsheet to reveal a modern light-wood computer desk, side unit for a printer, a high-backed office chair and two small filing cabinets, stacked one on top of the other.

'Ikea's finest,' she said. 'It didn't really go with the house, but of course, it was practical. Would it do for your workroom?'

'Yes, it's just the thing!'

'Those boxes in the corner contain his hard drive, a monitor and printer, all in good working order, so you could have those too, if you want them?'

'I've only got a small laptop, so it would be handy having a permanent workstation just for the museum work. As long as you're sure you don't need any of it.'

'No, it's all surplus to requirements. I took all Uncle Hugo's genealogical files off it and wiped the hard drive before I put it up here. I knew his password to get in.'

She checked her watch. 'Time flies when you're having fun, but we need a couple of strong men to heft the office furniture over to your workroom. Do you happen to have Simon and Thom's mobile numbers handy?'

'I do. I've got all the book group in my phone now, but they might both be in the middle of doing something important!'

'We'll see,' she said.

I'm sure Simon was, because he looked abstracted when he arrived with Thom and said he couldn't stay long. Derek must have been about somewhere, because he brought them up and stayed to help, while I dashed ahead to wedge open all the doors.

When I'd done that, I went back, but only as far as the bottom of the first flight of stairs, because the thumps and swearing from above were horrendous.

Eventually, however, it all arrived safely, and then Simon immediately dashed off.

'I must go too, or Baz will be wondering what's happened to me,' Derek said. 'Viv's taken Rory out, Honey. She said she needed a walk.'

'She speaks to you?' Thom demanded. 'She doesn't even seem to want to *look* at me.'

'She whispers, but I do feel honoured,' he said.

'I'll come back with you and lock up the passage behind me,' Honey said, and followed him out.

'Coffee?' I offered Thom. 'I feel I owe you something after all that!'

'I need to lock up the workshop properly and take Jester for a run,' Thom said. 'But I don't think either Simon or I would say no if you wanted to treat us to Welsh rarebit in the Pink Elephant teashop in an hour? I expect Simon will have finished whatever it is he's doing by then. I'll text him, but he can never resist the lure of food.'

'Is the Pink Elephant the café in the square?'

'Yes, and the décor has to be seen to be believed,' he said, sending his message. 'It's open till seven for light meals, though the repertoire is pretty limited to things on toast.'

'Sounds good to me!'

A message pinged back to Thom instantly and he read it and said, 'Simon's coming, and he's asking Pearl if she'd like to join us.'

'Good idea,' I said, thinking we really were, if not the Famous Five, the Famous Four.

Thom left and, as I locked the room up and went into the cottage, I sang: 'We are the Famous Four, and Go-li-i-ghtly the cat.'

Said cat gave me a withering look, then turned and headed for the utility room, where I found him pointedly staring into his empty dinner bowl.

He always managed to make me feel guilty: were all cats like that?

25

Away with the Fairies

The Pink Elephant was determined to live up to its name: the curtains were printed with processions of the creatures, a frieze of them ran round the top of the cream-painted walls and the menu holders were also pink and elephantine.

From five till seven, when they shut, they had a light supper menu of Welsh rarebit, and eggs, scrambled or poached, on toast.

We all opted for the Welsh rarebit.

'The bread's good and you get doorstops, so it's really filling,' Simon said enthusiastically.

'I find it a bit too filling and can never eat the second slice,' said Pearl, who had joined us.

'I'm always happy to eat it for you,' said Simon.

He did, too, then ordered a rum baba, something I had never come across, and which looked about a million calories a mouthful. It was just as well that Simon, like Pearl, seemed to have the kind of tall, rangy figure that never put on an ounce.

While we were having coffee afterwards – or Earl Grey tea, in Pearl's case – I had another email from Will, though I would have thought at this time of day he'd be revving himself up, ready for tonight's performance. I was quite right to, as I discovered when I quickly scrolled down it:

Just a quick one from my dressing room, darling, before I put on the slap and don the bells and motley.

Marco just came in and asked me if I was in touch with you and had your new address! He recognized your writing on the envelope of that note you sent here to the theatre with the taxi fare in it, so clearly suspected we might still be in touch.

He said he was so distracted with worry about you, because you weren't answering his calls or messages, that he'd gone out to your flat in Ealing and found you'd gone.

I told him you'd said in that note that you'd already accepted a new job out of town and were leaving almost immediately, but I had no idea where. Which is, of course, quite true, Garland darling, though I do think you could trust me with it.

All this concern for you has come a bit late in the day, don't you think? But I suspect he has an ulterior motive in wanting to find you – he has realized you were his muse. He said the management would only take his new play – which sounds like an arty mix of Swan Lake crossed with Metamorphosis – if he rewrote it in the style of A Midsummer Night's Madness, which was exactly the advice you had given him and it had been your idea to turn to writing supernatural thrillers in the first place.

So I said you were quite right and if the management thought so, too, that clinched it. Then he looked gloomy and went away – and I must don my wings and flit away with the fairies, too.

Oberon xx

That last bit made me smile, though in fact his costume was black and silver, so he was a very dark and dramatic Fairy King, which suited his devious role in the play.

I looked up to find the others had stopped talking and Thom was regarding me rather broodingly.

'Sorry,' I said, then explained to the others: 'That was an email from Wilfric Wolfram, one of the actors in my ex-fiancé's new play.'

'You've stayed in touch with him, then?' Thom asked.

'He was so kind when I . . . broke up with Marco, that I emailed to thank him and he's emailed back a couple of times. He doesn't know where I'm living now, though, and I'm not going to tell him.'

His expression seemed to lighten a little. 'Right. I thought it might have been from Marco.'

'Well, I wouldn't have been laughing at it if it had been!' I said, astonished. 'He *has* tried to contact me, but I've just ignored him.'

Pearl, who was obviously dying of curiosity but too polite to ask any questions, got up and said she had to get back, because she had work to do that evening, and I said I'd settle up our bill and walk back with her.

We left the two men debating whether to go to the pub for a quick pint. Simon must have the digestion of an ox.

*

To Golightly's disgust, I vanished into the workroom for a bit to set up the new computer and printer. The drawers of the filing cabinet were full of empty folders, so I put fresh labels on them, though had no idea yet what I was going to fill them with.

A rising crescendo of demonic shrieks eventually made me give up and go back to the cottage, where I amused Golightly with the feather toy for a while, before settling down to read more of Rosa-May's journal. She sounded an enterprising kind of girl . . .

*

I sent a quick reply to Will over my breakfast, which was porridge the following day as I felt I'd overdosed on toast the previous evening.

Hi Will

It was fine to tell Marco I'd moved out of London to a new job, but I don't intend having any further contact with him, about his plays or anything else.

I don't know about being a muse; I was probably just the voice of common sense while he was writing the last play and certainly advised him to follow it up with another in the same vein. Whether he takes that advice or not is entirely up to him. It sounds as if he is at least now thinking about it.

Wishing you continued success in your role as Oberon,

Garland xx

I still wasn't going to give Will my address, because after the current run of the play finished, I wouldn't put it past him to suddenly appear – and although I enjoyed his slightly waspish emails and appreciated his basic kindness after my Ripping Time, I wasn't interested in any romantic relationship, if that was what he had in mind.

I was probably wrong about that and flattering myself, but even if I weren't, it seemed likely that he was about to break into major stardom, while I was doing my best to sink into obscurity.

Feeling in need of a bit of fresh air and exercise after that, I set off to explore the rest of the small town, finding the large supermarket on the edge, as well as a good hardware store, a bakery and a small needlework shop, which might be useful for odds and ends.

I found the doctor's surgery too – I should register there the following week – and then at a small newsagent's I stocked up on address labels, felt-tip marker pens, highlighters and a few other things. Stationery was so irresistible.

On the way home I found Pearl's shop open and my feet took me inside it without conscious volition. The book of Venetian masks had vanished from the window, so I was probably fairly safe from expensive impulse purchases.

There were a couple of customers in the shop, so I browsed the shelves of Victorian novels in the backroom and couldn't resist an illustrated copy of *The Water Babies* . . . or keep myself from adding to my Enid Blyton hardback Adventure series collection, with *The Valley of Adventure*.

The child inside had stayed frozen in time after I lost Mum and Dad, so I'm always turning back to the books I loved before then, for some kind of comfort.

When the customers had gone, laden with bags of books and wearing the slightly stunned expression of those whose credit cards have taken a hit, Pearl came through and offered me a coffee, then admired my modest selection from the shelves . . . before producing the Venetian mask book, which she said she'd put away until I'd had a chance to look at it.

'But no obligation to buy it, of course,' she added.

But the photos in it were wonderful, and even if masks were a bit out of my field, I knew I had to have it.

Luckily another customer came in just as I'd finished my coffee, so I managed to pay for my purchases before Pearl persuaded me into buying anything else . . .

In the courtyard, Jester was lying on his furry cushion outside Thom's workshop, which had both halves of the stable door open, and thumped his tail when he saw me. Thom looked out and said if I still wanted to go and explore the junk shop, he'd come and collect me in about an hour.

I'd forgotten he'd said he would go with me and he must have mentioned it to Simon, too, because when I opened the door to his knock, they were both there.

'You don't mind if I come too, do you?' asked Simon, whose sandy hair was rumpled into an untidy crest. 'I've been working on a big consignment of fascinators all morning and they are *so* boring to make compared to hats!'

'Of course I don't mind,' I assured him.

'Good, because I love a good rummage around Arthur's Cave!'

It wasn't far, and they pointed out Terrapotter opposite, where the garden pots had come from.

Arthur's Cave was on a corner with windows on both sides filled with a very strange collection of objects.

'He keeps the good stuff in the main part of the shop, then there's a lean-to veranda thing at the back, an outbuilding and a yard full of garden stuff,' said Thom. 'Come on!'

We followed him in, stopping just inside while our eyes

adjusted to the dim light. The floors were wooden boards and a thin mist of dust seemed to hang in the air.

''Allo!' said a reedy voice from the gloom. 'What can I be doing you for?'

'We just want a rummage round, Arthur,' Thom said.

'Oh, it's you two, is it?' he said. 'I'm going to charge you for rummaging, if you don't buy anything this time.'

'We've brought a new customer with us today, so you never know,' Thom said, indicating me.

'And I bought all those antique wooden hat blocks from you only a few months ago,' said Simon, sounding aggrieved. 'They cost me a fortune!'

'I let you know about them, didn't I? Knew you'd be interested,' said Arthur, eyeing me curiously. 'And if this lady has any particular interests, and wants to leave me a contact number, I'll do the same for her.'

'Thank you! My name's Garland, and I just want a good look round, though I'm always interested in things connected with dressmaking and costume — tailor's dummies, old sewing equipment, that kind of thing.'

'Might still be a tailor's dummy down in the basement,' he said, rubbing his nose thoughtfully.

'If there is, we'll find it,' Thom said cheerfully, then suggested we go outside first and work our way back in.

There wasn't anything of interest in the barn-like building. It was all huge dilapidated Victorian mahogany furniture, and the garden section outside was mostly broken birdbaths, old sinks and a few rusty gates.

The glazed lean-to building looked a lot more interesting and I headed straight for a rack of doors.

'What are you looking for?' asked Simon.

'Honey said she'd seen a stable door and Garland wants one,' Thom explained. 'And here it is.'

He slid forward an old stable door, that had been stripped back to bare wood.

'Doesn't look bad . . .' he said. 'Have you got the measurements?'

I got my notebook out and a tape measure, and they wrote down the dimensions and compared them.

'I think it will fit,' Thom said. 'The width is fine but it might be a fraction too short, though I could fix that by running a wooden batten across the bottom of the doorframe to fill in the gap.'

'In that case, I'll have it,' I said.

'We might beat him down on the price, if we find anything else we want to buy,' Simon suggested.

Looking round, something struck me. 'Why are so many things painted with this horrible matt undercoat in Elastoplast pink or dirty sage green?'

'It's one of Arthur's foibles – don't ask me why,' said Thom. 'Just be grateful he didn't get round to the stable door before you got here.'

He pushed it back in while I examined the jumble of mostly sorry-for-itself furniture, old metal advertising signs, a battered jukebox and, under a dirty carpet, a low chesterfield sofa in a ripped linen loose cover that might once have been brightly flowered. You could see through the holes that underneath it was blue velvet.

I pulled the carpet off on to the floor and had a closer look at the little sofa, lifting up the loose cover. The velvet was worn, but the seat cushions firm, though when I cautiously sat on it, it rocked alarmingly.

'It's missing one castor,' said Thom, amused.

'It's not bad, other than that,' I said. 'You don't often see a small chesterfield. This would fit nicely into my living room and I could make a new cover for it really easily, using this old one as a pattern.'

'It *is* a bit doll's house-sized, like that little tub chair you had when you were a child, and you still fit into that.'

'I have grown a bit since then,' I said with dignity.

Simon pulled the sofa right out and we had a good look all over it. There was no sign of woodworm in the legs, or stuffing bursting out. It smelled a bit musty, but nothing a blast of fabric freshener and a good vacuum wouldn't fix.

Thom said, 'If you want it, Arthur will either have to come up with a matching castor, or a set of new ones.'

'The door was overpriced, but this is dirt cheap,' commented Simon, looking at a brown cardboard tag pinned to the cover. 'Arthur's pricing is always really random and you can usually beat him down a bit, or get free delivery. I can negotiate, if you like.'

'OK, but let's have a look round the rest of the shop first,' I suggested.

There were three floors of the shop, with the more valuable furniture and antiques on the ground floor, where Arthur lurked in a sort of cubbyhole.

I thought some of the brass bedsteads and china washbasin sets upstairs might have come from Honey's attic.

I found a nice old hall runner in rich dark shades of crimson, blue and green, and added that to my purchases. I only hoped my flat sale would be finalized soon, before I ran out of money!

In the basement I discovered the tailor's dummy Arthur had mentioned, but it had seen better days so I resisted that.

Thom was rummaging in a big open box of woodworking tools.

'We all have our guilty pleasures,' I said, coming up behind him.

'I do have quite a collection,' he agreed, getting up with an old plane and a couple of other wooden-handled tools in his hands. 'Are you done? I don't know where Simon has got to.'

We found him rocking himself in a big Windsor chair upstairs, while Arthur seemed to be making a small parcel up out of newspaper and string.

'Bought a small framed Regency fashion plate – bonnets,' he explained.

'Barely making a profit, I am,' Arthur grumbled, and when he turned away I gave Simon the list of things I wanted and asked him to do his best, which he did, getting the runner and delivery thrown in for free.

Arthur got Thom and Simon to help him load everything in his van before we left, and promised to bring them round when he shut at five.

*

Simon and Thom came over to the cottage as soon as Arthur's van appeared and helped carry everything in, once Golightly was safely shut in the utility room.

I put the runner straight down in the hall and we leaned the stable door against the living-room wall.

The sofa, looking small and grubby, lurked in the middle of the room like a visitor unsure of his welcome.

'I'll come back tomorrow and put that spare castor Arthur found on the sofa for you. I can have a go at fitting the door, too,' offered Thom.

'I'm sure you have other things you'd rather do on your day off!'

'You know I love doing that kind of thing,' Thom said, and gave me one of his rare, warm smiles.

'I wish I could help, too,' said Simon, 'but I always run Pearl to church on Sunday mornings and then she buys me lunch at the Devil's Cauldron as a reward.'

'I'll be here all morning, because I'm letting Golightly out for the first time and I want to keep an eye on him.'

'Hope it goes well,' Simon said. 'We'll all meet up at Pelican House at half three, shall we? Ready for another antique rummage. I can't wait!'

'Yes, as long as we don't have to heft any more heavy furniture about,' Thom said firmly.

Rosa-May

And so began the modest start of my career, with some months spent travelling up and down the country, staying in poor lodgings and playing in all kinds of venues. But I adored the life and learned so much in that short time, both about my profession and about people ... and Sara was right about my needing her protection.

I began with the smallest of roles, but by hard work and application, by the time we returned to London, I was being given ever more speaking parts.

Mr Joseph Blake must have reported back to his brother on my progress, for soon after our return to Town, I made my debut at the Cockleshell Theatre in my favourite role of Titania in A Midsummer Night's Dream, to the chagrin and jealousy of the older actresses of the company.

On the first night, I knew that my future hung in the balance, for the London audiences were notoriously difficult to please, but I had good advice from Mrs Aurelius Blake, a great actress in her time, which I received with gratitude.

By great good fortune, my performance seemed immediately to

capture the hearts of the audience and this, my first major success, was followed by other important roles.

I was hailed as the Fairy Queen of the North . . . and also as the Vestal Venus, since my chaste reputation remained unsullied.

Even the most successful actress is not showered in riches, but eventually I could employ Sara exclusively to attend me.

I finally gained acceptance by the older ladies of the company, perhaps because I was unsuited by nature to take on the great tragic roles in which they revelled.

*

You will know with what success my career continued, both at the Cockleshell Theatre and during my annual tours around the country.

It was quite an exhausting life, especially since I was determined to bring something fresh and new to the various roles I was allotted. Luckily, I had always been quick to learn and retain my parts, for we performed many different plays during such tours of the provinces.

As my earnings increased, I entrusted my finances to the advice of Mr Blake, so that I might accrue enough to fall back upon, should my voice give out – a constant fear – or my health decline, for I had quickly realized that my constitution was not as robust as many who, like Mrs Siddons, continued their profession into old age.

I did not give the matter much thought in the early years, but increasingly, these things became a concern.

Of course, marriage would have given me security and I had not been without offers of matrimony from enamoured young men . . . However, I had never been truly tempted, for my fear of the consequences outweighed the advantages.

I had a circle of friends, including dear Letty, now married with two children, on whom she doted. Her assurances that they were worth the pains of childbirth, however, did not convince me.

Despite having reprised my role as Titania in the autumn and winter of 1814 to great acclaim, as the year turned to 1815 and I passed my twenty-sixth birthday, I had begun to fear a little more for the future . . .

26

The Cat Sat on the Mat

After the horribly wet and dreary day of my arrival, the weather seemed to have switched to a bit of an Indian summer, and Sunday dawn was pale gold against celestial blue. A bird was singing its heart out in the small tree in the railed garden.

After breakfast, feeling like a mother letting her child go out to play on its own for the first time, I unlocked the cat flap, watched by Golightly, and demonstrated the way it now opened and closed.

He merely sat down and regarded me with an expression that clearly said: 'You don't get me like that twice!'

In the end, I picked him up and gently pushed him headfirst halfway through, then let go, then stood back to see what he would do next.

For several long minutes, this was absolutely nothing. If he hadn't been so skinny, I'd have thought he was stuck and I was just wondering whether to pull him in again when, very, very slowly, he inched forward and vanished, the flap slapping closed behind him.

I dashed to the living-room window and squinted sideways

at the open latticework of the porch, where I could just make out his ghost-grey shape sitting on the mat, statue still.

When I went back into the hall and, kneeling down, pushed open the flap and looked through, he turned and made a silent face at me.

'It's OK, Golightly. You can come back in any time you want.'

He made the hideous face again, then turned his back on me once more and, with a sigh, I opened the front door and slid out, closing it behind me, so I could demonstrate the amazing ability of the cat flap to open both ways, just like his old one. Then I went back in, closing the door quickly when he seemed about to follow me.

I stood in the hall listening . . . and then a blue-grey head slowly appeared and a pair of yellow eyes regarded me balefully. Then there was a rattle and he was gone.

This time, from the window, I watched him very slowly move across the cobbles before sliding through the garden railings and vanishing into the bushes.

He'd be safe enough in there, so long as he didn't emerge on the other side and leg it off into town.

There was no way I could settle to doing anything else, so I took a kitchen chair outside and put it by the porch in a spot the sun had just reached, then sat drinking coffee and waiting for the return of the traveller . . . or even some sign that he was still there.

Thom must have been up and working early, because the door to his workshop opened and he came out, tossing down Jester's cushion. Jester, hard on his heels, immediately curled up on it and Thom, turning to go back in, spotted me and waved.

'I'll be over in ten minutes,' he called, and it was only then I remembered he'd said he would fit the door and put the castor on the sofa today. Golightly's release into the wild had entirely distracted me.

'Sunbathing?' he asked, when he carried his big toolbox and several long strips of thin wooden batten over.

'I've just let Golightly out for the first time. He went in that direction.' I gestured at the garden.

'How did it go?'

'Well, he didn't exactly skip off to the theme tune of *Born Free*, but I'm hoping he just has a little potter round the garden and comes back again. If he's still *in* there.'

Thom, from his greater height, could see more of the garden than I could and peered across, shading his eyes.

'I think he just fell off the lowest branch of the cherry tree in the middle. But don't worry,' he added hastily, as I sprang up, 'there's a nice soft flowerbed right underneath.'

'He doesn't usually climb on to anything higher than a low armchair.'

'He's probably never seen a tree before, though, so maybe it was too much to resist. Or perhaps some innate instinct took over?'

'Maybe,' I agreed. 'I'll stay out a bit longer and watch him. Do you want a cup of coffee?'

'Love one. I'll drink it out here with you and then, if Golightly seems OK, I'll fit that door for you.'

I took out another chair for him and made more coffee. When I sat down next to him, he assured me he could see the entranceway to the mews and Golightly had not gone out.

'It's kind of you to keep doing all these handyman things for me, because you must have other things you'd rather be doing.'

'Not really. I enjoy it. I might do a little more to that Burmese puppet later, though, because I want to finish it so I can start on the Maria Marten marionette. The only other character they need is the stepmother and I've got a female marionette in stock that will do.'

We sat out there in the surprisingly warm sunshine, discussing the puppets and the costumes I would make for them.

'The Marinos should all be back by the end of the month and I'll introduce you and tell them you're taking over the costume making.'

'I'm looking forward to seeing some of their puppet performances. It will be a new experience.'

I'd been so interested in what we'd been discussing that I'd forgotten about Golightly, but when I remembered and turned to look, Thom said quickly, 'Don't worry about the cat – he hasn't gone out of the mews.'

'I think I'll stay out here a bit longer anyway and see if he comes back,' I said.

'I'll go and get on with the door. I can give you a shout if I need anything.'

He carried his tools and the wood into the house and I sat on, listening to birdsong ... and drilling, sawing and the sound of an electric screwdriver.

On my left, Jester snoozed on, curled on his cushion, but Golightly didn't emerge and I was just wondering whether to go and look for him when Thom called me in to admire his handiwork.

The sofa now stood solidly on four large antique wooden castors, which he said he'd oiled, to make moving it easier.

Then he demonstrated the new door. 'I've fixed the length by running this piece of batten across, like a sill. You can wax it when you do the door, so they match.'

'The stripped wood *is* nice. I think waxing would look better than painting it,' I agreed. 'I see you've fitted bolts top and bottom, too.'

'I had them spare and thought they'd do instead of a lock – and there's another vertical one so you can hold the two halves together, if you want to open the whole door instead of just half.'

'It's perfect!' I said. 'But you must let me pay you back for the bolts.'

'OK, and I've got a tin of antique-finish wax you can have, too, which is quite expensive, so that can go on the bill! You just rub it in with a soft cloth and it gives a nice, mellow finish.'

'Great!' I said, then added tentatively, 'I'll make us some more coffee, but while you're here, would you mind putting some picture hooks up for me? The new plaster on the walls is making me feel nervous! I've put sticky tabs where the hooks need to go. There's one in the workroom, too, for my big corkboard.'

'That won't take a minute,' Thom said, and after I'd pointed them all out to him it seemed no time before he joined me outside and picked up his mug of coffee.

'All done. Any sign of the furry marauder?' he asked. 'Jester doesn't look as if he's moved since I last saw him, so Golightly must have stayed quiet.'

'The nearest shrubs swayed a bit a few minutes ago, even though there's no breeze, so I thought that might be him exploring. I mean, he's never been in a garden before, so it'll all be new to him.'

'Like an exciting jungle,' Thom agreed. 'We could go and check up on him in a minute, if you still feel antsy about him.'

The town hall clock struck half past ten and, as if on cue, Simon and Pearl came out of their adjacent cottage doors, waved at us and then got into Simon's car and drove away.

'Off to mingle with the godly at St Gabriel's,' said Thom,

and then, as a backfire sounded from the direction of the square, added, 'And he really needs to get that exhaust fixed!'

The noise had been enough to startle Golightly into flight, for he suddenly shot out from between the railings and was halfway across the cobbles in the direction of home when he spotted us and slowed to a saunter, as if he hadn't been scared at all.

The backfire had woken Jester, too, and the movement as he sat up caught Golightly's eye. He stopped dead and stared.

Jester saw him at the same time and, getting up, tail wagging, he went to meet him.

'A new friend!' his amiable face seemed to be saying, but Golightly's expression must have been anything but friendly, for the dog's steps slowed to a halt as he neared him.

For a long moment they faced each other like a furry version of *The Gunfight at the O.K. Corral* – and then Golightly gave one of his high-pitched banshee shrieks and Jester did the only thing possible: he laid down and rolled over, all four paws in the air.

'Wuss,' observed Thom. 'Mind you, if I'd been a dog, I'd have done just the same that day when you came for the keys to the cottage, because scary doesn't begin to describe it.'

I ignored that. 'Discretion is the better part of valour – and look!' I exclaimed, for Golightly appeared to accept Jester's submission. Something must have passed between them, anyway, for Jester cautiously rolled over and got up, before they both headed back to his furry bed outside the workshop.

'That was a quick about-face!' I said, gobsmacked, as they settled down together. 'Do you think it's love at first sight, or does Golightly just think Jester is some strange kind of cat?'

'Neither. I think it's a takeover bid and Jester threw in the towel in the first round.' Thom got up. 'I somehow don't think you need to worry about Golightly any more and I'd put even money on him coming home in time for his dinner.'

'I expect you're right . . . and now perhaps I can get on with something else and stop worrying about him. I'll hang all my pictures and then skim through the basic catalogue of the dress collection that Honey's sent me.'

'I'll leave you to it, then,' he said, and when I'd taken the chairs and mugs back in, I resolutely shut the front door and hoped for the best.

*

I didn't have to wait until dinnertime for Golightly to reappear, for with unerring instinct he returned at lunchtime to share a tuna sandwich.

The excitement of his initial expedition seemed to have worn him out, because after that he curled up on the armchair and went to sleep and he was still snoring wheezily while I was getting ready to go over to Pelican House. He woke as I spooned gourmet cat food into his bowl and came in, slightly stiffly. I'd tried to do it quietly, but the spoon had rattled against the dish, which was as good as an alarm as far as he was concerned.

'Listen,' I said, waving the spoon at him. 'I've only put your dinner out this early because I'm going out for a few hours. If I were you, I'd leave some of it for later.'

I might as well have saved my breath, because he started wolfing it down as if he hadn't eaten for a week.

I left him to it and locked the cat flap, because I didn't want him roaming about while I was out. I intended locking it every night, anyway, so he might as well get used to it.

As I left, I heard the unmistakable sound of his bowl hitting the unit as he polished it shiny in the hope of a last morsel of dinner.

I caught up with the others at Honey's garden gate. She'd told us to come in by way of the kitchen door.

'We look as if we ought to be using the tradesmen's entrance anyway, since we're all wearing old clothes we don't mind getting filthy,' said Simon. 'Except Pearl. She only needs a Lambretta and she could be cast for a remake of *La Dolce Vita*.'

I could see where he was coming from, because Pearl was wearing pedal-pushers and a blue and white spotted scarf tied peasant-style over her hair.

'Oh, these old things,' Pearl said, though she smiled at Simon. 'And I'm only wearing the scarf because I've got a fear of spiders getting into my hair.'

'I'd never even thought of that one,' I said with a shudder. 'They're bad enough running about where you can see them!'

'We'll protect you!' said Simon, striking a heroic pose.

But it seemed Honey had already thought of that one, because when we followed her up to the attics we found a collection of long-handled feather dusters and brooms. Viv had brought up the rear, dressed practically in jeans and a checked lumberjack shirt that might have belonged to her husband: Charlotte Brontë trying to blend into the twenty-first century.

'Viv's got a notebook and she's going to list what we want to get rid of and anything that might be valuable that we need to check out first. I've cleared this room and put anything I want to keep in the old servants' rooms through that door,' Honey said, gesturing. 'The junk shop man, Arthur, has taken the rest, and my plan is that as we work through the older attics, we move anything I don't want to keep into here. Then he can come back and have a look at all that, too.'

'Fair enough,' said Thom. 'I see the electric lights extend up here.'

'It's all old and needs rewiring when we've cleared enough space,' Honey said. 'As there's just one light bulb in the middle of each of the other rooms, I've brought some torches up for the dark corners.'

I told Honey I thought I'd seen some of her old brass bedsteads at Arthur's shop the day before, and about the stable door and the sofa.

'We might find you a couple more bits of furniture, you never know,' she said. 'Come on, I'll show you the scale of the task before we get on with it!'

She led the way into the first of what proved to be three long gabled rooms, crowded with the dark shapes of furniture and lit only by single bulbs on loops of flex across the ceilings. A narrow passage had been left through each one, so you could squeeze through, but the final, much smaller room, was accessed by three steps down and a dog-leg corridor, in the inconvenient manner of old houses.

We only looked into that one from the doorway, because it was so tightly packed with what looked like luggage and small tea chests.

'I don't think that one's going to be very exciting, somehow,' Simon said, as we retraced our steps to the first attic.

'I don't suppose any of them will be,' Honey said. 'But you never know – and we'd better make a start!'

27

Table Talk

'So far as I can see,' said Honey, 'they filled up the attics in no particular order when they moved here from Up-Heythram Hall, so furnishings from different time periods are all jumbled up. Then the later generations have shoved all kinds of unwanted junk up here, wherever it would fit.'

'It does look like the bargain basement version of King Tut's tomb,' said Thom.

'Only not so much of the "wonderful things",' agreed Pearl, peering distastefully at a nearby bundle. 'That rolled-up rug has to be a moth feast!'

'I should think they'll have had a go at any soft furnishings,' I said. 'That rug only looks fit for the tip.'

'Let's drag it into the other room and just check it isn't the remnant of some fabulous Persian heirloom,' suggested Simon.

It wasn't, but it was certainly dusty.

'You know, I think I'll see if I can persuade Arthur to take *everything* away that I don't want, even the rubbish like this, on the understanding that I let him have some decent stuff at a reasonable price,' Honey said. 'I think he'll go for that and it'll save me a lot of trouble.'

We began slowly to clear one corner of the first room, moving monstrous mahogany wardrobes and Edwardian bedroom suites by pushing them across the wooden floor into the outer room, where Viv listed them all in her notebook, while Pearl dusted everything off.

'I think Uncle Hugo had a lot of the more monumental pieces brought up here,' said Honey. 'He liked a mix of comfortable modern and seventeenth-century furniture.'

'Of course, what I'm secretly hoping to find up here is some more of Rosa-May Garland's belongings – maybe even another journal that would give some clue about what happened to her after her twin boys were born,' I said.

'Now you've told us, it's not a secret hope any more,' Thom pointed out.

'I don't know how far you've read in the journal, Garland,' said Honey, 'but she does mention that her husband gave her two blank notebooks, and since she totally filled the first one, she might have started the second, so you never know.'

I suspected she was just saying that to keep me going, because by now even Simon's first flush of treasure-hunting zeal had worn off and we were all pleased when Viv, who had vanished some time before, came back up with a tray of coffee.

'The journal sounds interesting,' said Pearl, 'but it's amazing *one* volume survived, not to mention the costume you loaned to the V&A, isn't it?'

'The Titania costume was a great find,' I enthused. 'It's going to be the centrepiece of the Rosa-May Garland Room on the ground floor. The journal will be on display too and blown-up extracts round the walls.'

The coffee revived us a bit, and as soon as we'd drunk it, Honey said briskly, 'Come on, let's get going again! Forward, the Famous Five.'

I always suspected her of being a mind reader.

'*Six*,' came the merest breath of a whisper from Viv.

*

We all helped to push, pull and drag out the unwanted furniture, but found little Honey wanted to keep, until she came across a box containing the remains of a lovely tea set.

'Minton,' she said. 'I'll take that down with me when we go, Viv, and it can go in the glazed cabinet in the study, instead of those old school and university sporting trophies of Hugo's.'

She put it near the stairs and we carried on a bit longer, though we were flagging by then and couldn't raise a lot of enthusiasm when Thom discovered a Victorian scrap screen.

Simon helped him carry it into the other room and open out the folds.

'I'm not sure the light improves it,' I said dubiously, when the full glory of the pasted scraps under a thick soupy coating of yellow-brown varnish was revealed.

'If that was a nursery screen, those leering cherubs must have frightened the children into fits,' said Pearl.

'Oh, I don't know, I think it's sort of charming,' said Simon, surprisingly. 'And those cherubs aren't leering, they're puffing out their cheeks to blow clouds away, I think.'

'As far as I'm concerned, they can blow the whole screen into Arthur's Cave,' said Honey frankly. 'Although I think they're quite collectable now, so we'd better look them up on the internet first, Viv.'

Viv made a note. She'd now filled several pages and we'd barely started!

We worked on for another half-hour and when we finally called it a day, dirty and dishevelled, we'd cleared over a quarter of the room. The survivors of the cull now huddled together in the middle of the space, as if for protection.

We'd made a few more small finds and we all seemed to have come out of it with something: Honey had awarded Thom an ebony stick with a round silver handle that he'd admired, and Simon a red lacquered Chinese box that had taken his fancy.

Pearl succumbed to the offer of a china water jug painted with roses, but missing its washbowl, which she said would be perfect to put large bouquets in. 'Or big things like dahlias and sunflowers.'

'Since I've already had your uncle's office furniture, I feel greedy taking that cute little miniature chest of drawers, too,' I said, for it was a perfect piece of furniture in miniature, down to round white porcelain knobs.

'You're all welcome to any odds and ends you take a fancy to,' Honey said, then stretched. 'I think I'm going to ache tomorrow and we're all certainly grubby, but it's been sort of fun, hasn't it?'

It had, too, and once we'd washed some of the grime from our hands in the downstairs cloakroom, we all settled round the long table in the kitchen and demolished a huge Indian takeaway, which Honey had ordered, washed down with tins of lager.

Refined dining, it wasn't.

The wolfhound Rory watched every bite with wistful eyes, but wasn't allowed any because it would upset his stomach. In the end Honey gave him a rawhide bone and he retired to his bed and gnawed that to a soggy pulp instead.

'I'm ravenous,' declared Honey, helping herself to another piece of naan bread and a second helping of prawn biryani. 'I shouldn't be, because Viv cooked a wonderful Sunday lunch, but I am.'

'I think we all are,' said Thom. 'But hefting all that heavy furniture about must have burned off the calories!'

We were all so full afterwards that we declined the offer of fruit and cheese, and just had coffee in the sitting room instead, once we'd helped clear the table.

We could still hear Rory chewing his bone even from there.

The talk turned to the new museum again.

'Tomorrow will be my first official working day and I'll have to begin by quickly measuring up all the dresses so we can order the display mannequins,' I said. 'Then I can take my time working on them after that.'

'Well . . .' said Honey. '*Actually*, I've been wondering about the opening date, and now Priceless Interiors have promised to deliver the bulk of the display cases this week and next, I'm thinking of opening on Monday, October the fifteenth.'

I stared at her. 'But I haven't even *looked* at the costumes we're putting on display, and that doesn't give me much time to get them ready!'

'I don't think it really matters if they aren't all on display by then. The museum can be a work in progress,' she said. 'The Rosa-May material comes back at the end of the month and will be ready to go straight out on display, so that can be the first thing to set up.'

'Well . . . yes,' I said slowly, 'but—'

'Of course, you'll need to add your own wedding dress to the display in that room,' she continued, blithely ignoring my panic.

She explained to Pearl and Simon: 'Garland created a perfect replica of a lovely Regency evening dress that Rosa-May had had made in the style of her Titania stage costume, which she meant to use as her wedding dress, so if they were displayed next to each other, the visitors would be able to compare them.

Of course,' she added, 'you don't have to reveal the whole story of why you never wore it, if you don't want to, Garland.'

'I'm certainly not revealing *all* the details to the public,' I said, 'because I'm still ashamed of my part in what happened next.'

I looked at Simon and Pearl's surprised faces and suddenly realized their friendship already meant a lot to me and it would be a relief to tell them everything.

'I think I'd like you both to know everything – Honey and Thom already do.'

So I described what I'd overheard at the Cockleshell Theatre when I was delivering the Titania costume.

'Your fiancé actually let another woman borrow the wedding dress you'd spent so much time making, without telling you?' Pearl gasped.

'He did, but there was more betrayal to come, because it became evident from what Mirrie was saying that she and Marco had been having an affair.'

'Just to complicate things, Mirrie Malkin is the actress who starred alongside me and my stepbrother Leo, in the Silvermann films,' explained Thom. 'She and Leo married after the filming finished, but I caught her with Marco not long after that, so now they seemed to be taking up where they left off a few years ago.'

I heard Viv give a small, surprised squeak. I'd forgotten she was there!

'Mirrie was playing Titania in Marco's new play and he was also directing it,' I expanded. 'The actor I overheard her talking to was Wilfric Wolfram, whose email I got when we were in the Pink Elephant.'

'It's a small world,' Honey said.

'It is,' agreed Thom grimly. 'And full of betrayals.'

Our eyes met for a long moment, his unreadable. I don't know what he saw in mine. On the surface, our old friendship seemed to have resumed, but underneath my emotions seemed permanently to be not just mixed, but in turmoil.

I looked away and carried on with the story. 'Hearing her practically boasting about it all was such a shock that I dashed back into her dressing room, the room where I'd just hung the Titania costume . . .'

The next bit, admitting the enormity of what I'd done, was hard, but I screwed up my resolution and carried on. 'I have no recollection of the next few minutes, except that I suddenly felt furious . . . and the next thing I knew, the Titania costume was in shreds.'

'Gosh!' said Simon inadequately, his faded-denim-blue eyes widening.

I felt my face burn. 'It was so unprofessional of me that I can't believe even now I did it! All those hours of work I put into making it . . .'

'But I'm sure you couldn't help it,' said Pearl quickly. 'It must have been the shock!'

'I don't know, but I think Honey was very brave, offering me the job here. You've been so kind, Honey!' I told her, and she grinned at me.

'Not at all. I found what you'd done perfectly understand-able in the circumstances and you aren't likely to do anything like that again, so I got a costume expert for a pittance!'

'Garland always did have a fierce temper, even when we were children, although it always blew over quickly,' Thom said with a half-smile. 'We grew up together until we were nearly eleven and then didn't meet again for over ten years, but she hadn't changed.'

He looked ruefully at me. 'Then when we first saw each other again, I thought for a minute you were going to fly at me!'

'I nearly did, seeing you standing there after all that time not knowing what had happened to you. Perhaps I need anger management counselling?'

'You seem pretty chilled to me,' Simon said, puzzled. 'And why would you want to attack poor Thom?'

'Because poor Thom left London six years ago without a word to me and I hadn't any idea where he was, or what he was doing. He cut me off because I was seeing Marco and he always mistrusted him – he thought he was the most to blame for introducing his stepbrother, Leo, to drugs – but he never told me at the time that he knew Marco and Mirrie had had an affair a few years before.'

'I should have done and I can see now how cruel it was of me to leave you not knowing what had happened to me, but at the time, I thought I was acting for your own good. It was just after Leo overdosed, though, so I don't expect I was thinking very straight.'

Our eyes met again and held. The old connection would always be there, whatever happened, and I could forgive him with my head . . . it was just feeling the forgiveness right to the bottom of my heart I was still having trouble with.

Honey broke into the ensuing short silence.

'Well, it's all out in the open now and everyone knows everything,' she said expansively, and I saw Thom gave her a quick, suspicious glance, as if he suspected she might have known about our past history all along, which, of course, she had.

'I'm so glad you felt you were among friends and could share your story with us,' Pearl said. 'It's so easy to put your foot in it and say the wrong thing to people when you don't know their pasts. I could tell there had been something between you and Thom.'

'I couldn't!' Simon said, opening his eyes very wide.

'No, well, detecting subtle emotional undercurrents isn't exactly your strong point, Simon!'

'We've strayed a long way from discussing when the museum will open!' I said, remembering, with a feeling of panic, Honey's proposal that it should be on 15 October.

'Yes, we were talking about how much of your own story you wanted to reveal to the public – and I might expand on my own, because there's a little more to it than appeared in the papers at the time,' Honey said.

'I suppose the first dress I should concentrate on getting ready to display is Amy Weston's,' I said, when it became clear Honey wasn't going to expand on this now. 'You said she would be the focus of the opening display and you wanted to get maximum publicity for her story.'

'Who is Amy Weston?' Pearl asked.

'The Bloody Bride,' said Honey with relish, and explained all about Amy's disappearance and her mother's understandable hope that by putting her dress on display, she would finally find out what had happened to her daughter.

'Gosh!' said Simon. 'I never realized a wedding dress museum could be this exciting!'

'Oh, some of the dresses have even more bizarre or mysterious stories to tell,' Honey told him. 'Stranger even than Garland's series of unfortunate coincidences!'

'I don't think my story's strange so much as tragic,' I said. 'But at least I found out what Marco was really like before I actually married him!'

'He may eventually work out that you're here,' suggested Honey.

I shrugged. 'He seems to have the hide of a rhino and keeps trying to contact me, but since I'm not replying I expect he'll quickly lose interest. Will – Wilfric Wolfram – said in his last email that he thinks what Marco misses most is my advice on making his plays more accessible to wider audiences!'

'You don't seem to be ignoring *Will's* emails,' Thom said, and I looked at him, surprised by his tone.

'No, but you know how kind he was after that horrible scene at the theatre and he *is* amusing, in a sardonic kind of way. But I'm hoping he'll fade out now too, because my life is firmly fixed in Great Mumming and I don't really want constant reminders of the past.'

'They're not that easy to escape,' Thom said rather broodingly, and his expression must have unnerved poor Viv, who had been sitting quietly in Honey's shadow, because she got up and scuttled out of the room.

It had been quite an evening but I was glad I'd told Pearl and Simon everything, because it felt quite cathartic.

Perhaps now Thom and I really could start to build this new, different relationship he'd suggested . . .

Rosa-May

I resolved, while I had health and voice enough, to work as hard as I could and continue with Mr Blake's good advice to build up a sum sufficient to support me should I have to retire from the stage.

But you must not think that life was all work, for I had a circle of friends, both in the acting profession and in society, and London held amusement enough to satisfy anyone.

So it was that in early May of that year I went one evening with a small party of friends to Vauxhall Gardens, where we supped in a booth and then promenaded the various walks, which were lit like fairyland itself, with so many lanterns that my friends joked that, as Titania personified, I should feel quite at home there!

This was all the more apposite because I was for the first time wearing an evening gown modelled on the new stage costume Mr Blake had had made for my reprise in the role the previous autumn. It was extremely pretty and became me very well, so that I knew I was looking my best. Indeed, I received several admiring comments and our booth during supper had been the focus of many eyes.

While we promenaded, our party somehow merged with another, though that was not an unusual occurrence at these

300

affairs, when acquaintances were met with. Two wounded army officers, home on sick leave, were of the company . . . and both being young and handsome, and their wounds not seeming to impair their enjoyment of the evening, presented a romantic appearance . . .

One of them, Captain Guy Fairford, who was very merry and engaging, immediately attached himself to me. I had perforce to slow my pace to his, for he was walking stiffly, with the aid of a stick.

But we soon became so engrossed in conversation that we fell behind the rest of the party and noticed no more of the surroundings for a considerable time!

I had not thought myself capable of such tempestuous emotion, but from the very first moment my eyes met his merry hazel ones, my heart was quite lost and my fate sealed.

Nature plays such wicked tricks on even the most sensible of us!

28

Thirteen Dresses

I was up very early next morning, filled with anticipation at the thought of actually beginning work on the dresses today, but also some apprehension about having enough of them ready to go on display for the opening date!

I was sure Honey would have all the other arrangements in place by then, because I already knew she was someone who liked things done at once, and had the means to pay to make them happen. This was just as well, since I couldn't see the museum making enough money to pay my wages and the upkeep for quite a long time, if ever. It could be a very expensive hobby! But then, I suppose the natural history museum had been just that for her uncle Hugo.

After I'd fed Golightly, I unlocked the cat flap and he went straight out. Then, a few moments later, when I was eating my poached egg on toast, he came back in again.

This was reassuring, because it looked as if the central garden was now his new outdoor vantage point.

'You're a very clever boy,' I told him. 'You can just go in and out all day, as you please, while I'm working, and I expect Jester will be about later too, so you can hang out together.'

He didn't respond to that, just sat staring at me through slitted yellow eyes, until I got the message and gave him a cat treat.

I left the top half of the stable door open when I went into the workroom, and the one to the staff room ajar in case Honey came in. I thought I'd make a habit of this, so I was always accessible when I was working, to Honey or, when the museum was open, Ella, Kay and Derek.

Today, because they would be the first to go out on display, I'd have the treat of examining Honey's dress and the Bloody Bride's in detail.

I reminded myself that I really should stop calling poor Amy Weston the 'Bloody Bride', because she was a real, live – at least I hoped so – person.

Deciding to begin with Honey's dress, I removed it from its hanging cover, before carrying it in and carefully spreading it out on my new cutting table.

Then I opened Honey's basic catalogue of the collection on the computer, ready to start adding detail as I went.

I was about to scroll down to Honey's wedding dress, when I glanced out of the window and caught sight of Golightly, insouciantly sauntering across the cobbles to the garden, as if he owned the place.

With a smile, I looked down again and read:

Dress 1
Honey Fairford
Jilted, 1990

The bare bones of her story were already there, though it would seem not the whole of it. I wondered what else was to come, but then put the thought aside and turned back to the cutting table.

The dress, made from a smooth silk satin with a faint sheen, was floor-length and the skirt slightly fitted. Looking at it, I didn't think Honey could have put on an ounce since it was made for her!

The lightly beaded bodice had a sweetheart neckline, with a lace collar that rose high up to the neck, but was open at the front.

There was a short train, trimmed all the way down with the same lace and beading used on the bodice, as were the slightly puffed, wrist-length sleeves.

The underskirt layer was fairly minimal and I thought the effect would have been a sort of demure slinkiness . . . very Honey!

I took photos, including various construction details and then added those and a detailed description to the computer catalogue, along with the measurements.

Of course, the dress was marred by some ominous staining – the front hem of the skirt looked as if it had been dragged through blood, which was now a rusty red-brown, and a paler stain spread above it, about knee-height. I took pics of all that, too, before fetching the box of accessories and opening the lid. Honey had kept things simple for her big day: there was a light veil, obviously meant to just hang behind, attached to a beaded headband. The shoes were plain white satin with small heels, although they wouldn't really have shown.

If there had been anything borrowed or blue, it was not in the box.

I'd just arranged the dress over the slenderest of my dress-maker's dummies so I could photograph it from all angles, when the office door clicked open and Honey appeared in my doorway, yawning.

'Can I come in, or would I be disturbing you?'

'No, come on in! I've almost finished examining and recording the details of your dress.'

'So I see,' she said, interestedly eyeing the dress on the dummy, with its pearly sheen and ominous stains. 'You know, I haven't really looked at it for *years*. I had it hanging in my study for inspiration, while I was writing the first of my revenge thrillers in a white-hot rage, and I didn't have it cleaned first. But dried blood never does really come out of silk, does it?'

'It's hard to get it out of anything, once it's dried and set in,' I agreed. 'And . . . there's quite a lot of it.'

'I know! When my groom didn't turn up at the church and I drove to the cottage where he was staying, there seemed to be blood *everywhere*. The best man was groaning on the bed with a head wound and there was a wet and bloody towel hanging off the side of the bed, so when I leaned over it, that's how the dress came to be stained. I think my fiancé must have been trying to clean the head wound up, before he panicked and drove drunkenly off, instead,' she added, matter-of-factly.

'That would account for the paler stain up the front,' I agreed. 'I think I've heard that scalp wounds bleed a lot.'

'They certainly do, and I suspect drinking huge amounts of alcohol makes it flow more freely, too. Anyway, the owner of the estate the cottage was on turned up just then. It must have looked a bit Lady Macbeth, with me leaning over the bloody bed, so he called the police. After that, it all got a bit farcical – though not as farcical as when the best man told me what the argument and fight had been about!'

She grinned crookedly and added tantalizingly, 'But you'll have to wait a bit longer for the full story.'

'All right,' I said, and turned back to the dummy. 'It is – or was – a lovely dress, though.'

'I know! At the time it seemed such a waste. However, as it turned out, it did provide inspiration and led to my becoming a major bestselling novelist, so it served a purpose, even if not the original one.'

She looked in the open box. 'Is that my veil? The headband is quite pretty . . . and I had a bouquet of creamy yellow roses.'

She laughed suddenly. 'I was staying at Pelican House for the wedding in a local church and Uncle Hugo was giving me away. When the groom didn't turn up, I tossed the bouquet away – Viv caught it, though she was already married by then – and hared off back across the square in my wedding dress, jumped in my car and roared off to the cottage to look for him.'

'What did everyone do when you'd gone?' I asked curiously.

'Oh, Uncle Hugo said that since the function room and a buffet was already laid on at the Sun in Splendour, they might as well all go and have a party, which they did. They were still at it when the police let me go and I got back. I was ready for a stiff drink by then.'

'I can imagine,' I said, fascinated.

She yawned again. 'I was up writing till the early hours and I haven't really got going yet. I'll leave you to it. I'm expecting Arthur shortly, to look at the first attic gleanings, and I need some strong coffee before we do battle over the prices.'

When she'd gone, I completed my work on her accessories and, apart from one tiny tear to the edge of the veil, where it must have snagged on something, it was all ready for display. I thought I might as well mend that now, since it would only take a few minutes, and searched out the exact same shade of white silk thread as the veil. And, believe me, there are millions of shades of white, not just one!

Then I sat at the table, happily sewing minute fairy stitches into the delicate fabric.

Time flies when you are enjoying yourself and I was definitely ready for lunch by the time I'd finished.

I thought I might have to go and search for Golightly, but no. There he was, curled up in his favourite armchair. He only woke when he heard me in the kitchen.

*

After lunch, Golightly vanished into the great outdoors again and I mentally crossed everything and hoped he would confine his explorations to the courtyard, and also avoid what little traffic there was. The parking was private, but there were always delivery vans . . .

Golightly had answered the call of the wild and now it was time for me to respond to the call of the workroom. Next on my agenda was Amy Weston's dress.

In Honey's random way, she had allotted it the number 13: lucky for some, though not, it seemed, for Amy . . .

Her dress was on the rail in a zipped bag, and I took that and the box of accessories into the workroom before turning the computer on and scrolling down to her catalogue entry.

Dress 13
Amy Weston
The Bloody Bride
2017

Of course, I already knew the story and had looked at the scanned-in photographs, newspaper cuttings and Amy's mother's emails to Honey, the originals of which were in the box.

One of the photos showed Amy and her mother together, and since both were tall, with long, blond hair, they resembled each other and you had to look closely to see that one was glossily well preserved rather than young.

Amy's mum was quoted in a couple of the newspaper articles, saying things like: 'Many people thought we were sisters rather than mother and daughter.' I don't know about Amy, but I'd have hoped my own mum would have looked like one by now, rather than as if she'd borrowed my makeup and clothes . . .

Still, she was obviously doing her best to find her daughter and I hoped all the publicity the display in the museum generated would help.

I carefully spread Amy's dress on the table and contemplated it. It was of white matte silk satin and there was quite a lot of it, since it was long enough to drape on to the floor and also had quite a large train.

It was strapless and tightly fitted down to below the hips, where it flared out over layers of tulle, embellished with beads and lace, which had a subtle effect through the matte satin of the overskirt. There was more lace and beading on the bodice, which had a mesh back, so it looked fairly open.

I'd have looked like an overdressed Christmas tree fairy in it, but I expect tall, slender, blond Amy had been able to carry it off . . . or would have been.

Had someone carried *her* off – perhaps violently? Because there was no escaping the rusty spatter of small bloody droplets down the front of the skirt.

I knew the police had hung on to the dress for some time, and then her mother had not had it cleaned, since she seemed convinced it held some secret information that the police had somehow missed.

The dark drops marring the front of the skirt looked incongruous and, of course, my costumier's mind immediately started offering solutions to cover them up – a scatter of silk and lace roses, perhaps? But of course, it was futile to think about that, for no one would ever want to wear this dress again.

As far as measurements went, Amy was a fairly standard twelve, a stock size. The dress was creased, as if it had spent a lot of time folded in a box, before it was put on a hanger, so a little gentle pressing was really all it needed to make it display-ready.

There was no veil in the box, just a hair ornament of wire, beads and pearls to match the dress, and the shoes were high-heeled satin with more beading and pearls. I found the fake swansdown cape Honey had mentioned in there too, but I thought that would be better displayed separately.

When I'd taken all the details and photographs and added them on the computer, I returned the dress to the end of the hanging rail, next to Honey's. Two down, eleven to go. But still, I now knew the sizes of three mannequins to order, because of course I already knew my own. Since Honey had arranged to buy the two mannequins specially made for Rosa-May's Titania costume and evening dress from the V&A, I didn't need to worry about those.

George had kindly emailed me all his technical notes, giving details of fabric and construction, so those only needed adding to the catalogue at some point, although, of course, I already knew every tiny detail of the Titania-based evening dress.

I felt I was getting on really well and stopped for a coffee break, then braced myself to actually look at my forever-tainted Titania wedding dress.

I put it on the dummy I used when making my own clothes and it whispered into place like a dream . . . but a tainted dream, for I was sure it still held an alien trace of Mirrie's disturbing, musky perfume.

I'd taken copious notes on the fabric and construction while making it, plus lots of photos, so those were easy to add, under its catalogue number:

Dress 12
A Titania-Inspired Dress
Without the Fairy-Tale Ending
2018

Now it was just one more dress in the collection, and I made it feel even more impersonal by writing a brief outline of the story of why it was never worn in the third person, naming no names and missing out the shredded-costume interlude, of course.

At some point I'd write the wording for the small information cards that would be displayed next to today's dresses, and email them over to Pearl, who would print out and laminate them. Honey intended writing the big storyboards with sensationalized histories of the exhibits herself.

Looking out of the window, I saw that the courtyard was full of long shadows. It was definitely time to finish for the day and think about dinner.

And someone else agreed with me, for a horrible, ululating scream issued from the direction of the sitting room: Golightly was singing for his supper.

29

Box of Delights

It was only when the cat was tucking into his posh nosh that I realized quite how tired I was. The thought of cooking anything more adventurous than beans on toast seemed way too much of an effort.

However, before I'd even rummaged in the drawer for a tin opener, there was a ring at the door and I found Thom and Simon on my doorstep, bearing wrapped and mouthwateringly fragrant parcels of fish and chips.

'We've been to the chippy and thought we'd get enough for three, in case you fancied some,' Thom said.

'How can I resist, when the very smell makes my knees go weak?' I said, stepping back to let them in.

'Does it? Maybe I should try that on Pearl?' Simon said. 'Or on second thoughts, perhaps not, because she isn't a fan of them.'

They followed me into the kitchen where Golightly, who obviously was a fan of fried fish, appeared like a smoke-grey wraith in the utility-room doorway.

Ignoring Simon, he headed for Thom and wound himself sinuously around his ankles.

'He definitely likes you. He's only done that to me once,' I said, feeling slightly jealous.

'Or he knows I'm the softest touch?' he suggested.

'That's probably it, because I saw you feeding him prawns out of your sandwich at lunchtime,' Simon revealed.

'Snitch,' Thom said amiably, pulling up a chair.

'He was over at your place today, then?' I asked.

'Yes, he turned up just as Simon and I were having a late lunch in my workshop. Maybe Jester told him, telepathically.'

'He seems to be coming and going quite happily, and not straying away.'

'I think he'll hang around home territory, like Jester,' Thom agreed. 'I could see you through the workroom window once or twice, and I thought you'd be lost in costumier's heaven.'

'I was,' I said. I'd poured out orange juice while they were unwrapping the parcels. We didn't stop for refinements like cutlery, just ate the food straight from the cartons with our fingers, except for the mushy peas at the bottom of the tub when we'd finished dunking our chips: we needed spoons for that.

'This is great,' Simon said, sneaking the last few of my chips when I began to flag. 'And I much prefer the smell to linger in your cottage, rather than mine, because I'm always afraid it will waft down to the workroom and impregnate the hats.'

'*Impregnate*,' repeated Thom, then grinned. 'Sounds as if they might have very strange offspring!'

'Well, you know what I mean,' Simon protested. 'Maybe I should have said *permeate*.'

'How *is* the hat trade?' I asked, putting a big tub of peanut butter ice cream on the table by way of dessert.

'These days people mostly only want hats for race meetings, weddings and special events, especially royal ones. Of course, there's an endless demand for fascinators, but they're hardly any kind of creative challenge,' he said gloomily. 'I can make a little bonnet for the Maria Marten puppet, though, if you want me to. I'm just so grateful you've taken over making the marionette costumes!'

'That would be really helpful. I've researched the dress for that period and I'll show you a picture of the sort of thing I'd like after we've finished.'

'*My* order book is fairly full, especially considering I'm currently working single-handed,' Thom said. 'There are always repairs and restringing requests, too. Pearl's going to expand our website with a selling page when she's less busy setting up the museum site for Honey. I finally persuaded Bruno to let me sell marionettes online, though I'll need to build up a bit more stock before I go live with that.'

'We are really busy and I'll need to make some more miniature costume mannequins for the V&A shop as soon as I have time. Honey thought I should make some wearing replicas of the dresses in our collection too, but I'm not convinced any of our visitors would buy them!'

'Oh, I think they might prove surprisingly popular,' Thom said. 'She suggested *I* make marionettes for you to dress in replica wedding gowns, too, didn't she?'

'Yes, but I think both the mini mannequins and the marionettes will be a bit expensive for impulse buys from the museum shop, though they might sell better online later on,' I suggested. 'At the moment, I'm mostly planning ahead to when the museum is open and I go part-time, because I'll need to earn more from my own work. So it's good to have plans.'

I showed Simon the kind of simple bonnet I thought Maria Marten would have worn and forwarded him the link, before he and Thom went off to the pub together. I declined their invitation to go with them, because I wanted to skim through Honey's basic information on the remaining dresses again, so I'd be ready to measure them up for mannequins next day . . . and then, perhaps, if I wasn't too sleepy, read another instalment of Rosa-May's journal, which I did, until Golightly decided to lie on the laptop keyboard.

When I slept that night, Rosa-May's story and the strange, sad, mysterious, poignant or unexpectedly funny tales of bridal misfortunes were all jumbled up in my dreams.

*

I was up and in my workroom very early on Tuesday morning, feeling a bit like a child on Christmas Day: all those Pandora's boxes to open, even if only briefly, before somehow making myself close them again!

First, however, I sent over to Pearl the content for a couple more show cards. No sooner had I pressed Send, than up popped an email from Derek.

He must be an early bird, like me, and already in the Pelican House office, because he said he'd put in the order for those first mannequins. I thanked him and replied that there would soon be a whole lot more, but I thought I'd get the most urgent ones first.

Duty done, I was free to make a start on dresses two to eleven, and I thought I might as well tackle them in numerical order. The more modern ones would be quick and easy to measure, but there were also some antique costumes – not by any means the traditional white wedding dress we expect now – that would take much longer.

As I worked, laying out each one in turn on my cutting

table, I tried not to dwell on the intricacies of their construction, or their histories. There would be time enough for that later, although the condition of some of them made it hard to keep my mind focused on the task in hand. They appeared the products not so much of bridal misfortunes, but catastrophes!

The last one was especially poignant . . . but finally, by late afternoon, they were all safely returned to their boxes or garment bags.

Pearl rang just as I was packing up for the day to say she'd already printed out the information cards I'd sent over to her and would laminate them next day, but she also wanted to remind me it was book group night.

'I thought you might be so busy you'd forget.'

'I had, but I'll come. Golightly seems to be so much happier and more relaxed now he can go out during the day, so I don't feel so bad about leaving him.'

'I'm sure he'll be fine. The meeting is at Thom's cottage this time and we're going to discuss favourite children's books.'

'That sounds like fun!'

'What's that weird noise in the background?' she asked.

'Golightly. He wants his dinner, so I'd better go,' I told her and rang off.

When I'd fed him, I decided on impulse that I'd have a light meal at the Pink Elephant – I deserved it!

To my surprise, I found the Rev. Jo-Jo in the teashop, seated in one of the booths at the back of the room.

She beckoned me over. 'Do join me! I'm afraid having afternoon tea here is my guilty pleasure, but I'll feel so much better if you're indulging in one, too!'

'I was thinking more of something savoury,' I said. 'But now you've mentioned it, I don't think I can resist!'

'The full works, with finger sandwiches, scones and cakes?' she said happily. 'That's what I've ordered.'

'Then I'll have the same.'

I gave my order, then Jo-Jo explained that she usually had tea there on a Tuesday, before visiting a former parishioner who now lived in Great Mumming. 'There isn't time after that to have anything to eat before the book group.'

'I came here on impulse – I just felt I deserved it after a hard day's work. Also, it's a reward because I managed to resist dwelling on the stories that lie behind all the dresses in the collection while I was measuring them for display mannequins.'

'I look forward to finding out all about them when the museum opens, which Pearl tells me will probably be mid-October.'

'Yes, the fifteenth! That's what Honey has decided, and I suspect she usually gets what she wants,' I agreed. 'It doesn't give me long to get everything ready to go on display.'

'I've just been to see Pearl, because she had some books for me, and she told me about the family connection between you and Honey, and how you discovered it through an exhibition about a mutual ancestor – a Regency actress! It was all quite enthralling!'

'That's right. It was only because Honey found some items in the attic related to Rosa-May Garland and loaned them to the V&A Museum that we found out. Of course, I knew I was a descendant, because I was named Garland after her, but Honey had no idea of my existence till then.'

'And now you've left your job as a theatrical costumier in London for a new life here in Great Mumming? That must be quite a change? Of course, you are not entirely among strangers because as well as Honey, Pearl mentioned that you were previously acquainted with dear Thom, who we are all busily pretending we don't know was once a famous actor!' She beamed, her round face rosy. 'The plot, as they say, thickens!'

'Thom and I knew each other as children, then met again later in London, but until the day I moved here I hadn't seen or heard anything of him for six years and had no idea where he was. It was . . . quite a shock.'

'But a good one, I hope?'

I looked across the table at her and there was something at once so clever and kind in her grey eyes that I felt an unstoppable urge rise up in me to tell her the whole story of my life *and* Thom's, since they were inextricably intertwined.

Really, I don't know what had got into me lately! Ever since I'd met Honey, I seemed to have gone from preserving a clamlike silence about my past to babbling on about it at the drop of a hat.

Anyway, my mouth seemed to have taken on a life of its own, because before I knew it, I was explaining all the events in the past that had finally led me to this point in time – and I mean *everything*. Out it all poured: our happy childhood, then the trauma of my parents' deaths and our separation. Our new lives apart, in very different, but equally alien environments. How we'd eventually come together again in London and instantly been best friends, closer than any brother and sister.

Then there was the relationship between Thom, his stepbrother Leo, and Mirrie Malkin, which had been finally broken first by Mirrie's infidelity to Leo and then Leo's death, and, before that, how Thom had blamed Marco and Leo's other London friends for leading him into drug and alcohol dependency . . . which in turn, when I told Thom I'd fallen in love with Marco, led to our estrangement.

'And we still hadn't made up the argument before Leo died

from an overdose, after which Thom just vanished from my life.'

I petered out at this point and looked uncertainly at her. She had been nodding and making encouraging noises throughout, but it must have seemed a tangled and incoherent story.

'I'm so sorry for unloading all that on to you,' I said. 'I don't suppose it even made sense!'

'Oh yes, I managed to follow it perfectly,' she assured me. 'What a terrible trauma you and Thom suffered as children, when your parents were killed – and poor Thom had already lost his own mother by then, too.'

She shook her head sadly. 'It was bound to affect all your future relationships. And then, of course, I can understand why he would have been hurt and angry that you had taken up with this Marco.'

'He didn't believe me when I assured him Marco had changed. I was sure at the time that Thom was holding something back and now I know what it was: the affair Mirrie was having with Marco when she was married to Leo.'

'I see. And since the three of them had become so close on the film sets, that must have been a severe blow to him,' she said. 'But he should not have held that information back from you.'

'No, he shouldn't . . . though I was so madly in love with Marco at the time, it might not have made any difference,' I said honestly. 'I think if Leo hadn't died, Thom wouldn't have completely cut contact with me, although of course I can see now that with Marco around, our relationship could never have been the same.'

'Very true – but do drink your tea before it gets cold,' Jo-Jo urged me, and I suddenly realized that I must have been eating my way through my confession, because the cake stand before me was almost empty!

'So,' she said, pouring herself a last cup from the teapot, 'Thom vanished up here to make a new life for himself and you stayed in London with Marco, pursuing your own career?'

'We got engaged and I threw myself into my work. Then when the Rosa-May Garland exhibition opened at the V&A, I took Marco to see it and it inspired him to write a new play, *A Midsummer Night's Madness*.'

I stopped and looked uncertainly at her. 'If you don't mind listening to me going on, I think I'd better tell you about the last part of the sorry saga.'

'Yes, do go on if you want to,' she urged. 'I'm very happy to listen.'

'Thom, Honey, Pearl and Simon all know this part,' I said, and launched into the scene at the theatre, which had brought down the final curtain on my engagement and my career.

When I'd finished, Jo-Jo leaned forward and patted my hand, saying warmly, 'You poor child!'

There was such kindness and understanding in her voice that it brought tears to my eyes.

'I hope Great Mumming will provide a safe and happy haven for you, just as it has for Thom, and I'll pray that you find it in your heart to forgive him for leaving you in an agony of worry about him for so long.'

How well she understood me!

'I *have* forgiven him with my head, it's just my heart that's taking a little time,' I said wryly. 'When I saw him standing there in his workshop doorway on the day I arrived, I felt such a rush of mixed emotions that I wanted to kill him and hug him at the same time!'

'I can imagine,' she said with a twinkle. 'But I'm sure God

meant you to find each other again, and forgiveness will come in time.'

'I expect it will, but we can't turn back the clock and resume the same close friendship we had before, can we? Things seem the same on the surface but . . . perhaps not underneath.'

'No, you can't pick up where you left off, but there's no reason why you shouldn't create a new and stronger relationship, is there?'

'That is pretty much what Thom suggested the other day.'

'Then why not try? The foundations are there. If you accept that he did what he did because he thought it was in your best interest, however misguidedly, you should be able to forgive him.'

'I can try,' I agreed.

'I think you have something worth the attempt, Garland.'

She looked at the table, empty apart from used crockery and crumbs, and sighed deeply. 'My inner woman is replenished, and now I'm off to visit my former parishioner – and if it's a good day, she will know who I am . . . and if it's a bad one, she'll just eat the box of chocolates I take her and stare at me as if she's never seen me before!'

Then she added benignly: 'Thank you so much for sharing your story with me, and may the Lord bless you and help you find the way to happiness and contentment.'

The booth did feel as if it had been a confessional and I'd certainly indulged in a long bout of spiritual blood-letting.

As I watched her leave, I felt quite shattered, but also, quite suddenly, filled with a burst of probably totally unfounded optimism!

*

I detoured by way of Rani's Minimart on the walk home, to replenish my supplies of ice cream in case I should be in need of comfort food later. Simon seemed to be a bottomless pit, as far as ice cream was concerned, and after three helpings last night had scraped out the last bit in the tub.

Golightly demanded his dinner with menaces as soon as I appeared, but I locked the cat flap before I fed him. I wanted him to get into the habit of staying in after dinner, although actually his day's activities seemed to exhaust him so much that it probably never crossed his mind to go out again.

Tonight he fell asleep on the armchair while only halfway through washing the dinner off his whiskers and didn't even stir while I was getting ready to go out.

I was curious to see Thom's cottage. It occurred to me that if the book group rotated around all the members' houses, I'd have to get a couple more chairs, and make that loose cover for the sofa.

I arrived at Thom's front door at the same time as Simon and Pearl, and since the vicar, Baz, Derek and Ginny had all just appeared in the entrance to the mews, we waited for them.

'We look like a bunch of out-of-season carol singers!' Jo-Jo said, as Simon rapped on the door. I'd felt a little shy at meeting her again after pouring my heart out like that earlier, but she beamed at me so kindly when she caught my eye that the feeling immediately evaporated.

When Thom let us in, I was surprised to find his cottage was much bigger than mine. It stretched back a long way and I could see through a door at the far end of the living room into a kitchen beyond.

The room was cosy in a slightly Scandinavian way, with pale, natural wood floors, lots of sheepskin rugs, walls painted a sort of soft, misty blue-grey and a real log burner on a small stone hearth.

The furniture was all beautifully handcrafted in natural wood, and I recognized one or two pieces from his London house.

The warm day had turned into a chilly evening and the stove had been lit. Jester, who had been lying in front of it, got up to greet us enthusiastically.

'Sit down, and I'll make us some coffee,' Thom said. 'I forgot to go out and get anything to eat, but I've got some biscuits somewhere . . .'

'It's OK,' said the Rev. handing him a large white card cake box. 'I stopped at the bakery earlier and thought I'd buy a cake, because my house is too far away to hold the meetings there, and it's only fair I should chip in.'

'You didn't need to – but cake is always appreciated!' said Thom, opening the box. 'Chocolate, too – my favourite.'

'The book group will be at Simon's place next week – he has a flat over the workshop,' Ginny told me. 'Then Baz and Derek's, then me.'

'I could have the one after you in my cottage,' I suggested. 'It will be a bit of a squash, but there should be enough room – if we can persuade my cat to give up his favourite armchair.'

I offered to help Thom with the coffee out of sheer curiosity to see more of the house, and Pearl came, too.

The kitchen was long, very modern and well-equipped, with a dining table at the further end in front of glazed doors. I wandered down to look out on a small gravelled yard with pots.

'We're lucky on this side of the mews because we have tiny gardens at the back,' Pearl said, putting the cake on a plate, while Thom switched on the coffee machine. 'These cottages used to have their own outside loos, too – the height of luxury at the time.'

'I suppose it was,' agreed Thom. 'When I bought this house, it had a dingy little bathroom leading right off this kitchen, but I had that moved upstairs.'

'Honey did the same in mine, which is why I've got a utility room but only one bedroom,' I said.

Back in the living room, when we'd all been provided with coffee and cake, we settled down to a lively discussion about our favourite children's books.

When I confessed that I often still read my Enid Blyton, especially the Adventure series, Baz said he did too, and we rambled around Beatrix Potter, E. Nesbit, Arthur Ransome and many others, before moving forward in time to more recent offerings.

'I like Ursula Le Guin,' said Ginny. 'And anything with dragons in it . . . and of course,' she added, with a sly look at Thom, 'I *adored* the Silvermann books. So much better than the films!'

'I've never read them,' said Thom blandly and probably truthfully.

'I've only seen the films,' I said. 'And ages after they came out, because I was brought up miles from a cinema. They weren't really my cup of tea, either. A group of special children brought up in isolation from their parents . . . an alternative world with invisible monsters that might or might not exist – I found it all very baffling.'

'I haven't seen any of them, or read the books,' said Pearl. 'But I do reread *The Box of Delights* by John Masefield and the Narnia chronicles of C. S. Lewis.'

'How about *The Lord of the Rings*?' said Baz. 'Would you call that a children's book?'

'No, I'd call it a boring adult trilogy with a distinct lack of decent female characters,' retorted Ginny, and we were off again into a wider discussion.

After an hour or so, we all adjourned to the pub, only pausing briefly at Fallen Idle so Pearl could sell Jo-Jo a copy of *The Box of Delights*, which she had expressed an interest in reading.

Rosa-May

Captain Fairford told me that he had been staying at the home of his elder brother and his wife, who lived in a remote part of the Lancashire moors, in order to recover from a serious injury to his leg. He was lodging in town with his fellow officer, Captain Wentworth, in order to see a medical man, for he was eager to rejoin his regiment on the Continent.

Then he laughed and said his brother was such an old woman about his own health, that he had persuaded himself into becoming an invalid, while his wife was sour-faced and disapproving, so there was no fun to be had at Up-Heythram Hall!

He added, with a very speaking look, that he was now even more glad he had bolted to London for a few days, since he had met me. Then he squeezed my hand, which he had drawn through his arm, and I felt the strangest sensations . . .

As we wandered on along the romantically lit pathways of the gardens, I found myself confiding in him, as I had to no other, about my unhappy childhood at Nettlefold – not too far removed from his brother's house – and my escape from Bath to eventual success on the London stage.

He laughed and said I was a woman of spirit and he wished he *could see me perform, though he had heard much about me before we had so fortuitously met.*

When I remarked that our acquaintanceship must needs be short, for he would soon have to go back north, or rejoin his regiment, he said that he was not yet fit – and as to returning to his ancestral home, the longer he delayed it, the better!

Instead, he proposed to spend as much time in my company as I would allow.

All this was said with the most speaking glances from his hazel eyes. I felt a momentary doubt, for this was the kind of proposal I had only too often received. He may have felt my slight withdrawal, for he added that his intentions were strictly of the most honourable kind.

30

Bridal Paths

The first thing I did next morning was compile a list of the second and much larger order of mannequins, though I had to do some online searching of specialist suppliers first to find exactly what I wanted. Some of the dresses were far from standard modern sizes, and one of the brides in particular had been tall and quite substantial.

I added a couple of extra mannequins to have in stock, and also a much larger dressmaker's dummy than I already had, then sent the list and all the information to Derek, to run past Honey.

I'd be displaying some of the veils separately and I wanted to consult George about the best kinds of stands for the purpose, but I could do that later. I hadn't been through all the boxes of accessories yet.

Duty done, I was finally free to bring in the large archive box labelled:

Dress 2
Pregnant First World War Bride
Late November 1918

I'd only lifted out the dress from the top yesterday in order to measure it, but underneath, wrapped in tissue, were the surviving accessories and a copy of the written account of its history, which apparently had been passed down in the family. A great-granddaughter had donated it.

There were no wedding photographs, though that was hardly surprising, given that the bride went into labour at the altar and, after the shortest exchange of vows in living memory, gave birth in the vestry.

It sounded funny in retrospect, but I'm sure it wasn't at the time. The couple had got engaged during the groom's last leave and she found herself pregnant after he'd returned to his regiment. They were unable to marry until he came home at the end of the war. By then, the baby was due any day, a wedding had been hastily arranged, and the baby *just* managed to be born in wedlock.

They called her Mary, although there hadn't been anything of the Virgin Birth about her conception . . .

I spread the dress out on the cutting table, deeply grateful to whoever had had the presence of mind to wash it after the ceremony, presumably plunging it straight into cold water, for it was a lot less stained than you might have expected. There were signs of repair to rips in the skirt, too. Really, you could read the whole story of what happened simply by examining the dress.

According to the information with it, the bridal gown had been made by the village dressmaker for an older sister, and then adapted quite skilfully to the pregnant bride's fuller figure and large bump. The original dress was ivory silk taffeta and inserts of an *almost* matching fabric had been added to the skirt and bodice, along with extra ivory glass beading to fill in the gaps in the geometric pattern.

After that, the whole dress was covered in an overlay of chiffon, which rather cleverly pulled it all together.

I thought the original dress must have been quite loose-fitting and with a fairly straight skirt, so you really had to take your hat off to the dressmaker's clever remodelling!

I examined the long, fitted sleeves finished with lots of fiddly little self-fabric covered buttons at the cuffs. Then, turning the dress over, I undid the hooks and eyes that closed the back, some of which showed evidence of having been wrenched open and then mended. You can learn a lot from the inside of garments: the costumier or dressmaker's contrivings laid bare.

Perhaps it was the bride's sister, whose dress it had originally been, who had rescued and washed it – and maybe mended it, too, unless that was the bride herself, later – though I don't know why they did that, because obviously no one else was ever going to wear it. That part would have to stay a mystery.

Still, after all the drama, the marriage was apparently a long and happy one and the couple went on to have four more children.

While I was working I'd been taking notes and photographs, including close-ups of the fabric, any damage and repairs. Finally, I put it on to one of the dummies and took more snaps from all angles, thinking that really the marks of damage were surprisingly minimal considering.

I turned to the rest of the contents of the box. The white shoes were probably borrowed, since they showed signs of wear, but had been trimmed with taffeta and bead flowers to match the dress.

The only other thing in the box was a long, folded veil – in fact, very long, when I laid it out on the table, with a very pretty front of fabric flowers.

It was absorbing work and I'd only stopped long enough for

a quick sandwich and coffee at lunchtime, because the howling of my stomach sounded like a whole pack of ravening wolves.

Later, when I'd just carefully packed everything back into the box and replaced it on the shelf in the back room, I became conscious of the distant sound of workmen doing something or other, coming from the direction of the museum.

Then I heard Honey call from the staff room: 'Garland, are you there? If you aren't in the middle of anything, do come out and see the new sign they've just put up!'

'On my way,' I called back, and went out through the foyer, where both pairs of double doors were open, and down the steps, to admire the large new sign, which read:

THE WEDDING HOUSE
A LITTLE MUSEUM
OF BRIDAL MISFORTUNE

The logo of a wedding cake house, split down the middle, from top to bottom, was painted on one side and it gave the opening times and days underneath.

'Perfect,' I said. 'And those pots look wonderful too,' I added, noticing that they had now been planted up with large, bushy curry plants.

'I thought the whitish foliage and yellow flowers would look interesting against the antique effect of the terracotta pots,' Honey said. 'The gardener was all for clipped box trees but I find those so boring – and box smells horrible, anyway.'

She pointed out two car parking spaces for the disabled just outside the door. 'Those can be booked in advance via the website, and everyone else can park in the market square. Getting a wheelchair over these cobbles would be hell. I'm having a ramp made for one side of the steps, too.'

'You seem to have thought of everything!'

'There'll always be something I've forgotten and there are still a few small finishing touches to the inside of the museum to be done, too. The display units will have to be fitted when they arrive and the electricians will sort out the lighting inside them. I want a spotlight shining down on the Bloody Bride's dress.'

'Then all I have to do is fill them up with the dresses,' I said. 'Easy-peasy!'

She grinned. 'With all the ones you'll have finished by then, anyway. How are you getting on? Derek showed me the latest list of mannequins we need, so I know you've made a good start.'

'Well, they're all measured, but now I've begun a more detailed examination of each one, so that'll take a lot longer. Some of them are more complicated than others, or will need extra attention,' I said. 'I've just completed the first one, from 1918, and it really needs nothing much more than a gentle pressing before it goes on display.'

'I'm sure by opening day you'll have completed work on most of the dresses. And don't forget we'll already have the kernel of the collection ready to go out: the Rosa-May material, my dress, yours and the Bloody Bride's!'

'That's true,' I conceded. 'I hadn't thought of it like that. Everything still has to be set up, though – not to mention the reception desk and shop.'

Honey made a gesture as if brushing my objections away like cobwebs. 'The first of the renovated display units arrives this Friday and most of the rest at the start of next week, so, providing we meet all the rules and regulations relating to buildings open to the public, there should be no problem. I'll set Derek on to that. He so enjoys wrestling with bureaucracy.'

I hoped she was right and I said I, too, would do my best, but without cutting any conservation corners, since George, when he came to visit, was bound to notice.

'Fair enough,' Honey said breezily. 'And anyway, I expect once we open we'll get a stream of donated dresses, so your work will be ongoing. In fact,' she added, 'we'll probably start to get more once I mention the museum when I'm promoting my new paperback, *Bloody Young Men*. It comes out on October the fourth, not much more than a week before the museum opens its door.'

I was feeling a bit dazed by now, but she was unstoppable. 'Of course, I'll be including the story behind the Bloody Bride's dress, too. It would be great if the mystery got resolved through the museum, wouldn't it?'

'Yes, it would, but don't you think you should start calling her by her name, Amy Weston, rather than her tabloid tag? What with *Bloody Young Men*, it might all be a bit too much . . .'

'You're right, and of course I need to remember that she *is* a real person and not a fictional one. Still, any publicity might stir up people's memories and resolve the riddle.'

'Or it might just stir up a lot of murky stuff,' I said, and then shivered slightly, for no particular reason.

*

Before I finally stopped work for the day, I switched on the computer and updated the museum catalogue with all the new information from my notes.

Then, as I got up to stretch, thinking about my dinner and a quiet evening in, my mobile rang and it was Miss McNabb.

'Would that be you, Garland?' she asked, sounding even more Scottish than before, if that was possible.

'It would – I mean, it *is*,' I replied, thinking she'd probably rung to ask after Golightly again.

However, she immediately launched into an account of a phone call Marco had made to her that morning.

'He got my number from the letting agency, so they'll be getting a piece of my mind, and no mistake!' she said grimly.

It was like Marco to weasel private information out of people!

'What did he want?' I asked, though I was fairly sure I already knew the answer.

'My address, because he seemed to assume you were with me in Scotland, of all things! So, of course, I told him you were not, though he took a bit of convincing.'

'He's mad! I can't imagine why he should think I was with you,' I said. 'But I'm sorry he bothered you.'

'Nae bother! I told him I didn't know where you were, and wouldn't tell him even if I did.'

'Quite right. I *don't* want him to know, though he might work it out eventually. He's been trying to contact me and I've been ignoring him in the hope he'll lose interest and stop.'

'Since he is so persistent, perhaps it might be best to reply to him just the once, to tell him to cease bothering you?'

'I think I might have to,' I agreed, and then told her all about Golightly's adventures in the great outdoors.

*

Thursday was officially my day off, but I wanted to carry on working in the morning, before my trip to Jericho's End with Pearl, Thom and Simon.

First, though, since it was market day, I went out very early and bought fruit, salad and some rather nice cheese, before searching out the fabric stall I'd spotted last time.

It had had a lot of vintage-style furnishing fabric, and I hoped I might find something there I could cover the sofa in.

I fancied something over-the-top chintzy, and by great good fortune the woman on the stall had an end roll that was *perfect*, though I'd probably have to cover the cushions in something different, to tone with it.

I staggered back home with the bags and the bolt of cloth, which was almost as tall as I am, and as I thankfully let myself into the cottage Golightly nearly sent me flying by coming out to meet me and twining himself round my ankles.

There was a time for random gestures of feline affection, and this was not one of them . . . unless, of course, he really was trying to trip me up.

After I'd put everything away, I spread the fabric over the back of the sofa to admire the effect, which was everything I wanted. I'd wash and press the old cover, then take it apart to make a pattern from it and, once the pieces were cut out, it would just be a question of machine-sewing a lot of long seams.

But meanwhile, it was still early and the call of the workroom and the next of the dresses was irresistible.

Dress 3
The Bombed Bride
1940

This was another war bride, but a later one, and a sadder story.

The young couple were both Londoners and had been engaged before the start of the war. He became a fighter pilot, while she moved out of London to the country when the German bombing raids got severe, to work on her uncle's farm.

They decided to get married in the village church while he was on leave in mid-September of 1940 and the bride had already had her dress made from the silk of a damaged parachute her fiancé had given her.

Honey had made a note at that point, saying that so far as she could discover, this was the first instance of parachute silk being used for a wedding dress. Perhaps the newspaper reporting of the events that followed put other brides off the idea, in case it was unlucky, for one German plane, unable to get through to drop his bombs on London, instead released them over the village just as the wedding was taking place.

One landed right next to the church, at the moment when the groom was taking the bride's hand to put the ring on her finger . . . and when the surviving members of the congregation dug them out, they were still holding hands, crushed to death under the rubble.

They were buried together in the churchyard and the gravestone engraved with the words: 'In death, they were not divided.'

It was all so sad that as I carefully laid the dress out on the table, I felt tears come into my eyes.

Someone else had also taken care of the dress, for it had been cleaned before it was packed away, though the rips and tears in the ivory parachute silk bore mute evidence to the tragedy.

The dressmaker had made the most of the silk and it was cleverly cut in panels, which must have been difficult, given its origin.

The skirt was longer at the back and didn't flare out much, but instead was gathered in at the waist. The lightly boned wrap-style bodice had a high neckline, with no collar.

Self-covered buttons closed the back and the cuffs of the long sleeves, which were full at the top and then tapered to the wrist.

She must have looked lovely in it and I'm sure the groom thought so too. I hoped they'd had a moment of total happiness as he took her hand before the altar.

Like whoever packed the dress away, I was not going to make any attempt to repair the damage and it would be displayed as it was.

I made my notes and took my photos, then covered the table with a clean light cotton dustsheet. The rest would have to wait for tomorrow, because it was time for me to get ready to go out.

The prospect of ice cream and angels sounded an irresistible mix.

31

Veiled Illusions

We went to Jericho's End in Thom's car, since Simon's was an old Mini and it would have been a bit of a crush with the four of us.

Not that Thom's car, a Suzuki Swift, was that much bigger.

'I don't drive very far these days and I've never really been into cars, so this does me fine,' he said, as we headed out of town past Arthur's Cave and Terrapotter.

'My Mini's all I need most of the time too,' agreed Simon. 'Though sometimes I go a bit further afield. There's a great fabric shop in an old mill about an hour's drive away, Garland. If you like, you could go with me next time I'm over there.'

'Love to,' I said. 'I meant to look online for the nearest fabric and sewing supplies places, but I haven't got round to it yet.'

'Have you found Sew and Sew?' asked Pearl.

'That tiny sewing shop up a backstreet?' I said. 'I had a look, though it's mostly sewing machine repairs and embroidery kits.'

'Handy if you run out of anything basic, though,' Simon said.

'That's what I thought. Of course, I know all the big London suppliers and you can buy anything you need online now, but sometimes you just want to mooch around for inspiration and bargains.'

'Or feathers, in my case,' said Simon. 'I never seem to have enough feathers for rush orders.'

We'd left the town behind now, and the farmland on either side was turning from arable to scrubbier sheep grazing as we climbed towards the distant moors.

But after a couple of miles, Thom took a turn off to the right, down a lane so narrow I wouldn't have spotted it except for a cluster of signs at the entrance.

'This is the only way in and out of the village, apart from a really hairy back road,' he said.

'You don't call *this* hairy?' I demanded, as he shot down the narrow strip of tarmac, which had ditches and steep banks on either side.

'It's never very busy, except in the school holidays and at weekends,' Pearl assured me. 'And there are hardly any buses – two a day, I think.'

'*Buses?*' I was amazed anyone would try and get a bus down there!

Presently we rounded a bend and could see the village and the bright silver ribbon of a river in the valley below.

Thom pulled into a car park next to some ancient ruins on the outskirts and switched off the engine.

'Here we are,' said Simon. 'The village carries on up the hill, round that bend, but the physic garden, ice-cream parlour and Fairy Falls walk are over the humpback bridge to the right. I vote we have ice cream first, then do the waterfall walk.'

'You would want ice cream first,' said Pearl. 'But that sounds OK to me. I think we'd better leave the monastic ruins and the physic garden for another day, if we're going up to St Gabriel's church on the way home.'

'Good idea,' agreed Thom. 'I always want to spend hours in the garden. It reminds me of the Chelsea Physic Garden, which was about the only thing I missed when I left London.'

Then he gave me a wry sideways glance and a half-smile. 'Well, perhaps there *were* one or two other things.'

I said nothing, though I couldn't help remembering all the times I'd walked in that garden with Thom, and how we'd sit talking over lunch or tea in the café. Happy memories.

I remembered, too, that we'd seemed to be spending more and more time together before the row, although he *had* been away at his cottage for several weeks before it. I'd felt lonely without him, which was how I'd come to be at the party where I met Marco . . . and I really couldn't imagine now why I'd fallen so hard for him!

We walked down from the car park to the narrow hump-back bridge, which was on the opposite side of the road to a large and thriving-looking pub.

'It's called the Devil's Cauldron after the huge, deep pool below the bridge,' Pearl explained.

When I stood in the middle and looked over the parapet, I saw the mesmerizing rush of dark water cascading down into the pool, swirling and churning, as if stirred by a giant hand.

I'd probably have carried on standing there indefinitely, except that Simon's yearning for ice cream got the better of him.

The café, Ice Cream and Angels, had an old ice-cream seller's tricycle parked in front, the cold box over the front wheel now planted up with bright flowers, and there were tables outside. But we went in so that I could see the pictures for sale on one wall, painted by the proprietor's sister.

They were strange and semi-abstract depictions of what might have been waterfalls and small winged creatures . . . all illusion rather than substance.

'The whole history of ice-cream making is on the other wall,' Pearl said, as we sat down at a table in the window. 'They still have all their old equipment and make their own ice cream in really interesting flavours.'

'Their coffee's excellent too,' put in Thom.

He was right. We all had cups of frothy, delicious coffee, served with biscotti, and then big glass sundae dishes filled with the ice cream of our choice. Mine was rose, but Simon had three different scoops: mint chocolate, raspberry and lemon.

'That may not have been the healthiest of late lunches, but it was certainly delicious,' Pearl said, as we went to the counter to pay.

'Oh, all my ingredients are wholesome and natural,' said the small, elderly, turquoise-haired woman who had taken our order and now sold us the tokens we would apparently need to get through the turnstile to the riverside walk.

'It was really scrumptious,' I assured her. 'I need to come back several times, so I can work through the flavours!'

We went through an ornate Victorian cast-iron turnstile that clanked importantly, then made our way up a gravel path beside the river, while Thom explained how the scenic little valley had once been hugely popular with Victorian day-trippers, then, between the wars, became an artists' colony.

'It fell out of fashion after that and got a bit run-down, but it's become a real tourist hotspot again more recently.'

'There's more to attract the visitors too, now the gardens are open to the public,' Simon put in.

The path was becoming narrower and rougher, the further

we got, and it skirted round outcrops of rock, the thick roots of ancient trees and clumps of thorny gorse. The valley itself began to narrow, the trees closing in on either side.

We finally arrived at a viewing platform at the bottom of the Fairy Falls, which thundered down from a rocky precipice a long way above. The old painted iron railings along the edge were shiny and slick with damp.

We only stopped there briefly, before Thom led the way up an even steeper and rougher path that eventually brought us, hot and breathless, to a stone shelf that jutted out a little, edged for safety with more of the painted iron railings.

Once I'd caught my breath and looked around, I thought there was something magical about this spot.

The water poured straight out of an opening in the cliff face and rainbows danced in the sunbeams that slanted through the leaves. But the very air itself seemed to quiver, as if it was just a taut, invisible veil between ourselves and another, more ancient world . . .

I can't really describe the effect it had on me, but Pearl seemed to feel it too and moved quickly to lean right over the edge of the railings, as if she'd caught sight of something wonderful.

I saw Simon take her hand and pull her back a little, then retain his grip on it, as if afraid she might suddenly take it into her head to try to fly away.

I looked at Thom, only to find him watching me curiously.

'It's quite some place, isn't it?' he said. 'It has an atmosphere all of its own.'

'It certainly has – as if you've stepped into another, mystical world and anything outside it has faded away into unimportance.'

'Do you want everything else to fade away?' he asked gravely.

I said, honestly: 'Only the last six years, when I let Marco derail my life. I can see now that I was never truly happy during them, but it's hard to put them out of my mind completely when Marco is still haunting – or maybe that should be *stalking* – me.'

Then I told him how Marco had tried to track me down through Miss McNabb. 'I thought he'd finally got the message when I didn't answer any of his calls, texts or emails.'

'I think he's got a gall, trying to contact you at all, after what he did!'

'Oh, but he blames that all on Mirrie and says I misunderstood the situation. He's also magnanimously prepared to forgive me for ruining the Titania costume.'

'Big of him!' said Thom.

'Actually, before it happened, I'd begun to have some serious doubts about our relationship anyway. We were so different, I couldn't see how we would make things work. So, in a way, I suppose Mirrie did me a favour.'

'Marco must be missing you, though, to persist in trying to contact you.'

'What he seems to be missing is my input into his play writing! He used to bounce ideas off me and I finally managed to persuade him to turn his latest play into something more mainstream, not the sort that gets good reviews and short runs in tiny fringe theatres.'

He laughed. 'But it worked. This one is a success, isn't it?'

'According to Will, it is.'

'Will is still emailing you, then?' Thom said, and I thought he looked at me rather closely.

'I've only had a couple of one-liners from him recently, along the lines of "Great reviews and the theatre critics adore my performance as Oberon!" I don't feel any need to answer those, so I think his emails will slowly peter out.'

Thom smiled suddenly. 'I quite liked him when he worked on one of the Silvermann films.'

'He's kind under that waspish exterior,' I agreed. 'He'll fade out now I'm based so far from London and out of the theatre world, and if I can get rid of Marco too, there won't be anyone from my past to pop up and haunt me.'

'What about Miss McNabb?'

'She only rang to warn me about Marco's call. Now she's successfully landed me with the cat, there's no reason for her to keep in touch.'

'I like Golightly,' he said.

'If you want to adopt him, I won't stand in your way,' I told him. Then added, 'He always *loathed* Marco.'

'Good judge of character, then.'

'Yes, well, I've already *said* you were right about Marco all along, so you needn't rub it in! I do hope he doesn't suddenly turn up in Great Mumming, though.'

'I'll see him off for you if he does,' he promised grimly.

'It's not that. I'm worried that if he spots you, he'll tell everyone where you're living now.'

'You know, I think the others were right the other evening; it doesn't really matter any more if people know where I am. Those films were so long ago – *and* overtaken by the whole Harry Potter phenomenon! – that no one is going to really care that I was once Ivo Gryffyn.'

I thought he underrated public interest in what had happened to him, although probably not to the extent that Great Mumming would be besieged by avid fans.

'Let's hope he doesn't turn up anyway, seeing he's part of a past I've been trying to forget about. Miss McNabb suggested I should answer his email and tell him straight out to leave me alone from now on,' I said. 'Perhaps I should, since he doesn't seem able to take a hint, like being totally ignored.'

'She could be right. Threaten him with going to the police and informing them that he's stalking you. That should do the trick!'

Then Thom smiled down at me, his eyes like the darkest amber sprinkled with gold dust . . . and the air seemed to quiver again around us.

'I'm just so happy we've found each other again, Garland,' he said softly, putting his arms around me. 'And this time we won't let each other go, will we?'

'No, we must never lose each other again,' I agreed.

His arms tightened around me and he seemed about to say something else – but then I definitely heard the beating of wings and faint, far-away silvery laughter . . .

'Did you hear that, too, Thom?' I whispered. 'Wings and . . . voices laughing?'

'Are you away with the fairies, Garland?' asked Simon, breaking the spell. I hadn't heard the other two approaching, but there they stood, still hand in hand.

'Pearl swore she once saw one here – or an angel,' he continued.

I gave a sort of shiver, but it wasn't fear or cold, just a coming back to reality.

Thom let me go and said, 'It's a place steeped in old magic and it's easy to believe in an alternative reality up here.'

'That's how I feel, too,' Pearl agreed, and now I saw her more closely, she looked strangely abstracted, as if some new idea had come into her and she wasn't sure what to make of it.

'Come on, let's go and visit the real angels up at the church,' she added, seeming to give herself a sort of mental shake, but I noticed she didn't release her hand from Simon's until we reached the better path below the falls.

I suspected it had only just occurred to her that Simon was in love with her, and that she herself might have feelings other than those of friendship towards him. But mixed up with that was probably a feeling that, by acknowledging it, she would somehow be betraying the love she'd had for her late husband.

If so, that was at least a step in the right direction . . . so long as Simon didn't try and rush things.

*

Despite Pearl's protests, Thom drove us up to the church by way of the scary back road he'd mentioned earlier – and it really was scary, because as well as being narrow, rough and steep, with hairpin bends, there was a deep storm drain on one side and a sheer drop on the other.

Eventually it brought us out on the edge of the larger village of Thorstane, where, by some historical quirk, the ancient little church of St Gabriel's, with its squat, square tower and air of having grown there, lay just outside the parish boundary.

'Jo-Jo has two even smaller churches in the middle of nowhere, as well as this one,' Pearl said.

'If this is the parish church for Jericho's End, the parishioners must have had a lot of stamina to climb up the hill to it,' I said.

'Oh, there's a much easier path running up from behind the pub. They used to use that,' Simon said.

The church was unlocked. There was no sign of the vicar, or of anyone else, just a great sense of age and peace.

The interior was simple, with white-painted walls, dark wooden pews with carved ends, and beautiful old windows, especially the Gabriel one.

He occupied the window behind the altar, centre stage, as it were.

'You can tell who it is because he's holding a lily,' Pearl informed me.

'Yeah, and that banner with his name on is a dead giveaway, too,' put in Simon with a grin, and Pearl gave him a look. He said hastily, 'Nice white frock, though.'

'Robe,' she said, though the corner of her mouth twitched.

'I like all the jolly little angels flying around in the top part,' Thom said. 'The one in the pink robe is my favourite.'

I peered upwards. 'I think I like the one in yellow. He looks as if he's about to blow a raspberry.'

'I sit and look at that window every Sunday morning,' said Simon. 'Generations of villagers must have done that too, so it's not surprising there's this whole angel or fairy business over the waterfall.'

'Perhaps not,' I said, thinking the church would be a lovely venue for a wedding – one with just the closest of family and friends in attendance.

I crossed my fingers and hoped it might be Pearl and Simon's, one of these days.

*

When we got back to the mews, Pearl said she had some work to do and would see us all in the pub later, then vanished into her cottage, leaving Simon looking after her like a kicked puppy.

'I'll see you later, too. I must go and spend some time with

Golightly,' I said, and turned away, although Thom paused to say something to Simon before catching me up.

'What did you say to him?' I asked curiously.

'Don't rush things – give her space,' he replied.

Two minds with but a single thought.

*

At the pub that night I had the most delicious gnocchi for dinner.

Afterwards, I felt pleasantly tired and relaxed, which was probably the fresh air and exercise, but also, more surprisingly, I felt at home, so that I had to remind myself how short a time I'd been in Great Mumming.

As well as the immediate circle of Thom, Simon, Pearl, Derek and Baz, Honey and Viv had also come over for dinner and I spotted Ginny, too, with a group of very New Age-looking friends.

There were a few more vaguely familiar faces, probably from the local shops.

'You know, I already feel as if I've been here for months, if not years,' I said.

Pearl, who was looking cool and remote again, said I'd fitted in like a piece of the jigsaw they hadn't realized was missing.

'What a lovely thing to say!' I exclaimed.

'It's quite true, now I come to think about it,' Simon agreed.

'Yes, it only needed a small, explosive redhead to make life here complete,' Thom chipped in. 'Plus an alien being, masquerading as a cat!'

Rosa-May

In a matter of days, Guy had swept me off my feet. Indeed, it was like being caught up in a hurricane and my wits were entirely addled by love. The fear of losing him even overcame all my previous terrors arising from the married state . . .

Looking back, it was a kind of madness. Sara told me so, although Letty thought it all truly romantic.

Guy obtained a special licence and on 16 May we were quietly married. I was supported only by Letty and Sara, and the latter disapproved so profoundly that she issued dire warnings of the consequences right up to the altar.

I wore a pelisse and bonnet of celestial-blue velvet, which Guy said exactly matched my eyes, and a spotted muslin dress with the new style of sleeves.

Guy was attended by the friend with whom he was staying, Captain Wentworth, who thought it all a great jape and prophesied that I would enjoy the life of an army officer's wife, following the drum across the Continent, just as much as being on the stage.

Of course, there were many private matters that had to be settled in a rush. It was lucky that I had completed my current contractual obligations in London, without yet having signed one for my usual touring appearances.

Mr Blake, of course, could not be happy to lose me, and at such short notice, but with his wife's encouragement gave me a parting gift of the costume I wore as Titania – which, due to my small and slender frame would not have fitted anyone else – and a set of coloured plates depicting Oberon and two or three of the other performers in costume.

It was when Mr Blake said to me that he would now, of course, place my financial affairs in my new husband's hands that it came home to me how very much my life was about to change.

Apparel suitable to the rigours of my new life was procured and Guy presented me with a pair of small calf-bound books with invitingly blank pages, in which to write my impressions of my new life.

Guy had written to his brother to tell him of his intention to marry me and that this event would have come to pass by the time he received the letter.

To this, came a reply that although they could not approve of the marriage, yet since it was done, they would consent to receive us at Up-Heythram Hall.

I was sure he and his wife considered this a great act of condescension! But disapprove although they might of Guy's marrying an actress, the deed was done, after all!

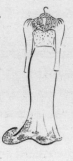

32

Taking Shape

That night I slept heavily and dreamed about Rosa-May again, which was hardly surprising since I'd read some more of her journal before turning in . . . not to mention having eaten rather a lot of rich sauce with the gnocchi, followed by a large slice of lemon panettone.

Rosa-May seemed to have shot to stardom and rapidly become the darling of the stage. At first it was evident she had such a fear of childbirth that she had never seriously considered marriage. But now, she had suddenly abandoned both her career and fears for love, and intended accompanying her soldier husband when he rejoined his regiment abroad. Up to this point in her journal she'd displayed a single-minded determination that had reminded me of Mirrie, but now I couldn't help thinking she was more like me, when I fell in love with Marco and lost the thing dearest to me – my friendship with Thom.

I'd woken just as early as usual and, although slightly less refreshed, felt keen to get back to my work.

Golightly appeared equally keen to wolf down his breakfast and then vanish outside, so he was happily falling into a routine, too.

The mews was quiet apart from a sudden flurry of birds taking off in the central garden, presumably as Golightly reached it. I took my second cup of coffee through to the workroom, setting it down carefully on the desk out of harm's way.

Dress 3 still lay under its dustsheet on the table, and I took that off for a last look, before carefully packing it up with lots of acid-free tissue paper and putting it to one side, while I explored the accessories in the box.

There were no shoes, but the veil had survived, although as torn as the dress itself. It was revealed to be very long and layered, when I spread it over the table, and I thought it was an old one, repurposed. A band of flowers made from ivory parachute silk had been added to the front, to tie it in with the dress and, just like the dress, it would not be mended but left to tell its own story.

As I was about to put it back into the box, I made a very poignant discovery: one white rose from the bridal bouquet had been pressed between two sheets of blotting paper and card, tied together with white satin ribbon.

When I'd restored everything to the stockroom, I checked my watch and decided I had time to make a start on the next dress before the first of the display units from Priceless Interiors arrived. They were coming from North Wales, so I didn't think they'd get here before noon.

These units were mainly from the ecclesiastical museum and Honey hadn't seen them, except the online photos, so I was curious. Besides, this first lot included all the display cases for the Rosa-May Garland Room, which needed to be finished and ready in time for the return of the exhibition material from the V&A, or George would be in a froth of worry.

I decided on another coffee and then I returned to work,

ready to deal with Dress 4, which was a lavish Victorian affair. The sheer size of the storage box alone gave me some hint!

Dress 4
An Unequal Marriage
Servant Girl and Elderly Magnate
1890

When I first saw that heading in the catalogue, it had sounded like a marriage entered into for the wrong reasons and I thought I could guess what they were: either an elderly and rich master, taking advantage of a young woman of an inferior social status or, on the other hand, a young woman taking advantage of an elderly, besotted and vulnerable master. The reality was totally different and, in its way, not really a bridal misfortune at all, for it had led to a surprisingly happy and successful marriage.

Luckily, letters written between the couple whenever they were apart, and other family documents, made the whole story and the relationship between them plain.

The wedding must have caused a scandal at the time and the couple seemed to have made a point of making it as lavish as possible, presumably with the intention of showing that this was no hole-and-corner affair.

The dress was very much the focal point of the show they were putting on and it was highly fashionable, but in an extravagant American style, so that I thought the groom must have had close business connections there.

It was of pale blue silk satin and faille. At that time, it was not unusual for other colours to be used for bridal dresses, and blue was popular.

The bodice was tightly corseted down to a narrow waist, one smaller than any of my dressmaking dummies, even my own.

The sleeves were puffed and gathered at the top, then quite tight to just below the elbow.

I spread out the skirt, which was straight down at the front but had a longer train at the back, admiring the contrasting textures of the silk satin and silk faille panels, which were repeated in the bodice.

The whole gown was embellished with beading and satin ribbon, which concealed the small, self-covered fabric buttons down the back and fastening the cuffs.

The construction was absolutely beautiful and I'd just turned it over to undo the myriad little buttons so I could examine the inside of the bodice, when an unmistakable commotion outside heralded the arrival of the display units and I had to toss the cotton dustsheet over the dress and dash off into the museum.

There was no sign of a van outside, which was presumably too big to fit through the arch, but four men were noisily man-oeuvring a large, blanket-wrapped display case over the cobbles on a wheeled trolley, watched by Honey.

There was some swearing – or it sounded like it, though I wasn't quite sure because it was in Welsh – as they carried it up the steps.

I flattened myself against the foyer wall, out of the way as they somehow managed to cram it into the lift with one of the men, while the rest ran up the stairs to meet it at the top.

'They started really early and made good time,' said Honey, who had followed them in. 'I've already given them coffee in Pelican House and showed them the attics, because there were a couple of ancient chairs and that huge glass-topped bureau thing in the next room to be cleared, which looked like their cup of tea. They're going to have a better look on Monday, when they bring the other units, so I won't let Arthur take any-thing other than the obvious junk until then.'

'Can't they take them now? It would make clearing the next room a lot easier.'

'No, they're off after this to collect some gigantic kitchen cupboards from a stately home further north. Besides, we might have found some other things in the first room for them to see by then. They offered me good prices for those two shabby old armchairs.'

'I hope you haven't already let Arthur take anything valuable by mistake.'

'No, I'm sure I haven't, but from now on I'll email pics of anything potentially interesting to Priceless Interiors.'

When the men came back down and trooped past us, one of them said to Honey, 'Those cobbles are a bugger!'

'Well, you knew what the access was like from when you collected the natural history museum furniture,' she pointed out.

'I expect we'll manage,' he sighed, and followed the others out.

*

Two hours later, everything had been brought in, unwrapped and placed in more or less the right position.

The wooden cases had been renovated and polished to perfection, the plate glass sparkled and the brass locks gleamed like gold.

Honey went out to see the men off and I skirted the huge, handsome, L-shaped reception desk that now sat in the middle of the foyer, along with some display shelving, and then went into the Rosa-May Garland Room.

It now contained two large, full-length glazed cases and three shallower, half-glazed ones, with cupboards underneath. There was also the glass-topped curio table that was to display the journal, and the big rectangular case in the middle of the room, which looked oddly like a giant inverted fish tank.

The place suddenly looked like a room in a museum now. In fact, it reminded me a bit of the Brontë Parsonage Museum in Haworth; it had that sort of feel about it.

Honey joined me there a few minutes later and eyed the fish tank speculatively.

'I'm certain the two trunks will fit in that, with the lids open,' she said. 'They're quite small.'

'Perhaps we'll find a few things from the right period, like parasols and gloves, to help dress them up with,' I suggested.

'Or perhaps fans?' added Honey. 'Though replicas would do because they'd only need to *look* right.'

'I think the Jane Austen Centre in Bath sells those and possibly other odds and ends that would be useful. I'll check out their website later,' I said.

'We'll have to sort out the keys to everything, although they're all labelled. The curio table, the desk and the shelves in the foyer weren't from the ecclesiastical museum, so they have a different set. I'll get a big key cupboard for the staff room.'

Then she went on, more briskly, 'Let's go upstairs and get an idea of how it will look when it's finished.'

Most of the big units for upstairs were still to arrive, but in the Bloody Brides room it was the same mix of full-length display cases and shallower ones as downstairs, though instead of a central fish tank there was a big octagonal glass case.

This would display Amy Weston's dress and you'd be able to examine it from all angles, because the door was of mirrored glass.

'When the rest of it arrives, we'll have plenty of space to display everything we have, but there'll still be room for expansion later,' Honey said.

'When are the electricians coming in again?'

'Allegedly this afternoon, to make a start on lighting the display cabinets,' she said. 'And I've invited Derek, Ella and Kay to a meeting here tomorrow morning at ten thirty, if that suits you, Garland?'

'Yes, of course – good idea. We're going to be a team, so it will be good to meet everyone.'

'I'm sure they'll all have lots of constructive suggestions to make, Kay especially, since she used to run that small folk museum.'

'Yes, she has to be the expert in the running of a small museum,' I agreed.

'I left Viv poring over the latest update you've made to the wedding dress catalogue – she's increasingly fascinated,' she said. 'But she'd already made a big batch of madeleines first thing, and said she might pop over with some for you – and right on cue, here she is!' she added, as Rory appeared from the Rosa-May Room, claws clicking on the parquet floor, closely followed by Viv, who was carrying a small plastic box.

'I just told Garland about the madeleines, Viv,' Honey said, bending to stroke Rory's grey head as he looked adoringly up at her. 'I don't remember inviting *you* in here, though,' she told him sternly, and he wagged his tail.

'I think he only came with me because he watched me put biscuits in this box,' Viv said – quietly, but not whispering today. 'These are for you, Garland.'

She handed me the box and I thanked her.

'These will be such a treat!'

'I just really enjoy baking and we can't eat it all ourselves.'

'I have a damned good try, though,' Honey said with a grin. 'It's just as well I have the kind of metabolism that burns the calories off.'

'Honey told me you'd seen the updates I've been adding to the catalogue,' I said to Viv. 'Would you like to come and see the dress I'm working on at the moment? I was in the middle of it when the furniture arrived and it's an interesting one.'

'If I won't be in your way?'

'Not at all! In fact, if you don't mind, you could write the notes for me while I'm examining it, so I don't have to keep breaking off.'

'Of course – I'd love to.'

'I'll leave you to it, then,' said Honey. 'I need some air and exercise while I work out a plot twist, so I'll take Rory somewhere we can both stretch our legs.'

Rory clocked the one important word, 'walk', and, giving a deep bark, ran ahead of her back to the house.

'Sometimes Honey makes me think of Emily Brontë,' said Viv thoughtfully, but I didn't tell her that she herself always brought Charlotte Brontë into my mind!

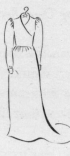

33

Roman Spring

Back in the workroom, I took the dustsheet off the dress and folded it away.

'There we are – dress number four, in Honey's rather random system, and quite a lavish and spectacular one, too! The bride and groom appear to have wanted to make a big show of their wedding, since it was a controversial one.'

'I think I remember the story, with the elderly business owner marrying the young daughter of his servants?' said Viv.

'Yes, that's the one.'

'I had a preconceived idea about the marriage, before I read the copies of the family memoir and their letters to each other, and discovered I was totally wrong.'

'Yes, me too,' I agreed. 'She'd been a clever child and he'd taken a fatherly interest in her – had her educated above her station and then she'd become a sort of secretary to him, if they called them that then. A lot of women were entering that kind of field at the time,' I said. 'But it's evident she had a real business head and became more and more involved in the business. Then, when his health began to fail, he wanted her to be able to take over the firm, since his relatives were only interested in his money. He thought the safest way to ensure her position was to marry her, but it was a marriage in name only, though a very successful partnership, with shared interests.'

'In their own way, I think it sounds as if they had fun,' said Viv.

'The family memoir says she sincerely mourned him and it was not for some time that she remarried – to the son of the junior partner in the firm, another kindred spirit! It's the descendants of that second marriage who donated the dress. They sent a photo of a painting of her wearing her wedding dress and a sapphire necklace her husband gave her.'

'I saw that and it was spectacular!'

'With those sapphires and the dress, she was certainly wearing lots of blue, like in the rhyme,' I said, 'and possibly something borrowed, if the necklace was a family heirloom.'

I handed Viv the pen and notebook, and gave her a quick update on the notes I'd already made about the fabric and construction, before undoing the dress and dictating more notes about the inside of the bodice. Viv was very useful when it came to taking close-up photos, too, holding back the fabric for me.

'It is very lovely, in an over-the-top kind of way,' Viv said when I'd finished and was neatly packing the dress with tissue paper before wrapping it up again.

'It is, and makes a good example of a marriage that was very happy, despite the way it looked to others. It's been stored very well, too: no damage by moths or anything else. I haven't looked at the veil and shoes yet. We could do that now.'

'OK,' she said, and I unfolded the gauzy layers of the veil first.

'A long simple veil, made to hang behind,' I dictated as she scribbled. 'The silver beading matches that on the dress . . . and the edges are ribbon trimmed . . .'

I moved on to the shoes, which were made high to the ankle, with a button closure and low heel.

'Now, these are unusual for the time because, like the dress, they're high fashion in the American style, not the English.'

'They look more like ankle boots,' she suggested. 'And not very comfortable!'

'No, they're so narrow and pointed, aren't they? But they were specially made in the same mix of silk satin and faille as the dress,' I pointed out. 'And embellished with yet more silver beading.'

'No expense spared,' Viv said, writing all that down as I took a few last snaps before packing everything away in the box and restoring it to the rack in the storeroom.

I looked at my watch as I came back and was surprised at the time.

'You've been here for *hours*!'

'I've enjoyed it and it was all interesting,' she said. 'I only hope you can make out my writing.'

'After reading Rosa-May's journal, I think I can decipher anything,' I said.

Viv declined my offer of coffee in the cottage, saying she must get back – possibly because Golightly had struck up an unearthly solo performance.

'But I'd love to meet Golightly another time,' she added, tactfully.

*

Next morning, I had a good catch-up session on the computer, adding the new notes and then writing the information cards to send over to Pearl and her handy laminating machine.

After that, I went into the museum and opened the outer

doors, because the first three mannequins – mine, Honey's and Amy Weston's – were to arrive between half past eight and half past nine.

I left the inner glass doors locked till they arrived, but it was a beautiful morning out there, the sky a pale celestial blue with a few fluffy snow-white clouds. The light streamed into the foyer through the glass doors and the window next to it, making it look light and airy, despite the dark wooden floor and furnishings.

There was no blind on that window – but then, there would be no costumes on display there to be damaged by direct sunlight . . . though actually, it would be enticing if you could see a wedding dress displayed inside, when you looked in.

Not one from the collection, of course, or of any value – sentimental or otherwise – but perhaps something suitable could be found in a charity shop?

I decided to put the idea to Honey. I was sure she would agree, and if we couldn't find anything suitable, I could always run one up myself.

It was still quite early and no sign of Honey yet, not surprising when she usually worked late.

The three mannequins duly arrived in their allotted time slot and I put them in my storeroom, till needed . . . which, at the rate everything was moving, wouldn't be all that far off!

*

I went back to work for a while, until I heard the others arriving in the staff room for the meeting.

Derek, who was armed with a clipboard, grinned at me as I entered.

Honey introduced me to Ella, who was a wiry woman with short, sleek, grey hair and the face of an eager greyhound, and her sister, Kay, who was larger, plumper and had her silver-streaked dark hair done up in a French plait.

'I think I told you that Ella was the librarian here, so she's had lots of experience dealing with the public and also knows all about tills and computer records,' Honey said. 'And so does Kay, having actually been the custodian of a small folk museum in Devon, so you see how lucky we are that they're prepared to take on all the day-to-day running of The Wedding House.'

'It'll be fun,' said Kay. 'I've just moved back here and I'm living with Ella while I look around for a cottage to buy, but we both need something interesting to fill in our time.'

'And *I'll* enjoy being caretaker and general museum dogs-body, because I can fit it round my other work for Honey and a bit of extra income is always welcome,' Derek said. 'Baz and I are saving up to get married and we want it to be *mega*.'

'I really do feel I ought to be paying you and Kay, too, Ella,' Honey said.

'We've already had all that out and we're happy to volunteer – plus perks,' Ella said briskly.

'Yes, the perks are *very* important,' agreed Kay, nodding. Dimples appearing when she smiled.

'What perks?' I asked curiously.

'The main one is that Honey's going to make an arrange-ment with the Pink Elephant tearoom, so after we finish work here every day, we can go straight there and have lunch or tea – whatever we want.'

'And the other stipulation is that a supply of orange pekoe tea is provided for us here in the staff room . . . and dark choc-olate finger biscuits,' Ella said.

'I love those too,' I said, 'but I promise not to touch yours!'

'Some chairs in here would be nice, too,' Ella said slightly acerbically, since we were all standing about.

'Already on the list,' Derek assured her. 'Plus a table large enough to pack orders on, ready for when we start selling gifts online. Then you'll need a desk, chair and a computer in here too, but not a safe, because I'll be coming in at closing time to transfer the takings to the one in the house, leaving only the float for next day in the till.'

'You've got it all worked out!' I said. 'I was afraid I'd have to do most of the running of the museum too, and I've had no experience of that kind of thing at all.'

'Your expertise is better directed elsewhere, Garland, although, I think I mentioned, you may have to take any booked parties round the museum.'

'I don't mind that; I'm always happy to talk about costume.'

I let them peek into my workroom and explained I would leave the door ajar if I was working in there when the museum was open, so I'd be handy if they wanted me. Then we went on a tour of the rest of the museum, Derek making notes of any suggestions, like a strong lamp for the desk in the foyer, which would be in the darker area by the stairs.

'And then I'll need to stock up the big cupboard next to the toilet with cleaning materials, loo paper and paper towels,' Derek said. 'And I fancy one of those big floor polishing machines.'

'If that floats your boat, you can have one!' Honey told him.

'We need a well-stocked first-aid cupboard in the staff room,' said Kay. 'Ella and I have both done basic first-aid courses.'

'We'll consult on that one,' Derek promised, making another note and putting a big ring round it.

When we'd run out of ideas, we went through the passage to Pelican House, where Viv produced tea, coffee and some of her delicious madeleines.

'So, we're all fine with an opening day of October the

fifteenth?' Honey said, and of course we all agreed, which was just as well, seeing she'd already made her mind up to it!

'We'll have a training day when the till has arrived and everything is in place, but you'll all have keys to the museum before that, because of setting up the shop and reception desk and, in Derek's case, playing with the humidity controls and counting his rolls of loo paper.'

'Like a squirrel counts nuts,' he said with a grin.

By the time we parted, I think we were all feeling equally excited about the opening day, though in my case it was slightly tempered by the thought of all the painstaking work still to be done.

It was too late to start anything new before lunch, and anyway, it *was* officially my half-day, so I locked up and went back into the cottage, where I found Golightly fast asleep in his cardboard box in the utility room, snoring wheezily. Curled up there, he looked quite cute in a slightly moth-eaten kind of way . . .

*

I'd just finished washing up after lunch when Thom came round and said he was going to take Jester on a woodland walk and invited me to go with them.

'It's only a couple of miles away and you'll get to see a bit more of the countryside.'

'All right,' I said, thinking a change of scene and some exercise sounded good, and soon we were heading out of Great Mumming in a new direction, with Jester panting excitedly in the rear seat.

We parked near a pub with the intriguing name of the Screaming Skull – apparently some local legend – before hiking up through some ancient and quite overgrown woodland, coming out into a flat, open area where there were the ruins of a small Roman bathhouse, the pool still filled with water and open to the skies.

Thom said you could pay to go in and swim in it, if you wanted to, and there *were* little wooden changing huts.

'I think I'll give it a miss till next summer,' I said with a shiver.

'People swim in there all year round – it's always warmer than you expect.'

'I'll take your word for it,' I said, and we carried on up the path to the village of Halfhidden, where we had coffee and toasted teacakes at a teashop with an open Victorian glass veranda, before hiking back down again.

It had been a really nice, relaxing trip. While we hadn't talked much, our silences had been amicable.

Pearl had texted me while we were having tea and, when I'd told her I was in Halfhidden with Thom, she invited us both to supper that evening, to be followed by a film.

'I suspect Simon invited himself and we're playing the role of double gooseberries,' Thom said.

'Probably, but I expect it will be fun – and another evening when I don't have to strain my cooking repertoire!'

'It'll be fun as long as we don't let Pearl choose the film, because she goes for the ones with sad endings and I've had enough of those.'

'Me too. I'll take a favourite romcom and subvert her,' I said.

*

We had a nice evening at Pearl's. As I was leaving she suggested I might like to go to church with her and Simon next morning.

I said perhaps I would one day, but I wasn't really a church-goer and also had quite a lot to do.

Simon looked relieved. I was sure he looked forward to having Pearl to himself for a little while every Sunday morning!

It might be peaceful and relaxing to go to a service at Jericho's End some time and sit looking at that lovely window, but this morning I planned to cut out the pieces for the sofa cover and start tacking them together.

I spent the whole morning working on it, with the radio to keep me company, and the only time I went out was when I had a sudden impulse to look at the railed garden in the centre of the mews. Golightly escorted me, in a proprietorial kind of way, as if keen to point out the finer points: the ornamental cherry, with a crescent of bedding plants on either side, and the various shrubs. I recognized a rhododendron, but that was about the extent of my gardening knowledge.

Thom appeared at lunchtime bearing the gift of a freshly baked loaf for me – apparently baking bread was now one of his hobbies – and the smell of it was too delicious to resist. I suggested he and Jester come in and I'd find cheese and pickles to go with it.

Jester went to explore Golightly's dinner bowl and practically jumped out of his velvety skin when the cat suddenly popped up out of his box.

Cat-in-the-box again – I think if anyone made them, they'd be a real seller. I put this idea to Thom, who said you could probably buy the mechanism and maybe he'd give it a go one of these days.

*

Our second attic clearing session, like the previous one, was exhausting but fun.

Honey decided we wouldn't try to clear a way to the things in the second room that Priceless Interiors had spotted, because she said they could do that themselves, if they were really interested, and it would make it much easier for us to work in there once they'd taken what they wanted.

Instead, we concentrated on finishing the first room, which went a lot quicker than last time, mostly because there were no more pieces of monumental Victorian furniture to shift.

Once again, we didn't find any hidden treasures, though Honey took a fancy to a small marquetry table, and said she'd find somewhere to put it. There was a dismantled ancient carved four-poster bed, too, which she decided to get Priceless Interiors to renovate for her.

'It can go in one of the guest bedrooms,' she decided, and I thought how much George would love that!

My only bit of excitement came when I opened a battered tin trunk and found it filled with an odd jumble of clothes and other items.

Thom suggested it might have once been a dressing-up box for the children of the house, because there was such a mishmash of things: a parasol; gloves; a long black cloak, a little moth-eaten; a hat with a cockade; and a large cartwheel hat, adorned with puffs of net and disintegrating fabric flowers.

I picked out some gloves, two fans and the parasol, then discovered a large paisley shawl at the bottom.

'I think these are more early Victorian than Regency, but they'll do for dressing Rosa-May's trunks when they go on display.'

The moths must have attacked the cloak before it was put in the trunk, because everything else was mercifully free of holes, but I thought I might just try the old trick of sealing everything in a plastic bag and leaving it in a freezer for twenty-four hours, just in case. Honey said there was room in hers and we put them in when we went downstairs.

George would probably faint at the thought, but there was nothing in good condition, or of any great value.

Later, over our takeaway, Thom said he'd heard from Bruno.

'His rheumatism is much better since he's been going to a thermal spring for hot mud baths,' he said with a grin. 'He wanted to know how I was doing with the orders and what new work had come in.'

'Hetty's just the same,' Simon said. 'She might have retired, but she hasn't lost interest. I'll tell her about the cartwheel hat. She probably wore one just like it when she was a girl.'

Honey had given him the hat, since he was very taken with it, but she said mildly now, 'I don't think Hetty is quite *that* old, Simon!'

Then she asked Pearl how the museum website was coming along.

'It'll be up and running well before you open and we can add the online shop later, if you want to,' she said. 'I've been laminating the information cards as Garland's sent the copy over. I'm trying to keep on top of those.'

'I still have several dresses to go, so there'll be quite a few more,' I told her.

'Great!' said Honey with satisfaction. 'And I'm writing the story of each dress for the big storyboards that will be dotted around the rooms . . . and maybe we could have each one printed on a separate sheet to sell in the shop.'

'I could print those as A4 landscape and then fold them into three,' suggested Pearl.

'That would look good. Even if we only charge fifty pence for them, it all adds up,' I said. 'Not everyone buys an expensive glossy guidebook.'

'I'm still working on that, too,' Honey said, 'not to mention, making plans for the opening day. I thought I'd have a book signing session in the foyer for my new paperback, *Bloody Young Men*.'

She turned to me: 'Speaking of bloody young men, Garland, Marco rang me earlier.'

'How on earth did he get your number?' I said.

'He managed to weasel it out of my agent, by spinning her some story, though it's not like her to give out personal information, so let's hope she isn't getting loose-lipped in her old age . . .'

Viv, the silent member of the party, now made a small squeak, which might have been agreement.

'I suppose he wanted to know if you knew where I was?' I asked.

'He assumed you'd have kept in touch with me, although fortunately he didn't seem to know about the museum, so he didn't suspect you were living and working here.'

'I did try to tell him about the museum once, but he wasn't listening, so I gave up. He was only ever interested in costumes and my work when it was directly connected to one of his plays.'

'He sounds very self-absorbed,' said Pearl.

'He is,' I agreed. 'I take it you didn't tell him I was here, Honey?'

'No, and luckily I'm immune to charm offensives. He really *is* a silver-tongued snake, isn't he?'

'That does sum him up pretty well.'

'I told him I hadn't heard from you for ages and I'd been too busy with my latest novel to chase you up,' she said with her twisted grin. 'I can lie wonderfully well, when I want to.'

'Thank you! I really don't want him turning up here. He's already tried to get my address out of my old neighbour.'

'He's very persistent,' said Simon.

'Miss McNabb – that's the old neighbour – suggested the only thing that might get through to him is if I reply to one of his emails and tell him what he's doing amounts to stalking and he needs to stop.'

'Worth a try,' Honey said. 'The penny is bound to finally drop about your whereabouts when the publicity for the museum reaches him.'

'But he may not see it,' I pointed out.

'Oh, I'm going to be *everywhere* before publication day. He won't be able to miss it,' Honey said. 'What with a new book, the museum and the story of the vanishing bride, I'm going to get a lot of press attention.'

'Thom and I will see this Marco off for you, if he does turn up,' offered Simon.

'I'm more worried about him seeing Thom,' I said. 'He'd go back and tell everyone where he's living!'

'Don't worry about me,' Thom said. 'There are new kids on the block when it comes to fantasy films. I just hope that, unlike me, the child actors really want to be in them.'

Viv gave another of her small squeaks, then suddenly scuttled out of the room.

'What did I say?' asked Thom.

Rosa-May

My lodgings had been given up, my belongings all packed and dispatched north, where Guy said that what I did not need to take with me could be stored.

I said a fond farewell to my friends, especially Letty, and promised to write, but was in every expectation of seeing her on my return to London on our way to rejoining Guy's regiment once he was fit to do so.

We soon set off for the north and Sara came too, as my maid, for she was determined to be with me until I departed for the Continent, when her sister would once more require her assistance. I would be sorry to part with her, for she had always been such an important part of my life.

I was sorry to leave London, too, but my husband was in great good spirits and told me we would return very soon, for not only did he find the company of his brother and his wife uncongenial, he was increasingly eager to get back to active service.

*

Up-Heythram Hall was a long stone building with mullioned windows, and set in an isolated spot on the outskirts of a small village.

The park around it seemed to consist only of scrubby grassland grazed by sheep and a few windblown and spindly trees and shrubs. It quite cast down my spirits, for it was even bleaker and more remote than the parsonage where I had been raised . . . and on the long journey north, after the rush of getting married and arranging to leave my old life, I had time to ponder the enormous step I had taken.

Guy's brother, Rafe, and his wife, Sophia, received us coldly but civilly. Where Guy was wiry and energetic, Rafe was spindly and languid – a confirmed invalid, as Guy had told me and seeming to revel in it. His wife was sour-faced and haughty, although she might have been pretty had her expression been pleasanter, but there was no sweetness in her disposition to make it so.

They were childless and, since they had been married some fifteen years, likely to remain so. Now that my sanity had returned a little, I privately hoped my fate would prove the same.

Guy is merry and laughs at his brother, teases Sophia and calls the house a mausoleum . . . with which opinion I would have to agree.

I was discovering much more about my new husband: he had a most impetuous nature and was in high feather at having succeeded in so summarily carrying me off, against my better judgement and the advice not only of my devoted Sara, but that of Aurelius Blake, who had spoken to me with sincerity and kindness on the subject, before it became clear that nothing could alter my course.

Our marriage accomplished, Guy now began to fret that if he did not get back to his regiment soon, he would, as he put it, miss all the fun, although I would not describe the heat of battle thus!

34

Totally Chilled

The electricians were back early on Monday morning, working in the Rosa-May Room, and when I popped out to tell them I'd unlocked the staff room door so they could make tea, I found someone had screwed a handsome brass plate on the door that read:

**The Rosa-May Garland
Collection**

I'd expected the next delivery from Priceless Interiors to come late in the morning, like the last one, but I'd barely started on Dress 5 – a sixties mini-dress – when Honey sent me a text to say they'd arrived and, after that, the rest of the morning was all bustle and chaos.

When they'd finally departed, bearing some of the contents of Honey's attic away with them, she and Derek came back and we had a good look at the new units upstairs, before I helped strip off the red tape from the floor, which had marked where each was to stand. We left the smaller areas of yellow tape for the moment, because Honey hoped Priceless Interiors would find her a few smaller cabinets to fill in the gaps.

'It's so exciting now the museum's really taking shape!' I enthused.

'Yes, a couple of days for the electricians to sort out the lighting up here and then it's pretty well finished,' said Derek.

'Perhaps by midweek, you might be able to start setting up the first displays?' suggested Honey, with her usual optimism.

'I'll have to wait for all the workmen to leave first, because of dust. Then it'll need a good clean through, but yes, after that, there's no reason why I shouldn't make a start.'

'I've got Viv to help me finish writing the stories behind the dresses for the big display boards now,' Honey said. 'We'll send the stories to Pearl as well, because that idea of hers for a three-fold leaflet was a good one. There's the first glossy guidebook to work on, too. I'll include some of your new information and photos in that.'

'If it's going to be printed in time for the opening, I don't suppose I'll have completed all the collection in time.'

'That doesn't matter, I'm going to subtitle the first brochure as a work in progress, with behind-the-scenes information and photos. I'll just keep updating that as we get more exhibits. There can be a proper guidebook later. And it'll all add to the museum revenue.'

The electricians had now moved upstairs, so we left them in peace and went down again.

'Priceless Interiors told me they might already have found a couple more dark wood display units for the shop and, if they look suitable, they're going to send me some pics when they get back,' Honey said. 'I want one of those rotating metal stands for my paperbacks in the shop, too. We'll look those up in the office, Derek, so come on, we've got work to do!'

*

After the Victorian excesses of the last costume, the white Swinging Sixties mini-dress looked more like a child's party frock!

It had quite a funny story behind it, too, which had made the local newspapers.

It had been a very small, quiet church wedding, with no family present, just a few friends. When the vicar got to the part where he asked the congregation if anyone knew of any reason for the marriage not to take place, a man and a woman, who were sitting separately right at the back of the church, suddenly stood up simultaneously and said they had! Confusion reigned and then the vicar took the young couple, plus the two objectors, into the vestry to sort it all out.

It transpired that both the groom and bride had made very early and short-lived marriages, but not told each other about them, thinking that since they were so long ago and they'd since started new lives in a different place, they would get away with it!

So, this was a dress from a marriage that never was, but it did have a strangely happy ending, because after a while the four protagonists retired to the nearest pub and, after a few drinks, things calmed down. The fact that an instant attraction seemed to have sprung up between the estranged spouses might have helped, because eventually there were two divorces and then two weddings!

I only had the dress from the first wedding, the one that never quite happened, but I did have a wedding photo from the second ceremony, when the bride had gone for the whole hippie look in flowing muslin.

The dress I had in front of me was short and simple, made in a slightly stiff plain white taffeta, with quite a high neckline and some shaping to the waist and bust. The sleeves finished above the elbow, but were overlaid with a layer of white voile that flared out and extended them to the wrist.

Instead of a veil, the bride had worn a floppy white hat adorned with fabric daisies, and long white boots, made of some shiny PVC-style material, that had stiffened and cracked a little.

I thought boot trees would be a good idea to help preserve them, but, for now, I stuffed the insides with tissue paper to give them shape, then put them in a box of their own.

It was the bride herself who'd sent Honey the dress and she'd included a recent photograph of the couple, so it had all worked out well in the end.

*

After a few days without any further direct communications from Marco, he sent me an email late that evening, claiming he was now seriously worried about me, since no one appeared to know what had happened to me – or if they did, they weren't telling him. Then he went on to say that he only wanted reassurance that I was OK and that he was sure if we could meet and talk to each other, all our differences could be resolved. He was missing me more every day and had come to realize how big a part I'd played in his life.

If I gave him a second chance, he continued, he was certain we could make it work this time.

He'd changed his tone in this email to something slightly more conciliatory, but still, I read it with incredulity: did he really think it was likely I'd ever want to see him again, let alone resume our relationship? And what was I supposed to do in London, when no costumier would be likely to employ me?

I decided Miss McNabb and the others were right and it was time to confront him with brutal frankness, because evidently nothing else was going to work.

I began my email without preamble.

Marco, I would have thought it was perfectly clear from my lack of response to your previous attempts to reach me that I do not want any further contact with you. However, evidently not.

I have moved out of London to a new job and have no intention of ever returning.

I am sorry I destroyed the Titania costume, but only on a professional level. After what happened there can be no question of our ever getting back together. I am starting to feel that you are stalking me and if you continue to pester me, I will report it to the police.

Garland

'That should fix him!' I muttered, sending it off, and Golightly woke with a start, before saying something emphatic in Cat, which might possibly have been agreement.

*

The next dress I began, on Tuesday morning, was in the worst condition of any so far, so I'd had to email George, asking for advice.

Meanwhile, so much else was going on that by late Wednesday afternoon, I was in that state beyond mere tiredness, where you feel permanently spaced-out but still wired.

After I'd fed Golightly his dinner – at his very vocal insistence – and talked to him for a while, I found myself wandering back into the workroom, where I'd slipped Dress 6 on to the new large dressmaker's dummy that had arrived the previous day, along with the rest of the mannequins, although they were still aimlessly standing about in the Rosa-May Room.

As well as being in poor condition, this costume had been challenging in more ways than one. The bride was a widow who had had her first wedding gown remodelled in 1910 for her second venture into matrimony.

During its chequered existence since then, not only had it been afflicted by moths, but the descendant of the original owner, who had donated it to the museum, had confessed that she'd tried to eradicate the reek of mothballs (presumably put in a bit too late) by washing it.

This hadn't entirely succeeded, for a faint, distinctive reek persisted, but on the other hand, the dress had survived the process remarkably well.

Luckily, the donor had provided photographs of both weddings, as well as a copy of a memo from the daughter of the first marriage, so it was possible to trace its evolution into the dress before me now, though many clues had also lain under the inner lining.

The original dress was of light green cotton taffeta, with glazed cotton trimmings, made in the style popular in the early 1860s, and intended to be worn for best after the wedding. It had featured elbow-length sleeves, lots of fussy ruffles and a fitted, rigidly boned bodice, the edges of which overlay the separate, bell-shaped crinoline skirt.

I expect there had been some signs of wear and tear from its subsequent use, but if so, they had been hidden by the radical makeover for the owner's second wedding in 1910, though the elderly bride had not chosen a particularly up-to-date style for the remodelling.

The cotton taffeta had been dyed a much darker green and the crinoline removed, so that the skirt now went straight down at the front, with a short train behind. Most of the ruffles and boning had been removed from the separate bodice and it had then been attached to the skirt. The sleeves were shortened and the whole effect of the dress very much simpler.

Given its history, it was amazing it had survived at all, even if it was a bit moth-eaten, as well as limp from washing. I was hoping some gentle and careful steam pressing might revive it slightly.

I hadn't, of course, attempted to restore it in any way, but merely mended the worst of the pulled seams and detached trimmings.

There wasn't much left to do to it now, other than update the details on the computer, but I was still standing gazing in a rather glazed way at it, when the ringing of my phone jangled me back to consciousness.

'Garland?' said Pearl's voice. 'It's well after six and I can see you're still in the workroom from my window.'

'I just came back in to have another look at the dress I've been working on.'

'You must be shattered, because you were already tired enough to fall asleep on Baz's shoulder at the book group last night. Thom said you reminded him of the sleepy dormouse in *Alice in Wonderland*.'

'I was a bit past it,' I admitted. 'It was nice of him to see me home before you all went to the pub, though. I'm even more tired now, but also sort of edgy and restless, if you know what I mean.'

'I do, so I want you to come over and have dinner with me. It's just fish pie and I'll put it in the oven now. You don't have to talk much, or stay long, if you don't want to. It'll just save you having to cook anything.'

'That's really kind of you and I'd love to,' I said gratefully, and went to change and tell a zonked and unresponsive Golightly that I was leaving him to his own devices for a bit.

Pearl had a glass of red wine waiting for me and made me sit down in her cosy sitting room, while she finished off the dinner. We ate it in her kitchen, which was much longer than mine, with a table at the back in front of the window on to the tiny yard, just like Thom's, and probably Simon's, too, if I'd been awake enough to notice my surroundings the previous evening at the book group.

We talked books while we ate, but when we'd finished off the meal with apple tart and thick cream, and returned to the sitting room with our coffee, Pearl said, 'Now, if you feel like it, tell me what's been happening in the last couple of days. You were too shattered to make sense at Simon's last night.'

'Oh, all kinds of things. It's been non-stop since Monday morning,' I said. I filled her in on the delicate Victorian dress I was working on, and everything that had been going on at the museum, before taking a gulp of wine. 'Honey and Derek have been constantly popping in and out of the museum, though they don't usually bother me – unlike Marco, who emailed me on Monday evening, suggesting we should get together again. He seems to think if we could meet, he'd be able to explain everything.'

'That would take a bit of doing!' she said. 'He must be deluded.'

'I'm sure he does believe his own version of events, though even if it was true, it doesn't excuse his actions in letting Mirrie

380

borrow my wedding dress and having an affair with her, however much or little it meant!'

'So, did you reply this time?'

'Yes, threatening him with the police if he kept on stalking me. I think that should fix him once and for all.'

'Quite right too! That has to be the end of it.'

'I hope so. I've got more than enough to think about without him hanging around my neck like an albatross . . . and I don't know why albatrosses should hang around necks anyway.'

'I suppose now the electricians have finished, you can start putting some of the costumes on display, as you finish with them?'

'I can, now Derek's had a clean through after them. When he'd finished, he insisted on showing me all the different ways you could angle the spotlights inside the bigger display cases, although, to be honest, I was totally past taking it in by then. All I really wanted to do was get back to working on that dress!'

'You said it had been a challenge!'

'That was mostly due to all the remodelling when the bride had the dress from her first wedding altered for her second.'

'Frugal!' commented Pearl. 'And a bit . . . weird.'

'I know, but she wasn't wealthy so perhaps she was just being practical. Hers is a bittersweet sort of story, really. She was widowed young and never really got over it. Not to mention that her late husband made her promise on his deathbed that she would never remarry.'

'I think that's a very selfish thing to do,' said Pearl. 'Neil told me he hoped I'd find someone else and remarry. Not that I've even given it a thought since . . .' she added.

'He sounds a lovely man,' I said warmly. 'But it took the

Victorian bride decades to get round to remarrying. Her groom was a former suitor who'd become a devoted family friend when she married her first husband.'

'Faithful Dobbin, like in *Vanity Fair*?' suggested Pearl.

'Yes, but he didn't get his reward until they were both quite elderly and frail. She was increasingly struggling to manage on a reduced income and he was wealthy and wanted to look after her.'

'Sweet!'

'It was, and they seem to have had a few happy years together, even if she didn't exactly sound like a ray of sunshine: apparently she'd worn mourning all those years and although she came out of it for the wedding, that was only as far as dyeing her original light green dress a very dark emerald.'

'Maybe she lightened up a bit after that,' Pearl suggested. 'She wouldn't have to reuse old clothes any more. She could go berserk in lavender, grey or heliotrope.'

'I expect she did, but it's such a lucky chance that we have not only the wedding dress, but both sets of wedding photographs, although the first one is in faded sepia.'

Pearl shared the last of the wine between us and said, 'I still have my wedding dress, though I don't look at it any more. It was made for me by an aunt, so it was exactly what I wanted – plain and unfussy.'

'I'm sure you looked lovely.'

'Neil thought so, anyway,' she said with a sad smile. 'And we were very happy, even if we didn't have long together. We both wanted a second-hand bookshop, so when we opened Fallen Idle we were living the dream. Simon was living nearby with his girlfriend when we first moved here, and working for his grandmother, although before that he'd been with a well-known hatmaker in London. His girlfriend missed the bright lights, however, and went back to the city.'

'And after that, Thom came?'

'We used to see him before he moved here permanently, when he came to work with Bruno from time to time. Then later, he and Simon were so kind to me after Neil died and we became such good friends . . .'

'I could see straight away that they are both very fond of you.'

'And I'm fond of them,' she said, turning the stem of her wineglass round and round, then looked up at me. 'I just hadn't realized until last Thursday that Simon feels differently about me. It never even entered my head until we were at the waterfall. I don't know if you noticed anything?'

'I thought something had changed between you and, yes, I'd realized he had strong feelings for you.'

'It was a bit of a shock, somehow, as if the familiar ground suddenly became shaky underfoot, and I'm not sure I'm ready for any kind of new relationship yet.'

'I'm sure Simon won't try and rush you into anything, but I do think he loves you.'

She sighed. 'I need time to think about it all, because whatever Neil said about my finding someone else, it still feels a bit as if I'm being unfaithful to his memory even thinking about the possibility.'

'Maybe you should have a talk about it with the Rev. Jo-Jo?' I suggested. 'I bared *my* soul to her the other day, when I ran into her in the Pink Elephant, and I felt a whole lot better for it.'

'You know, that's a really good idea! I could ask her to come and have coffee with me,' Pearl said, and tactfully refrained from asking me what I'd wanted to talk over with the Rev.

'I hope you're going to take the day off tomorrow,' she said, changing the subject.

'Just the afternoon, I think, because I have a few odds and

ends to clear up first. What I'd really like to do in the afternoon is go on a hunt round some charity shops for a second-hand wedding dress.'

I explained about my idea of displaying a wedding dress in the foyer, and how it had to be one that didn't matter if the light faded it, or visitors touched it.

'That would be fun and I'd love to go with you! Ormskirk would be the perfect place, because it has a really good dress agency as well as several charity shops. It's their market day too and it's a much bigger one than ours.'

'How do we get there? Is there a bus?'

'There is, but you'd have to change and it's quite a way, so it would be so much simpler to rope in Thom or Simon to drive us.'

I didn't think Simon would take much persuading, but when she rang him, he said he had to wait in for a consignment of hats to be collected, and even from my chair I could hear he sounded disgruntled about it.

But Thom, her next port of call, said he'd be delighted and would treat us both to lunch.

'Is that OK?' Pearl asked me, looking up.

'Never refuse a free lunch,' I said, and I could hear Thom's laughter.

35

Scouted Out

I completed my work on the green cotton dress, finishing with a little cautious steam pressing, but then replaced it on the dummy to air a little more, in the hope the last faint smell of mothballs would finally vanish.

It looked less of a wreck than it had before, even if the signs of wear and tear and the holes were still there.

I pinged over the updated catalogue entry to Honey and then went back to the cottage for a quick coffee, before changing into smarter jeans and comfortable trainers, because I suspected we'd be doing a lot of walking during our charity shop wedding dress quest in Ormskirk that afternoon!

I'd been really looking forward to it, and it wasn't a huge surprise that Simon had managed to change the collection slot for his hat consignment to slightly earlier, so he could come with us.

Ormskirk was a busy little town and the large open market enticing, but over a quick sandwich and coffee lunch, we decided to concentrate on the real reason we were there and we started on our search.

It turned out that Pearl was a connoisseur of charity shops

385

and knew them all, but after three I was starting to despair that we wouldn't find what we were looking for.

It wasn't that we didn't discover any wedding dresses, because the second shop had three, but two of them were so hideous I dismissed them instantly, while the other was a beautiful vintage silk dress that was just too good for our purpose.

I noticed a young woman who appeared to be following us around and I presumed she was on the same quest, though for a more personal reason. I thought that vintage dress might have tempted her, but no, we found her cruising the rails in the next shop, although I spotted the only wedding dress in the place first, hanging on a rail between two peach taffeta bridesmaids' frocks.

Since it was a huge white net meringue, it looked as if it was doing its best to elbow the other two aside.

When I lifted it out, there were actually three hangers tied together: the dress, a long slip that was slinky to the hips and then a mass of ruffled net, and a bag containing a veil.

I untied the string and handed the other two bags to Thom, then, pushing back the thin clear plastic covering the dress, got Simon to hold it aloft, so I could examine it.

It was an off-the-peg one and made entirely of polyester, but the general effect was good, in a ballgown style. The satin top had wide straps, and was fitted to the hips, after which it flared out in layers of gathered tulle and net.

The topmost layer had been hitched up at one side and pinned by a large, limp, white fabric rose. The back closed with a concealed zip and the skirt was a little longer at the back, giving a slight train effect.

'Plastic boning in the bodice . . . and the hook and eye at the top of the zip has been broken,' I muttered, having got Simon to turn it around. 'I think it's been washed, but they should have taken that rose off first, because it looks really sad now.'

'The whole thing looks a bit limp to me, like a dead jellyfish,' Simon observed, only his head and feet showing behind it.

'That's because it needs the petticoat Thom's holding to puff the skirt out and give it enough volume,' I explained.

'I don't think it's Simon's style,' said Thom gravely.

'No, but it will do perfectly for what I want. I can tart up the rose and add an embroidered belt, perhaps,' I mused. 'Let's get the veil out and have a look at that, too.'

It was a short one and quite pretty, with white fabric flowers between layers of tulle.

'There's nothing subtle about the ensemble, but it would make a bold statement standing in the entrance foyer of the museum, or glimpsed through the window,' I said.

'It would certainly be hard to miss,' said Thom. 'Do you want to check out a couple more shops before you decide?'

'No, this is the one,' I said positively. 'I'll buy it.'

'Come and look at this,' called Pearl, who had lost interest in wedding dresses and was riffling through the vintage rail instead, so I left Thom and Simon draped in bridal wear and went to see what she'd found.

'I think this would really suit you,' she said, and when I saw what she was holding up, I knew she was right. The fitted, sleeveless dress even looked my size!

There was a matching bolero jacket with three-quarter sleeves, both in a textured, heavy tusser silk in the particular shade of old gold that really does things for my pale skin, red hair and green eyes.

'Try it on,' she urged, and when I came out of the changing cubicle wearing it, Thom said I looked beautiful.

Simon wolf-whistled, so that everyone in the shop turned round to look, before saying loudly, 'Nice legs!'

'It's perfection! You could wear it for the museum opening,' suggested Pearl.

'I don't know – it might be a bit over the top – but I can't resist buying it anyway,' I said. 'Simon, show her the wedding dress, while I change back.'

When I came out again, Pearl said, 'A big puffy meringue dress wouldn't be *my* choice, but I can see it's perfect for what you want.'

'Excuse me,' said a voice behind us, and I turned to see the young woman with short, spiky, candyfloss-pink hair and matching fingernails, who I'd noticed in the other shops, looking curiously at us.

'I couldn't help overhearing what you've been saying: am I right in thinking you don't want the wedding dress to wear yourself? It's just for a display in a *museum*?'

I gave an inner sigh and hoped she wasn't going to say the dress was exactly what she was looking for and ask me to give it up to her.

'That's right, The Wedding House: A Little Museum of Bridal Misfortune in Great Mumming,' I told her. 'We open in October.'

'Bridal misfortune?'

'Yes, all the dresses on display belonged to brides who had unfortunate bridal experiences of one kind or another. I need a modern dress to go on display in the entrance foyer, where the light might damage older fabrics.'

I thought I'd put that quite tactfully, if she thought this was the dress of her dreams. 'Are you looking for a wedding dress for yourself?'

'No! Like you, I have another reason,' she said, eyeing us with a strangely speculative expression. 'And I think my boss,

Cassy Chance, might be interested in . . . well, a slightly different angle to what we usually do.'

We stared blankly at her.

'You've never heard of her?' she asked, sounding incredulous, and we shook our heads.

'Well, it's like this: I'm Milly Brownlow and I'm a scout for a TV series called *The Upcycled Bride* – you must have heard of *that*?'

'No,' Pearl and I said in unison.

She looked disappointed. 'I suppose it is low-budget and not prime time, but it's very popular. Look, do you think we could go for a coffee and have a chat in that café-bar across the road? Bring your husbands, or whatever, with you.'

She gave Thom and Simon, who were still patiently standing holding their burdens, an appraising look.

'They're just friends,' Pearl said quickly, and I saw Thom's mouth quirk up into a grin.

Milly's gaze sharpened on Thom and she said, slowly, 'You look really familiar . . . just like that actor who used to play Gus Silvermann in those old fantasy films! What was he called? Ivo something.'

Thom sighed and said, in a flat Lancashire accent, 'I know, I get told that all the time.'

We agreed to meet Milly in ten minutes and she went out of the shop, already talking into her mobile, leaving us speculating about why she was interested in the wedding museum – background scenery for an episode, perhaps?

We paid for our purchases – Pearl had found a light blue cashmere cardigan – and then Thom and Simon volunteered to take the clothes back to the car before joining us at the café.

Milly was already there and said she'd spoken to her boss, who was very interested in the museum.

When Thom and Simon appeared and we ordered coffee, she explained that the show featured a bride from a different area of the country in every episode. Cassy and her team helped her to find a second-hand dress and accessories, and also, sometimes, outfits for the bridesmaids or the mother of the bride.

'The bride we had lined up for this area has pulled out at the last minute, so I'm up here trying to find another happy couple and also suss out the local dress agencies and charity shops while I'm at it.'

'I see! I thought you were just a bride looking for a dress, when I noticed you seemed to be on the same quest as us,' I said. 'What happens in your show once they find a dress?'

'Cassy suggests ways of restyling it. She's really good at that kind of thing.'

'I'm not bad myself,' I said modestly. 'Before I took this job at the museum, I worked for a theatrical costumier's.'

'Cool,' said Milly.

'It all sounds like fun,' Simon said patiently, 'but I don't see where Garland and the museum come in, unless you want it for a bit of background?'

'No, I think it would make for a deliciously different episode in itself, and so does Cassy!' she said to my surprise, and turned to me eagerly. 'We can help you find the dress for the display and tart it up, but also "discover" an outfit for you to wear when your museum opens – that gorgeous vintage suit you were trying on. I mean . . .' she added uncertainly, 'I did get it right and you said the museum would open in October? And I suppose there will be some kind of ceremony?'

'It opens on October the fifteenth and I expect there will be a bit of a ceremony,' I agreed.

'And you're the – what do they call them? Curator?'

'I'm the curator-conservator, but the museum belongs to my boss, so you'd have to talk to her about anything like that. She's Honey Fairford, the bestselling novelist.'

Milly's brown eyes widened. 'Better and better!' she exclaimed, then excused herself and went over to a quiet corner, where she spoke urgently into her phone.

'I didn't think we were that exciting,' I said, but it seemed I was wrong, for by the time we left, Milly had Honey's contact details and had headed off purposefully to where she'd left her car for more prolonged consultations with her boss.

Her parting shot had been, 'Don't do anything to that suit or the wedding dress till you hear from us! We'll probably want to plant them back in the shop, for you to find on camera.'

'Isn't that cheating?' I said to the others when she'd gone.

'It's certainly manipulating circumstances to make a good episode,' Thom said. 'I expect a lot of that goes on.'

'I hope they think better of it. I really don't want to be on TV. I'm strictly a backroom girl.'

'It'll depend on Honey,' Pearl pointed out. 'What do you think she'll say?'

'A resounding yes,' I said gloomily, firing off a text to Honey, giving her advance warning in case this Cassy person contacted her before we got back. 'But then, if she does, perhaps she'll take centre stage instead of me!'

*

That evening in the pub, over a lasagne like none I'd ever tasted before, Honey told us all about her long phone discussions with Cassy Chance. As I feared, she was all for the television programme and the brilliant publicity it would give to both her books and the museum.

'But this episode will be a real last-minute rush, because of the original bride pulling out so late.'

She paused to fork in more lasagne, then added, 'So Cassy is dashing up here tomorrow to see the place and thrash out all the details.'

'That is keen!' said Thom.

'It had to be tomorrow, because Viv and I are off down to her cottage on Monday to see about packing it up and we won't be back until Wednesday. One of her husband's nieces is going to rent the cottage for six months, so it's turned out well, and we'll see how we get on, won't we, Viv?'

Viv made a tiny, affirmative squeak, a bit like a toy that had been trodden on.

'A breathing space, to decide if she'd like to stay on at Pelican House, or find a place of her own in the area.'

'That's great,' I said, and Viv smiled at me.

'Anyway, I'll bring Cassy over to meet you sometime tomorrow, Garland.'

'*I* won't have to be in it, will I?' I asked.

'Oh, yes, we *both* will, and apparently you've already found a wedding dress for the foyer and a lovely vintage suit you can wear for the opening. They'll only have to source something for me to wear.'

'That scout, Milly, told me not to do anything to the dress and suit, in case they went ahead with the episode, because the programme is all about this Cassy Chance upcycling the outfits.'

'Yes, she explained that to me, but I told her you were a qualified costumier and I was sure you'd want to add any embellishments.'

'I certainly would! No one is touching my suit. It's perfect as it is.'

'Don't worry, she said she didn't mind if you did the work, so long as it *looked* as if it was all her input.'

'OK, then,' I sighed resignedly. 'I definitely don't want anyone else working on the wedding dress either. I've got my own ideas.'

'Great, I'll tell her,' said Honey brightly. 'I insisted everything was filmed up here, including the reveal scene when Cassy shows off the upcycled dress, which is usually done in London. I'll be too busy then promoting my new book and the museum, and I knew you wouldn't want to lose a couple of days' work on the collection.'

'Absolutely right!' I said emphatically.

Honey grinned at Thom. 'I expect *you'll* want to keep a low profile.'

'Yes, head her off if she shows any signs of wanting to come over to the workshop, though I don't see why she should,' he said. 'I'll keep out of view till she's gone.'

'Viv is going to lay low, too,' said Honey. 'But I don't suppose she'll be here long tomorrow, just in and out to get the lie of the land and sort out the final details.'

'I'll be around,' I said. 'I thought I'd set up my own wedding dress in the Rosa-May Room first thing tomorrow. Then when the material comes back from the V&A next week, it can go straight out without being stored. That will be the first room to be finished.'

'Wonderful,' said Honey.

'I hope to put your dress and Amy Weston's on display in the Bloody Brides room soon, too.'

'Is it really called that?' asked Simon.

'Definitely. I've ordered a sign and it'll be in the glossy

guidebook. No one has ever accused me of letting good taste stand in the way of publicity!'

'There's another slightly bloodstained dress that could go in there, too,' I said. 'The one where the bridegroom rather unfortunately had a massive nosebleed all over it, as he was putting the ring on the bride's finger.'

'Romantic!' said Thom sardonically.

'Put it in there – the more the merrier,' said Honey inappropriately, then hummed a snatch of music.

'You know, I'd really like to have that Billy Idol song, 'White Wedding', playing very quietly in the background in that room.'

I'd listened to that on YouTube after she'd mentioned it before and I really hoped she was joking . . .

*

The first thing I did next morning was to detach the fabric rose from the charity shop wedding dress, then put the dress in a big net bag and wash it in the machine on a delicate cycle.

I was certain it had been washed once already, but a faint aroma of nicotine hung around it and I wanted to get rid of it. Anyway, it was entirely polyester and I was sure would come out perfectly well.

It was finished by the time Golightly and I had eaten breakfast, and then I hung the dress in the doorway to the utility room to dry.

The pale shape swaying there on a hanger reminded me horribly of the Titania costume . . .

I'd found a cleaner's label still pinned inside the gold suit when I got home yesterday, so I'd put it straight into a zipped plastic cover and hung it with the wedding dresses in my storeroom.

I was in love with it! It was so perfect, it might have been made for me, and there was no way I'd let this Cassy woman tart it up for her programme!

I had another cup of coffee before starting work, while reading an agitated text that had just arrived from George, who was overseeing the packing-up of the Rosa-May exhibition and fretting about whether everything was ready to receive it here, as if we were expecting visiting royalty.

I reassured him that the room was finished and ready, and then, once the rattle of the cat flap signalled Golightly's departure into the great outdoors, I went into the museum to find the mannequin for my Titania dress among the many still standing silently in the Rosa-May Room.

There is an art to putting a costume on a mannequin that I was sure George had mastered much better than I had, but with careful easing, the replica gown slid on to it and was fastened – and once it was in its display case, it looked beautiful.

Even if the dress *was* for ever tainted for me by Mirrie's having worn it, it was still an excellent piece of work!

I placed the laminated information card in its clear Perspex holder in front of it, locked the glass door and thought: one down, thirteen – or perhaps that should be fourteen now, if you included the charity shop dress – to go.

Time to get on with the next . . .

*

Dress 7
Hippie Wedding
1970

This was a bridal outfit rather than a dress, and had quite a funny story behind it.

The young couple had gone together to the 1970 Isle of Wight pop festival, where, after smoking a lot of pot, they had decided to get married on the grassy slope facing the main stage. A fellow reveller, who claimed to be a minister in some obscure American church, offered to officiate . . .

The bride and bridegroom wore whatever they happened to have on . . . or not, in the groom's case, because he was only wearing jeans, an embroidered headband and a beaded leather thong necklace.

The bride wore frayed, cut-off jeans, a cheesecloth midriff-tie shirt and a brightly flowered kaftan, open down the front like a coat or a dressing gown. She too had an embroidered headband, and her bare feet were decorated with henna.

It was the bride herself who had sent us the clothes – minus the husband's jeans – and a lovely description of what happened, as well as a photo of the happy couple right afterwards. There was a much more recent snap, too, which I wouldn't have guessed was the same couple, except for the familiar puckish grin on the wife's face.

She wrote:

It was a lovely wedding . . . But afterwards someone suggested we drop some acid . . . and then the police arrested about fifteen of us and held us in a sort of pen for hours, before they let us go. But it didn't spoil it, and when we got home again, we had a registry office wedding too. We're still together and have three children and ten grandchildren, who'll all be mortified if they ever find out what we got up to in the past!

The cut-off jeans and midriff top had seen some wear, but had been washed and pressed before she sent them. I think the kaftan had just been stored away ever since the wedding, because it was in much better condition and still smelled faintly of patchouli.

The only other things to survive were the two embroidered headbands and the husband's leather thong necklace, and, rather touchingly, the fragile ring of woven grass, used at the ceremony.

It didn't take me long to examine those, and after lunch I updated the catalogue and was just putting the archive box away when Honey brought Cassy Chance over to meet me. It was just as well the charity shop wedding dress had already drip-dried by then, because she wanted to see it.

Cassy was a tall, fair, athletic-looking woman of about my own age, with a disarmingly freckled face and friendly smile, but also with a pair of cool and calculating grey-blue eyes and a brisk let's-get-on-with-it manner. Not that that was having any effect on Honey, of course, who seemed to have arranged everything to suit herself.

Cassy had had a tour of the museum and heard some of the stories behind the dresses and the Rosa-May collection. She said she *loved* my Titania dress and wasn't I a clever little thing?

I really *hate* being called 'little' . . .

'Cassy wanted to check out your workroom, to see if it would be suitable for the reveal,' Honey said.

'The reveal?'

'You know, when I bring back the upcycled outfits and some accessories and show them to you. Then you put them on and are blown away by what I've done with them, that kind of thing,' explained Cassy. 'This room will do very well,' she added, looking around appraisingly. 'And Honey says you'll do the changes to your outfit and the wedding dress yourself.'

'Yes, I'd prefer that,' I said, and then fetched the dress and suit to show her.

'I don't want to add anything to the suit, but I have some Bakelite jewellery that will look interesting with it, so I'll only need shoes.'

'I can sort those, if you give me your size . . . and maybe you could make some kind of fascinator or hairband?'

'Hairband, possibly,' I agreed, then told her what embellishments I intended adding to the wedding dress.

'Fine, you can go ahead with that once we've done the shoot of you and Honey finding your outfits in the shop. We've been doing an internet search for something for Honey to wear, so we'll bring an outfit up with us.'

'They're coming back next Friday, Garland, and they'll film us in Ormskirk finding our outfits, then come back here for shots of Cassy arriving to meet us for the first time and discuss what we need. Then that's it until they return for the reveal and some filming inside the museum when it's almost ready to open,' Honey explained.

'Isn't that going to involve a lot of acting?' I said dubiously. 'I mean, we're going to have to pretend to find the dress and our outfits, and *then* pretend we've never met you before when you come back here!'

'You'll be fine,' Cassy said breezily. 'It'll only take a couple of days to film, too, and then later a crew will dash up to catch the actual moment the museum opens, with you both mingling with everyone, and the wedding dress on display in the foyer, too, of course,' Cassy reeled off. 'The credits will roll over that at the end. It's going to make for a great and unusual twist on the regular kind of story!'

I must have looked as reluctant as I felt, because Honey said encouragingly, 'It really won't take up much of your time, Garland, don't worry.'

'I wish the museum was opening earlier so we could move this episode to the start of the series,' Cassy said. 'But maybe if we get most of it in the can, we can add the closing scenes quickly and still get it out earlier.'

'Is that even possible?' I asked, surprised.

'If you're determined enough, anything is possible,' she said, showing all her tombstone-sized white teeth in the kind of smile the wolf probably gave Little Red Riding Hood before gobbling her up.

Rosa-May

Guy had visited his medical man again just before we left London and was persuaded that on our return there, two weeks hence, he would be passed fit for service.

Indeed, he now began to burn with impatience to be off and, as I wrote to Letty, I too longed to shake the dust of Up-Heythram Hall, with its grim, chilly air, lack of congenial society within easy distance, and grudging hospitality, from my feet.

Sophia constantly found fault with my attire, deeming it showy and not at all the thing for the country. But most of my possessions remained packed up, to be stored here – and I certainly had no occasion to wear the beautiful evening dress, inspired by my Titania costume, in which I had first captivated Guy! Sara carefully laid up my finery with lavender against the moths, and we hoped that would keep them at bay till our return.

*

But only a few days after our arrival, events took a sudden turn and our plans were totally overset, for Guy was urgently recalled and was packed and gone the same day!

He left with the promise that he would send his man back for me as soon as possible, but he turned a deaf ear to my entreaties to take me with him as far as London, where I could lodge with Sara and her sister until I could join him. He said it were better I was here, with his family, but I found it hard to believe that he could abandon me to those who were still uncongenial strangers, so soon after I became a bride!

But so it was — and as days turned to weeks, my only amusement has been the writing of this account of my life to date.

36

Will to Succeed

I met Pearl, Simon and Thom in the Pink Elephant just after five on Friday, to tell them how the meeting with the TV person went. Having a light early supper there saved me the effort of cooking anything later, too.

I also asked Thom and Simon if they could come over after lunch next day to help me move the rest of the display mannequins upstairs. That being a Saturday, I thought they'd be working in the morning, but they both said they didn't mind closing up for a while earlier. Pearl, of course, didn't shut her shop till four on Saturdays.

They were to come at ten, which gave me enough time to prepare Amy Weston's dress for display. This was mostly a matter of a little gentle pressing, and finding the information card, plus the right size of Perspex holder for it.

When the mannequins had first arrived, I'd labelled them with the numbers of the dresses that would go on them, apart from a couple of spare ones, which were already in my storeroom.

I knew where they were all going to be placed, so as Simon and Thom took them up in the lift, two at a time, I told them which were to go in where, according to Honey's room plans: Bloody Brides, Great Wedding Disasters and Almost a Bride, which covered most of the exhibits, though the first room by the lift and stairs was left unnamed for anything that didn't seem to fit elsewhere, or was on temporary loan . . .

The silent crowd in the Rosa-May Room, some headless and some not, rapidly dwindled until it was empty apart from the expectant glass cases and the soft silk gauzy shimmer of my Titania dress.

Simon had to go back to his workshop to finish a hat off after that, but Thom said he didn't have anything urgent to do and so would stay and help me set up the Bloody Brides exhibit, if I wanted him to.

'It would be great if you could, because it's always easier with two,' I said gratefully. 'Especially since I usually have to stand on something if I have to fix a veil.'

'No problem,' he said, although actually Amy's dress slid on fairly easily and, once I'd fastened it, it was just a matter of tweaking the skirts that flared out from just below the hips and arranging the train in a swirl behind.

I stepped back to run a critical eye over my handiwork: the final layer of silk tulle over the satin and beading gave it a subtle matte finish and, apart from the spatter of rusty-red marks across the otherwise pristine whiteness of the skirt, it looked rather beautiful.

Thom had to fix the crystal and satin flower headdress on the model's head – Amy hadn't gone in for a veil – and then it was just a case of placing her matching satin and lace shoes next to it and putting out the information cards.

'There,' I said, as he angled the spotlights to best effect. Then I went right to the other end of the building to see what the effect was like from the top of the stairs.

The distant dress hung like a glimmering ghost in its subtly lit central glass case, seeming to draw the visitor towards it. It was only when you were quite close that you could see the ominous stains.

'I wonder what *did* happen to her,' Thom said as I rejoined him.

'I hope nothing horrible, although it is almost a year since she vanished,' I said. 'But perhaps the publicity from this *will* finally solve the mystery, one way or the other.'

I locked the cabinet – I now often carried around so many bunches of keys that I was thinking of switching from jeans to combat trousers, just for the extra pockets – and said, 'Well, that's done. Thank you so much for helping, Thom, but I'm sure I've taken you away from your work long enough for one day.'

'I enjoyed it! You can always give me a ring if you need any help, and if I'm not in the middle of something, I'll pop over.'

'I'm not sure how happy your boss would be about that!' I said dubiously.

'Oh, Bruno wouldn't mind, so long as I'm putting the hours in and the work gets done. And, like you, I'm usually up and working early. Anyway, I hope you're going to take the afternoon off?' he asked, as we made our way back downstairs.

'Sort of. Honey's arranged a meeting at Pelican House with Derek, Ella and Kay, to discuss things like stock for the shop, bags, wrapping paper and price labels, which I'd never even thought about. We're lucky Ella and Kay have so much relevant experience, because it's not really my field.'

'You can't be brilliant at *everything*,' he said kindly.

'Apart from the costumier side of things, I don't seem to be good at anything, not even basic skills like cooking,' I said ruefully, then brightened. 'But Viv's promised to make chocolate brownies to cheer things along at the meeting.'

'Tell her you know a starving marionette maker,' he suggested hopefully. 'Meanwhile, why not come and have lunch with me and Jester now? It's soup *à la* tin, bread and cheese.'

'OK, thanks, I will,' I agreed.

After I'd locked up and we were walking across the courtyard, Golightly squeezed like grey ectoplasm through the garden railings and tagged along.

Another opportunist . . .

*

I had a busman's holiday after lunch, because I began to sew up the long seams of the new sofa covers, using Mum's old and trusty machine. I'd carried it through from the workroom and set it up on my small desk in front of the living-room window, because Golightly had chosen to accompany me back from Thom's cottage, and it would have felt a bit mean to abandon him to his own devices again.

Not that I thought he appeared bothered about having me around any more, now he could come and go as he pleased, and had his new canine chum.

He condescended to play with the feather on a stick toy for a few minutes, when I trailed it enticingly under his nose, but then he lost interest and went to sleep in his cardboard box, so I could get on with my sewing.

I *hate* putting in zips!

*

The meeting in Pelican House was very productive, even if I felt I didn't contribute a lot of ideas.

Honey showed us the rough draft of the glossy brochure she

was to have printed by a local firm, ready for opening day. The title was 'The Wedding House: A Little Museum of Bridal Misfortune: a work in progress'. It described the inspiration for the museum and the process of setting it up, with some of my behind-the-scenes photographs, showing how close examination often revealed hidden secrets about the dresses' construction, or remodelling. She'd also included a few of their stories, although if the visitors wanted more detail, they'd have to buy the separate leaflets for each one.

Once I'd finished work on all the wedding gowns, there would be the standard guidebook too, which could be updated every year with new acquisitions.

'And I'm making notes for a new non-fiction book based on the stories behind the collection,' Honey said.

I was starting to wonder if she ever slept!

As to the finer points of packaging, labelling, the best kinds of electric tills, credit card readers, price labelling and all the rest of it, not to mention the souvenirs we were having printed with our logo, it was just as well that Ella and Kay knew what they were doing!

It was all quite fun and helped along by the delicious chocolate brownies Viv brought in for us, but back at the cottage, once I'd fed Golightly, I felt both tired and restless. So when Simon rang and said Thom and Pearl were with him and they were ordering pizza and why didn't I come over, I agreed, first making a slight detour to the Minimart for a bottle of wine.

I'd been too tired to take much in about Simon's flat when I'd been there for the book group, but I saw now it was very cosy, although still a bit Hetty-ish in its décor, with pleated silk lampshades and flowery carpets.

While we ate the pizza, we watched the David Suchet version of *Murder on the Orient Express*, which we all agreed was the best. Afterwards, when Thom asked if anyone had plans for tomorrow, it transpired that Pearl and Simon were going to have lunch together at the Devil's Cauldron in Jericho's End after church, but they didn't suggest Thom and I join them there, which I thought might be significant: perhaps Pearl's talk with the Rev. Jo-Jo had helped her untangle her feelings for Simon . . .

She was certainly looking slightly self-conscious, and if Simon had been a dog, he'd have been wagging his tail.

Thom must have been aware of the unspoken undercurrents, because he caught my eye briefly, raising one eyebrow, and very tactfully didn't suggest we met up with them himself.

*

Even though I hadn't stayed late, you'd have thought from Golightly's expression when I got back that it was at least midnight and it took me a good ten minutes of abasement before he deigned to take any notice of me, even when I shook the cat treat bag. But after that, he climbed on to the kitchen table via my lap, which he'd never done before, and tried to sit on the laptop while I was deciphering the next instalment of Rosa-May's story – and it had just got to an interesting point after her marriage, when the reality of her new life was starting to sink in, so I began to wish he'd stayed miffed.

I had to remove him from the keyboard twice before he gave up and stalked off into the living room, but my eyes were too tired by then to read any more of Rosa-May's tiny crabbed writing. Before I turned off I checked my emails and found one from Will. I'd only had a couple of one-liners from him recently, and thought he'd soon forget all about me, but no, this was another long one.

Garland darling!

Do tell me where you are, and if it's within reach of London, I'll come and take you out for lunch one Sunday, the Cockleshell Theatre's closing day.

You must know by now that you can trust me not to divulge your whereabouts to anyone, especially not to Marco.

For some unknown reason, he appears to have suddenly appointed me his new best friend and yesterday confided that he'd now totally broken off relations with Mirrie – whatever they were – and frankly, darling, I was surprised they were still limping on. It seems she was very jealous of you and suspected Marco of still being in contact with you and wanting you back.

Which, of course, he does seem to – and who wouldn't, darling? Though oddly, what he still appears to miss most about you is your input into his plays!

He said you'd been his muse and how difficult he was finding it to rewrite his new play for the Cockleshell Theatre management without you. I told you the management loathed the first version, which Mirrie had assured him was wonderful, didn't I?

Then he went a bit lachrymose and said he wished he'd written down your advice when he first ran the idea for his new play past you, because he couldn't remember it. So you can imagine how aggrieved he is that when you finally replied to one of his many messages, it was only to tell him to leave you alone, or else!

But here, darling, I have a big, big favour to ask you, because I think there might be another big, juicy part for me in the new play, if only he can pull it off. So, dearest

Garland, out of the goodness of your heart, could you give me some advice to pass on to him if I promise not to divulge that it came from you?

If you do, I suspect I'll have to take on your pervious roles of propper-up and muse (though not any other of them, for I am not that way inclined), but as long as I also become his first choice for leading man, I can put up with that.

Will xx

I enjoyed Will's acerbic asides, but learned nothing new from the email, except that Marco had lied when he'd said there had been nothing but a quick fling between him and Mirrie and it was all over by the time I found out about it.

However, I liked Will, despite all the blatant self-interest, and since he'd made such a hit in his current role, I'd like him to go on to get other leading parts. So, after thinking it over, I decided to send him the advice I'd given Marco . . . or what I could remember of it, anyway.

I still wasn't going to give Will my new address, though, even if I was hardly within day-trip distance of London. I expected he'd find out eventually, once Honey's big publicity push for her new paperback and the museum got going, because then even Marco was bound to put two and two together, realize Honey had lied and guess where I was.

*

After breakfast on Sunday, I opened my laptop, which was still on the kitchen table, and began my reply to Will, only to be immediately interrupted by Golightly who, having demolished his own breakfast, now repeated his trick of climbing on to the table and lying on my keyboard.

'Bad cat!' I scolded, putting him back on to the floor for the second time, and he pulled a very affronted face at me, said something short and probably rude in Cat and went out, tail up.

After deleting the gobbledegook he'd left behind, I began again.

Dear Will

It was lovely to hear from you, as always, but I'm afraid I'm living way too far from London to make it practicable for you to get here and return in one day, kind thought though it was.

Although I'm now totally indifferent to Marco's affairs – of any kind – I do see your point about building on your huge success in A Midsummer Night's Madness with a leading role in the next Marco Parys production, if it can be turned into another box-office success.

So, here is, more or less, what I was trying to drum into Marco's head.

He needs to follow the success of A Midsummer Night's Madness with another supernatural thriller, because that's what the audiences will now expect. As I said to him, just forget the clever literary allegories and allusions, tedious symbolism and all that arty stuff. This play needs to be subtly dark and chilling: the audience must be unsure if the leading female character is really turning into a swan, or if it is all in her imagination ... or possibly that of the leading man – your role. We could simply be seeing what he sees – but is it real or not? Keep the audience guessing.

Is she literally the ugly duckling who turned into a swan at the end? Will she fly away – or crash?

You get the idea, anyway, Will. Like the current play, it should all be down to suggestion, atmosphere, costume, makeup and lighting.

There really should be another good role for you in it, if Marco gets it right, one where the audience won't know if your character is the hero or the villain of the piece, till the end . . . and maybe not even then.

I hope that all makes sense and you can drip-feed it into him when he seems receptive.

Garland xx

37

Pattern Pieces

After I'd sent off the reply to Will's email, I put the new sofa covers on – and very bold and beautiful they looked, too. The roses were *vast* and it's no use telling me they don't come in a blue variety, because they do and I've *seen* some.

It looked like an entirely new sofa and I thought my little sitting room was coming together nicely. I liked the mish-mash of bright colours against all those creamy white walls.

Thom had told me yesterday that he'd be in his workshop this morning because he wanted to string the Maria Marten marionette, but he rang just after Simon and Pearl had left for church, to say Simon had dropped a box off with him before he left, which was for me.

'It's full of the patterns for marionette costumes that his grandmother made over the years, which he thought you'd find useful.'

'I certainly will – that's great!'

'Shall I bring them over, or do you want to come for them? I'm about to have a break and a cup of coffee anyway, so you can join me.'

'OK, I'll be right over,' I said.

Thom's workshop door was open and Jester, who was lying just inside it, with Golightly curled up beside him, thumped his tail in welcome. Golightly ignored me.

There was no sign of Thom, but I could hear him in the back room, making coffee.

Looking round, the first thing that caught my eye was the William Corder marionette, which was hanging on one of the pegs against the wall. It was now not only jointed and strung, but had been painted – and with its glossy black hair and light brown eyes, it looked disconcertingly like Marco.

Then my eyes fell on the sections of the Maria Marten puppet, also now painted, but not yet fully strung, which lay on the bench.

Thom had given her golden hair, a simpering expression, big blue eyes and a definite look of Mirrie, so perhaps his subconscious had been busily exorcizing his demons?

'I see you've finished the William Corder marionette,' I said when Thom emerged, carrying two mugs and with a packet of chocolate Hobnobs under his arm, which I took from him before they fell.

'Yes, that one's finished and Maria is well on her way. The Marino family from the puppet theatre prefer the Continental style of horizontal control bars, like Bruno, so we make most of our marionettes with those, unless we get orders for the vertical type that's more common in the UK.'

'It's fascinating. There's so much I didn't know about puppets,' I said, carefully not mentioning the resemblance of his two most recent ones to Marco and Mirrie.

After placing the mugs on the bench, Thom bent down and hauled out a cardboard carton from underneath it, which seemed to be full of big brown envelopes.

'Hetty put the pattern pieces for each costume in an

envelope and marked on the outside what it is,' he explained. 'I had a quick look and there are lots for the stock characters we make all the time, like those from fairy tales, so I should think they'll be very useful.'

I had a rummage, opening one or two envelopes to peer at the contents. Hetty had obviously been very professional, for all the pieces of each costume were cut from good quality dressmaker's pattern paper, and labelled.

Snow White was near the top, and I assumed the Seven Dwarfs were in the box somewhere.

I probably looked like a child opening a particularly magical present on Christmas morning, for Thom, watching me, was smiling.

'Hours of harmless fun,' he said.

'Definitely! I'll really enjoy going through these and I'll file each pattern separately. I've got loads of space in that big cabinet Honey gave me.'

I reluctantly returned Snow White to the box. 'They'll be so helpful, because I need to know where the strings go so as not to impede the mobility of the puppet's limbs.'

'I can bring these two marionettes over to your workshop when I've finished stringing Maria, so you can fit their costumes there. But there's no rush. I don't want to burden you with anything extra when you're so busy with the museum work.'

'Oh, that's all right, they'll be something fun to do in my spare time, like the mini costume mannequins. I've already looked up costumes for 1827, the year of the murder.'

'I expect you'll have much more time for your own work once the museum's open.'

'I hope so. Then I'll make some mini wedding dress mannequins for the museum shop and see if they sell, and I could do the same for a couple of marionettes. I mean, we may not sell many in the shop, but there would probably be a bigger market for them online later.'

'We always keep a stock of marionettes in – we make them between orders – so any time you want to do that, you can just let me know.'

He smiled at me and there was something in the depths of his very dark amber eyes that seemed to draw me in, so that I couldn't look away . . .

'We have lots of time to make plans for the future, don't we, Garland?' he said softly. Then added, seemingly inconsequently, 'The Rev. Jo-Jo popped into the workshop for a coffee while you were at your meeting yesterday. She usually has coffee with Pearl when she's in town, but she said the shop was really busy.'

'Jo-Jo?'

That jarred me into breaking eye contact. I looked hastily down into my mug, remembering how I'd opened my heart to her in the Pink Elephant and hoping she hadn't mentioned it to Thom. But no, of course she wouldn't have! That café booth had felt like a confessional and I'm certain she would have treated anything I'd said in strict confidence.

Thom glanced over at where Jester and Golightly lay asleep together in a contented heap.

'Now it's starting to get colder and I won't be able to leave this door open all day for Jester, I'm wondering whether to install a cat flap so his new friend can come and go, and maybe in the cottage door, too. I wonder if you can buy dog-sized ones?' he added.

'Possibly, but then wouldn't a burglar be able to get through it?'

'Only a seriously skinny one. I'd only have one that big in the workshop door, which I could lock when I was out and at night. I'll have a look online.'

I got up to go. 'Why not come over to the cottage in a bit and have lunch with me? I'll make an omelette, since it's the only thing I cook really well.'

'You always did make great omelettes, especially when you put grated Parmesan in the middle.'

'I have a lump of Parmesan, so your wish is my command,' I said, picking up my box of paper treasures.

*

Thom said he'd bumped into Al and Joe Marino in the court-yard on the way over, two of the Pelican Puppet Theatre family.

'They come and go, because they store stuff at the theatre. They have three Punch and Judy booths on the road all summer, and then a marionette show going up and down the seaside resorts, too. They finish all those at the end of September, then take October off.'

'I expect I'll meet them at some point,' I said. 'Didn't you say they open the theatre at the start of November?'

'Yes, starting with *The Murder in the Red Barn*, which will be an early evening performance aimed more at adults, but there's always a children's play on Saturday afternoons, too.'

'I'd like to see both.'

'Well, I'm sure you'll be able to.'

Then he added: 'I wonder how Simon and Pearl are getting on. I got the feeling this lunch after church was sort of their first real date, didn't you?'

'I did. I hope it goes well, because I think Pearl has been struggling with the idea of having feelings for Simon ever since we all went up to the Fairy Falls. I expect it feels a bit disloyal to her late husband to be thinking about someone else in that way.'

'Neil was a nice man and I'm sure he'd want her to move on and be happy.'

I remembered what Pearl had said about her husband and was certain he would, too.

'I could tell Simon was in love with her the moment I first saw them together – but also that she had no idea!'

'Simon doesn't hide his feelings very well and he adores her, though he was just the supportive family friend during her husband's last illness.'

'It would be so lovely if they could find happiness together now,' I said.

'Perhaps we'll be able to tell how they got on when they get back,' Thom suggested.

'Maybe . . .' I said, although it wasn't always easy to read Pearl's expression. Then I made Thom go and admire my new sofa covers, even though he insisted he was not a chintz person, and anyway, it had been impossible for him to miss seeing those giant blue and pink roses on the way in.

*

There was still no sign of Simon's car when Thom and I went over to Pelican House for the attic clearing, but he and Pearl turned up a few minutes later, breathless and apologetic . . . and, in Simon's case, cheerful. Pearl was harder to read, but I noticed that they kept catching each other's eye, half-smiling and then looking away again, which was promising.

We were making steady progress, and were on to the second of the three largest attics, where there was a bit more room since Priceless Interiors had removed a few pieces of furniture.

Like the last room, we cleared one corner, then moved

anything into it that Honey wanted to keep, before sorting the rest into Arthur's spoil heap and a few more items for Priceless Interiors to consider. Honey took photos of those to send to them.

We came across a mahogany glazed cabinet that Honey thought might fit into one of the remaining gaps in the museum, or possibly the shop, and then there was an exciting moment when I thought we'd discovered something that might have been Rosa-May's: a leghorn hat in an ancient black shagreen hatbox.

Unfortunately, Simon declared it definitely Victorian.

'But the style didn't change much from the Regency, did it?' I said. 'So we could display it as part of the Rosa-May collection, possibly on top of one of the open trunks.'

'Why not?' said Honey, and Simon offered to take it back to his workshop and replace the moth-eaten ribbon and ostrich feather plume.

'I'm starting to lose hope that we'll find any more of Rosa-May's belongings, especially the second journal,' I confessed.

'Well, it was always a long shot. I only really suggested it to lure you into helping me with the clearing!' Honey said.

'It's too soon to lose hope when there's another big attic after this one, as well as that small room off it,' said Thom encouragingly.

'I'd love to know what happened to our ancestor, Garland, and why she vanished,' said Honey. 'Hugo said that, according to family rumour, she'd run off with a lover, but it's odd nothing was ever heard of her again.'

'A bit like Amy Weston, the Bloody Bride,' I suggested. 'Although Rosa-May left her children behind her, rather than her wedding dress.'

'Twin sons, who must only have been a month or two old when she left,' Honey agreed. 'At that time, she wouldn't have been able to keep her children with her if she left her husband. She'd have had no legal right to even see them ever again.'

'Women were still mere chattels then. It must have been dreadful if you were in an unhappy marriage,' said Pearl.

'I don't know how far you've got with her journal, Garland,' Honey said. 'But her sudden lack of any control over her money and the loss of her independence hit Rosa-May hard not long after her impulsive marriage.'

'I've got to the bit where her husband has gone back to his regiment without her and she's stuck at the Hall with his brother and his wife, feeling increasingly unhappy.'

'I'd like to read this journal,' said Pearl.

'It starts as more of an autobiography,' explained Honey. 'Then turns into a spasmodic journal. When Derek's less busy I'm still thinking he can type it up. Then I could get it published as a little book to sell in the museum.'

'That's a good idea, but it would have been even better if we'd found the second volume – if there is one,' I sighed.

Honey said bracingly that there was still hope, then rallied her troops and we set to work again. However, we found nothing at all other than unwanted furniture and spiders as big as saucers.

*

Over our takeaway dinner, Honey told us about all the promotion her PR had set up for her new book. In fact, she'd already recorded three radio interviews for book programmes, and one with the arts editor of a Sunday newspaper supplement, which would appear next weekend.

'It'll be a non-stop round for a few days in the run-up to publication day on October the fourth, when *Bloody Young*

Men will burst forth – though not literally, because then they'd have to be zombies and that's not my genre.'

'A different kind of book,' agreed Thom gravely. 'Does all the fuss die away once it's out?'

'No, it carries on for a bit, because I usually hog the top of the paperback bestseller list for ages,' she said with satisfaction. 'And of course, I want to keep it going till the museum opens anyway, because I'm featuring that and Amy Weston's story in most of the publicity I'm doing. I've kept Amy's mum updated,' she added, 'and she knows the museum's opening date.'

'I expect she'll want to be there,' I said. 'I only hope *The Upcycled Bride* crew arrive early enough to get their filming over with before we open to the public.'

'I think they mean to rush the final sequence back to the studios as soon as they've shot it,' Honey said.

'Will you have to go away for any book events?' asked Thom.

'I have a book launch in London on publication day, so I'll go down the night before, so I can spend the day doing even more events before it.'

'Hectic,' said Pearl. 'I'd *hate* doing that kind of thing.'

Viv laughed, which was such a surprise that we all turned and stared at her.

Honey said, 'Viv knows me too well! I'm a total media tart.'

Then she asked me if I'd heard any more from Marco and I said no, but I had from my actor friend, Will.

Looking up at that point, I caught Thom giving me one of his dark, unfathomable looks, although I had no idea why.

I told them what Will had said and the advice I'd given him to pass on to Marco, but without revealing it came from me.

'So perhaps now he'll rely on Will for advice and won't need me any more, so it won't matter even if he does twig that I'm working at the wedding museum,' I finished.

'Threatening to report him to the police for stalking probably finished him off anyway,' Pearl suggested.

Honey told us that Derek was chasing up the final paperwork for the museum, so that everything would be completed in good time.

'The health and safety, public liability insurance and all the rest of it are signed off.'

Everything did appear to be coming together very quickly – it was just that there seemed so little time left until opening day!

'Viv and I are off tomorrow to pack up her cottage,' Honey reminded us. 'Back Wednesday evening. The Rosa-May material arrives back on Tuesday, Garland, but Derek will be on hand to help if you need him. He's looking after the house and Rory while we're away.'

'*And* the Genealogy Society?' suggested Simon with a grin. 'I take it they all still turn up on Monday evenings, whether you're away or not?'

'Regular as clockwork,' she agreed. 'Old habits die hard and, for a couple of them, the sandwiches, cake and sherry are a major draw. The family history runs a distant second!'

Rosa-May

11 June 1815

I began this account of my life on 22 May, the day after my husband's departure for the Continent, when the full realization of my changed circumstances most forcibly struck me – and now it is 11 June and here I still remain, awaiting the summons to join him there.

Guy is not the best of correspondents, such letters as he sends being short and hurried, and though he says he longs to see me again, he does nothing to bring about this happy event!

Instead, he appears much more excited by the prospect that things were, as he phrased it, 'shaping up towards a big battle with Old Boney!' This is hardly news to gladden a wife's heart.

In my last letter, I earnestly entreated him to permit me to return to London with Sara, where I might await his summons in more congenial surroundings and with the comfort of having friends nearby, but this received only a flat veto.

How long must I be stuck here in this godforsaken spot? Even my friends now seem to be forgetting me, for none of my recent letters has received a reply.

My spirit rebels at being incarcerated here but, as a mere wife, I am now subject to the decisions of a husband, rather than being the mistress of my own destiny.

When I said as much to Sara, my only confidante here, she replied: 'Those who throw their caps over the windmill, must come home by Weeping Cross,' which, as I roundly told her, was neither comforting, nor helpful!

*

15 June

A hasty scrawl arrived from Guy, enclosed in a letter to his brother, saying that Bonaparte seemed to be massing his forces for a great battle. But we have heard nothing since and I feel so very cut off from any news here, which perforce must take much longer to reach us than if I were in London.

38

Soul in Torment

I assumed Viv and Honey got away OK early next morning, because her car had vanished from the mews.

Derek messaged me later to say a desk, chair and filing cabinet were arriving for the staff room today, but he'd take care of that, which left me free to put in a long day's work on the next dress. I wanted to complete it quickly because once the Rosa-May collection returned tomorrow, I'd be too busy setting it all up on display for anything else.

Dress 8 was another candidate for the Bloody Brides room, though it had an entirely different story behind it from Honey's or Amy's. There was no mystery either, other than the unfathomable workings of the heart and mind.

When I'd removed it from its very big box there was certainly a lot *of* it, because it was a 1982 wedding and the bride had gone for the whole white silk taffeta and lace Lady Di look, right down to the long train – though mercifully not quite as long as the royal original – and a glittering tiara to hold her veil.

The bodice of the dress was fitted and lightly boned to the waist, but then a crinoline under the billowing skirt made it a huge meringue.

The sleeves were puffed and full from shoulder to elbow, then lace to the wrists.

She hadn't gone for the big, frilly collar of the original, but that was the only main difference.

The bride herself had packed and sent her dress to us, with a letter telling the whole story of her wedding disaster . . . and also inadvertently revealing a lot more about her character and motivation for marrying than I'm sure she ever intended!

As well as being old enough to be her grandfather, the groom had extremely high blood pressure, and the excitement of the day led him to have a massive nosebleed at the altar, before collapsing into her arms with a minor heart attack. She wrote:

> But luckily, it happened just after we'd been declared man and wife and he was bending to kiss me. As you can see, the whole front of my dress was soaked in blood, right through to the petticoat, and of course, I couldn't change it until I got to the wedding reception venue hours later, where we were also to spend that night! I had to go in the ambulance with poor Archie just as I was, so you can imagine how everyone stared at me in the hospital! Archie was OK, but they wanted to keep him in overnight, and since all our guests had gone on to the reception, he insisted I should go and join them.

Not surprisingly, the first thing she did when she got there was to change out of her wedding dress, which she stuffed into a suitcase, along with her stained satin and lace shoes. Then she tossed in the veil for good measure, even though it had escaped largely unscathed.

You might think this was a classic gold-digging young woman and a besotted elderly groom, but there was a happy-ever-after, of sorts.

Archie joined me at the hotel next day and we spent a quiet honeymoon there. Of course, his family were against the wedding, not only because of the age difference, but because he'd very sweetly altered his will in my favour just before the ceremony. But of course I was very, very fond of him and made him extremely happy for the rest of his life ... unfortunately only just over a year from our marriage.

Fiona Stornaway might have been a gold-digger, but one with a heart, and probably she really had been fond of her elderly husband and made his last months happy, even if marrying her had speeded up his demise!

Fiona continued,

Anyway I saw the article about your museum and, since I had no idea what to do with the dress, I thought you might like to have it and put it on display, though it's a total wreck! I've enclosed a photo of me wearing it, before I set out for the church.

Fiona had had the Lady Di hairdo, too, though not the pink cheeks and the sweet and nervous smile. Instead, her pretty face wore what I could only describe as an expression of triumph.

When I told my mother what I was doing, she insisted on sending the dress to be cleaned before we gave it to you, but after so long stuffed in that suitcase, it hasn't exactly come up like new, as you can see.

That was an understatement, for there was still heavy staining visible and, since she had packed it in a box to send to us, even more crumpling of the skirt than when Lady Di got out of her wedding carriage, so I thought perhaps a little very cautious steam pressing was in order.

*

Next morning, when I'd finished working on Fiona's dress, I took it straight upstairs and set it up in one of the cases along the wall in the Bloody Brides room. I found it a bit of a struggle, since the billowing folds, not to mention the huge crinoline, kept threatening to swamp me like a tsunami.

I was also constantly interrupted by calls and texts from George, who was anxious to know that everything was ready to receive the Rosa-May collection – the lighting, humidity, etc., etc. . . .

After what I hoped was the final call, I fetched a stool from my workroom to stand on while I fixed the sparkling tiara and veil on to the mannequin's head – and then there she was, seemingly poised for action . . .

I arranged the stained satin and lace shoes so that the toes just peeped out beneath the skirt, and then there was only the information card to put out before I locked the cabinet and went back downstairs.

There I found Derek, who had brought in a delivery of Honey's books, both non-fiction and novels, though not copies of the new one, which hadn't yet arrived.

He had Rory with him, who seemed pleased to see me, but then, like Jester, he seemed pleased to see anyone! Both dogs had endearingly friendly natures, although Rory looked dignified, too, while Jester's expression was permanently slightly comical.

'I'll leave the books for Ella and Kay to put out. Now they've a key to the main doors, they can come and go and arrange everything in the reception area just as it suits them.'

'Kay's experience of running that folk museum will be a real asset, I should think,' I said.

'I'm sure it will,' Derek agreed, then added, 'Honey says Viv is bringing her husband's old PC tower and monitor for the staff room, since it's a good one and she's already transferred everything on it on to her own. We'll need one in there for stock checking and online orders when the shop website goes live.'

'There are so many practical aspects to running a museum I've never even thought of till now!' I confessed.

'No reason why you should, since your area of expertise is costume making,' he said comfortably. 'Leave the nitty-gritty to me and the Golden Girls.'

I wasn't entirely sure how Ella and Kay would take to being called the Golden Girls, but on the whole I thought they'd probably like it.

*

The Rosa-May collection arrived just before lunch. It was all, as I knew it would be, immaculately packed and the costumes ready to go out on display.

I had everything taken straight into the Rosa-May Garland Room, but before I began to unpack it, I texted George to reassure him that all had arrived safely.

Then I lost track of time in the delights of actually getting my hands on the real Regency Titania costume and the evening dress I'd copied – a near twin to mine in its nearby display case.

I wanted to get those, and the two silk dominoes, on to their mannequins as soon as possible, and entirely forgot that Pearl had messaged me earlier to say she would come over and help me when her shop shut at four. She turned up just in time to assist me with the evening dress, which, with its fragile fabric, had to be carefully eased on to its mannequin.

When it was done, I sent a couple of photos to George, who was probably chewing his fingernails, or his beard, or both, and then we closed up the museum and retired to my cottage for coffee – and to give Pearl a chance to unburden herself about Simon, if she wanted to.

And she did, for after admiring the sofa covers and addressing some respectful remarks to Golightly, who only pulled a moderately hideous grimace at her, she said, 'You know Simon and I went out for lunch on Sunday after church? We were late getting back because we'd been for a walk up to the Fairy Falls and then into the physic garden.'

'That sounds like a lovely day out! I loved those falls and I really must see the garden at some point, too. Did you have a nice time?'

'Well . . . we talked a lot,' she said, going slightly pink. 'And I told him that although I'd recently realized my feelings towards him had changed, I needed time to adjust to the idea before I could think of another relationship.'

'Fair enough,' I said. 'I'm sure he understands why you aren't ready to rush into anything.'

'That's what he said, and that he was happy to take things very slowly . . . and by then we'd got to the waterfall and there must be something in the air up there—'

She broke off and I suspected there had then been a romantic interlude.

But I was sure she was right about the magical effect of the falls, because something in the atmosphere up there had made me re-evaluate my confused feelings for Thom, too. There had been a seismic shift of some kind, even if I wasn't yet ready to cross any fault lines.

'So, are you officially going out with each other?'

'Since generally we seem to socialize in our cottages or at the pub, it's more a case of staying *in* with each other,' she said, with her sudden, rather beautiful smile. 'But I suppose we have moved on from being just friends to . . . loving friends.'

That sounded *very* Rev. Jo-Jo to me!

She dashed off after that to change and grab a snack before book group, which was at Baz and Derek's tonight, with a general discussion of what we'd been reading lately, although in my case that was only the information that had come with the donated wedding dresses and bits of Rosa-May's journal.

*

Baz and Derek lived behind the art shop and Rory was there, looking twice as big in their small sitting room, but perfectly at home, even down to trying to grab one of the warm home-made cheese scones Baz had put on the coffee table.

Despite the delicious scones, I was still hungry when we adjourned to the pub, probably because I'd somehow forgotten to eat lunch and dinner, so I decided to order a ploughman's.

While I was eating, I listened to the others talking. Baz asked Thom if he'd heard any more from Bruno, who said his boss was still happily stewing himself in hot mud puddles for his rheumatism.

'At this rate, he might not want to come back, if it's helping that much,' Simon suggested.

'I don't know. He still asked lots of questions about how the order book was looking and whether I'd finished the *Murder in the Red Barn* marionettes,' said Thom.

'Which you *almost* have,' I said, 'and then I'll run up the costumes in no time. Simon, I don't think I properly thanked you for that box of Hetty's patterns, did I? They'll be so useful!'

'That's OK, I'm just so relieved you've taken all that over, especially now, when I've got other things I want to concentrate on in my spare time.'

And then he smiled across the table at Pearl, who blushed very prettily, the Snow Queen warmed to vivid life.

*

I spent all of Wednesday setting up the rest of the Rosa-May collection, and at various times Derek, Thom, Simon and Pearl popped in, if only for half an hour, to give me a hand.

By late afternoon everything was unpacked and in place: the hand-coloured prints of the costumes for the fairy scenes in *A Midsummer Night's Dream* in the glass-topped table, flanking the open journal, which I'd opened to the page where Rosa-May described her first major success as Titania on the London stage, and with a few other odds and ends of hers, including a pair of gloves and some satin shoes.

I'd spent a good couple of hours getting the central display with the two open trunks quite right, with an artful profusion of parasols, gloves, shawls and other odds and ends from the dressing-up box we'd found – and the leghorn hat, which Simon had now refurbished, resting on one open lid as if tossed down there by the owner.

Honey would have the big laminated storyboards that George had sent with the collection fixed to the walls, and then the room would be entirely finished. Or for the moment it would be, because I quite fancied trying to make that replica of

Rosa-May's wedding dress and pelisse, which she had described in the journal, and also, perhaps, a couple of ballgowns to go under the silk dominoes.

I hadn't noticed that Honey and Viv had got back until they walked into the Rosa-May Garland Room late in the afternoon, just as I was taking a last satisfied look round, before going back to the cottage.

They were amazed at how much I'd done in so short a time, but I explained about all the help. Then I had to dash off and leave them to have a good look at everything on their own because, by then, Golightly's Soul in Torment impersonation could probably have been heard in Ormskirk.

39

Director's Cut

Apart from popping out to the market very early for some fresh fruit, salad and a chunk of the Lancashire Crumbly cheese to which I was now addicted, I worked on all day, because it seemed likely that the following day would be entirely taken up with Cassy Chance and the crew of *The Upcycled Bride* filming some of our episode. I was really dreading it and would be glad when it was over and I could climb back into my own little world again.

Besides, there was so much still to do. The next dress on the list, a very wrecked mermaid, was calling to me.

Still, at least this dress, dating from 2004, was a lot less voluminous than the previous one. Mind you, it would be hard to make one *more* voluminous!

But Dress 9 was quite a simple design, in white matte silk satin, the strapless bodice boned to give it structure and then the fabric pleated around the bust and to the waist. It was tight to below the knee and then flared out, particularly at the back. It fastened with concealed hooks and eyes, all in good order, which was more than you could say for the rest of the dress.

Not only was it extensively water damaged, but it was also covered in what looked like streaks of soot, mud and a quantity of brown dog hair.

The short and simple two-layered white veil hadn't fared much better and as for the high-heeled white silk satin shoes, they were coated in reddish mud and one heel had broken off entirely. It looked as if the bride had caught her heel in the tulle flounce of her petticoat, too, for part of it hung down. The front of the veil had also partly pulled away from its flower-ed silk headband. It was all a sorry mess.

But I like a challenge and I was well on with mapping out the scale of the catastrophe and taking close-ups of the bodice, when Thom walked in, by way of the staff room. Ella and Kay, who were unpacking books in the foyer, must have let him in.

'What on earth happened to that?' he said, gazing down at the bridal wreckage with astonishment.

'A series of unfortunate events that sound like slapstick, although I don't suppose the bride thought it funny as it unfolded. It must have been like a wedding disaster in a sitcom!'

'I'm guessing fire, flood and a mudslide, at the very least.'

'Quite close. The bride and bridesmaid were travelling to the church in a vintage Bentley belonging to a friend of the groom, but the engine caught fire on the motorway and he pulled on to the hard shoulder. They had to get out and move up the grassy bank for safety . . . and it had just started to rain. Then the driver, who was more concerned with his car than his passengers, threw open the bonnet and the wind blew sooty smoke all over the bride and bridesmaid. At that point, the heavens opened and torrential rain soaked them to the skin in seconds.'

'Was that followed by a plague of frogs, by any chance?' Thom asked, grinning.

'If it was, they arrived too late, because a passing breakdown truck spotted them and stopped, put out the fire, loaded the car on to the back and then managed to squeeze the whole party into his cab, along with his *very* friendly dog.'

'I can see from all the hair on the skirt just *how* friendly it was!'

'The truck driver kindly made a detour to drop the bride and bridesmaid at the church, where everyone was still waiting. The bridesmaid had managed to ring the bride's mother to say they had broken down, but were now on their way, but she lost the signal before she could mention what state they were in. Their dresses were a complete wreck, they looked as if they'd swum there through a bog, and the heel of one of the bride's shoes was broken off, so she limped and squelched down the aisle to "The Wedding March".'

'I'm impressed she wasn't having hysterics by this point and calling the whole thing off.'

'She said in her letter that by then she'd gone sort of shell-shocked and just wanted to get the ceremony over, so she could get to the venue and change – but once she saw the groom's expression as he turned to see her walk down the aisle, she started to laugh – probably that *was* hysterical – and so did he.'

'I should think the wedding photos are interesting, to say the least,' Thom said, grinning again.

'They are – she sent one.'

I rummaged in the box and produced it. 'Honey's using it for part of the display. It's a cracker!'

'But a bridal misfortune with a happy ending, I hope?'

'Eventually, because by the time she got to the hotel where the wedding reception was being held and could shower and change into clean, dry clothes, she'd caught a chill and a honeymoon spent in Iceland in search of the Northern Lights put the finishing touches to it, so she was ill in bed for most of that. But she said they can laugh about it all now and are very happy.'

I put the photo back in the box. 'She left the dress and everything just as they were when she took them off – and I'm not going to attempt to clean them up, just make a couple of small repairs to the underskirt and veil. Like some of the others, you can read the story through the damage to the dress.'

'Are you carrying on now? I came to try to persuade you to come for a walk with Jester and me. Pearl and Simon have gone off on their own again somewhere and I thought by now you'd probably need some fresh air and exercise – and it *is* your half-day, after all.'

'You know, I think you're right,' I decided. 'I've done enough for one day.'

*

In the pub that evening, Honey told me that we were meeting Cassy Chance and her team in Ormskirk at what she called 'the ungodly hour' of half past eight.

'They've bribed a couple of the charity shops to let us in early, so they can film that sequence of the wedding dress search before anyone else is about. I think we pretend to look in two shops, before finding the wedding dress in the third, like we did in real life. So that will be the big find scene, and then Cassy spots your outfit on the vintage rack in the same shop, Garland.'

'I'm not at all good at acting,' I said, doubtfully.

'You won't have to do much,' Honey said encouragingly, 'and the next part is all about me, because we move on to a nearby dress agency, where *I'll* find *my* outfit, another vintage one. They've run some clothes past me and I think I know which one I'll choose.'

'It does all seem like cheating,' Pearl commented. I'd noticed she was holding hands with Simon under the table, though I don't think anyone else could see. 'But the audience won't know, I suppose.'

'I don't think it's usually quite as contrived,' said Honey. 'They were just let down at the last minute by the potential bride they had lined up originally, so it's a bit of a rush, and also, Cassy would like to get our episode out early in the series.'

'Do you think the filming will take all day?' I asked.

'Not *all* of it. We'll be back home by lunchtime and then, after that, they film the bit to go at the start of the programme, where Cassy arrives at the museum and we meet her for the first time. Then we go into your workroom and explain why we want a wedding dress and what we'd like to find, and also that it would be a bonus if we both discovered outfits to wear at the museum's opening ceremony, too.'

'It's all back to front, but I suppose they just slice it up and then splice it back together again,' said Baz vaguely.

'I don't actually think they use reels of film any more,' said Thom.

'OK, I'm a dinosaur,' said Baz amiably.

'I think that's all the filming they're doing, until they come back for the "reveal" scene, supposedly bringing the altered clothes with them,' said Honey. 'Only, of course, you will have made any changes or additions to the dress and your own suit, so that won't exactly be a surprise. I think they're going to take my outfit away after we find it in Ormskirk, though, and do something with it, so a bit of that reveal will be genuine.'

'So, the filming tomorrow might be finished by midafternoon?' I said, seizing what was, to me, the important bit of what Honey had said.

'I expect so.'

'Good, because once they've gone, I can get on with blinging up the wedding dress a bit and sorting out my accessories. I'm not touching my suit. Cassy wanted me to wear some kind of hairband, although that's going to be more of a token gesture.'

'I'll make that for you,' offered Simon. 'I know what you want: something unobtrusive and not too much like a fascinator. I've got some bits of silk ribbon in two shades of old gold that should match the suit and I'll cover a narrow band with alternating stripes of those and then add a few *tiny* flowers and maybe a little beading up one side. You'll hardly know it's there, and I don't mind if this Cassy person pretends she made it, either.'

'Thanks, Simon, that would be wonderful,' I said gratefully.

'I suspect letting someone else do the work and taking all the credit will suit Cassy perfectly,' said Honey drily.

*

We met the TV crew in the Ormskirk car park early next morning, then retraced our footsteps around the three charity shops we'd previously visited, only on this occasion the streets and the shops were deserted, except for the staff.

We made our 'finds' in the third, though this time Cassy pounced on a pair of white satin shoes with small heels, magically in my size, and told me, on camera, that they could be dyed to match my suit.

I knew very well that this would cost more than everything else we'd bought put together, but I said nothing on film.

Our finds were all taken back to their van to be transported to the museum, while we went on to a dress agency in search of Honey's outfit. It was quite a big place, occupying the upper floor of what might once have been an old barn behind a pub. There were some interesting little shops on the lower floor, which I'd much rather have explored.

I'd already realized Honey was a natural in front of the camera and Cassy was in danger of being completely upstaged.

True to form, as soon as we got there and the filming began, she said, 'Like Garland, I want to go totally vintage for my outfit, only in a different style.'

'The vintage rail is over here,' said Cassy, leading the way and then starting to riffle through the clothes, pulling things out for Honey to see, including two velvet trouser suits.

Honey immediately pounced on one of them. 'Yves Saint Laurent – and I'm *sure* it would fit me!'

Cassy suggested she try on both trouser suits and also a slinky dark red dress with sequin detail, but Honey dug her heels in over that last one and said she never wore dresses in winter any more because she couldn't be bothered with tights.

The boxy jacket of the dark blue trouser suit had shoulder pads and the shape didn't suit Honey in the least. The YSL one, on the other hand, was perfect!

It had high-waisted, straight-leg trousers and a jacket cut on long, fluid lines, with three buttons.

'That's it!' said Cassy. 'And I'll find you a lovely vintage top to go underneath – but you'll have to wait for the reveal to find out what that's like!'

Honey rather regretfully watched her lovely suit being borne off to the van by one of the team, and then we got into her car and headed back home for a quick lunch and change of clothes for the next shoot, although as Honey pointed out to Cassy, that was pointless in her case since she almost always wore black jeans and a T-shirt.

I just changed my top to a moss-green one and added dark green malachite earrings, which would have to do.

Cassy and the crew turned up and, after a quick look around, shot the scene where Honey and I go out on to the museum steps to meet Cassy for the first time. The sun helpfully came out from behind a big, lavender-grey cloud at the appropriate moment.

After that they invaded my workroom and shot the scene where we were supposed to tell Cassy all about the museum, the wedding dress we needed for the foyer and how lovely it would be if she could help us to find outfits for the museum opening.

I found the whole experience very bizarre, especially doing it out of sequence, but Honey was in her element.

When they'd stopped filming, I explained to Cassy how I meant to embellish the wedding dress and about my hairband thing, while Milly stood by scribbling notes, so Cassy would be able to present it all as her own work when she came back for the next session.

'That's it, then, for the moment,' she said finally, but accepted Honey's offer of sandwiches and coffee in Pelican House before they set off back to London.

I heaved a big sigh of relief once they'd all headed off through the Rosa-May Garland Room towards the passage. Honey might thrive on this kind of thing, but I felt like a bit of chewed string. Even though it wasn't yet quite four, I closed up the workroom and retired to my cottage to chill. Early dinner and a quiet night in with Golightly, while watching an old romcom, sounded the perfect antidote to me.

*

Before I went to bed I thought I'd read a bit more of Rosa-May's journal, which seemed to be developing darker and more ominous overtones, but Golightly scuppered that by jumping on to the keyboard, so I gave up.

He curled up on my knees instead and began making the weirdest noise yet, which quite worried me until I realized it was another variation on his purring.

*

I was up early on Saturday to repair the minor tears in the mermaid dress. Then it was going out exactly as it was, fascinatingly and totally wrecked.

When it was completed, I arranged it on its mannequin upstairs and had just gone back down again when Thom rang to tell me he'd finished the Maria Marten marionette and suggested he bring it over, together with the William Corder one.

So I said fine and went to let him in by way of the cottage. There were a couple of free pegs under a shelf on one wall of the workroom and I got him to hang the marionettes there, so I didn't forget them.

'But as I said, there's no hurry to make the costumes.'

'Now I've finished my sofa covers, I need another project. This will make a nice change. I found—'

I broke off as Honey appeared in the doorway to the staff room. One glance at her face told me she was furious about something!

'What's up, Honey?'

'You know I let Amy Weston's mother know the museum opening date and about all the publicity I'd be doing over the next couple of weeks, including talking about Amy's story?' she said. 'Well, instead of waiting for my publicity campaign to start, she went and pre-empted me by giving the story to a local paper! She emailed me with links, as if I was going to be pleased about it.'

'That's a pity, but if it's only a local paper, that's not so important, is it?' pointed out Thom soothingly. 'It won't lessen the impact of *your* publicity.'

'I suppose you're right,' conceded Honey, coming right in and dropping on to the office chair.

'You know, Honey, after I'd read the emails she'd sent to you about Amy, she did come across as a bit of an attention seeker. They were all about how she felt rather than focusing on Amy.'

'She must be, because this newspaper article is exactly like that, too. Sonia – that's her name, Sonia Weston – also said she'd had an anonymous letter the day after it appeared in the paper!'

'A nasty one?' I asked.

'Definitely. She sent me a screen shot of it, all block capitals written in something like a felt-tip pen.'

Honey had brought her tablet with her and now got it up on the screen so we could both read it.

YOU EVIL, PUBLICITY-SEEKING OLD WITCH! GET THAT DRESS BACK ASAP AND SHUT UP ABOUT IT, OR YOU WILL BE SORRY.

'Short and to the point,' Thom commented. 'Who do you think sent it?'

'Maybe the fiancé,' Honey suggested. 'He won't want it all raked up again, will he?'

'Did she show it to the police?' I asked.

'No, she seems strangely reluctant to do that and she's adamant the dress should go on display, so the story of Amy's disappearance isn't forgotten.'

She sighed. 'I'd better tell my PR about that newspaper article. She won't be pleased, but I'm sure you're right and it won't matter really, unless it gets syndicated. It wouldn't surprise me if Sonia contacted the national press herself next, once all my publicity gets under way, but that won't matter by then.'

'No, it'll probably help, if anything,' Thom said.

Honey got up. 'She probably thinks she's going to hog all the limelight at the museum opening ceremony, but if so, Thom, you and Simon will have to corral her in the corner till I've had my say!'

*

After Honey and Thom had gone, I finished off a few odd jobs and tidied up in the workroom.

Thom had offered to drive me up to Jericho's End after lunch, to see the beautiful physic and rose gardens, an offer I couldn't resist.

For once, I didn't feel any desire to linger in the workroom, because the two marionettes hanging on their pegs freaked me out, especially the one that looked like Marco.

On my way out, I turned their faces to the wall.

Rosa-May

23 June 1815

Rumours have now reached us of a great battle that took place on the eighteenth, but no word of Guy, so we are all on tenterhooks.

*

26 June

It is confirmed. There was indeed a great battle on 18 June, at a place called Waterloo, and, though our forces were victorious, yet we suffered very heavy losses.

Rafe wishes the state of his health permitted him to go to London, where he might more readily discover news of Guy – and I too wish I could! However, he would not hear of my travelling there alone.

I wrote again to Letty, begging her to send me any news without delay, in the hope that she would this time reply. Her continued silence is very unlike her, so that I fear my letters may somehow have gone astray.

I am restless and full of fears and forebodings . . . I pace my chamber and cannot settle to any occupation.

*

27 June

Today, several letters arrived all at once, having clearly been delayed somewhere along the road, for first Rafe opened and read aloud to us the dreadful news that Guy was dead, only to immediately learn from the next missive that he was alive, although badly injured.

He has been taken into a private house in Bruges, together with some other wounded officers, including his friend Captain Wentworth, with whom, once they are recovered enough, he will eventually be conveyed home by easy stages, with a doctor in attendance.

I felt so dazed with the shock of first hearing that Guy was dead, only to learn moments later that he was alive, but grievously wounded, that I had to beg Rafe to read the last letter again.

Guy has sustained an injury to one side of his head and face but, most terrible of all, has lost his left arm. As if this were not enough, in falling from his horse he broke the leg that was only recently mended.

Rafe looked through the rest of his letters to see if there was anything further and, in doing so, let drop one addressed to me in Letty's familiar hand.

I pounced upon it and read it later in my own chamber, and it seemed that she had not received my recent letters and wondered at my silence!

Letters do go astray, but that several should do so is very odd.

40

A Bit of Bling

I woke on Sunday feeling tired after my hectic week and just lay there for a while, thinking about what we'd already achieved in the museum – and everything that still needed to be done.

I'd managed to work through the dress collection amazingly fast, but still had two to go, not to mention several still to put on display, which was time consuming.

The most urgent task for the next couple of days was bling-ing up the charity shop dress, which I'd labelled as Dress 14. The work had to be completed before the TV crew returned yet again on Wednesday.

It didn't give me much time and I thought I'd better get on with it the next day.

Today, though, I wanted to draw up the patterns for the marionettes' costumes, which I could base on some I'd found in Hetty's box. Once that was done and the pieces cut out, I could sew them up at my leisure.

The puppets' faces were boldly painted, so I thought I'd choose strong contrasting colours for their clothes.

Adapting the patterns to the right style of the period took

little time, so after that I sorted through my large collection of fabric oddments.

All the while, I was strangely conscious of the two marionettes hanging behind me, even if their faces were now turned to the wall, so before I cut the material out, I moved them into the stockroom.

I think I may have been watching the wrong kind of films . . .

*

Pearl had invited me and Thom for Sunday lunch, because she said Simon was hankering after traditional roast beef and Yorkshire pudding like his mother used to make, though she'd warned him the Yorkshire puddings would be frozen ones, since hers always came out thin and hard, so it wasn't worth the effort of making them.

But, frozen or not, they were perfect, and we had a lovely meal, sitting at the table overlooking the small paved back yard, full of pots and tubs, the space she said was once the home of the outside loo, at a time when not having to share one with your neighbours was a luxury!

The four of us seemed to share a lot of meals. Perhaps that was a bonding process and why I so quickly became friends with Pearl and Simon. Having close friends other than Thom in my life was a novelty.

After lunch, Simon gave me a small box full of white tissue paper, in which was nestled the gold silk hairband he'd made for me. It was very slim and delicate, with just a hint of feathers, flowers and beading embellishing one side. It was barely visible among all my copper curls, so I didn't feel it would look over the top on opening day.

Simon seemed pleased I was so delighted with it and said he

hadn't forgotten he'd volunteered to make a hat for Maria Marten too. When we left, he walked back to the workshop with me to collect some material I thought would be perfect for it.

'I'll make it straight away. It'll be a nice change from fascinators: I've had yet another big order,' he said gloomily. 'The only good thing about those is they take no time to make and you can charge a lot!'

'I expect they're your bread and butter, so you have to make them.'

'True, although I'm already designing hats for next year's weddings and race meetings, which is a lot more fun!'

*

I suspected we'd all really have preferred to spend the afternoon in a coma of repletion after our lovely lunch, but instead we dutifully gathered at Pelican House for another attic clearing session.

We didn't make any terribly exciting discoveries, but at least all the trotting to and fro and dragging furniture about must have burned off some of the calories.

Mind you, when Viv produced some Eccles cakes she'd been trying her hand at baking for the first time, we fell on them as if we hadn't eaten for a week. They were irresistibly delicious, too: golden and crispy on top and moist with fruit inside. And we still managed to do justice to an Indian takeaway later, so I suspect my calorie intake for the day was the equivalent of what I usually eat in a week.

We'd been sitting around the kitchen table chatting generally and I was feeling full, happy and a bit sleepy, when Honey startled me awake by saying, brightly, 'Just think, only two weeks tomorrow until the museum opens!'

I groaned. 'I've been trying *not* to think about it, because it seems to be rushing towards me.'

'I know – it's very exciting!' she said enthusiastically. 'I'm finalizing the arrangements for the day and I've decided to invite selected guests for a champagne reception at half past eleven in the foyer, before opening the doors to the public at twelve thirty. Kay and Ella suggested admittance should be free for the first afternoon, which seems a good idea.'

'I suppose the private event will give the TV people a chance to film us with guests,' I said. 'Then the closing shots when the public come in.'

'Yes, I think it should work very well, and I'll invite some press, too.'

'Who else are you asking to this private reception?' Pearl asked.

'All of you, of course, the Rev. Jo-Jo, the mayor and lots of local people, including Baz and Derek, Ginny, the Marinos from the puppet theatre if they're around then, the landlord of the Sun in Splendour and his wife, and Rani from the Mini-mart,' she listed. 'And, of course, your friend George from the V&A, Garland, who I hope will stay a night or two.'

'He's been so involved with the collection, I'm sure he'll want to be here,' I said.

'Sonia Weston will be there too, of course . . . and I know I've forgotten to mention several people just now, but I've got a list,' Honey said. 'I hope all the local shopkeepers come because the museum should attract more visitors to spend money in the town.'

'I hadn't thought about that, but you're right, it could be good for local businesses,' said Pearl eagerly. 'Hmm . . . I must think about a special display in the bookshop window, although, of course, I'll have to close for part of the day if I come to the drinks party.'

'You can put a sign on the door, saying when you'll be back,' suggested Simon.

'I hope George *can* make it,' I said. 'It's ages since I last saw him.'

'I expect he will, and we'll also have another guest staying with us, because I've invited Lyn Kirk, my and Viv's agent, as well.'

'You share an agent?' Thom said to Viv, looking surprised. 'I would have thought agents who represented poets were very specialized?'

As always when Thom spoke or even just looked directly at her, Viv went pink and seemed to shrink into her chair, as if trying to become invisible. The fork dropped from her hand and she dived under the table to retrieve it.

Rory was lurking under there, and I could hear him enthusiastically welcoming her. She emerged looking ruffled.

'It's unusual for an agent who represents novelists to also take on a poet, but Lyn was at university with us, so it's just a favour, when Viv needs any advice or representation,' explained Honey. 'In fact, when we were students, the three of us used to hole up in a cottage and write during the summer vacations, but then Lyn decided her forte was more in looking after authors' interests than being one.'

I remembered something she'd once told me. 'Wasn't your agent originally your ex-fiancé, Honey?'

'He was. That's how we met. I chose him out of *The Writers' and Artists' Yearbook*, because he specialized in thrillers and psychological suspense, but of course, after he jilted me, I switched my business to Lyn, who by then had set up her own agency.'

'Are you going to invite your ex-fiancé to the opening event, too?' asked Thom, curiously.

'Oh, I think so – *and* his partner. It seems only fair when I'm going to reveal the full story of why he jilted me, along with my wedding dress!'

I think we all looked expectant, because she laughed and said she supposed she could tell us the whole tale now.

'Some of the circumstances were a little humiliating at the time, so I kept them quiet.'

Of course, I'd already heard most of it before: how, when the groom didn't turn up at the church, she'd jumped into her car and hared off to the best man's cottage, where they had both been staying, to see what had happened to them.

'The door was wide open and when I went in, there were bloodstains everywhere and no sign of Nick Riddick, my fiancé. Then I heard groaning and found the best man, Charlie Neston, lying on the bed with a bad head wound.

'The owner of the estate the cottage was on, a cousin of Charlie's, turned up and rang the police and it all got a bit confusing once they arrived, because there I was with the front of my wedding dress covered in blood, although actually most of that came from a wet towel Nick must have been trying to clean up the head wound with.'

'The police actually thought you'd bashed the best man?' asked Simon, with interest.

'Only briefly. Luckily, before they carted Charlie off in an ambulance, he said he'd had a fight with Nick and kept asking for him.'

'I think at this point, we'd all like to know where he'd got to,' said Thom.

'He'd drunkenly driven off the road and through a hedge, so it was a while till he was spotted. He *said* he'd gone for help, but I suspect he thought he'd killed Charlie, lost his head and was running off back to London.'

'So, it was just a drunken fight?' Pearl asked.

'Yes, and Charlie actually got his head wound by falling against the corner of the coffee table. So no one got charged with anything and the story just fizzled out.'

She looked at me. 'I've told you all this already, Garland, but what I *didn't* say was that when I arrived at the cottage it was clear Nick and Charlie had been sharing the bedroom and, from what Charlie let slip in his ramblings, had been having a long affair. The argument was because Charlie threatened to stand up in church and tell everyone. He was, not surprisingly, jealous.'

'But . . . if Nick is gay, why was he marrying you?' I asked.

'He is bisexual. He told me so when he turned up a few weeks later to apologize. He said he loved me, though actually, I think my money was a big part of the attraction. I'd inherited a lot from my father and was in line to be Uncle Hugo's heir, too. That's when I hit him,' she added, with satisfaction. 'I felt *so* much better after that; I quite forgave him, especially since it added a bit of spice to my novels and led to my huge success!'

She grinned round at us. 'There's a sort of happy-ever-after to the story too, because eventually Nick and Charlie got back together again and settled down. I see them at events sometimes.'

'So if they're together, I don't suppose they really mind you telling the whole story now,' Simon said.

'No, because it's not like I'm outing them or anything. I think Charlie, at least, saw the funny side, so I expect they'll turn up to the opening.'

'It's going to be a memorable day in more ways than one!' Thom said.

'I saw your article in the Sunday supplement this morning, Honey,' Pearl said. 'It was very clever how you tied the new book in with the museum and the vanishing bride.'

'I've done a lot of publicity already and there's even more lined up next week, including a trip to London for the book launch on Thursday, publication day. It all helps sell books and if it also helps solve the mystery of what happened to Amy Weston and promotes the museum at the same time, that's an added bonus.'

Then she described the donation box for the foyer she was having made in the shape of the wedding cake house we used as a logo.

'It might part the visitors from their spare change. Derek has been trawling the internet for even more amusing wedding-related gifts we can sell in the shop, too.'

'I'll have the museum website finished in the week before opening,' promised Pearl. 'There's a page for the online shop, but we can go live with that later.'

'*My* big job for the next two days will be blinging up the charity shop wedding dress, ready for when the TV team come back on Wednesday,' I said.

'What are you going to do to it?' Honey asked.

'Well, it washed beautifully, but I had to remove the fabric roses from the skirt and veil because they'd gone a bit limp and grey, so I'll have to replace them.'

'I can help with those,' volunteered Simon. 'I may even have something to match in stock. I'll come across tomorrow and take the old ones, to see what I can do.'

'Simon, you're being such a help!' I said gratefully. 'If you can come up with new roses, then there's only a jewelled belt for me to make, and perhaps a scattering of crystals on the skirt, under the first layer of tulle.'

'Will there be time for that?' said Thom.

'There will if I use Hotfix crystals – but don't mention to George when he's here that I glued anything on!'

'I still think it'll take time, so I've got a feeling we won't see much of you for the next couple of days,' he said.

'But it's bound to be finished by Tuesday evening, so you can come to the book group?' Pearl suggested.

'It will have to be finished then, with the TV shoot the next day – so yes, I'll be there!' I said.

*

Not surprisingly, I was up and working on Dress 14 at the crack of dawn on Monday morning – and actually, dawn didn't so much crack as delicately expand itself behind the rooftops in pale candyfloss pink.

I shook out a few creases – oh, the joy of polyester! – and then slipped it on to a dummy over the voluminous under-skirt.

It was eye-dazzlingly white, but after some rummaging in my boxes of remnants, I found a piece of white silk satin in exactly the same shade, which I turned into a belt, wider at the front and made to tie at the back. Then I began to embellish it with clear crystals and pearls, sewn on by hand.

It was slow work and I took a mid-morning break when Simon rang and suggested I take the original roses from the dress over to his workshop, to see if we could match them, though he'd make new ones if not. Luckily, he did have some white velvet and silk roses ready-made that were just right: a large one for the skirt and several smaller for the front of the veil.

I carried my booty back and temporarily abandoned the belt in order to add a bit of sparkle to the centres of the roses with crystals and pearls, before attaching them.

I sewed the largest rose on to the skirt where the top layer of tulle was hitched up at one side. Adding the small ones to the front of the veil took a lot longer. Still, when it was done, the effect was pretty and made the dress look much more special.

I'd been so absorbed in what I was doing that the time had flown by and I jumped when my phone rang again.

This time it was Thom, tentatively asking if I'd had any lunch and, if not, whether I would like to go and have some with him.

I looked at the clock and saw it was already after one, so no wonder it sounded as if a ravening wolf pack was prowling round my stomach!

I accepted gratefully. 'But I want to check on Golightly first, because I haven't seen or heard him since breakfast.'

'No need, he's here with Jester. Neither of them liked the fine rain much.'

I hadn't even noticed it had started to rain!

Thom had made tuna mayo sandwiches, which both Jester and Golightly expressed interest in, and I'd brought chocolate finger biscuits as my contribution to the feast.

Thom asked me how the blinging-up was going, before showing me the face of a Pinocchio puppet he was carving.

'We usually have one or two marionettes for the most popular fairy-tale characters in stock, but this is an order for the larger size and with the vertical type of control bar.'

Then he stirred his coffee with another melting finger biscuit and told me he'd sourced a big enough cat flap on the internet to let Jester squeeze in and out of the workshop and would be installing that after lunch, before he started work again.

'And I got an ordinary-sized one for my cottage door from the pet shop.'

'That's a lot of expense to go to when he's not even your cat!' I said. 'You don't have to let him come into your cottage, or in here.'

'I don't,' Thom said. 'He just seems to materialize out of nowhere. I often only realize he's there when he demands to be let out again.'

'Golightly has an insidious way of making everyone do exactly what he wants – and I'm starting to think *we* are just *his* puppets!'

41

The Bartered Bride

The following morning I put the finishing touches to the belt and then pinned back the uppermost layer of tulle on the skirt and spent several happy hours gluing Hotfix crystals randomly over the layer beneath, so that they would lend a subtle sparkle to the dress as it moved.

Quite often in theatrical costume making you just want the instant effect, and historical accuracy isn't important.

There would now be quite a fairy-tale sparkle about the dress when it was standing in its corner by the window.

I left the gown on the dummy, but covered with a cotton dustsheet. I'd have *loved* to have put it straight out on the mannequin, so it was a pity I'd have to wait till after the TV reveal scenes had been filmed the following day.

Even after I'd packed away everything I'd used, there would still have been time to make a start on the next dress, but by then I could hear Golightly exercising his claws on his scratch board and thought he deserved a bit of company and attention before I went to the book group, otherwise I wouldn't put it past him to call Catline to complain about my neglect.

*

The TV crew had stayed somewhere local on Tuesday night, so they could arrive quite early. I wouldn't have time to do more than refresh my memory about the next dress on the list, before their arrival.

This one, Dress 10, would be time-consuming anyway, since it was not so much a dress as an ensemble, dating back to the 1840s.

The bride seems to have been a bargaining chip, used to seal the alliance of a businessman who had seen that steam power was going to be the way forward, and a more socially important family who wanted to come into the firm as partners. The plan was that the businessman's daughter should live with the upper-class family and be launched into society. Then, at eighteen, she would be married to the son and heir, uniting money with class.

From the copies of some pages from a privately printed family memoir, it sounded as though the young couple bonded in their mutual resentment of this arrangement and eventually it turned into a love match. They were married for over fifty years and had several children.

The wedding portrait showed a young woman with a very determined air, whose handsome, amiable, young husband appeared to be gazing adoringly at her, as did a small spaniel at her feet.

She'd been dark-haired in the old photograph, so probably suited her head-to-foot crimson costume.

White was not then the most popular colour for a wedding dress, especially if, like this one, it would be put into regular use later.

While I was still contemplating the strange ways of love, Honey came in via the staff room, yawning heavily, and said this was way too early for her and she'd be glad when things calmed down in a couple of weeks and she could sink back into her nice, comfortable routine of killing people in print.

'It's after half past nine, not that early,' I pointed out, but she said it *was* if you were usually wide awake into the early hours.

'But the post has been and *I've* had a printed anonymous letter that looks just like the one Sonia Weston got, except it doesn't call me an old witch.'

'Really? What does yours say?'

She shrugged. 'Just that if I don't take Amy Weston's dress off display and shut up about it, I'll be sorry.'

'That's definitely a threat,' I said worriedly. 'And after all the museum publicity, everyone must realize you live here in Great Mumming. Are you going to take it to the police?'

'I don't think so. Amy's mum didn't. Besides, I've had far worse threats on social media, obviously thinking I was some kind of man-hater.' She gave that slightly wicked, tilted grin and added: 'But I *do* like men, even if I couldn't eat a whole one.'

'Seriously, Honey,' I persisted, 'I do think you should give it to the police.'

'No, I feel sure it's only an empty threat, probably sent by Amy's fiancé, though it *is* interesting.'

She didn't say in what way, but just then we were interrupted by the arrival of the TV van pulling into the disabled spaces in front of the museum and after that the pace was just non-stop.

*

Three hours later, we'd done the scene where we greeted Cassy on the steps of the museum, the one where the clothes were being carried in from the van, as if they had brought them with them, and then the 'reveal' scene in my workroom, where the wedding dress and veil went back on the dummy I'd just removed them from, to be admired by us.

After that, Honey and I took turns to go behind a screen and emerge wearing our new outfits. The shoes they'd had dyed to match my dress and jacket did look lovely, as did Simon's hairband, which I had to admire as if I'd never seen it before!

They'd found Honey a blackberry-coloured sequined top from the fifties to wear under her black velvet YSL trouser suit and she wore her own black suede boots with it. She looked very striking, with her bobbed black hair, dark eyes, natural pallor and bold red lipstick: a very *couture* vampire.

Before the reveal I'd explained to Cassy what I'd done to the wedding dress and about the hairband, so she could relay that back to us as if she'd carried out the work herself . . . and it all got just as confusing as the day we filmed in Ormskirk, so I only hoped they managed to put all the bits together in the right order.

The final footage they shot was of me in the foyer, putting the wedding dress and veil on to the mannequin in the window; then that was it, as far as I was concerned. Honey took them round the museum so they could film some of the costumes already on display, and then they were to have sandwiches and coffee in Pelican House before setting off back to London.

Honey had woken up again and was still full of energy and enthusiasm when I retreated into my workroom and thankfully closed the door behind me, limp as a wet lettuce.

She was setting out for London later too, as soon as the TV crew had gone, although I didn't think she'd be hitching a lift with them. The back of a van certainly wasn't her style!

*

Thursday dawned bright, sunny but cooler. There was definitely a hint of autumn and woodsmoke in the air now.

I hoped the weather was the same in London, and that Honey would have a lovely day of events leading up to the evening's launch of *Bloody Young Men*.

She'd be back on Friday, and the thought of how pleased she'd be to find I'd finished the penultimate dress of the collection spurred me on.

The box for the Bartered Bride's costume was huge, even though it didn't contain the modest hooped petticoat it needed under the skirt. That hadn't survived, but I'd ordered one after my earlier brief examination, and it was already on the more generously proportioned of my new dressmaker's dummies.

The waist of the bodice wasn't tiny, but the dress was definitely made for someone with the generous hourglass figure that was fashionable in the mid-Victorian era.

I caught a hint of old lavender when I opened the lid and began to take out the various parts of the costume. This was a dress with several separate elements, a sort of Victorian mix-and-match.

The separate bodice, sleeves and skirt of the dress were made in bright crimson silk satin, trimmed with red lace. The bodice, which had small cap sleeves, was corseted and curved down into a point front and back over the skirt, which would flare out over its hooped petticoat.

That was the basic gown, but there was also a pair of long, close-fitting sleeves, with white lace at the cuffs, designed to fit under the cap ones, and appear part of the dress.

And then, as if this were not enough, there was an overdress of very thin red muslin with self-coloured floral embroidery and red and white lace trim, which went high up to the neck and down to the end of the sleeves.

The veil had not survived, but there was a little square,

tasselled drawstring bag in matching crimson silk, which was designed to be worn tied to the side of the bodice.

While both the bodice and skirt showed signs of regular use after the wedding, I thought the long sleeves and overdress had been made just for the occasion and then packed away.

There was some moth damage, not extensive, and a few small rents in the red and white lace that I'd have to repair, but on the whole, it would need surprisingly little work before it went on display.

It took quite a while to examine and evaluate. I took notes and photos of all the parts separately, before reassembling them on the dressmaker's dummy. It looked much better with the hooped petticoat holding out the skirt.

I snatched a quick sandwich lunch before beginning to mend the lace, but I hadn't got very far before Thom, Pearl and Simon arrived. This being their half day, I'd drafted them in to help me get some more of the dresses I'd already finished out on display and then forgotten about it!

Ella, Kay and Derek were having a blitz in the shop and staff room too, unpacking stock that had arrived and setting up the new, scarily gleaming till.

Kay was at the staff-room computer, entering stock because, as she said, she was going to count it all in, and then count it all out again, as it sold.

With the others' help I filled some of the shallower, shelved cabinets with accessories and their matching information cards. Pearl had brought a stack of the A4 paper leaflets with her, so afterwards we retired to my cottage living room to fold them into three, and since Pearl had thoughtfully cut four pieces of rectangular card to fold them around, it wasn't as fiddly as it might have been.

*

We went our separate ways once the origami session was over, but were to meet later at the pub, though I called in at Pearl's a little earlier to look at a wonderful old fairy storybook with lovely illustrations that she'd happened to mention . . . and which, of course, I bought.

I seem to be a sucker for fairies, and possibly now angels too, since my trip to the Jericho's End waterfall.

Still, it also gave Pearl a chance to unburden herself about her lingering sense of guilt at having fallen for Simon . . .

*

By the time Honey returned from London late on Friday afternoon, I'd finished the repairs to the Bartered Bride's dress and reassembled it upstairs on its special mannequin, where the deep crimson made a bold and beautiful statement.

And when Honey came to look around at what had been done in her absence, exhausted but still wired from her trip, she was amazed at the progress we'd all made.

There was just over a week until we opened – and one more dress, a bittersweet story, to end with.

Rosa-May

27 June

In my reply I unburdened my heart to dear Letty. But then, having a sudden, although perhaps unfounded, suspicion that Rafe was keeping back my letters, I had Sara enclose it in one of her own to her sister and requested that Letty reply in the same manner.

I did also send a short note to Letty in the usual way, because if Rafe was indeed intercepting them, then I did not want him to suspect I was now corresponding with my friends by a different means.

I have now also secretly written to Mrs Aurelius Blake, begging for news of old friends and hoping that she had not quite forgotten me, since I had had no response to my last two letters to her . . .

Today I again told Rafe that I wished to return to Town and begged him to assist me to do so, but he would not hear of it and I have not sufficient means to make the journey alone, especially since I am very sure he would do all in his power to prevent it, and we are so very isolated here.

There would be neither sympathy nor help to be got from the vicar in the nearby village, for he is Rafe's kinsman and has shown me by his manner how much he disapproves of my former profession.

I am unaccustomed to having my freedom curtailed in this manner, and my spirit rebels, so that I have begun to try and think of a means of making my departure with Sara.

I feel certain that once Guy reaches London he will be pleased to see me and I would be able to obtain the best of medical assistance to help me nurse him back to health.

If I were to appeal to Letty, we might devise some way to secretly arrange my journey . . .

*

30 June

Since I wrote in this book, a new and very dread fear has overtaken my mind!

I had put down some recent queasiness and lack of appetite to a passing malady, but now further signs make me suspect I may be with child!

I pray that it is not so, and that this so-called blessing will be conferred upon Sophia instead, who yearns for it.

I had thought those with child only felt sickly in the mornings, but Sara says some women may feel so all the time, so that I must entertain the possibility.

I have of late often seen Sophia's eyes upon me when I refuse food, or have to suddenly retire from the table, so I think she may also suspect.

If it should be so, I would desire even more urgently to be in London, where Letty and other friends could give me the best advice, for I have such a mortal fear that it would go ill with me.

To be within reach of an eminent doctor well-versed in the difficulties of childbirth would be at least a little reassurance.

Guy, too, would benefit from being able to call in the services of a good doctor and I have written to him to point this out . . . though without mentioning my own fresh reasons for wishing for it.

42

Bittersweet

I took Saturday afternoon off, because I had a feeling I'd be working flat out from Monday and spent it sewing the mario-nette costumes. Simon brought me Maria's tiny blue bonnet, perfect in every way, down to a miniature plume.

Then, in late afternoon, I had another email from Will, reporting on progress:

Darling Garland

I cunningly filtered your excellent advice into Marco's ear and it was very well received, because he has been burn-ing the midnight oil in an attempt to revise his play into something that the management might actually want. As a consequence, he now looks a lot more like a Byronic poet than ever, pallid and somewhat hollow-eyed.

As predicted, I have now had to take on your mantle as best friend and muse, so it was me he came rushing to tell when he discovered your current whereabouts.

You didn't tell me you were related to the bestselling novelist Honey Fairford, but Marco says you are cousins, but only realized it at that Rosa-May Garland exhibition, where it turned out that the actress was a mutual ancestor.

How very thrilling! Of course, we all know that A Midsummer Night's Madness was inspired by that exhibition, too ... He hasn't revealed which muddy duck pond had inspired his current swan lake epic, and probably just as well.

Even I had noticed that Honey Fairford had been all over the media lately, talking about her new book and also a wedding dress museum she had set up in her hometown in Lancashire. So of course, Marco realized you must be involved in it and that was the job you had left London for, though he said he'd rung Honey Fairford to ask if she knew where you were and she'd told him she had no idea.

I do wish you weren't in Lancashire, which is so far away!

I said to Marco how relieved he must be to know you were happily employed by a relative and quite safe, but he only said he didn't know why you had been so secretive about it, when all he had wanted was to assure himself of your wellbeing, though of course we both know now why he really wanted to find you!

I would love to come up some time and see this amazing museum, which I gather features bridal misfortune, rather than the happy-ever-after variety ... and perhaps meet Honey Fairford, because I am a great fan, although actually, I think she looks really scary.

Anyway, darling, it didn't sound as if Marco was about to jump into his car and rush up north – and I shouldn't think he's ever been further north than Milton Keynes – so you can relax.

Do tell me all about the museum and whether your own bridal misfortune features in it.

Will xx

I sent him a brief reply, saying that yes, my new job *was* at the wedding dress museum and I was very happy living and working in Great Mumming. I told him I'd known the penny would drop once Marco saw the publicity about it, but hoped he would have lost interest in me by then, so was glad to know that this seemed to be the case.

Then I finished by wishing him continued success in his role as Oberon and said at some future date, if he was in the north, it would be nice to see him.

'Nice' is such a pleasantly non-committal kind of word, isn't it? And after all, if Will did turn up and had romantic inclinations, I could always call on Honey to scare him off . . .

*

Amy Weston's mother *had* got herself into a Sunday paper, but this time Honey didn't mind, because the publicity was all out there now, anyway. Honey's PR still had some more events planned, but locally, in Liverpool and Manchester, which she could easily manage in a day.

I had done a little work on Sunday morning, but then Thom drove me up to the Pike with Two Heads, on the moors near Thorstane, to meet Simon and Pearl for lunch after they'd been to church. Then we had a walk in the pine woods round a nearby reservoir to burn off some of the calories, and Simon and Pearl held hands, so things there seem to be developing nicely.

On the surface, Thom and I appeared to have slipped comfortably back into our old friendship, but it could never be quite the same – undercurrents are stirring and I have no idea where they will take us, except I'm sure neither of us could bear to lose the other again . . .

*

When we met for our usual attic session, we made a big push to clear the third large attic, because we knew we'd be too busy to come over on the following weekend, right before the museum opened.

It was frustrating to leave the final small room untouched, when we had so nearly finished. Not that it looked very exciting: just a tightly packed jumble of more recent cast-offs, like hat stands, standard lamps, tea chests of books and lots of old luggage.

'It doesn't seem likely we'll discover any more of Rosa-May's things now,' I said regretfully as, tired and grubby, we headed downstairs for our takeaway treat and a lot of cold lager to soothe our dusty throats. 'And I'm almost at the end of her journal, too, with only a few more scrappy-looking entries to go, so if she did start a new one, it must have been lost. Pity, because her husband was injured at Waterloo and she's waiting for him to return – and now I'll never know what happened.'

'We can tackle the last little attic on the Sunday after the museum opens, if we've still got the energy, so you never know what we might turn up,' Honey said encouragingly.

If anyone would have any energy left by then, it would be her!

Over our dinner, I told them about Will's latest email and Honey said it was a pity he would be working on the day the museum opened, or she would have invited him. As so often with Honey, I wasn't sure if she was joking or not . . .

*

The next week was as hectic as I'd expected it to be and the museum a hive of activity, with Derek, Ella and Kay in and out setting up the shop, reception desk and office.

I'd quite often find Viv somewhere upstairs, sitting on a camp stool with notebook and pen in hand, or wandering around like a modern-day Miss Havisham, though if she came across me arranging accessories on the shelves in one of the display units, or dressing a mannequin, she would quietly lend a hand. She always spoke to me quite normally now, when we were alone, or with just Honey, and I got to know her much better. I quickly realized she and Honey shared a similar dark sense of humour, despite her gentler, Charlotte Brontë appearance, but then, all the Brontë sisters had had cores of steel, too.

On the Tuesday evening she and Honey joined the book group, which was at Ginny's house this time, so we could celebrate the good news that *Bloody Young Men* would be in the next weekend's *Sunday Times* bestseller chart – straight in at number one! Honey arrived bearing champagne and a large fruitcake, baked by Viv, with the book title iced on top in bright red. The 'n' in Men was running down the side of the cake like blood – nice touch . . .

Later, at the pub, Honey bought us all drinks, so I was feeling slightly jaded and had a bit of a headache when I began work next morning on Dress 11, the one with the bittersweet story behind it.

Luckily, this one needed little more than recording and photographing, before some careful pressing.

The couple had married in 1992 when they were very elderly, but had actually been childhood sweethearts, parted by the war. The man had been reported missing in action, although actually he had just been injured and eventually returned home, but by then his fiancée and her family had moved away and he'd been told she'd been working in a munitions factory that had been bombed.

Each thinking the other was dead, they eventually married other people and got on with their lives – until the day when, by one of those strange twists of fate, they met again many years later when they were living in the same retirement home.

They married in their eighties, with the blessing of their families, and lived there together until they died within a week of each other almost ten years later.

For the wedding, the bride had worn a lilac cotton sateen dress with a ruffled cowl-style neckline and short sleeves, only slightly fitted. She had a matching fascinator with flowers and feathers and soft, comfortable lilac pumps with a small heel. In the wedding picture she looked very sweet, with curly silver hair. Her new husband, dressed in an obviously new dark suit, held her hand.

It brought a lump to my throat: our grandparents' generation had gone through so much, to ensure that their children and grandchildren could live in safety.

*

Given my slight hangover, it was a pity that this was the morning Kay and Ella had chosen to instruct me in the ways of the till and credit card machine, because even with a clear head I'd have had trouble grasping it all, particularly the till, which I jammed every single time. I just hoped there would never be an emergency when I had to take over the desk!

I was glad to escape back to my own work and, by early afternoon, I'd put the final dress on display and was just heading downstairs again to the foyer, when Honey came in from the house, carrying three large packages.

'I hate to do this to you, Garland,' she said with a grin, 'but I'm afraid some more dress donations have arrived!'

43

Alien Intrusions

'They're all relatively modern, from weddings within the last fifty years, so nothing terribly fragile or precious,' she said, handing them over. 'They can wait till after the museum opens.'

While that took the pressure off me a bit, I still spent Thursday morning measuring each one for a mannequin, before carefully packing it away with its accessories in a proper archive box.

Honey had already opened the parcels, so she could thank the donors, which was a help, and I added them to the catalogue.

I sent over an order for yet more mannequins to Derek, then quickly scanned in any information and photos that had come with the dresses, resisting the urge to read their stories. There would be time for that later.

When I'd finished, I had a cup of coffee in the staff room with Ella and Kay. Ella had been pricing up the latest batch of souvenirs, while Kay was answering some emails, for the new website had gone live.

'So far, they're all asking about things that they can find out on the website,' she said. 'What days we're open, the times and where we are. It was just the same in the museum I worked in before.'

Then I had to admire the big donations box, which had arrived and been placed in the centre of the foyer, a giant wedding cake house, with a crack opening up between the figures of the bride and groom on top, together with a slot for the money we hoped would roll in.

When I returned to my room, wondering what to start on next, I looked idly across the courtyard and, since it was a bright day, wasn't entirely surprised to see Jester lying on his cushion outside the open door to the puppet workshop.

I'd finished the final touches to the marionettes' costumes the evening before, so on impulse I decide to take them over to Thom. At least they would no longer be quietly hanging around!

Afterwards I was going to treat myself to lunch at the Pink Elephant and thought he might like to join me – maybe Pearl and Simon too, so I sent them a text. Then, if they weren't doing anything else on their half-day, I could take them round the museum to show them how it was all looking now.

I had some goodies from Viv to share with Thom: almond finger biscuits. I put those in my shoulder bag, then unhooked the two marionettes and set off, finding them quite heavy to hold high enough to keep them clear of the cobbles.

When Thom had admired the costumes, I handed him the box with his share of the biscuits.

'Viv suggested I share them with you, like she did the last time.'

'I don't know why she's suddenly started sending me goodies when she appears to be scared to death of me,' he said. 'Do you think it's like offering up a sacrifice to a monster, to keep it sweet?'

'Maybe . . . She seems a lot more scared of you than Simon, although actually, it would be hard to be scared of Simon, because he's like an overgrown schoolboy, full of goodwill, enthusiasm and kindness.'

'I don't think I'm frightening, am I?' he asked.

'You can be, a bit . . . sort of reserved and intense,' I said. 'And you really *were* quietly frightening in the Silvermann films, though I shouldn't think Viv has seen them.'

'In the films, I was supposed to emerge as the actual manipulator of events behind the scenes, even though Leo's character was the handsome, brave, monster-slaying hero.'

'But it was you who ultimately saved the world – or one of them, because there seemed to be several overlapping realities. I can't say I ever really got the hang of it,' I confessed.

'I think the books were cleverly written, but hard to get over on film,' he said, and then added, slightly bitterly, 'Mirrie played her devious, double-dealing character to perfection. It must have come naturally to her, given what happened later with Leo.'

'It doesn't do to dwell on the past,' I said. 'Not the bad parts of it, anyway.'

'No, you're right, Garland, we should only remember the happy times, like when we were children,' he agreed. 'And those few years we had after we met again in London, when we were best friends – those were good.'

He was looking down at me very seriously so I said, trying to lighten the atmosphere a little, 'And now, here we are, together again! I can see now that you were right when you said that although we can never go back to the relationship we had before, we *can* build something good and new on the foundations.'

'Something permanent this time,' he agreed. 'We both had

our lives ripped apart when your parents died, and I can see now I caused you great hurt when I left London and cut off contact, even though I thought I was doing it in your best interests.'

He gave a rather wry smile. 'I'd come back from a long stay here with the intention of finally telling you where I kept vanishing to, but there you were, confessing you were madly in love with Marco Parys!'

'You were actually going to tell me about your cottage here and what you were doing?'

He nodded. 'Yes, because I'd made up my mind to move here permanently after my part in that last play finished. In fact,' he added, 'I'd only kept my house on and taken the occasional role because of you. You were doing so well in your job and seemed permanently fixed in London.'

'You had been spending more and more time up here and I missed you when you were away. I think that's partly why I fell for Marco so hard: I was lonely and he was just . . . *there*.'

'These things just happen, but I knew Marco wasn't worthy of you . . . and we both lost our tempers in that last argument, didn't we?'

'Mine's easily lost,' I said ruefully, 'but I'm sure we would have made it up again if I hadn't had to go up to Scotland at the crucial moment when Leo overdosed. I should have been there for you, but I didn't even hear about it until days after it happened, and by the time I could get back, you'd vanished.'

'Like I said, it did seem the best thing for you . . . but I had a long talk with the Rev. Jo-Jo the other day and she made me see how cruel it had been to cut you off dead like that.'

'I've talked to her, too,' I admitted, thinking we all seemed to have been baring our souls to the vicar!

'At first I thought you just needed time and I kept waiting

for you to get back in touch with me. But you didn't, and I had no idea if you were alive or dead, happy or—' I broke off and swallowed hard. 'You were always in my mind.'

'I see that now, and of course it was different for me, because Mal and Demelza let me know any news of you, so I knew you were engaged to Marco and doing well at Beng & Briggs.'

'I was in line to be head of the historical costume department, once Madame Bertille finally retired.'

'Jo-Jo said I should have trusted you not to tell anyone, even Marco, where I was.'

'She was quite right! Just being able to email you would have been something. There were so many times when I wanted to talk to you, or share something funny that had happened. We always had the same sense of the ridiculous. Marco never shared that or understood why sometimes I needed to get away from everything and be alone, in that old caravan I used to rent.'

'The one on a farm, with no mod cons?' he said with a grin. 'You described it to me, but, like me with this place, you never said where it was. But I understood why: you needed that privacy.'

'We both respected each other's need to keep our sanctuaries secret,' I said.

Thom looked down at me, his dark eyes searching mine. 'I missed you so much, Garland.'

'And I missed you – it was like a physical ache sometimes, as if I'd lost part of myself.'

'I felt just the same, and when you turned up on my doorstep that day, I thought I was dreaming!' Then his mouth quirked up in a smile. 'For a minute I thought you might lose your temper and fly at me!'

'I nearly did! I was just so confused – stunned *and* angry! Part of me wanted to hit you, and the other wanted you to sweep me right off my feet in a bear hug, like you used to do when we hadn't seen each other for a while.'

'You mean, like this?' he said, picking me up and tightening his arms around me.

I looked up, laughing, into his intent, dark amber eyes in which flecks of gold dust always seemed to shimmer . . . and saw some deep emotion stirring there.

My heart gave a great leap. Then, as if irresistibly drawn together, we were kissing as if we'd never stop and I couldn't have told you if my feet were on the ground or not.

'Garland, you don't know how long I've wanted to do that,' Thom said with a shaky laugh, when we finally broke apart. 'I knew I loved you long before I left London, but I was just too afraid that although my feelings for you had changed, yours for me hadn't.'

'No, I still thought of you as somewhere between a brother and best friend, right up to the moment I arrived in Great Mumming and you opened the workshop door. After that, I was totally confused about how I felt, though that talk of my own with Jo-Jo helped.'

'It's just as well I never did tell you, then.'

'I suppose so. But we've wasted so much time we could have spent together!'

'We'll make it up,' he said, his arms closing around me again.

'How *very* touching!' said a furious, familiar voice from behind us, and I looked up to see Marco framed in the doorway, white-faced with rage.

He seemed so out of place, so much part of a long-distant past, that it took me a moment to take in his sudden, demon-in-the-pantomime appearance. Then I exclaimed, 'What on earth are you doing here?'

'Pursuing a lost cause, evidently,' he said, coming right in. 'I was looking for you and when I found the museum shut up and saw this door open, I came to ask if anyone knew where you were – and heard your voice.'

His brown eyes regarded us coldly. 'Sorry to interrupt this pretty little scene, but you didn't waste any time, did you, Garland? But then, I suppose you must always have known where Thom was, even if you told me you didn't.'

Thom had let me go, although he still kept one arm around my waist.

'You're wrong. Garland didn't know,' he said. 'And she's already told you you're finished and she doesn't want to see you again, so you've had a wasted trip.'

'Evidently,' said Marco, but he was now looking curiously around the workshop at the hanging marionettes.

'Is this where you've been all this time – making puppets, of all things?'

'Yes, I'm a partner in the business.'

Marco turned to me. 'Well, I don't believe you didn't know where he was. In fact, I realize now that all those times you said you needed to get away on your own, you were here, cosying up with *him*!'

'Oh, don't be silly, Marco. Of course I wasn't! It was a huge surprise to find him here.'

'A likely story,' he sneered. 'And so much for the "platonic friendship" you said you had.'

'I never lied to you about anything, Marco, and I genuinely fell in love with you, but that's all over. Now, my feelings towards Thom have entirely changed.'

'So I see! And I suppose he's been poisoning your mind against me with a lot of lies, and that's why you haven't answered any of my messages.'

'Thom had already warned me, when I told him I was going out with you, that you hadn't changed your old ways since you used to hang out with Leo and Mirrie and that crowd,' I said. 'But I thought he was wrong. He didn't tell me then that he'd caught you and Mirrie together, when she was still married to Leo. I found that out later.'

'That meant nothing at all, like our recent fling,' he said dismissively.

'Your moral compass and mine seem to be on entirely different settings,' I said coldly.

'But I told you the truth about kicking the cocaine habit, Garland. I mean, it was just a recreational thing we all did at the time.'

'I don't think that was quite the whole truth,' said Thom, a steely note in his voice I'd never heard before. 'I knew you were dealing cocaine to your friends years ago and that's where Leo got it from.'

'I wasn't really dealing, just doing a favour for friends,' Marco said quickly.

Thom ignored that. 'After Leo died, I discovered there was over an hour not accounted for, between him trying to see me at the theatre and going back to my house, when he must have got hold of the drugs that killed him.'

'Well, what about it?' said Marco, but suddenly he was looking wary.

'His phone was missing, but when my house was packed up, it was found behind the spare room bed, the battery dead. I charged it up – and guess who his last messages were exchanged with?'

'Not – Marco?' I said, aghast.

'I'm afraid so. And Marco's replies made it plain he was willing to supply the drugs Leo wanted.'

Marco began backing away a little now. 'You can't prove that!'

'I've still got the phone and the messages are damning. It was only for Garland's sake I didn't give it to the police. I hoped, also for her sake, that Leo's death would give you a scare and stop you dealing too. You can't have needed the money, after all.'

'I wasn't dealing by then!' Marco exclaimed revealingly. 'OK, I might have done when I was younger, because my mother kept me short of money,' he said, as if this was perfectly reasonable. 'But once I came into my inheritance I didn't need to. The stuff I gave Leo was just for my own personal use.'

I stared at him: he was so not the person I'd thought he was at all. How could I ever have been so fooled by him?

'All those times when you wouldn't take your dark glasses off and I thought you'd drunk too much, you'd really been shoving fairy dust up your nose?' I said with distaste.

'It's nothing – everyone does it for fun.'

'It wasn't fun for Leo!'

'But I couldn't have known he'd take the whole lot at once, could I?'

'You must have seen what state he was in when he collected it, and you knew he was always emotionally volatile,' said Thom.

'You *disgust* me, Marco,' I said, which seemed to sting him to anger again.

'Perhaps this wasn't entirely a wasted journey, because I imagine a lot of people will be interested in Ivo Gryffyn's whereabouts!'

'I doubt it, but you go ahead and tell them. And then I'll have a little talk with the police about that phone,' Thom said. 'Unless you'd rather that didn't come out? It would hardly do your career much good, would it?'

Marco blanched and stared speechlessly at him for a moment, then swung round to make for the door – and almost fell over a blue-grey shape that blocked it.

Golightly had *always* loathed Marco and now, clearly, his invasion of a place he felt was his own made him furious.

With a banshee scream, he threw himself at the intruder in a whirl of teeth and claws, and Marco fled, one trouser leg shredded, slipping and stumbling over the cobbles.

Golightly sat down and began calmly washing himself, as if nothing had happened.

Jester sidled in, discretion obviously being the better part of valour, as far as he was concerned.

'Some guard dog you are,' Thom told him. 'You'd let anyone in.'

'You don't need a guard dog when you've got Golightly,' I said, bending to stroke him.

The room filled with a rumbling intermittent noise, like a faulty engine.

Golightly was purring.

'I really do think he needs a new gasket,' said Thom, amused. Then he took me in his arms again. 'Now, where were we . . . ?'

Rosa-May

4 July

Rafe sent my letter to Guy enclosed in one of his own. I hope Guy is recovering his strength . . . and also that my suggestion now finds favour with him.

Sara coaxes me to eat and I try to do so, and also continue my daily walks in the shrubbery, which is at least a little protected from the harsh winds that blow off the moors.

We have heard more news of Guy's progress and hope he may be strong enough to begin the slow journey back before the end of the month. He should by now have my letter, so I very much hope that before then he will write to me and to Rafe, so that all may be arranged for my arrival in London in time to meet him there.

*

11 July

I continue to feel ever more sickly, so that food quite disgusts me and this, together with other things, makes my condition certain.

Sophia had, of course, guessed and passed her suspicions on to her husband. When he asked me if it was so, I said it was, but begged him not yet to impart the information to Guy.

*

Sophia has become strangely solicitous for my health, despite disliking me as much as ever.

Sara's sister is in sore need of her assistance in the lodging house and she fears she will not get more work at the theatre if she is absent for much longer, but despite this, she is resolved not to leave me, especially as I daily grow weaker from lack of nourishment.

Rafe sent to the nearest town for the doctor, but he was an elderly man who barely listened to me and wanted to let my blood, although Sara told him roundly that she would not allow it, for it would only weaken me still further.

If I were in London, Letty would know the best person to advise me, as well as trying to allay my fears, for already I have nightmares about the birth.

*

A letter arrived today from Letty, enclosed in one to Sara, in which she said she had not received the note I had told her I was sending in the usual way. Nor had I received the one she sent, ditto – so it seems quite clear that Rafe is intercepting my correspondence.

The fact that I have also heard nothing from Mrs Blake confirms me in this conclusion.

I do not know why he should wish to separate me from my friends in this way, for although he might disapprove of Mrs Blake's theatrical connections – although she and her husband are of impeccable character – he can have no objection to Letty, who is more than his equal both by birth and marriage.

Trisha Ashley

I have confided to Letty all my fears about my condition, as well as my hope of hearing a favourable answer from Guy as to my return to Town.

To know that I have at least one good friend to help me, other than my faithful Sara, gladdens my heart.

44

Open Doors

We arrived late at the Pink Elephant and Pearl and Simon were already there.

'Sorry, we were talking and lost track of the time,' apologized Thom.

'Yeah, we saw you "talking" through the open door of your workshop and we thought we'd leave you to it,' said Simon, grinning, so there went any hope of keeping things quiet while we explored our new relationship!

'Busted!' said Thom, but Pearl said she'd seen it coming.

'*I* hadn't,' said Simon, predictably.

'You wouldn't see a double-decker bus until it ran you over,' Pearl told him.

'I like that! *You* were the obtuse one, where we were concerned,' he pointed out indignantly.

'That was different. But it's lovely that everything has turned out right for all of us, isn't it?' she added. 'Just like a Shakespeare play, where all's well that ends well.'

'It's more of a new start than an ending,' said Thom, and gave me the smile that did things to my heart.

*

At the pub that night, over a wonderful spaghetti carbonara, we told Honey and Viv all about Marco's visit – and I do mean *all* of it because there didn't seem any point in holding anything back at this stage.

Baz and Derek, who were sitting at the same table, looked baffled but interested.

'Garland's already told me a bit about your stepbrother and how he died, Thom,' Honey said, 'and I can see why you never liked Marco. But I can't understand why you decided not to tell Garland your stepbrother got the drugs that killed him from Marco and, instead, simply vanished from her life!'

'She's right,' I said. 'I might not have *wanted* to believe you, but the phone evidence would have convinced me and I'd have known Marco hadn't really changed, at all.'

'I can see it was a wrong decision now, but I wasn't exactly thinking straight at the time,' Thom said.

'Water under the bridge now, anyway,' said Honey. 'And with the threat of that phone evidence hanging over his head, Marco isn't likely to bother any of us again.'

Then she eyed Thom and me thoughtfully and added, 'Not that his visit seems to have bothered you two that much, anyway!'

Baz and Derek turned and stared at us and I felt myself blushing: was it that obvious?

It was Simon who came to our rescue, through pure greed. Waving the menu, he said, 'Look, there's Italian tutti-frutti ice cream as tonight's special dessert!'

'You're such a boy about ice cream,' Pearl said, though fondly.

None of us could resist it and, while we ate, Honey told me that her agent, Lyn Kirk, had offered to drive George up with her on Sunday and then give him a lift home on Tuesday.

'That's really kind of her.'

'She said she'd be glad of the company. They'll arrive late afternoon and by then we should have everything in the museum ready for the opening on Monday.'

She'd already roped in Thom, Simon and Pearl to help with all the last-minute preparations, and Derek was bringing Baz, who was a dab hand at lettering and had volunteered to add a little more to the message on The Wedding House donations box, to encourage people to contribute.

'Ella and Kay will be there too, of course – they're so efficient and organized,' Honey said. 'I just feel it's all going to go with a swing on Monday and be a *huge* success!'

*

When I woke early on Monday morning, I had a fluttery feeling of anticipation in my stomach that was fairly equally caused by the thought of seeing Thom later and the opening ceremony at the museum.

I also felt really tired, because by the time we'd finished getting everything ready the previous afternoon, George had arrived and wanted me to show him around and explain what I had – or hadn't – done to the costumes in the collection.

Honey had finally come to my rescue, dragging him off to join Viv and her agent, Lyn, for dinner, but by then I was dead on my feet and glad to retire to my cottage and cat . . . and a pizza delivery from Thom, though he wouldn't stay, because he saw how tired I was.

'And tomorrow, as Scarlett O'Hara said, is another day!'

'You've read *Gone with the Wind*?'

'No, but I saw the film. That Ashley was a wimp,' he said, and then left me with a kiss.

Golightly had watched this with what looked like benign approval, although maybe that was because the large tin of gourmet cat food he'd just put away had softened him up a bit.

There was no time to lie there and think about Thom, so I sprang out of bed, showered and then tried to eat some breakfast, my stomach tying itself into knots of nervousness by then.

Golightly left with a rattle of the cat flap. I hoped all the visitors arriving wouldn't upset him, but if they did, he'd probably just come home again.

I went back upstairs to put on my *Upcycled Bride* outfit – and Honey is quite right about tights, they *are* a pain.

Still, when I was in my subtly shimmering gold dress and jacket, the hairband adding a hint of sparkle, makeup on and, the final touch, had added a Bakelite necklace in moss green and honey yellow, I gazed at my reflection in the mirror and thought I looked like a completely different person!

Or maybe it really was me, but on a good day?

I slipped the strap of a small gold bag I'd borrowed from Pearl over my shoulder, feeling half naked without my big tapestry one, with everything but the kitchen sink in it, put on the gold satin shoes and then I was good to go.

Through the front window I saw Ella and Kay already letting themselves into the museum and I went to join them.

*

By the time the invited guests began to arrive, the *Upcycled Bride* people had already filmed some of the exhibits, as well as Kay and Ella behind the reception desk, with Derek standing by, all wearing shiny enamel 'Staff' badges.

My badge said 'Curator', which made me feel a bit like Head Girl, although actually I never even made prefect, having drifted silently through school, trying to pretend I was invisible.

The film crew moved to position themselves outside, ready to film me with Honey, who was looking stunning in her Yves Saint Laurent trouser suit, on the museum steps welcoming our guests in.

I glimpsed them slowly panning out . . . and then it was all over and they jumped into their van to dash back to London for the final cutting and pasting, or slicing and splicing, or whatever they did with film these days.

Honey greeted her guests as they arrived, introducing some of them to me – including her ex-fiancé, Nick Riddick, and his long-term partner, the erstwhile best man, Charlie Neston. I knew Nick was several years older than Honey, but he looked *ancient* and also had the air of a bad-tempered and dyspeptic camel, so I thought she'd had a lucky escape there.

Charlie, on the other hand, was small, portly and cheerful, with a fringe of faded gold curls around a bald pate. He was wearing the kind of vermilion canvas trousers favoured by older sailing types and immediately headed for Baz, who was rocking the same look, although in his case teamed with a piratical earring and bandanna. I was pretty sure that when it came to boats, however, he wouldn't know his prow from his stern.

Nick gravitated towards Lyn, a fellow literary agent, who had George, looking distinguished and ambassadorial, in tow.

Amy Weston's mother arrived late, when most of the guests had already been handed a glass of champagne and the noise level in the foyer was quickly climbing.

I'd noticed in the newspaper photos that Sonia Weston strikingly resembled her daughter. Tall, leggy and with long, blond hair, she wore a very short skirt, a waist-length jacket and very high heels. It was only when Honey introduced us that I noticed that her slenderness verged on the scraggy, her flowing locks owed much to hair extensions and the carefully applied makeup couldn't conceal the rays of lines around her big blue eyes and her mouth.

It's not a crime to want to look younger than you are, but I thought a daughter might find a Peter Pan mother a bit of a trial!

I knew I should feel deeply sympathetic towards her, as a mother searching for the truth about her lost child, so it was irrational to take an instant dislike to her . . . Or maybe it was just the way she'd clocked Thom, who was looking very handsome in a well-cut dark suit, then made a beeline for him.

I bet she was the twentieth person that morning to tell him he looked just like that actor Ivo Gryffyn!

Over Sonia's blond head, he caught my eye and winked, and I felt a sudden rush of happiness: he'd already told me I looked beautiful when he'd arrived.

Simon was wearing a suit too, although his was obviously old and comfortably baggy round the pockets and knees. Pearl had on that lovely misty-blue linen outfit she'd bought from Spindrift.

I checked my watch and found it was almost time to open the doors to the public – and I could see a surprisingly large number of people gathered outside.

Honey clapped her hands for silence and invited the Rev. Jo-Jo, who had been sitting on the corner of the reception desk, glass in hand, to say a few words.

She put her glass down and got up. Then, bowing her head, she said, 'God bless this museum. May it flourish and add to the prosperity of our little community. Amen.'

We all echoed the Amen, though perhaps Pearl and the other shopkeepers did so a little louder than the rest . . .

Derek and Baz began to collect up all the glasses, while Ella and I pinned back the big engraved glass doors: the museum was officially open!

*

I circulated, answering any questions until Honey, who had been upstairs being interviewed for the *Views Northward* TV programme, came down to do her book signing at a table that had been placed next to the wedding dress by the window. A queue of people clutching copies of *Bloody Young Men* had already formed.

On her way over, she asked me to take Sonia Weston up to the Bloody Brides room, where a local journalist wanted an interview and a photo of her standing by her daughter's wedding dress.

Sonia was all for it; she'd clearly been sulking because she'd failed to get herself included in the *Views Northward* Interview.

She whipped out a mirror, so she could check her makeup and add another slather of red lipstick, a shade that really didn't suit her born-again-blond fairness.

The journalist was waiting upstairs. Luckily, there was no one else in the room, so I could temporarily loop the rope barrier across it. I was relieved he didn't want any input from me, but thought I'd better hang around until after he'd finished.

Sonia went through the story of her daughter's disappearance and then, when asked where she thought Amy was now, she said, a catch in her voice, 'I – have to hope she's still alive. Perhaps the police will now feel it's time to re-examine the evidence and interview her former fiancé again.'

She smiled sorrowfully and I was just wondering what the ex-fiancé would make of that, if he saw the article, when a thin, dark, intense-looking man stepped over the rope, followed by a very statuesque auburn-haired woman, who seemed to be trying to restrain him.

He stopped right in front of Sonia, who cowered back, and he said, furiously, 'The police cleared me! There was no way I had anything to do with Amy's disappearance!'

'It's *you*!' gasped Sonia, now clutching the journalist's arm. 'I don't know how you dare to show your face here, Len Paget. And I *know* it was you who sent me that anonymous threatening letter, too, trying to get me to stop Amy's dress going on exhibition or telling her story.'

He frowned, staring at her, fists balled at his side. 'What letter? I've no idea what you're talking about. And I never harmed a hair of Amy's head!'

'Deep breaths, Len,' I heard the woman with him murmur soothingly, laying a hand on his arm. 'Deep breaths!'

He glanced at her, relaxed slightly, and said more quietly, 'It wasn't me, Sonia, and although I'd rather it wasn't all raked up again, I've moved on. In fact, Pippa and I are married.'

He turned his head and smiled at Pippa, who patted his hand and, with the expression of an approving nanny, said, 'That's right. Len came to me for help with anger management – and we just clicked!'

Sonia seemed nonplussed. 'I don't believe you,' she said uncertainly.

'It's quite true,' said Pippa. 'And I'm happy to say Len's anger and jealousy issues are entirely a thing of the past.'

'Well, they weren't when he and Amy were living together, because she told me he was jealous and controlling – and I still think you had something to do with her disappearance,' she added to him, accusingly.

'Oh, come off it, Mum!' loudly exclaimed an entirely

different voice, and out of the enthralled circle of watchers crowding round the doorway stepped a tall, leggy, young woman with long black hair, who was wearing, rather oddly for indoors, dark glasses. She whipped these off now, revealing large blue eyes.

Sonia went so white her makeup stood out like a mask and then she clutched at her heart.

'A-Amy?' she stuttered.

'Yes, it's me.' She pulled off her dark wig and her hair underneath was golden-blond and cropped short.

'And don't try to pretend you're amazed to see me, because I left you a letter so you've known all along I was alive. But then, you'd do anything to get your picture in the paper and a moment of fame, wouldn't you?'

'I never got a letter,' said Sonia quickly, then rearranged her features into an expression of delighted relief and held her arms out towards her daughter.

'Darling Amy, I'm *so* overwhelmed to see you again that I hardly know what I'm saying! Do come and give your mother a hug.'

'You keep off,' warned Amy. 'Save your play-acting for those stupid enough to be taken in by it. I didn't run off just because I'd decided I couldn't face having Len organize the rest of my life for me, but because I was fed up with you as well, always wanting to hang out with my friends when I lived at home, and borrowing my clothes, as if you were my sister and not my mum! And I said all that in the note I left, so maybe that's why you didn't want to show it to the police?'

The journalist, who had been scribbling away, now looked at Amy with interest. 'So, your mother has actually known all along that you left of your own accord?'

'That's right,' agreed Amy. 'I didn't tell her where I was going, though.'

At a nudge from his wife, Len now cleared his throat and said, 'Amy, I want to sincerely apologize for the way I treated you. Pippa helped me to understand what I'd done and why, and I'm a changed man.'

'Glad to hear it,' said Amy crisply, then looked at Pippa, who was nodding approvingly at her husband, in that severe-but-kind nanny way, and added, with a faint grin, 'I'm sure you've married the perfect woman for you.'

'So, how *did* you get away and stay hidden for so long?' asked the journalist. 'And why was your wedding dress bloody?'

'I planned the disappearance with my best friend, my brides-maid, Daisy. We taught at the same sixth-form college. I had a mobile phone Len didn't know about. I came into the house after the hen party, changed into some old clothes I still kept there, put the note on my mother's pillow and left by the back garden. I just had to walk down a lane to some allotments and then my friend's brother, Huw, was waiting there to pick me up.'

She turned to the watchers and beckoned a stocky, weather-beaten young man to join her.

'This is Huw and I've been living on his farm in Wales ever since – and now we're going to get married and I'm tired of wearing a wig and pretending I'm someone else, so we might as well put the record straight now.'

'And she hasn't done anything illegal by running off, so the police can close the case,' Huw put in.

'But what about the blood on the dress?' the journalist per-sisted, gesturing at the spattered wedding gown in the case behind him.

'The dress was hanging on the outside of the wardrobe and

I threw it on the bed so I could open the door and get at the jeans and sweatshirt I had in there. I remembered I'd pinned an old sapphire bluebird brooch that was my gran's inside the bodice before I made up my mind I couldn't go through with the wedding – something blue, you know? – and managed to jab the pin right into my finger, getting it out. The blood dripped on to the skirt and . . . it was sort of fascinating against the white, so I sprinkled a few more drops on it.'

'Right,' said the journalist, scribbling. 'When you saw the publicity about your disappearance and realized your mother had concealed the note you left, didn't you think it was cruel to let your ex-fiancé be under suspicion?'

'No, he deserved it. For ages I was afraid he might track me down.'

'She's right, I *did* deserve it,' admitted Len. 'But I'm really glad you're alive and happy, Amy.'

'So, it's a wedding dress story with a surprisingly happy-ever-after ending,' said the journalist brightly, snapping his notebook shut. 'Could I take a quick pic of you and your new fiancé, Amy?'

While they were doing that, I looked around for Sonia and found her backed against the wall, looking strangely deflated and shrunken.

All the watchers on the other side of the rope barrier had been silent all this time, but now a buzz broke out, rather as if a play had ended and the lights gone up.

I could see Thom, Pearl and Simon among the audience and I made my way over to them, pausing by the now tearful Sonia Weston.

'Why don't you come along with me, Sonia, and I'll give you a nice cup of tea in the staff room, before we call a taxi to take you to the station?' I suggested.

'Oh, yes, please!' she gasped gratefully, and let herself be ushered out and downstairs.

When she was in the staff room, she recovered some of her composure and tried to tell me she'd never had any note from Amy, so the accusations had all been unjust.

'And I really don't know why she should tell such fibs!' she finished.

I made soothing noises, but it was a huge relief when Derek, having heard what had happened – and by then I should think everyone in the building had – came in and offered to run her to the station.

'You are a star!' I whispered in his ear as he followed her out. He grinned and hissed back: 'Exit, bag and baggage!'

45

Flight of Fantasy

I stayed in the staff room and had a soothing cup of coffee myself, then Thom came in and told me that Amy, her fiancé, her ex and his wife had all adjourned together to the Sun in Splendour.

'And Amy says you can keep the dress on display, so long as you change the end of the story.'

'Well, that's good!' I said, then sighed. 'I'd better go and circulate among the visitors again, I suppose. Is Honey still signing books?'

'Yes, and Viv's been standing next to her, opening them ready for her to sign. You'd think her agent would have done that, but *she's* more interested in talking to your friend George.'

'I noticed they seemed to be getting on really well, too,' I agreed.

'Love seems to be in the very air of the museum, doesn't it?' he said. 'Despite the whole doomed-bride scenario.'

'They weren't *all* doomed. Some of the stories are tragic, but several are funny or have a happy ending of one kind or another.'

'I hope *we'll* have a happy ending of the traditional variety,' he said, putting his arms around me and pulling me close for a kiss. 'Did I tell you how very beautiful you look today and how much I want to marry you?'

I looked up, startled, and he kissed me again, then said ruefully, 'This wasn't the moment I meant to ask you . . . I know you need time to get used to the idea of our new relationship and I wasn't going to rush you, but . . . well, I couldn't help myself!'

He took a small box from his pocket and opened it. On a bed of dark green velvet lay an amber Bakelite ring.

'Oh, how lovely!' I said. 'How can I resist it?'

'I was hoping it was *me* you couldn't resist. I don't know if it will fit your finger or not, although it is quite small.'

But it did fit, sliding on easily, the most perfect engagement ring ever! I knew then that Thom and I were the perfect match, even if it had just taken us a very long time to find out.

We had to go back out eventually and I couldn't bear to take the ring off, so our sudden engagement wasn't going to be a secret for very long.

Honey had just finished signing for the last of the very long queue and said almost all the copies of the new book had gone – and so had Viv, who'd retired to the house to start preparing for the buffet supper Thom, Simon, Pearl and I were all invited to.

'She'd had enough of crowds for one day, anyway.'

'I think I have, too, but it's going very well,' I said, as Thom went off to find the others. Then I told Honey the whole saga of Amy turning up, alive and kicking. Of course, being Honey, she found this highly amusing.

'And I could get a plot out of it . . . only perhaps the Bloody Bride should sneak back after she's happily married to her farmer, and kill her ex?'

'Why would she want to, if she's happily married to someone else?' I objected.

'The ex will have done something to deserve it,' she said confidently. 'She can kill him with some kind of ancient farming tool . . .' she added vaguely.

I said doubtfully, 'Isn't there something called a mattock?'

'I'll look it up,' she said, but true to form had already pushed up the black velvet sleeve of her YSL jacket and was writing up her arm, with the gold pen she still held from her book signing.

I tried to read it upside down and she seemed to be trying out various titles: *Culling the Bloodline*, *Furrowed Death* and *Slaughtered Dreams*.

Then she pulled down her sleeve and, glancing up, spotted my ring.

'O-ho! Is there something my little cousin isn't telling me?'

'Thom and I just got engaged,' I confessed. 'I mean, *literally* just! I didn't even know my feelings had changed towards him till just before Marco turned up, but now we know we're in love with each other, so it seems pointless to waste any more time, doesn't it?'

'Definitely, and everyone else could see you were in love from the moment you got here, what with all those antagonistic undercurrents – very *Pride and Prejudice*!'

I laughed. 'I think I could see Thom in the Darcy role, but I'm no smart-mouthed Elizabeth Bennet.'

'I'd better go and talk to my guests, I suppose,' she said resignedly.

'And I'll go and answer even more visitors' questions . . . although my feet are hurting! I haven't worn heels for ages.'

'We all have to suffer for our art, and today has really gone with a swing, hasn't it?' Honey said, and then drifted off, tall, slim and elegant, her black bobbed hair shining under the bright foyer lights.

Pearl and Simon came to congratulate me before they left, Pearl with a potential customer for the bookshop in tow. Thom also went soon after to walk Jester, and the crowd began to thin a little.

I'd just retreated into the corner next to the charity shop dress to surreptitiously ease one painful foot out of its shoe, while listening to the hum of visitors, like happy bees, and the merry jingle of the till, when a slightly husky gin-and-cigarettes kind of voice accosted me.

'Blimey! That looks just like my wedding dress!'

A latecomer, a buxom, rosy-faced young woman with bright, bubble-gum-pink hair, had stopped dead and was staring at the wedding dress in the window.

Then she glanced at me, clocked my badge and said uncertainly: 'You know, for a minute I thought that really *was* my wedding dress! It's almost identical.'

'If you happened to have given it to a charity shop in Ormskirk, it probably *is* your dress!' I told her.

'Actually, I *did*, but my dress was plainer.'

'It was quite plain, but I added new roses because the old ones were a bit limp, the jewelled belt and a bit of bling on the skirt.'

'Then it is mine – but it looks a lot prettier. I wish *I'd* thought of getting them to bling it up a bit!'

'Why did you give it to the charity shop?' I asked tentatively.

'Course you can! In fact, I only came to look round the museum because of what happened to me! I'm Rachel, by the way.'

'Garland,' I said. 'Please do tell me your story, because I'd love to hear it.'

'Well, my wedding day started off to plan. My parents spent

a fortune on it and booked a lovely country house hotel for the reception. It was a perfect, fairy-tale wedding – right up to the point where I found my husband and my bridesmaid – who was also my best friend – in a very compromising position in a walled garden.'

'What an awful shock! You must have been devastated?'

'Nah – I was absolutely *livid*! I shoved them both in this big lily pond they were standing next to, then ripped off my dress and veil and tossed those in after them.'

She grinned suddenly and engagingly, showing a gap between her front teeth. 'Bev, my ex-friend, was screaming and they were both struggling about under all that wet material, but I left them to it and went back to the reception in my slip – it was like a thin, slinky dress, anyway – and danced the night away. My dad and my brothers saw my soon-to-be ex-husband and Bev off the premises.'

'That was . . . very brave of you,' I said weakly, trying not to laugh.

'Mum and Dad paid a lot for that wedding, so we had to get our money's worth out of it. And Mum went and fished the dress and veil out of the pond later and washed them when she got home. They came up fine, so we gave them to the charity shop.'

'Do you mind that *we* bought it, to put on display?' I asked, and told her it had also featured in an episode of *The Upcycled Bride* TV series.

'I watch that!' she exclaimed, thrilled. 'You keep it and tell people the whole story of what happened.'

When we'd exchanged phone numbers, she said, 'I've got a new fiancé now and I've told him if he cheats on me, my brothers will see he talks in a very high voice for the rest of his life.'

Then she went off to explore the rest of the museum and I glimpsed her later wearing a sparkly plastic bridal tiara from the shop.

*

We all gathered that evening at Pelican House, tired but happy, for the opening had been a huge success.

As well as Thom and Pearl, Honey had also invited Kay and Ella, the Rev. Jo-Jo, and Derek and Baz. George and Lyn were there too, of course, since they weren't leaving till next day.

Viv had laid on a lovely buffet in the dining room, and the double doors between the rooms were thrown open.

Rory, being big enough to snatch things off the table, was shut in the kitchen, but occasionally sneaked out whenever anyone forgot and left the door open for a moment.

Honey had broken out the champagne and, in a mood of tired euphoria, we all enthusiastically toasted the success of the museum, Ella and Kay's sales prowess and, finally, my engagement to Thom.

I think we were all a bit tiddly after the toasts, but I suspected Lyn had had a few drinks before the rest of us arrived, because she raised her glass again and said, slightly slurring the words, 'We should toast our bestselling novelist's new book too – straight to number one, Honey!'

She gave a small hiccup. 'Or perhaps we should toast *both* my bestselling authors, because I suppose now you're living in the same place as the star of those films based on your books, Viv, everyone knows you wrote the Silvermann Chronicles.'

There was a silence while we all took this in, before turning as one to stare at Viv, who was shrinking back into her chair.

Honey said resignedly, 'No, everyone *didn't* know, Lyn, but they do now. What happened to your vow of secrecy?'

'Whoops!' said Lyn, and gave a very unprofessional giggle. 'But Thom must surely have guessed that Viv is Gus Silvermann?'

'No, why should I? It never even crossed my mind!' Thom exclaimed, still staring at Viv, who avoided his gaze and looked as if she might bolt at any moment.

I think only Kay and Ella had no idea what Lyn was talking about, because the vicar said benevolently, 'How very clever of you, Viv!'

And then Baz and Derek both said 'Cool!' at the same time, then laughed.

'Did you *really* write them, Viv? Wicked!' said Simon, admiringly. 'If I had, I wouldn't have kept it secret.'

'Viv never wanted any publicity, so apart from her husband and Lyn – and myself, of course – it's been kept secret for years,' Honey said. 'She and her husband liked a simple, quiet, country life, and they wouldn't have had that if hordes of fans had known who she was.'

'No, they certainly wouldn't,' agreed Thom. 'And I suppose that's why you've always seemed nervous around me, Viv? You were afraid I might somehow find out?'

'What she was really afraid of was that you'd blame her for ruining your life, after I told her how you hadn't wanted to be a child actor and had to grow up in front of the cameras, not to mention being mobbed wherever you went.'

'But that was hardly your fault, Viv,' he said. 'It was my stepparents who made me take the role. But eventually, after the films finished and all the fuss died down, I met Bruno and discovered what I really wanted to do with my life.'

'And now he's going to marry Garland, Viv, so really, you haven't ruined his life at all,' Honey said bracingly.

Then she asked Simon to top everyone's glasses up again. Frankly, I thought most of us were afloat already and would soon be washing up in odd corners, like bits of flotsam.

'Come and get a bit more food to mop up all the booze,' Thom suggested in my ear, and we loaded our plates with more sandwiches, cheese puffs and quiche.

Simon was already on to the desserts and, having been unable to choose between chocolate gateau and trifle, had helped himself to both.

'You are so talented!' Simon told Viv when we went back into the sitting room. 'A brilliant cook as well as a mega-selling author.'

'She's a really excellent poet, too,' said Honey.

'Yes, but there's no *money* in poetry these days, unless you're a performance poet, out on the road the whole time,' objected Lyn, who looked as if she was only staying upright because George had his arm around her.

'She doesn't *need* the money, Lyn!' pointed out Honey. 'She can write what she likes.'

Apart from an extra brightness in her dark eyes, Honey seemed entirely unaffected by the champagne, and went on, 'What an action-packed day it's been, hasn't it? The museum opening day couldn't have gone better, and then all the drama of Amy Weston turning up alive and well was the icing on the wedding cake.'

'And then the bride whose dress we bought in the charity shop suddenly appearing at the end!' I put in.

'Not to mention you and Thom getting engaged – and then, finally, Viv's outing as the acclaimed author Gus Silvermann!' Honey said.

Viv, still huddled into her armchair, made one of her alarmed squeaks, but Lyn said, bracingly, 'I'm sorry I gave you away, but you really should learn to be proud of those books, Viv. I mean, the sales were *enormous*, especially after the films. But that was all ages ago and now there isn't that much interest in the more Dungeons and Dragons end of the fantasy market.'

'I'm sure Viv would still prefer us to keep it to ourselves,' Honey said, and Viv nodded fervently.

'Of course we won't tell anyone else,' Jo-Jo agreed, for all of us. She grinned suddenly, her rosy cheeks bunching up into dimples. 'After all, we've had years of pretending we don't know who Thom really is!'

'*Was*,' said Thom, firmly.

*

When Thom and I were leaving, Jo-Jo took our hands and blessed us, then said she'd love to perform our wedding ceremony, if we'd like that.

The thought of marrying Thom in that lovely little whitewashed church, with the angels flying in the window overhead, made my head spin even more than it had been doing, but in a happy kind of way.

Rosa-May

28 July

My nausea ever increases, so that I retch when trying to eat and grow ever weaker.

Sophie has instructed the cook to make dainty morsels to tempt an appetite I no longer possess, and Sara coaxes me to sip clear broth or warm milk.

It was evident that my journey to London would have to be undertaken in easy stages, which would be costly, but I have pinned my hopes on Guy's agreement to my plans and to his giving Rafe instructions to enable me to travel – and for the sake of my health, the sooner, the better.

*

Today my hopes have been entirely dashed! It seems that against my wishes, Rafe told Guy that I was with child and Guy writes that I must continue at Up-Heythram Hall, under Sophia's care, and await him here!

The letter was both short and couched in the coldest terms, not at all in his old, slapdash and affectionate manner, but I reasoned that he must still be suffering great pain, which would account for it.

He has informed Rafe that he would shortly set out for England, in the company of his friend Captain Wentworth, whose family had engaged a doctor to accompany them.

I fear I must be resigned to staying here for the present, at least, though I comfort myself with the recollection of how much Guy dislikes the place, so that once his health is regained, I am sure he will be as eager to leave it as I am!

*

August

Sophia constantly urges me to eat, but I know her concern is only for the child and not for me, especially since she unkindly informed me that since I have become so thin and lost my looks, Guy will hardly recognize his wife.

There is some truth in this, for the mirror shows me a pale and wan face, the eyes dark-circled.

As I enter into my third month, Sara assures me that many women lose their sickness soon after this, so that I must hope I am one of them!

I do not sleep well, for my dreams are filled with terror and foreboding.

'So we just have to organize the reception now, but only a small one, since we're not inviting a lot of guests,' I said later that afternoon to Honey and Viv, when the six of us had once more gathered at Pelican House for what we intended to be our final onslaught on the attic clearance.

I'd noticed that since Lyn had outed her pen name, Viv seemed a lot more relaxed around Thom. Maybe one day she'd even speak to him!

'Why not hold the reception in the museum?' suggested Honey. 'Your wedding is at two, so if we closed it for the morning it would give us plenty of time to get everything ready. In fact, I'll hire caterers in to do it all for us! We'll throw open the whole ground floor and a buffet can be set up in the staff room.'

'That's *so* kind of you, but of course, we must pay for it all, Honey,' I said.

'You're my only relative, Garland, and I really want to do this for you, so don't spoil my fun!' she said, with her twisted grin.

'Having the reception in the museum would certainly be different,' Thom said. 'I think it's a great idea!'

'How many people are you thinking of inviting?' asked Pearl.

'I'll have to make a list, but not many. Thom's inviting Sir Mallory Mortlake and his wife, who are old friends, and of course I want George to be there – and perhaps your agent, Lyn, might like to come too, Honey?' I suggested.

'I suspect George and Lyn would be up for another road trip together,' agreed Honey. 'I get the impression from Lyn that they're seeing a lot of each other.'

'Yes, I gathered that from George's last email.'

'Our other guests will just be local friends,' Thom said.

'*I* think you should invite that actor friend of yours too,

Garland – Will Wolfram!' said Honey. 'I've been checking him out on the internet. He's rather dishy and looks just my type.'

'If you're serious I could invite him,' I said, looking at her dubiously.

'Dead serious!' she assured me.

We'd arrived at the attics by then, the three large ones now cleared and the things Honey wanted to keep neatly stacked against the walls.

We made our way through them to the small, packed room and surveyed it from the doorway without a lot of expectation.

'The things in here look a lot more recent than in the other rooms. I suspect Hugo used it to shove odds and ends in, when he was trying to find more family papers,' Honey said. 'It was probably empty before that, because those steps down and the sharp bend in the corridor would make getting anything large or heavy in here difficult.'

'I can see a couple of big cabin trunks stacked up on each other, right at the back,' said Simon.

'Yes, but those are cumbersome rather than really heavy,' she said.

We moved three tea chests of old books into the first attic, where Pearl could look through them more comfortably, while we sorted the rest out . . . starting with a hideous hat stand constructed out of antlers.

'One for Arthur's Cave,' said Honey, as we dragged it out and Thom and Simon manoeuvred it up the steps.

Except for a couple of nice oil lamps, we found nothing terribly interesting, and any slight lingering hope that we'd find any more of Rosa-May's belongings faded and died.

Soon, only the two huge cabin trunks were left against the furthest wall.

Pearl rejoined us, a smudge of dust across one cheek, and said she had one small box of books to take back to the shop and check out further, but the rest were all things like collections of sermons, which no one would want.

'Arthur will just have to take them away, then,' Honey said. 'I'll let him have that old mirror with the good frame for free.'

'Yeah, but it makes anyone reflected in it look as if they've got leprosy,' Simon pointed out.

'I think mirrors can be re-silvered,' Thom suggested. 'Right, shall we get on? Simon, help me lift down the trunk stacked on top.'

When opened, it contained only a pair of huge green velvet curtains, sun-faded along the folds. The trunk that had been beneath, however, was heavier when they pulled it into the middle of the room.

The weight was explained when they lifted the lid to reveal that a smaller and much older-looking chest of dark wood had been put inside.

On top lay a fat, brown manila envelope, on which had been written boldly in black ink: 'Open this, before you look inside the chest.'

'That's Hugo's handwriting!' exclaimed Honey, pouncing on it. 'How curious!'

She tore it open and took out a sheet of paper. With it came a small book with a brown calfskin cover.

'But . . . that looks just like Rosa-May's journal!' I cried. 'Honey, could Hugo have found the missing second volume?'

'He must have,' she said, opening it. 'This is her writing – but how odd of Uncle Hugo to hide it away like this!'

She turned a few more pages. 'She doesn't seem to have written many more entries and the light in here is too bad to make out her tiny handwriting. Let's see what Hugo has to say.'

She unfolded the paper, scanned it, then said, 'Listen to this.'

> To whoever finds this – quite possibly my great-niece Honey Fairford, since I'm sure the clutter of the attic will be anathema to her and she won't rest until it is all cleared out.
>
> I discovered the old wooden chest some years ago, while searching the attics for more family documents, and there seemed to me to be no point in stirring up old secrets that reflected badly on the family. So in the end, after removing the enclosed journal, and locking the chest, I had it placed inside in this cabin trunk and stored here with the other old luggage.
>
> The thought of it has occasionally weighed on my conscience, but I leave it to whichever descendant discovers it to decide what course to take.
>
> Hugo Fairford

Even before Thom and Simon had lifted the old wooden chest out and prised open the lid, I think we all had a foreboding of what we'd find inside.

Honey lifted out a small leather valise and there, curled underneath it, was the pathetically tiny body – withered and mummified to little more than a skeleton. The uppermost side of the small skull was dented in and broken . . .

'Well, I think we can now have a fair guess at what happened to Rosa-May,' said Honey, and even she sounded shaken.

*

Probably due to all the research she did for her books, Honey knew that however old a body appeared to be, the police must be informed and she rang them right away.

Then, since she suspected they would take away the journal and letter as well as the body, she sent Viv and Pearl to scan them into the computer in her office, before the police arrived.

After that, we all went downstairs and had a stiff drink.

*

Later, once the formalities were over and the sad remains had been removed, we had a very late and rather subdued supper.

Honey ran off a few copies of the final journal pages while I helped Viv make the coffee. Then we all retired to the sitting room to read them.

Honey gave the others a brief résumé of Rosa-May's life to the point where the final journal entries started, but after that there was silence in the room, except for the crackling of paper or the chink of a coffee cup in its saucer.

Even though I was used to reading Rosa-May's handwriting, it wasn't easy, because these last entries had obviously been hastily written at a time when she had a very troubled mind. And, as I read on, I was not surprised.

47

Last Words

12 August 1815

This afternoon my husband returned to me, accompanied by the doctor who had attended him on the long journey home.

I had braced myself not to recoil when I first saw him – lame, suffering from the loss of his arm and perhaps disfigured from his head wound . . . but what I had not expected was that he should be so changed in his character and his manner towards me.

In this wasted, bitter man, a long scar puckering one side of his face in a way that made him seem a stranger, I could find no trace of the lively, merry, young man I had so incontinently married.

I know my own sickness has much changed me, too, and when I first saw him he stared at me as if he did not know me and then was very cold and distant in his manner.

I had hoped that, once he had recovered somewhat from his injuries, he would be my ally in wishing to leave the Hall and soon agree to our moving to London. As a younger son, he did not have much income of his own, but I could return to the stage once I had delivered my child – a prospect that still made me shudder with apprehension – and recovered my looks and health.

I pray some of his old affection and cheerful spirit will return to him soon . . .

*

Today I begged an interview with Dr Bowen, who was staying with us for some days to see Guy settled, and he assured me that the effects of such injuries as Guy had sustained often caused a temporary change in character. But with patience and good nursing, he would soon become more his old self.

After this, I ventured to ask him about my own condition and the weakness the endless sickness caused me, which the local physician had ascribed to mere hysteria! He was most kindly and said he disagreed, for he had heard of other cases of a similar kind, where the situation had improved once the three-month stage was passed. This was very much as Sara had suggested and I hoped it would be so. Meanwhile, I was to rest – although I had little energy to do anything else! – and eat small amounts of whatever I felt I could stomach, at as frequent intervals as possible.

*

The good doctor has left, but I managed, without anyone seeing me, to slip letters to Letty and to Mrs Blake into his hand and begged him to see they reached my friends when he returned to London. He assured me he would and stowed them away in his coat pocket.

I was very sorry to see him go.

Guy keeps to his rooms and, although I go in each evening to wish him goodnight, he evinces little interest in seeing me and turns the scarred side of his face to the wall.

I must be patient . . .

*

There is little evidence of summer to cheer my days, for as August moves into September, the sun seems to be permanently obscured by cloud.

I think Sara and the good doctor were right in saying my health would soon improve, for, while I remain sickly and often nauseous, I can retain a little more nourishment.

Guy says that I could be well if I wished, and most women with child did not fall into such a sickly state! He is not kind and said I had entirely lost my looks . . .

He himself grows stronger, but still keeps to his rooms, especially when there are visitors, although in this remote spot that is a rare enough occurrence. He appears to have a great dread of people seeing his disfigurement. Nor does he seek my company and my only amusements, when I am well enough, are to take short walks in the shrubbery, or read the novels that Sophia devours.

*

October

A dressmaker was summoned to make looser garments for me, for although I have put on no flesh elsewhere, my stomach is now already very big . . .

Sophia says it is often so with small women, and also said spitefully that women of such small stature have great pain and difficulty in the delivery of their children, which has only added to my terror, for I remember the trials Mama suffered and her permanent poor health after several confinements.

I am shut up here in this godforsaken place, with nothing to do and no congenial company, other than Sara – and no hope of escape, for when I tentatively asked Guy if, when he was a little better, we might return to London and make our home there, he told me we would be permanently fixed at the Hall, where, once he was well enough, he would take over the management of the estate for his brother.

I was in total despair at this news, and feel so very trapped, both by my condition and my married state, which renders me penniless.

Or almost so, for I still have a little gold hidden away in the trunk containing my lovely Titania costume . . . and I have hidden the first volume of my memoir and journal there, too.

I cannot stand the prospect of living here for ever, with a husband who seems to hate me, and Rafe and Sophia, who both despise me.

That is, if I survive the travails of childbirth . . .

When I said this to Sara she told me I should not be maudlin, for there were many small women who had brought children into the world and survived to tell the tale! Also, that I must try and look forward to the arrival of my babe, for once I hold it in my arms, I will think all was worth it.

I cannot confess even to her that I resent the child I carry for ruining my health and keeping me here, and my longing for the day it is born is solely due to the prospect that I might then escape, for I know even Sara would think this unnatural.

Guy does not grow warmer towards me, but seems now almost to hate me, so lately I have even wondered if perhaps he would agree that we might separate, difficult though that might be for me: penniless, and with my way in the world to make again. Though, of course, with good friends to assist me . . .

Sara points out that if I do so, then my child will stay here and

I will probably never be permitted to see it again, but that price I am willing to pay for my freedom.

*

November

I am in great distress, for Guy says Sara has been mollycoddling me and encouraging me in my airs and megrims, and has sent her back to London!

This is beyond cruel and I am reeling from the blow. The young maid, Mary, who is to wait on me now, is kindly and helpful, but can never be my friend and confidante, as Sara was.

And yet, since she is betrothed to one of the grooms, she might yet be of use to me . . .

*

December

It is so cold and the house draughty that I keep to my rooms very much . . . and without Sara find myself sinking into a deep gloom I cannot rid myself of. I am now very big and the babe lively, which also predisposes me to dark despair at the thought of the ordeal to come – and my appetite, only capriciously returned, has vanished.

Sophia worries and urges me to eat for the sake of the child . . .

*

Today I could have embraced Sophia, for she has persuaded Guy to allow Sara to return!

It was for the good of the babe, of course, and since Rafe and

521

Sophia have no children of their own, it will be the heir to the estate. I had not thought of this.

*

Oh, joy! Sara has returned and, despite much scolding of me for my lack of spirits and appetite, has already chased away some of the black clouds and given me a little hope. Also, she brought letters from dear Letty, assuring me of her affection and her hope that, once my confinement is over and I am fit enough, I might be able to make a long stay with her in London.

If I am allowed to do so, then I am determined I will not return, despite knowing that leaving my husband would be a bold and terrible step to take.

*

February 1816

How long it is since I have written here – and how relieved I am that the terrors of childbirth are now a thing of the past!

I felt increasingly unwell and uncomfortable over the Christmas season and then, well before the time, my labours began and I gave birth to twin boys, who, although very small, were healthy enough and thrived once a wet nurse had been found for them.

For myself, I was in a high fever for a fortnight and knew nothing.

It is such a relief to have that behind me, and although I have now seen my babes, they do not feel at all a part of me, nor do I feel the love everyone thinks I should towards them, and which Sophia, who has taken on the role of doting mother, seems to feel.

No, I am strangely detached . . . and determined never to go *through that experience again. I wish only to be well enough to make my return to London, one way or another.*

*

My appetite has returned and, although the weather is cold, I take a turn in the garden every day.

My mirror also tells me my looks are not forever lost to me and I may yet one day take flight again as Titania on the London stage.

*

Guy too has been leaving his rooms more often and this morning happened to come into my chamber when I had got Sara to put me into the Titania costume, to see if it still fitted me – and I was laughing and pirouetting around the room like a giddy girl, when he came upon us, perhaps attracted by the unaccustomed sound of my laughter.

He flew into an irrational fury and said I should forget my former life and strive to be a good wife to him, instead – and then, to my horror, declared that if I was well enough for such nonsense as play-acting, I could resume my wifely duties . . .

I was so horrified by this that I said straight out that I would never do so: that our marriage was a mistake, for I was not fitted by nature for childbirth. Then I begged him to let me return to London.

This made him even more furious and he said he would not stand for the dishonour of having a wife leave him and go back on to the stage. Then he struck me with such force that I was sent flying across the room and did not know where I was until I came to my senses sometime later, with Sara bathing my bruised face with lavender water and crying.

I have locked my bedroom door against him, and once more, as I did so many years ago, I am planning to run away. Sara now wholeheartedly agrees that this is the only course I can now take.

*

Sara has been sent back to London again, but that suits us very well, for she is to arrange with Letty, to whom I have appealed, how I may be conveyed to London. She will return and stay in the nearest town once everything is in train, and send word when a carriage will await me by the Hall gates, once all is arranged, by means of the young maid, Mary. I gave her the little gold I have stowed away, although she said she would in any case have helped me for the affection and pity she had for my situation, for, of course, the whole household knows that my husband was violent towards me.

I have begged Sara and Letty to make the arrangements at the first opportunity, for fear of what Guy will do if I continue to deny him.

*

1 March

It is tonight! I am both excited and fearful.

Mary will help me slip out of the house at midnight and there will be a carriage – and Sara – waiting for me by the gates.

I can carry little, just one small valise, but that does not matter. Nothing matters except to get away.

I did go to look at my babes in their cradles this evening – they thrive, despite being so small – and wished them well, but did not feel truly that they were mine. Sophia will find her fulfilment in taking my place as their mother.

I will take this journal with me, but dare not go up to the attic, where the box containing my Titania costume has been banished, in which I hid the first volume.

I feigned sickness this evening and did not go down to dinner, but stayed in my room instead, for I feared they might see my nervous state and wonder at it.

And now it is almost time to leave. Mary is here, ready to help me into my cloak and see me safe through the dark house to the side door on to the shrubbery – and the freedom that beckons beyond . . .

*

That was the last entry. When I'd finished reading it, I looked up and waited for the others to reach the end, too.

Honey, Viv and I were first, probably because we had read her previous journal and were used to her handwriting, but when the others, one by one, looked up, I said, 'So it seems we'll still never know exactly what happened to Rosa-May – only that she never left Up-Heythram Hall.'

'The conclusions are pretty obvious, though,' pointed out Honey. 'I mean, she didn't hit herself over the head and lock herself in a trunk, did she?'

'Since she wrote the final entry just before she was to make her escape, it seems obvious something happened to her that very night,' said Thom. 'But she could have met with an accident.'

'Unlikely – and why then hide the body?' said Honey sceptically. 'No, it's evident what happened: her husband's head wound caused him to become unbalanced and prone to anger and violence, so I think she met her death at his hands. His family must have helped him cover it up.'

'I suppose if he discovered her in the act of running away, that might have been the scenario,' agreed Simon. 'He probably didn't mean to kill her, but she was a tiny little thing, wasn't she?'

'Very much the same size as Garland,' said Honey, 'but of course, she had suffered a lot during her pregnancy and been ill after the twins were born, so she must have still been very frail.'

'Poor Rosa-May,' Pearl said gently.

'The interesting thing is,' said Honey, a gleam in her dark eyes, 'that if Guy Fairford killed his wife, then Garland and I are descended from a murderer!'

'Thank you for that thought!' I said. 'And given my temper, Thom might think twice about marrying me, now.'

'You always were a fiery little creature,' he said with a grin. 'But you never resorted to physical violence.'

'Destroying the Titania costume was violence by proxy,' I pointed out.

'I still think I'm safe,' he assured me.

'What happens now?' Simon asked Honey.

'When the police have finished their work, I expect they'll release the body and I thought I'd ask Jo-Jo if she could hold a quiet service for her and then allow her to be laid to rest in the churchyard there.'

'I'm sure she will, and that's a lovely idea,' said Pearl. 'Then her soul will be at peace.'

It was more than *mine* was after the day's revelations, and I *really* didn't want to be alone that night, so Thom fetched Jester and his basket over to my cottage and stayed with me, the very *best* kind of comfort blanket . . .

Epilogue

Pure Gold

1 December 2018

Thom stood at the altar of the little church of St Gabriel with Simon, his best man, at his side. Turning as the organ started to play, he watched his beautiful bride walk down the aisle and thought he was the luckiest man alive.

Garland was wearing her vintage tusser silk dress and jacket, and they shone like cloth of gold in the slanting sunlight. The hair ornament Simon had made for her sparkled in her bright copper hair, but she wore no ring, for the Bakelite one Thom had given her was in his pocket, waiting to be presented to her all over again: she had wanted no other ring.

As she moved towards him on Honey's arm, with Pearl in attendance, the angel window briefly cast a harlequin pattern of colour over them, like a bright blessing.

He didn't think it would be possible to feel any happier than he did at that moment: marrying his best friend and the woman he loved, and looking forward to their life living and working together, happy and fulfilled.

Garland smiled at him, green eyes shining, and he thought,

amused, that with her fiery hair and temperament, she was no angel – but then *he'd* never been the fantasy hero of the films he'd made, either.

Grinning, he turned back to face the front as she took her place at his side.

The Rev. Jo-Jo, beaming and spreading her arms wide, as if to embrace them all, began 'Dearly beloved . . .'

*

Outside, they paused only briefly to lay Garland's small posy of yellow roses on Rosa-May's simple grave, for the clouds had closed in and feathery snow was falling.

'Rest in peace, Rosa-May,' Garland said.

'I think she will, now,' said Thom, then took her hand and drew her away towards the car.

'But it's time for *us* to live – and I love you, Garland Fairford!'

'I love you, too, Thom Reid,' she said gravely, and they kissed, with cold lips, before breaking apart and running back to the car over the thin layer of soft white snow.

'Those satin shoes of yours will be ruined,' he said as they reached it.

'It's all right,' she assured him. 'I'm not going to need wedding shoes *ever* again!'

Postscript

18 June 1816

I, Mary Marshall, lately maidservant at Up-Heythram Hall, now finding myself near death and believing that the wasting sickness that has so grievously afflicted me is a punishment from God, most urgently desire to unburden my soul of a great evil I have witnessed – and indeed, was party to.

The wife of my master's younger brother, Guy Fairford, confided in me that she was deeply unhappy in her marriage and had resolved to seek refuge with friends in London. I was very shocked, for though all knew that since his return from the great battle against Bonaparte last summer he had treated her ill, it is a wife's lot to bear such things and find consolation in her children. But I was weak and the gold she offered persuaded me to assist her to leave the house late one night when a carriage was to meet her at the gates.

We were both in fear and trembling as we made our way down through the dark house to a side door, though not from the same cause: for, having bethought me that I would be turned off from my position without a character, should my part in the affair be found out, I had told Mr Guy Fairford of his wife's intent – and he was awaiting us below stairs.

In a fury he smote her such a great blow to the head that she was felled to the ground and stirred no more. Then the master also came on the scene and told me to go to bed and speak not to anyone of this matter, so that I fled the terrible scene.

I did not gainsay it when next day it was said that Mrs Fairford had eloped in the night with a lover, though I knew in my heart that, small and slight as she was, she could not have survived such a blow, and this knowledge has weighed heavily on my soul.

Acknowledgement

With thanks to my son, Robin Ashley, for all his technical support, research and so much more invaluable assistance.

About the Author

Trisha Ashley's *Sunday Times* bestselling novels have sold over one million copies in the UK and have twice been shortlisted for the Melissa Nathan Award for Romantic Comedy. *Every Woman for Herself* was nominated by magazine readers as one of the top three romantic novels in the last fifty years. Trisha lives in North Wales.

For more information about Trisha and her books, please visit:

TrishaAshleyBooks

trishaashley

Recipes

Garland's Perfect Parmesan Omelette

Ingredients:
- 2 large eggs
- 1 heaped tbsp of grated Parmesan cheese
- 1 tbsp butter, cooking fat or oil

Method:
1. Beat two large eggs in a bowl.
2. Season with a pinch of salt and black pepper to taste.
3. Finely grate a heaped tablespoon of Parmesan cheese into a separate bowl.
4. In a non-stick frying pan, heat a small knob of butter or cooking fat, or alternatively a little oil.
5. When a tiny drop of the egg mixture sizzles when you drip it into the pan, pour in the beaten eggs and tilt the pan gently in each direction until the egg covers the base of the pan.
6. Keep lifting the edges of the omelette with a spatula and tilting the pan to let the mixture run underneath and puff up.
7. Once the egg has set, flip the omelette over using a spatula.
8. Sprinkle the grated cheese into the middle of the omelette and then fold it in half.
9. Lightly fry for a minute or two on each side to melt the cheese.
10. Serve immediately.

Viv's Chocolate Brownies

Ingredients:
- 240g/8.5oz unsalted butter, melted and cooled
- 2 tbsp vegetable oil
- 260g/9oz caster sugar
- 200g/7oz light brown sugar
- 4 large eggs, at room temperature
- 1 tsp vanilla extract
- 130g/4.5oz plain flour
- 100g/3.5oz good quality, unsweetened cocoa powder
- ¾ tsp salt
- 200g/7oz chopped dark chocolate

Method:
1. Preheat oven to 200°C/fan 180°C/gas mark 6.
2. Lightly grease an 8 x 12-inch (20 x 30cm) baking pan with butter. Line with greaseproof paper and set aside.
3. Add the melted butter, oil and sugars together in a medium-sized bowl. Whisk well to combine.
4. Add the eggs and vanilla. Continue to whisk until the mixture turns lighter in colour, around 2 minutes.
5. Sift in the flour, cocoa powder and salt into a separate bowl.
6. Gently fold the dry ingredients into the wet ingredients until just combined. Do not overmix as it will affect the texture of your brownies.
7. Fold in three-quarters of the chocolate pieces.
8. Pour the mixture into the prepared pan. Smooth the top out and sprinkle with the remaining chocolate pieces.
9. Bake for 25–30 minutes for a fudgier texture or 35–40 minutes if you like your brownies firm.

10. After 15–20 minutes, carefully remove them from the pan and allow to cool to room temperature before slicing.

11. Serve while still warm with a scoop of ice cream for a decadent treat. Alternatively, they will keep in an air-tight container for 5 days and be the perfect accompaniment to a cup of tea.

Fruitcake

Ingredients:
- 700g/1.5lb dried mixed fruit (you can use dry fruits of your choice and add candied peels, glacé cherries or nuts according to your preference)
- Zest of 1 lemon
- Zest of 1 orange
- 230g/8oz plain flour
- 1 tsp baking powder
- 1 tsp each of mixed spice and cinnamon
- 230g/8oz unsalted butter
- 100g/3.5oz soft brown sugar
- 3 tbsp molasses
- 180ml/6fl oz water
- 3 eggs
- ½ tsp salt

Method:
1. Preheat oven to 160°C/fan 140°C/gas mark 3.
2. Lightly grease an 8 inch (20cm) cake tin with some butter and line with greaseproof paper.
3. Chop the dried fruit and place in a large bowl.
4. Zest the lemon and orange into a small bowl and set aside.
5. Sift the flour, baking powder and spices into a medium-sized bowl.
6. In a saucepan, combine the butter with the mixed fruit, brown sugar, molasses and water and bring to a boil.
7. Simmer over a high heat for 3–4 minutes, stirring occasionally to ensure the mixture doesn't stick.

8. Remove from the heat and let stand until it is cool.
9. Once cool, beat in the three eggs.
10. Add in the flour, baking powder and spices, and salt, and the zest of the citrus fruits.
11. Mix well until everything is just incorporated.
12. Transfer the batter into the prepared tin.
13. Bake for about 75–90 minutes. The cake will be ready when a toothpick inserted into the centre of the cake comes out clean.
14. Let the cake cool completely before taking it out of the tin.

Serving suggestion: this fruitcake is best served the day after baking. I would recommend following Simon's advice and eating it with a chunk of cheese, Lancashire Crumbly is my favourite.

Easy Eccles Cakes

Ingredients:
- 320g/11oz roll of pre-made puff pastry
- 200g/7oz dried currants
- Zest of 1 lemon
- Zest of 1 orange
- 100g/3.5oz soft brown sugar
- 1 tsp cinnamon
- 1 tsp allspice
- 2 tbsp unsalted butter
- 1 egg white, beaten
- 20g/0.7oz granulated sugar

Method:
1. Preheat the oven to 180°C/fan 160°C/gas mark 4.
2. Prepare a baking sheet by lightly greasing it with butter and lining with greaseproof paper.
3. Place the puff pastry roll onto a lightly floured surface. Roll out the pastry until it's 0.5cm (0.2 inch) thick.
4. To make the filling, mix the currants, zest of the lemon and orange, brown sugar and spices in a large bowl and stir to combine.
5. Then, melt the butter in a small saucepan over medium heat. Once melted, add the butter to the currant mixture.
6. To assemble the Eccles cakes, use a cup as a guide to cut out eight circles from the puff pastry.
7. Place a heaped tablespoon of the fruit mixture in the centre of each circle.
8. Moisten the pastry edges with water. Then gather the pastry around the filling and squeeze it together.

9. Remove greasepr
   minutes until the
   small holes or cra
10. While the pastry
    frying pan and t
    start to brown. R
11. Dice 38g (1.3oz
    Scatter the diced
    tom of the pastry
12. Using a spoon,
    continually mixi
    mix in the beate
13. Season to taste
    shouldn't need m
    meg. Pour three
14. Half-pull the ov
    sheet. Quickly p
    case. Scatter the
    push the shelf ba
15. Lower the oven
    about 25 minute
16. Let the quiche s
    tin. Serve imme

9. Flip each Eccles cake over so the smooth top is upwards and gently flatten each round, making sure not to break the pastry.
10. Brush each cake with egg white and sprinkle generously with granulated sugar.
11. Make three parallel cuts across the top of each cake, then transfer to the prepared baking sheet.
12. Bake for 12–15 minutes or until golden brown.

Classic Quic

Ingredients:

- 175g/6oz
- 100g/3.5c
- 1 egg yolk
- 200g/7oz
- 50g/1.75c
- 200ml/7f
- 200ml/7f
- 3 eggs, be
- Pinch gro

Method:

1. First, pre
   cold butte
   cessor. Us
2. Tip the p
   ball. Plac
   For the b
3. Take the
   you can.
4. Preheat tl
5. Ease the
   bottomec
6. Trim the
   the tin. P
   with a for
7. Put a bak
8. Place grea
   and bake

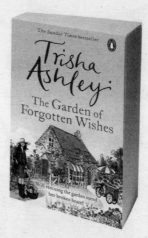

THE GARDEN OF FORGOTTEN WISHES

All Marnie wants is somewhere to call home.
Mourning lost years spent in a marriage that has finally
come to an end, she needs a fresh start and time to heal.
Things she hopes to find in the rural west Lancashire
village her mother always told her about.

With nothing but her two green thumbs, Marnie takes
a job as a gardener, which comes with a little cottage to
make her own. The garden is beautiful – filled with roses,
lavender and honeysuckle – and only a little rough around
the edges. Which is more than can be said for her
next-door neighbour, Ned Mars.

Marnie remembers Ned from her college days but he's far
from the untroubled man she once knew. A recent
relationship has left him with a heart as bruised as her own.

**Can a summer spent gardening help them recapture
the forgotten dreams they've let get away?**

ONE MORE CHRISTMAS AT THE CASTLE

This Christmas will be the most special of them all . . .

Elderly widow Sabine knows this will be her last Christmas in her beloved home, Mitras Castle. Determined to make it just like the ones she remembers from her childhood, she employs Dido Jones of Heavenly Houseparties to help with the big day.

Dido is enchanted by the castle as soon as she steps through the imposing front door. And as Christmas Day approaches, her feeling of connection to the old house runs deeper than she first thought.

But when the snow begins to fall and Sabine's family arrive at the house – including Dido's teenage crush Xan – tensions rise around the castle's future and long-buried mysteries begin to unravel . . .

As past secrets come to light, can this still be a magical Christmas to remember?

THE CHRISTMAS INVITATION

Meg is definitely not in the Christmas mood. She's never gone in for tinsel, baubles and mistletoe, and right now she's still getting over an illness. Yet when she's invited to spend the run-up to Christmas in the snowy countryside, rather than dreary London, she can't refuse.

Arriving at a warm and cosy family home in a small hilltop village, Meg soon begins to wonder what a proper Christmas might be like. But just as she's beginning to settle in, she spots a familiar face. *Lex.*

Despite the festive cheer, Meg suddenly wants nothing more than to get as far away from him, and their past secrets, as she can. **But if she stays, could this be the year she finally discovers the magic of Christmas?**

THE HOUSE OF HOPES AND DREAMS

When Carey Revell unexpectedly becomes the heir to
Mossby, his family's ancestral home, it's rather a mixed
blessing. The house is large but run-down and comes with
a pair of resentful relatives who can't be asked to leave.

Still, newly dumped by his girlfriend and also from his job as
a TV interior designer, Carey needs somewhere to lick his
wounds. And Mossby would be perfect for a renovation show.
He already knows someone who could restore the stained-
glass windows in the older part of the house . . .

Angel Arrowsmith has spent the last ten years happily
working and living with her artist mentor and partner. But
suddenly bereaved, she finds herself heartbroken, without a
home or a livelihood. Life will never be the same again – until
old friend Carey Revell comes to the rescue.

**They move in to Mossby with high hopes. But the
house has a secret at its heart: an old legend concerning
one of the famous windows. Will all their dreams
for happiness be shattered? Or can Carey and Angel
find a way to make this house a home?**

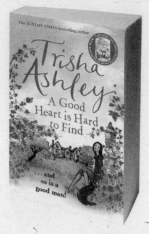

A GOOD HEART IS HARD TO FIND

'It is a truth universally acknowledged that a single man of over forty is in possession of a major defect . . .'

Cassandra Leigh has woken as if from a bad dream: desperate for a baby, and finally out of patience waiting for her 20 year affair with Max to end with happily ever after. Maybe Max is not the only man for her?

Perhaps she could find love with her friend Jason – though he's perhaps a little *too* rugged, and there's something strange about the way his wife disappeared. Or there's Dante, the mysterious stranger she meets on a dark night in his haunted manor house . . .

Cass must throw caution to the wind and claim the life she's always wanted. Suddenly, it's a choice between Mr Right, Mr Wrong or Mr Right Now . . .

A LEAP OF FAITH

Sappho Jones stopped counting birthdays when she reached thirty but, even with her hazy grip on mathematics, she realises that she's on the slippery slope to the big four-oh! With the thought suddenly lodged in her mind that she's a mere cat's whisker away from becoming a single eccentric female living in a country cottage in Wales, she has the urge to do something dramatic before it's too late.

The trouble is, as an adventurous woman of a certain age, Sappho's pretty much been there, done that, got the T-shirt. In fact, the only thing she hasn't tried is motherhood. And with sexy potter Nye on hand as a potential daddy – or at least donor – is it time for her to consider the biggest leap of all? It's either that or buy a cat . . .

WIN

A champagne afternoon tea for two experience with

Afternoontea.co.uk is the UK's premier guide to over 500 venues across the country where you can enjoy a traditional Afternoon Tea, with free online booking and exclusive offers. The lucky winner will receive a voucher for 'Champagne Afternoon Tea For Two', at a venue of their choice from the Afternoontea.co.uk website.

To enter visit:

www.trishaworld.com/weddingdresscompetition

Competition ends on 31st July, 2023